In the beginning . . .

The beginning was to be recorded by the scribes so that all of the children of Israel might know of their early days, and learn to revere their hero Joshua, the man who turned a wandering horde of bedouin—desert nomads—into a proud and virile nation.

It would take nearly three thousand years.

But in the beginning, he was to teach them that, surrounded by enemies on all sides (the Hittites, now called Syrians; the Moabites, now called Jordanians; the warriors of Babylonia, now known as Iraqis; the Amurrus, now called Lebanese; and the Egyptians, still known by that name . . .), their survival lay not in their very considerable contribution to the culture of the known world, but in their military prowess.

That prowess was small; but in the face of adversity, it grew. And this is how it all began.

The scribes wrote:

> *And Joshua took Makkedah, and smote it and its King with the edge of his sword; he utterly destroyed every soul in it, he left none remaining. Then Joshua passed on from Makkedah, and all Israel with him, to Libnah. He smote it with the edge of the sword, and every soul in it; he left none remaining, and did to its King as he had done to the King of Jericho. He passed on to Lachish and assaulted it, and took it on the second day, and smote it with the edge of the sword and every soul in it. Then Horam, King*

of Gezer, came up to help Lachish, and Joshua smote him and his people, till he left none remaining. And they passed onto Eglon and took it on that day, and every soul in it he utterly destroyed, as he had done with Lachish. He went up from Eglon to Hebron, and smote it with the edge of the sword, and its King and its towns, and every soul in it, he left none remaining. Then Joshua, with all Israel, turned back to Debir and assaulted it, and he took it with its King and all its towns; and they smote them with the edge of the sword and utterly destroyed every soul in it, and left none remaining; as he had done to Hebron and Libnah and its King, so he did to Debir and its King. . . .

Thus it came about after the Exodus from Egypt, that Joshua led his people across the Jordan and into Canaan . . . and into the hands of their enemies.

ALAN
CAILLOU

JOSHUA'S
PEOPLE

PINNACLE BOOKS   NEW YORK

Although the main characters in this book were real people,
and the events herein depicted did take place, in some in-
stances both the people and the events have been fictionally
intensified to add to the drama of the story.

JOSHUA'S PEOPLE

JOSHUA'S PEOPLE

Prologue

The great blaze of the sun, redder now than it had ever been before, had finished searing the desert for one more broiling day and was retiring over the horizon to work its blessings or its evil on other lands.

Here the sun was a constant enemy; though its early warmth brought seeds blossoming from a parched earth, its gathering heat then shriveled them up as they struggled for survival.

The Israelites watched its setting and breathed a sigh of relief as it sank, malevolently, over the distant mountain, gilding the rugged hills with awesome majesty as it gave way to the cool breezes that began to stir with the coming of the evening. The western sky was a brilliant copper color, the peaks below it harsh and forbidding in spite of their reflected gold, and they were very far away. For a hundred miles and more around the oasis with its life-giving springs and pools, there was only dry and dusty sand in which nothing could live save a few sparse patches of wretched scrub here and there.

And yet, for forty years—a whole generation—fifty thousand men, women, and children had managed to survive out there. They had spent these forty years wandering, not because they did not know where they were going (they knew this very well indeed), but because the problems of getting there were almost insuperable. And it was all a matter of *water*, without which there could be no food either.

A man needed at the very least a pint of water a day to survive in the desert's murderous heat, though this was the barest minimum. Eight times as much, a full gallon, would have given him the strength he needed, though this—beyond the oasis—was a luxury only to be dreamed of. Often, a father would crouch, weeping, over his dry and brittle waterskins, not knowing how distant, nor even *if,* fresh supplies of water might be found, knowing only that it meant that yet another of his children would die now from dehydration.

But they had come, thankfully, to the great oasis of Kadesh-Barnea, where there was good sweet water in abundance, even for fifty thousand intruders. There were five springs here, spread out over an area some twelve miles long by three or four wide, and each had its own name—Azmon, Karka, Kadesh, Ein Mishpat, and Hazar-Addar. There was grass growing here, and there were dates in fine profusion, and millet ready for harvesting when they arrived. . . .

They had walked—a great, untidy, and thirsty column—for more than eight hundred miles in a desert where nothing could live save at the infrequent oases; between these places of safety, there was only sand so hot that it burned through the leather soles of their sandals, so hot that time and time again people lay down on it, suffering its burning, and just . . . gave up, their parched lips and dried-out skins becoming one with their bones, which would very quickly bleach under that murderous sun.

But now they had reached the greatest of all of

3

Sinai's oases, and there was a haven for them here. And in the first eight days of their long sojourn under the welcoming shade of the palm trees, seventy-two of the starving Israelites died from too much food and water, too quickly ingested into their shrunken stomachs. And their tens of thousands of goats, as hungry as their herders, were uprooting the shrubs and devouring them in a frenzy.

It was part of the goat culture, which was always disastrous. The goats never bit off only the edible shoots so that the plant could grow again, as other browsing animals did. Instead, they tore the whole bush out of the ground, roots and all; and not content with this, they broke up the thin crust of the soil with their sharp hooves, reducing it all to dust wherever they went.

Because of their destructive habits, the goats were the enemy of the people; but the people did not consider this, because the goats provided them with milk and meat, without which they would have died. They provided them with leather for their clothing and sandals, and with skins to make into bloated water bags.

And so, the cycle went on: The herdsmen searched out the scattered, pathetic pastures, and the goats destroyed them. They moved on when the ground became barren and no more food was forthcoming; and they would never learn that with their hurtful goats, this would always be the pattern of their lives.

But now they were camped at the oasis in their tents (also made from the hair the goats provided), and most of them would have been content to spend the rest of their lives here, rather than venture once again into the terrifying wastelands they had been wandering through for so long, lands which were

4

known, all of them, by names in which there was a common denominator signifying the aspect which bound them all together; the *Wilderness* of Paran (sometimes called Sinai), the *Wilderness* of Shur, the *Wilderness* of Zin, the *Wilderness* of Edom, and the *Wilderness* of Moab. . . .

They wanted to have no more part of all these wildernesses; but their leader would have none of this. He told them fiercely, *"Beyond all these empty deserts lies the land of milk and honey, which will be ours . . ."*

His name was Moses, and he painted a splendid picture for them: *"A good land, a land of brooks and water, of fountains and springs flowing forth in valleys and hills, a land of wheat and barley, of vines and figs and pomegranates, a land of olive trees and honey, a land in which you will eat bread without scarcity . . ."*

He was eighty years old, and a man of the most extraordinary character, as befitted his equally extraordinary background. Born in Egypt's Nile Delta at a time when the Pharaoh ordered the killing of every male Hebrew child, his mother Jochevet set him adrift on the river in a rush basket sealed with pitch, and he had been found by Pharaoh's daughter herself, to be brought up as a young prince at the royal court. But he overstepped his authority one day when he killed an Egyptian slavemaster whom he found flogging an Israelite slave half to death (he had always known his own true heritage) and fled his royal home.

Now he was leading the Israelite slaves out of Egypt and toward the promised land, a formidable and angry man who would brook no interference from anyone, a man with an obsession, a man blessed with that strange, mystic quality that prompted others to *listen* to him, even though he spoke so hesitantly and in such faltering tones that he was constrained to have his words translated for him by his elder brother Aaron, so that they would be understood. (There was a language problem too: The Aramaic he spoke was that of the Egyptians, quite different from the Canaanite Aramaic of the Israelites.)

He led them from the city of Rameses to Succoth and on to Etham at the edge of the desert, moving very fast for fear of pursuit. There was a pillar of fire in the sky at night to guide them, a pillar of clouds by day, and the ground itself was shaking. (*"The planets,"* said the seers, *"have lost their course and are passing close to our Earth. . . ."*)

They came to the Reed Sea—which later historians would mistakenly report as the *Red* Sea—and in the terrestrial convulsion the waters parted for a miraculous crossing and closed again on the pursuing Egyptian hordes. They saw the thousands of dead bodies, soldiers and horses alike, tossing on the crushing waves with upturned, shattered chariots, and knew that under Moses' leadership they were safe.

They sang a thanksgiving song, and Moses' sister Miriam, in spite of her great age, led the women in a dance as she beat out a rhythm for them on her tambourine.

To reach Canaan, they should have turned to the left now; but ahead of them in this direction there were outposts of the Egyptian empire, all the way along the coast as far as Gaza, and Moses said, *"No. We move south now, to avoid them. . . ."*

The people murmured against him, knowing that to the south there was nothing but waterless desert;

but Moses cursed them and said, *"Follow me, and we will reach the Promised Land. . . ."*

There was no defying his vehemence, and they turned south to Marah, the place of bitter water, and into the Wilderness of Shur and on to Elim, where they found a dozen small springs and seventy date palms, then on to Dophkah in the constant search for one tiny oasis or another.

The ground would not stop trembling, and sometimes red-hot hailstones fell from the skies.

They caught quail that rested overnight on the long migrations in the sparse, gray-green scrub, but they were very few. They found coriander growing wild, a stinking weed with seeds that were sweet and tasted of honey wafers, and they called it *manna*, which meant "a dish to eat."

It was very little; a hand could hold perhaps a hundred of the seeds, but a hand was larger than a grown man's stomach. . . . From day to day, they lived on the hard seeds, because there was just no other food.

They trekked still further south, always following the smoke that hung in the sky ahead of them, convinced that it had been sent by their one and only God to guide them, and came to Rephidim. The wells here had dried up, and almost no one among them had any water left.

The sign of well-being in the desert was a wetly shining, bloated goatskin, tightly stitched and filled with water, black and slippery and even cool to the touch; but there were none of these to be seen now among the multitude, and the children were crying from their thirst.

But the rocks here were honeycombed, like sponges, their steep sides covered in parts with a coating of copper-sulphate residue that glistened in the sunlight with a glorious red-green sheen, a brittle paste that bottled up the water the great honeycombed rocks had gathered over the centuries. Moses hacked at the coating with his staff and broke it, and watched the water trickle out under his blows; and soon, the goatskins were full again.

But here, a new threat showed itself.

This was the home of a fierce tribe of desert nomads who called themselves Amalekites; and the intrusion into their territory by so many thousands of hungry and thirsty strangers, using up their meager supplies of food and water, was more than they were prepared to tolerate.

Surrounded, the Israelites were in despair; but Moses sent for a young man named Joshua ben Nun, who had distinguished himself in other matters, and told him to prepare the untrained, disorganized bedouin he led for battle. It was the first time the Israelites had been forced to fight against human enemies, but Moses told them the Lord was with them. Moses himself would hold up his staff to encourage them in their endeavors, a visible emblem of their fearlessness. . . . .

At dawn, the battle was joined as Moses sat on a hilltop with his rod raised high above his head. Toward afternoon, his ancient arms wearied and the totemic staff began to droop; Aaron and a man named Hur, who was Moses' brother-in-law, were at his side at once, holding up the hands that held the sacred rod, holding them there till nightfall.

And by dark, the Amalekites were routed utterly.

It was the Israelites' first battle, and their first victory. There was great relish in the camp that night, and they moved on to Mount Sinai, where Moses fought his way up the mountainside, an erupting vol-

8

cano, to find the Lord in Whom he had such faith. He remained there for forty days, and in his absence his people on the plain below grew restless, sure that the man who had led them out of Egypt was gone forever. They melted down the gold earrings and chains the women wore, and the goldsmiths among them fashioned a Golden Calf as a new God to worship.

And then Moses returned. . . .

He was in a fury when he saw what his people had done. He broke the tablets of the Law he had fashioned up on the mountain, and he smashed the Golden Calf too, causing it to be ground up into powder, which he mixed with water and made his followers drink. Even this was not enough for him; he rounded up a large number of the idol-worshipers and put them to the sword.

Chastened, the people of Israel followed him once more, into yet another wilderness; and very soon, there was a desperate hunger on them again. But the earth was shaking still, the skies were opening, cinders were raining on the earth and a monstrous wind was blowing across it from the east. Great flocks of quail were blown in from the sea and fell to the earth, exhausted, so many of them that their bodies fell one on top of the other. They lay in the sparse scrub, fluttering helplessly, as fifty thousand starving men, women, and children descended on them, picked them up, and broke their necks. . . . The fires were lit, the birds roasted; and for two days the Israelites gorged themselves on the succulent flesh, till their bellies swelled up. And once again too much food stuffed into stomachs that had been too long empty, caused hundreds of them to fall violently ill; and many of them died.

Now, they turned north at last, to the sea at

Ezion-Geber, and then inland again until they reached the oasis of Kadesh-Barnea.

They were to stay here for forty years, while a whole generation died out and a new one took its place, a generation of bedouin, born only to the deserts and life in goat's-hair tents.

And when at last they moved on, at Moses' insistence, they came to a mountain named Nebo that towered out of the arid desert on the northeast corner of the Dead Sea.

They climbed it, and from this great pinnacle, the people could look down onto the raging waters of the River Jordan, and beyond. . . .

Beyond them was a land called Canaan, which Moses had said was their Promised Land, to be the Israelites' home for all eternity.

And here, at the age of one hundred and twenty, his great dream of entry into that Promised Land unfulfilled, Moses died. The sages wrote of his death: *"And to this day, no man knows where he is buried. . . ."*

In his final days, he had chosen his successor, who was henceforth to lead the Israelites in their search for a homeland they could call their own.

It was not quite a new country for them; Abram, the father of all the Jews and the founder of the Hebrew nation, had come to Canaan from Ur of the Chaldees where he was born, on the banks of the Euphrates River, more than five thousand years ago, settling first in Syria with his wife Sarai and his nephew Lot, and then (at the command of his God) moving to Shechem in Canaan, which would later be called Nablus. But there was famine in the land, and they moved on to the region's granary, Egypt, in the constant search for food.

10

But now, a new leader was taking his people home again: He was Joshua, the son of Nun, an Ephraimite, and a man of very fiery temper.

It was a name that in all of history would never be forgotten.

Chapter One

Igal ben Gahar of the tribe of Issachar stood on the east bank of the River Jordan and stared disconsolately down on the raging waters, raising his hand to shade his eyes from the glare of the burning sun. Even though it was low in the sky, it was still searing the land.

He was tall and very thin, with a strange kind of angularity that made him walk awkwardly, as though one leg were shorter than the other. He was heavily bearded, and his eyes were a little wild, black and penetrating over sunken cheekbones and a large, hooked nose. But he was a handsome man in his prime, some forty years old, though he could never remember his exact age; it mattered little.

He wore a short-sleeved tunic, brown with embroidered bands at the hems, and a wraparound skirt of heavier, darker cloth, both of them woven from goat's hair. There was a wide cloth belt at his waist, which carried his short copper sword and all his valuables, and leather sandals on his broad, splayed feet; the sandals were worn thin with the constant abrasion of sand and rock. He sat down and took them off and studied them morosely, knowing that the time had come yet once again to stitch on a new

sole, even though goat's leather was almost inde-
structible.

He turned and stared to the north, wondering
where the devil Caleb was; Caleb, that devious old
man whose mind was filled with knowledge on almost every subject under the sun. . . . But then he
decided that wondering would do him no good at all,
and so he stretched out on the sand and went to
sleep.

He was a good father, and he dreamed of his children, only nine out of fourteen surviving the rigors
of their desert wanderings. There was the eldest son,
Elam, a strapping twenty-five-year-old, powerful,
impetuous, and a troublemaker. There was Barkos,
seventeen years old and a very good herdsman,
though not as well disciplined as he might have been.
And Dibri, two years his junior, strong but easygoing, a cheerful youth, still only lightly bearded, who
always seemed to find humor in the most adverse of
conditions.

There were others, whose names he could never
remember, save one. . . .

The images that came to him in his deep sleep
were mostly of Elisheva, sweet and pretty and de-
lightful and now reaching puberty at the age of
twelve. He dreamed of her when she was only seven,
racing, very fleet of foot, after a cheetah cub she
failed to catch; there was a fantasy of her at ten,
weeping because a baby gazelle she had found, its
mother killed by a hungry hunter's arrow, had died
in spite of the care she gave it; Elisheva at eleven,
just a year ago, bathing in a pool at one of the tiny
oases they had discovered on the eastern edge of that
fearful Valley of Salt. He remembered her as he had
come upon her unexpectedly: naked, fragile, vulnerable . . . and *weeping*. She had been sitting in the

15

freshwater as she splashed herself and *wept,* and he had gone to her in great apprehension, crouching down beside her as she scooped up water in her child's hands and poured it over her head.

He had gently reproached her: "But why are you crying, child?" and she had answered, the tears streaming down her face, her lovely young mouth contorted: "So much water, after so long. . . ."

It had seemed to her to be an adequate reason for her tears, and he had sighed, knowing that he would never understand her. Her child's breasts were just beginning to fill out, very full for her age; and in his sleep, he sighed.

He awoke with a start in darkness, a half-moon high in a beautiful starlit sky, and he looked up into the eyes of his companion Caleb, crouching over him with a quizzical look on that crafty, weathered face.

Caleb looked a hundred at the very least, but he was only eighty-five years old and had left Egypt (the source of all his knowledge) as a grown man in his forties; moreover, he had been one of the twelve scouts sent by Moses to spy out the land of Canaan, a country about which, Igal sometimes thought unhappily, he seemed to know *everything.*

His old eyes on fire, Caleb said, "What—you are asleep? We are surrounded by our enemies! My gentle touch could have been, instead, a sword through your heart."

Igal rubbed the sleep from his eyes. Joshua had put him in command of this two-man patrol (much to his surprise) in spite of Caleb's years, and he felt he had to assert his authority. Scornfully he said, "What enemies? There are no Canaanites on this side of the river."

"You cannot be sure of that."

"I am sure of it. There is no son of man who can

16

cross that raging torrent. They cannot, and we cannot."

Caleb's old eyes were crafty, and he was smiling; his teeth, very few of them left, were yellow and broken. He said, "Whether we can or not . . . we must."

"No. Instead, we will return to the camp and tell Joshua: 'We cannot cross the river here. We must move north and find a more suitable place.' "

"I have come from the north," Caleb said, "and I have examined the river very carefully. To the north, there are cliffs a hundred cubits high. We cannot climb down them even if the water were quieter there, which it is not. No. We cross over here."

Igal said hotly, "*I* give the orders, old man! Joshua put *me* in charge of this patrol, and you will do as I order!"

"Ah yes, of course . . . And do you have a good flint? Mine is too small for what I must do now."

"A flint?" Igal said, startled. "Yes, I have a very good flint."

He fumbled in his waistband and found it, an irregular stone the size of a small girl's flattened hand. He gave it to Caleb and said again, "A very good flint."

Caleb felt the edge with his callused thumb and, smiling, said, "Good, but not sharp enough for what I have in mind."

"Which is?"

"A tick . . . May I split it?"

"Of course! If you can improve it . . ."

Caleb examined the flint with great care; he was very expert in these things. He found a small piece of granite, for a mallet, and laid the flint on a flat rock and struck it once, very hard, in exactly the right place. The flint split in two, and he thumbed the new

17

edge and said, "There, as sharp as a man could wish for! A tick has found a home under my toenail and has laid its eggs there. I have no wish for them to hatch."

Igal nodded. "No, indeed." He watched as Caleb sliced into the flesh of his toe and found a sliver of wood with which to lever out the poisonous eggs.

As he worked, Caleb said, chuckling to himself, "Do you perhaps know *why* Joshua put you in command of me? Even though my knowledge of the country is ten times that of yours?"

"Yes, of course," Igal said hesitantly. "He knows me to be the better man."

"No. You are being tested."

Igal stared. "Tested?"

"Yes. Joshua wants to find out if you have the qualities necessary for leadership. The trials ahead of us . . . He must find men who can command."

"Oh." Igal blinked. "It is the truth?"

"The truth. And I am expected to report to him on your capabilities. But have no fear, I decided a long time ago what I would say. I decided that I would tell him: 'Igal is a born leader, Joshua. . . .'"

Igal could not contain his astonishment. "I am? You will tell him *that?*"

"Because it is the truth. Permit me to say that your qualities are not always immediately apparent. But I am a very perceptive man, and I can recognize them, hidden though they may be."

"Well . . . !" Igal stared, almost hypnotized, at Caleb's bloodied toe, split down almost to the base of the coarse nail. He said, "I suffered once from the ticks, but I used a burning ember from the fire."

"Oh yes," Caleb nodded. "A hot coal is good too. But it seems to me there's always one egg that the fire misses. And really, once a single egg hatches, it can be quite painful. I like to make sure I've destroyed every one of them."

The surgery was finished, and Caleb tore a piece of cloth from his gown to bind the awful wound, and he said gently, "We cross the river *here*, Igal. If we return to Joshua with our mission unfulfilled . . . he will kill us both." He showed his broken teeth. "Your life, perhaps, is of no importance. But mine is. Can you swim?"

"Swim?" Igal said. "No! Of course not! How should I be able to swim?"

"I myself," Caleb said smugly, "learned how to, in Egypt. And in Kadesh-Barnea, where you were born, you never learned?"

"No, I did not. Why should I?"

"But you saw the dogs swimming there in the pools?"

"Yes, on occasion."

"And observed, perhaps, how they use their legs to paddle?"

"Yes . . ."

"Then you do exactly the same thing. That is how a man swims, and that is how we will cross the river. Tomorrow, at dawn."

The earth resumed its fearful shaking, but, inured to the pattern, they were not afraid. For fifty years (and it would last for fifty more) this had been part of their daily life.

The ground shuddered, and shook them, and Caleb murmured, "The seers tell me that a new planet is being born in our heavens. They say that it is passing very close to our Earth. They say that the Earth is being tipped off balance. They say that the sun, which revolves around the Earth, will soon be stopped in its course, that there will be five nights without day. And that in the lifetime of our great-grandchildren or a little later, the world will come to an end. And that meanwhile . . . cinders raining down from the sky, and smoke, and fire, and dreadful winds will make our life very hazardous. They call it . . . a terrestrial disturbance."

Igal, in spite of his faults, was a thinking man, and he murmured, "The pillar of clouds by day that we follow? And fire by night?"

"All part of the same condition," Caleb answered gravely. "We follow what portends the end of the world. Men of simple understanding, as you and I are, must listen to the wisdom of the seers. It is how we learn."

The seers were the Egyptian astrologers who accompanied the Israelites on their Exodus, wearied by the oppression they had suffered at home and searching for a new life with these refugees.

Postulating gravely as they sat around the nighttime camp fires, their long gray beards nodding, they had said, "The planet is called Mars by the Assyrians, and a piece has broken from it. Its tail is passing now very near the Earth and raining devastation on us. Within a hundred years, the Earth will explode into an immense cloud of dust. . . . Till then, there will be earthquakes without number as our Earth seeks to join the new planet."

They were always conscious of the terror they could strike in the hearts of lesser men, and they went on, accepting the bread and raisins which the women, frightened out of their wits, pressed on them: "There will be winds strong enough to pick up a man and his whole family, and hurl them out into the heavens to everlasting damnation. There will be coals of fire raining down from the skies, and sometimes hailstones the size of fully grown figs hurtling down with a force strong enough to shatter the skull of even the strongest man. The end of the world is upon us, it will come in the time of our children's children's children. . . ."

Caleb told all of these things to Igal in that wonderful period between darkness and the time for sleep, which was the hour for telling tales. . . .

But at last, they slept, wrapped up in their goat's-hair robes on the soft sand, to dream of terrifying showers of red-hot coals from the sky that suddenly turned to icicles from which there was no escape.

Chapter Two

When the slanting rays of the sun struck their faces, they arose and ate more of Caleb's bread, flavored now with honey, carried in a tiny pottery jar stoppered with a piece of rag which the ants would not leave alone. They slid down the steep bank to the river, and Caleb cautioned, "Remember, now, how the dogs swim."

Igal gritted his teeth and jumped into the churning water.

There was a long moment of panic, and he was carried for more than a mile downstream before, paddling furiously and inexpertly, he reached the western bank. He fell down on his hands and knees and moaned, and prayed to his God, thanking Him for his salvation. He turned over on his back and just lay there, staring up at the lightening red of the eastern sky and waiting to be found.

Caleb came to him at last and said, "We are here. Come, let us proceed. We move to Jericho now."

Igal sat up, and remembering the old man's reproach and trying once again to assert a halfhearted authority, said, "*Now,* the enemy is all about us. Not before."

24

"No longer," Caleb said cheerfully. "We are now merchants from the deep south in search of trade."

"The deep south?"

"Where we came from. It will account for the differences in the language we speak."

"But I am not a merchant! And neither are you!" Igal said, astonished.

"A story," Caleb said gently. "A mild deception to justify our presence here."

"Ah, yes, a story. A deception. Of course." There was a terrible problem gnawing at his mind. "And if we meet with the *Anakim*, the giants? It is said that they tear their enemies apart, limb from limb, and eat them."

"It is not true."

"It is also said that in comparison with them, we are like grasshoppers."

Caleb sighed. He said carefully, "As you know, I was one of the spies Moses selected to journey through Canaan and study the land and its people. It was I who brought back the story of the *Anakim*. I said they were big men, four cubits in height or more. But in the retelling, they became larger, five cubits tall, even six . . . It is not true. They are giants, yes. But all I saw of them leads me to believe that they are *gentle* giants."

Igal looked at him curiously, a new aspect on Caleb's character. He said slowly, "You have no fear at all, old man, do you? Not of the earth-tremors nor the cinders that rain from the sky . . . Not of the river's raging waters, not even of the *Anakim* . . ."

"More than that," Caleb said. "I do not fear death itself. The Lord God of our people will take me when he decides that my time has come. Meanwhile, from six wives, I have fathered forty-seven children, of whom thirty-five are still living, most of them sons, though I cannot remember the exact count. They all carry my blood. The Lord God will take me, yes! But the strain . . . it lives on, through constant copulation. This is how the Angel of Death can be defeated. When he comes to take me, my sons will laugh and say, 'But *we* are still here to plague you. And when you come for us, we will have left behind us our own sons, and their sons too!' By this means, Igal, death itself can be defeated, and is therefore not to be feared."

"Blasphemy!" Igal said, terrified, and Caleb nodded. "Yes, blasphemy indeed. Come. We move to Jericho now."

For an hour, they climbed the hill ahead of them, and they came at last to a collection of mud huts, their roofs thatched over with rushes, and the village was deserted. There were two narrow streets here, and one of them had been paved over with slabs of granite; a village of some importance.

But it was empty, and they wandered awhile among the houses, entering some of them and picking up neglected clay pots and other cooking vessels, staring at the skins stretched out on pegs in the sand floors that were the beds and wondering who had once slept there; cockroaches were crowding everywhere by the hundreds, and a neglected goat was bleating pathetically.

The two men had separated, and in a little while Igal called out, "Caleb! Over here . . . !"

He had found an old man sitting under an olive tree with a spear embedded in his stomach. He was still very much alive and conscious, though his old eyes were clouded with pain.

The two of them squatted on the ground beside him, not quite knowing what to say. At last Igal said, "Do you wish me to remove the spear, old man? If I

26

do, you will bleed more, and the end will come sooner."

He shook his head. "No. The pain is already enough for me to bear. And I am dead, there is nothing to be done now."

"Yes. Dead now, I think so. Your name, if we may know it?"

"I am Guni of Gilgal, a Canaanite."

"Of Gilgal?"

"Of Gilgal. It is the name of this village. Gilgal."

"Ah yes . . . We thought it might be Jericho."

"No." A long, rattling moan came from his throat. "Jericho is the city you see on the hill across the valley there. This is Gilgal, a village of no consequence at all."

"And will you tell us," Igal said, making conversation, "who it was that killed you?"

The old man chuckled, and the sound that came from his throat was horrifying. He whispered, "Jericho—Jericho attacked us. And two—two young men took—took advantage . . . Do you have water? My mouth is dry."

Caleb unshouldered his bloated goatskin and said gently, "But drink with discretion, friend. A little water will be good now, but too much. . . ."

He pulled out the rag stopper and held the bag to those withered lips, and Guni sucked on it till he began screaming with the sudden access of pain.

Igal drew his sword and said politely, though with a touch of irritation, "Surely you would wish me to put an end to your suffering now? A quick and painless death?"

But Guni shook his head, gasping. "No," he said, "though I thank you. But there are visions in my mind now of my youth, and I wish to enjoy them while I still live." He was even laughing quietly, and

27

he whispered, "As a young man, I used to prowl the women's tents in the darkness, quite skillfully, you understand. There was a girl named Micah, I remember. Ah yes, the lovely Micah . . . And another whose name was Merab, I think—her thighs were twin pillars of the purest alabaster. Merab, I wanted so much to take her to wife, but my father had no money. . . . Yes, Merab . . . and where will she be now?"

The crows, settling on the thatched rooftops, were shattering the silence with their raucous cries, and Caleb said roughly, "Enough of your women! While you still live, tell us about Jericho, Guni."

Startled out of his reverie, Guni answered, "It was from Jericho that they came."

"They?"

"An army to punish us for infractions we were not even aware of. Jericho is very strong, and we were weak; they destroyed us in two days of fighting. But among them, there were two brothers—"

He tried to laugh, but his face was contorted with his pain. "I seduced their sister, her name was Tamar, she was thirteen years old and very beautiful, a gazelle with great heat in her blood, with tiny breasts and long, supple legs. . . . They came to me in the midst of the battle, and one of them drove his spear into my stomach and left me here to die, as I soon will, in great pain."

"I can ease it for you," Igal said gently. "A quick thrust of my sword through your heart—"

"No." Guni shook his grizzled head, and he sighed. "While I still live, let me dream of Tamar."

"The men of Jericho," Caleb asked. "It is said that they are good soldiers. Is it true?"

"Good? They are strong, yes, and evil to a man. When they descended on us . . . we were poorly

28

armed here, and could offer no resistance, so we surrendered immediately. They dragged off our ruler and disemboweled him, and they laughed at his screams. They killed all our men, and then they rampaged through the city, taking our young women in the streets, shamefully, with no regard at all for who might be watching. They herded the old women into houses they then set fire to, and with the edge of the sword cut down those who tried to escape the flames. . . ."

He was gasping, the talk too much for him; but there were things that had to be said. "Never anger the men of Jericho," he whispered. "They are cruel and brutal beyond—beyond imagining. In their arrogance, they repay insult a hundredfold, they delight in tearing babies from their mothers' arms and impaling them on their lances . . . they show mercy to no one."

"Then they shall be shown no mercy either," Caleb said quietly.

But the old man's mind was wandering; "Tamar," he mumbled, "the lovely Tamar . . . it may be that she carries my son now . . . and the name Guni will live forever. . . . It is my hope." His eyes were glazed. "Cruel and evil men . . . the monsters of Jericho . . . a disgrace to all men . . ."

Igal held up his sword. "The point is good," he said earnestly, "a thrust to the heart would be quick and really quite painless."

"No," Guni whispered. "Death will come in time. And the pain . . . I am a strong man, I can bear it while I dream my dreams. Leave me now, good friends that you are. I wish to think only of Tamar. . . ."

Igal sighed and sheathed his sword, and Caleb said abruptly, "Come. We will leave him to die when his time comes. You and I . . . we have work to do now. In Jericho."

They gripped the old man's forearm and left him there with his own private thoughts, knowing that he could not last much longer.

There was a small spring at the bottom of the valley, a brook streaming from it, and they stopped there to refill the goatskin bag and to drink; and Igal said, staring up at the city above them, "Even from here, one sees that the walls are strong."

But Caleb shook his head. He had the eyes of a hawk, and he said, "No. I see cracks in them everywhere, the earth is shaking them to rubble. And are you hungry? I have bread and garlic."

"Garlic too?" Igal stared. "I have only bread left, and very little of it."

"A wise man does not travel without enough food for the whole of his journey. And in these matters, I am wise indeed." He took his sword and pounded the cloves, tore open the flat bread to stuff the pulp inside, and they sat and ate with great satisfaction.

It was the middle of the day when they reached Jericho, at last, a busy time for the bustling market at the gates. The crowds were very thick, and Igal thought he had never before seen so many people in one place, all of them, it seemed, talking at once.

It was Igal's first sight of a city, and though his own people were very numerous, they had always been spread over vast distances, so that it might take a man a full day to walk from the tents of Dan to those of Zebulon. But here, there were more than a hundred thousand people crowded between walls encompassing no more than ten acres of hilltop land, a mere eight hundred paces around.

A hundred thousand of them! Crowded together like the quail that dropped, exhausted on their migrations, and piled up one on top of another. How could they live like this?

The merchants in the market square at the gate sat on the sand under rickety shades of twigs and thatch, guarding their produce: strings of onions, melons, the little hard figs of the sycamore tree, peppers, leeks, cucumbers . . . There were pots of honey, rag-wrapped bundles of raisins, fresh grapes and cactus pears, and jars without number in all shapes and sizes, containing oil or rose water or vinegar or wine; there were heaps of walnuts everywhere, and crescent-shaped pancakes stuffed with a wide variety of fillings, and everywhere the constant shouting-out of wares and prices.

And there were milling crowds everywhere! The men, for the most part, wore short kilts of embroidered cloth, with heavy, thonged sandals of goat leather, and the women, save for the slaves, were dressed in the long gown they called an *abba,* very similar to that worn by the Israelite women, though more expertly stitched. The slave women, well muscled and sturdy, wore only loin-skirts and went barebreasted and barefoot too as they carried huge *jarras* of wine or oil, or clay-encased combs of honey on their hips or shoulders, or great piles of firewood on their backs.

Moving slowly by the wall, Caleb ran his forearm, a cubit, along it and murmured, "Four cubits thick, but it is rubble, no more. . . ."

Indeed, a hundred or more slaves, clad only in ragged skirts or loincloths, were hefting great fallen stones back into place where they had tumbled to the ground. They stared at the broken wall, wondering how old it might be, and Igal murmured, "The wall is nothing, thick though it is. But did you ever see so many soldiers?"

31

He yelped suddenly and turned as he felt an iron grip on his shoulder. It was a guard, muscular and bare-chested, wearing a short skirt of embroidered linen, with a long fluted sword at his leather belt and a circular shield strapped to his left arm. Igal looked in alarm to Caleb for help, and the guard growled, "Strangers . . ."

He made it sound like an offense, but Caleb's ancient face wrinkled in smiles. "Merchants, Your Honor, merchants from the south, seeking out new markets for our sesame oil and our honey."

The guard glared. "I do not like merchants, they are all thieves."

"Some of us," Caleb said easily, "flatter ourselves that we are honest men. It is admittedly a rarity, good sir. We seek only trade, beneficial not only to us . . . but to this lovely land of Canaan as well."

"You have money?"

Caleb smiled cautiously, "A little, Captain, just enough for our immediate needs, no more."

"I am not a captain, but a simple soldier, as you see. I do not like flattery, either."

"An honest mistake, sir. A man of such imposing militancy, I thought . . . a captain at the very least."

The guard grunted, but he was mollified. He repeated, "Strangers. And how long will you stay in Jericho?"

Igal felt it was time to assert himself, and he said, "One day only. Tomorrow, we will move to the east to find our caravan."

"And where will you sleep this night?"

"On the street," Caleb said at once. "Our money is not sufficient for the luxury of lodgings. We will find a sheltered corner."

32

The guard laughed. "Go to the Street of Brothels," he said. "You will know it by the three fig trees that stand at its entrance, hard by the city wall. And once there, search out a woman named Rahab, tell her I sent you. My name is Adriel, remember it. Adriel."

"I will not forget it," Caleb said. "Adriel."

As he turned away, the guard said harshly, "Wait!"

They turned back, and Adriel said, "I have given you information of great value, a small gratuity is customary."

"What gratuity?" Igal began, but Caleb dug into his belt and found a shekel and handed it over.

The guard looked at it without enthusiasm and said coldly, "A better man would have paid a better price."

"Alas, we are but humble traders," Caleb said swiftly, before Igal could utter the curse that rose in his throat.

Adriel left them to their devices, and they wandered through the town, finding that it was made up of good stone houses, many of them splendidly decorated with ornamental tilework of the highest quality. Igal was amazed and could only stare, openmouthed.

He was one of the desert bedouin, born in a desert oasis, brought up in desert wanderings, a man to whom home meant a tent and nothing more; and he had never seen houses such as these. He remarked on them to Caleb, and the old man nodded, conscious of the huge gap that separated their backgrounds. "In Egypt," he said, "there are houses like these. Even more elaborate."

"A tent is better," Igal said. "If a man lives in a

tent, he can move whenever he so wishes, packing up his home on the back of a mule. But if he lives in a stone house . . . ? No, it is very foolish."

They returned from their examination of the town and came back to the marketplace at the gates. They had seen troops without number, heavily armed with swords, daggers, javelins, and bows. And many times, chariots had raced past them, drawn by fiery horses, two to each of them, carrying bowmen with filled quivers of reed arrows topped with copper heads; and Igal muttered: "This is the city that Joshua wishes to conquer. How can we fight against them? We cannot!"

The marketplace was the source of all gossip, and they wandered there till the broiling sun was low in the sky and the evening breeze began to soften the rigors of the day. They found a drinking place where wine and beer were being sold, and Caleb said abruptly, "My old bones are tired, and my mouth is dry. We will sit here and rest for a while, and we will listen to what we can hear."

Igal was furious. Caleb was giving the orders again! Restraining his anger, he said, "Old man, there is something you must know! If we sit here and drink, it will cost money! We have no money. Therefore, we cannot sit here and drink."

Caleb said calmly: "I have three *minas*."

Igal was startled, and his mouth dropped open. "You have?"

"Three *minas*, and fourteen shekels."

"Oh."

He thought about it for a moment, then said, "Well, in that case, perhaps we should sit here for a while and listen to the local gossip. Good. It is an excellent idea, and I congratulate you, Caleb. My mind is already filled with what I will say to Joshua, but there is always room for a little more of the information he wants."

They sat down on the wooden bench outside the shop, and when the owner came, Caleb said grandly, "We are thirsty. A jug of your best beer, landlord."

"Your servant, good sirs . . ." The tavern owner was bald, pudgy, and very florid-faced, with a leather apron spread over his huge paunch. When he returned with a pottery pitcher of fomented barley water and two mugs, he sat on the bench beside them and stared at Caleb, then said, "You are merchants, I think?"

Igal nodded. "Yes, from the south, offering oil and honey to the good people of Jericho, at very favorable prices."

"Ah . . . Our honey, here in Jericho, is the best in all of Canaan. But this year, our wine . . . There was a blight on the grapes, and it affects me grievously, since I supply the troops with their wine. It raises very considerable problems for me."

Caleb said amiably, "But will you not honor us by sharing our pitcher of beer?"

"You are very kind," the landlord said. He snapped his fingers and a young girl hurried to him at once; she seemed frightened, a sad little thing dressed in a long *abba* of the coarsest goat's-hair, but quite sweet and pretty, perhaps twelve years old.

"My daughter," he said to them, "and I cannot marry her off because she has the vilest temper imaginable, and everyone knows it."

He turned to her and said abruptly, "Another mug. And put your sandals on—what is this place, a brothel? No, it is a respectable tavern!"

She brought the mug and poured for him, and when she had gone, three musicians came to their table, two young men with flutes and a girl with a tambourine, swinging her slender body from side to side as she beat out the rhythm.

They listened in silence for a while, and when they had finished and were standing there, expectantly, the landlord said, "They are very good, are they not? Perhaps you should give them five shekels. You are merchants, and therefore men of wealth."

Caleb shook his head. "No," he said, "their music is very pleasing to the ear, but I am sure that a single shekel will be pleasing to their stomachs."

He fumbled at his waist-cloth and found his little leather bag, and selected a coin to give to the girl, fondling her behind affectionately as he did so; and when she made no objection he reached up and touched her breasts and murmured, "If only I were forty years younger . . ."

She laughed and twirled away and said happily, "If there is still desire, old man, there is still life. . . ."

She went on her way, and Caleb turned back to the landlord, saying, "You were telling us . . . You have difficulty providing the troops with their wine. Perhaps we can come to your rescue, at a very fair price indeed. How much would you need for the soldiers?"

"Four hundred skins every week," the landlord said.

Caleb nodded. "I am sure it can be arranged. In a few days' time we will return here. And if we can speak again . . . ?"

"If the price is right, yes."

"And the soldiers' ration of wine is a generous one?"

"No." The landlord scowled. "I have drunk very heavily with the high command in an attempt to increase it. But they are adamant. One skin a week to every fifty men—it is not enough. It allows them only to whet their appetites!"

Now that he had found out what he wanted to know, Caleb changed the subject quickly. "And your Street of Brothels, landlord? Where would that be?"

"Hard by the gates," he said. "You will recognize it from the fig trees there. But you should know . . . the left-hand side of the street is for the poor only. Find a house on the right. If they ask for a *mina,* give them only twenty shekels, it is enough."

"*Ten* will be enough," Caleb said, "I am sure of it."

A chariot rounded the corner and knocked over three tables as it raced on, drawn by two powerful horses, the three men aboard it armed with javelins and bows. Igal watched it as it sped from their sight, and trying hard to show his approbation he murmured, "In all the cities we have visited in our long journey south—"

"North," Caleb corrected.

Igal went on. "Yes, north. I have never before seen one so well armed. It is good."

"We are constantly at war," the landlord said earnestly. "The soldiers are part of our daily life. The other cities, Bethel, Ai, Gibeon, they are all jealous of us. Even Gilgal, which has learned its lesson and is no more . . . But we are strong here."

He called for his daughter again and said, "I am sure that my friends here would enjoy another pitcher." Not waiting for her to bring it, he smiled benignly and left them.

They did not know it, but he had caught the eye of a local resident who was sitting over his wine at a nearby table, and there was a certain imperiousness in those dark and angry eyes. . . .

He was a very big man, more than six and a half

feet tall, one of Canaan's *Anakim,* the giants. He left the table as the landlord approached, looking back just once with an unspoken message. Alarmed, the landlord followed him till they were out of earshot, and then the giant turned and said, "Who are they, friend? I overheard some little of their conversation, and it troubled me. The old man there wanted to know how many skins of wine you supply the troops, and what is their daily ration. It means . . . he wants to know the strength of the garrison. Who are they?"

The landlord gestured broadly. "Who are they? They are merchants from the south."

"And you know who I am?"

"I believe your name is Anak, good sir. An honorable citizen of our fair city. Yes, I know who you are."

"And these so-called merchants?"

"Offering us oil and wine. Traders from Edom."

"By their speech," Anak said, "they are not from Edom. Have you learned of the great horde across the river?"

The landlord nodded. "Thirty, forty, perhaps fifty thousand of them; the market seems to gossip about nothing else these days. But they are bedouin, they cannot harm us."

"How so?"

He shrugged. "They would have to cross the Jordan, which they cannot do. And we are far too strong in Canaan to concern ourselves with a rabble of desert nomads."

Anak was frowning darkly. "The two strangers crossed the river," he said, "I am sure of it. One of my slaves saw them emerging from the jungle of the Jordan. It means they have come from some distant place we can only guess at."

The landlord looked back and saw Caleb and Igal talking earnestly with one of the local wine dealers, a man who was known to be very talkative. Worried now, he said slowly, "If that is so . . . could it mean they are spies from the east?"

"That is the thought that occurred to me. Their speech is different from ours, and I do not know where they came from. I propose sending one of my herdsmen among them, a man in whom I have great confidence, to find out just who they are. And, meanwhile, these two should be questioned."

"The guards, then," the landlord said, and Anak nodded.

"Yes, call the guards, landlord. If they are indeed peaceful merchants, no harm will come to them. If not . . ."

He left it hanging as the landlord hurried off.

But by the time the soldiers came, Caleb and Igal had left the drinking place and had been swallowed up in the city's pressing crowds.

Darkness was falling, and they found themselves a niche in a broken corner of the wall, and wrapped themselves up in their robes, and shivered in the cold night air of the hilltop as they slept, unnoticed among hundreds of other pilgrims sleeping on the streets to husband their precious coins.

And in the morning, as soon as the gates were opened at sunup, the hordes came streaming in and out—farmers, builders, pottery-makers, water-carriers and traders . . . As the raucous bustle of a new day began, Igal and Caleb slipped out and wound their way down to the river, there to swim across once again and to collapse, exhausted, in the bosom of their families.

Chapter Three

Igal went straightaway to his tent; he wanted desperately to see his family and tell them of his adventures.

Most of all, he wanted to be with the sweet Elisheva, and she sat on the ground at his feet and held his hand as all the other children gathered around him and listened, openmouthed. All, that is, save Elam. Elam scorned such open shows of affection, and he stood a little apart from the others, his hands on his hips, tall and straight and bearded even more heavily than his father. He was only fifteen years younger than Igal, and considered himself almost the head of the family, a presumption which irritated Igal considerably.

"I will buy you a bride," he would say wrathfully, "and then you can be head of your own family."

He fondled Elisheva's hair now, thick and dark and a little frizzled, and said proudly, "You will find this hard to believe, but I *swam* across the river."

Her childish eyes were wide. "You *swam?*"

He nodded, very pleased with the impression this statement had caused. "I even showed Caleb how it could be done. While we were in Kadesh-Barnea, I saw dogs swimming, even a few of the local children, and I thought, 'If they can do it, surely I can too.' And so I learned. And the water was really quite fearsome. Poor Caleb was swept for more than a mile downstream, and I was constrained to go and look for him."

"I can swim," Elam said. "And well. I too learned in the oasis."

"Yes," Igal said, a little annoyed. "Well, be that as it may." Elisheva was holding his hand against her smooth young cheek, and he said to her, smiling, "And what did you do in my absence? Did you miss me?"

"Oh yes, so very much!" Her olive-skinned face was turned up to him, her eyes shining; they were almond-shaped and very lustrous. "And I wove a piece of cloth for you, Father. May I give it to you now?"

"Yes, please do."

She went to the wooden chest against the wall of the tent where the family's possessions were kept, and produced a square of pale brown goat's-hair cloth embroidered with a geometric design in red; handing it to him, she said shyly, "I made the dye for the decoration myself, from kermes."

"Kermes?"

"Yes, Dibri collected them for me."

Dibri laughed shortly and held out his hands, heavily stained in red. "A thousand insects at least," he said, "which I scraped off the trees and crushed, and it was never enough, she wanted more. So, another thousand, and still another . . ."

There was a great warmth in Igal's heart, and he murmured, "I thank you both." He examined the square carefully, and found it to be excellently loomed. "I will have your mother sew this onto my gown for me," he said, "so that all our neighbors will

43

know how skillful and devoted my children are." He stooped and kissed his daughter on the cheek, hugging her tightly, and his wife Azuza said morosely, "You spoil that child too much, husband. And we will eat now, the bread is ready."

In the opening of the tent, a fire of thorn-root charcoal was burning in a grate made with three large stones. On it, upturned pottery platters were covered with a paste of barley flour and water in which raisins had been embedded. Azuza peeled off the thin sheets of bread and handed pieces of them around, and as Igal ate he gesticulated with his food, waving it about in an excitement which he knew they all felt too.

"Jericho is a fine city," he said. "Four or five of their streets are paved with blocks of granite more than half a cubit square, and fitted together most carefully. They have been there for a very long time; there are ruts in them where the wheels of the chariots pass, very deep indeed."

Elisheva's eyes were bright. "Chariots? Drawn by horses?"

He nodded gravely. "Yes, by horses, just like the Egyptian chariots our Elders have told us about, the first I have ever seen! And they carry two or sometimes three men, so heavily armed that it is quite unbelievable! Swords, daggers, shields, bows and arrows, javelins for throwing . . . Yes, the chariot is a very formidable weapon. There are thousands of people in the marketplace at the gates, thousands! And their pottery! It is on display everywhere, jars and pots and platters in the most exquisite forms imaginable, many of them glazed with some strange shining material that was quite new to me. In comparison, our own platters are merely . . . sheets of burned clay. It is a very highly cultured city, there

44

can be no doubt about it. And yet . . ." He lowered his voice. "Yet it seems that they have a whole street devoted to brothels—it is very hard to comprehend."

He was conscious that Azuza's sad eyes were on him, and he said at once, "I hasten to add that we merely heard of this, we did not find out for ourselves, as Caleb will tell you. No, it was merely mentioned to us in the course of our inquiries. But can you imagine? A whole street devoted to harlotry!"

And then there was a sudden bellow of anger outside the tent, a single word shouted: *"Mutar . . . ?"*

The word meant, in effect, *"Is it permitted,"* or *"May one enter?"* It was the purely conventional warning that someone was coming, so that any women in the tent who might be uncovered could cover themselves and scurry to their own quarters, leaving the men to their ponderous business. Once the word was spoken, it was mandatory for the visitor to wait until the reply was made: *"Mutar,"* it is permitted.

But this was not a request. It was, instead, a command from a very angry man in authority. And a moment later, without waiting for the obligatory response, Joshua himself lifted the flap of the tent and strode in; and he was in a fury.

He was a man of some sixty years, of medium height and physically very powerful, his black beard streaked with gray, his eyes very deep and penetrating. There was a leather band around his forehead to hold his unruly hair in place, and he wore a long gown of coarsely-woven goat's-hair, bound at the waist with a leather girdle in which he carried his sword and dagger, both made of copper and sheathed in leather. He also carried a staff cut from the branch of an almond tree, which he used ferociously to gesticulate with when—as was often the case—he was angry. He was a man to whom temperance was an unknown quality, and as he advanced on Igal, he shouted, "I sent you to Jericho to bring me news! You returned from Jericho, and where is that news which I await? Where?"

Igal was terribly embarrassed; his whole family, even Elisheva, was watching in alarm. He rose to his feet and said, "Your pardon, Joshua . . . it seemed necessary first to report to my family that I had escaped the great dangers that Canaan offers."

"What great dangers?" Joshua said scornfully. "You were in danger there?"

"Oh yes, indeed! We saw one of the *Anakim* there, the dreaded giants who eat their own children."

"The *Anakim* do not eat their children!"

"Well . . . We spoke at great length with the landlord of a small drinking place, where we consumed just one, single, small pitcher of beer. We were seeking out information, as you instructed us. And then . . . he went to speak with this giant, hiding himself very discreetly from our sight, and I said to Caleb, 'He is suspicious of us, it is better we leave at once.' "

"And that," Joshua said, "is exactly what Caleb tells me he said to you."

"Well," Igal said, flustered, "I do not recall whose idea it was, and frankly, I don't think it matters very much. What does matter is that we left at once and hid ourselves in the very considerable crowd. It seemed to me, as leader of this patrol, to be the wise thing to do. We were very discreet, as is befitting for spies."

He laughed shortly, self-deprecatingly, and said, "Really, I cannot be expected to remember *whose*

46

idea it was, I had much more portentous matters on my mind."

But Joshua's attention had been distracted by the lovely Elisheva, standing there in awe of a great man she seldom saw but knew to be the most important man she was ever likely to meet. He was studying her intently, impressed with her great beauty.

Scowling even over this trivial matter, he said, "She is of age now. Why do you not find her a husband? The children of Israel need . . . children."

"A matter," Igal said earnestly, "to which I have given great attention. I thought of Mordechai of the tribe of Reuben, but he is known as a whoremonger; or of Dan of the tribe of Levi. But I do not like the Levites, they prevaricate too much. So . . . I must give the matter more thought."

"Come with me," Joshua said brusquely. "We will talk about Jericho."

They left the confines of the tent and began the slow descent into the Valley of the Jordan, the sun very high in the sky now and burning the land. Here, there was only desert; but a mile or so ahead of them, the valley was green with lush vegetation. They fought their way through the dense shrubbery and came at last to the steep bank at the water's edge; and Caleb was waiting for them there, sitting on the hard red rock and staring out to the distant mountain range which was the first barrier Canaan was to offer them.

Joshua said at last, "Caleb tells me that it is here that you crossed over. Do you agree?"

"Oh yes," Igal said. "Just below the palm trees there."

"And the water is deep?"

Igal made an expressive gesture: "How can I tell? I could not stand in it. I know only that, as you see, it is very fast and violent. I know only that you cannot lead fifty thousand people over it—men, women, and children too."

For a long time, Joshua held his silence; he was brooding again. He said at last, "To the south of us?"

"The Dead Sea itself, we are very close to it here."

"And the north?"

"I traveled for perhaps ten miles to the north," Caleb said. "There are very high cliffs there. Maybe there is a way down them . . but I think not."

"How high, Caleb?"

"A hundred cubits at the very least."

Joshua nodded and thought about it for a very long while. He said at last: "Then, when the time comes, this is where we will cross over into Canaan."

Igal echoed him irritably. " '*When the time comes!*' How can the time *ever* come?"

But Joshua ignored him and turned to Caleb instead. "And in Jericho itself," he asked, "how were you received?"

"With suspicion," Caleb said instantly.

"Can I send a hundred men in there, posing as Canaanites?"

"No. They saw at once the difference in our speech, our clothing, even in our weapons. There was a merchant there we spoke with, a very loquacious man. He wanted to know where my sword was cast, because of a different design in the hilt."

It seemed to make Joshua very angry. "Our speech," he said coldly, "is that of the Jews we left behind us five hundred years ago, the speech of Canaanite Jews."

"No." Caleb shook his head. "In all those genera-

48

tions, it has changed. We use Egyptian words as though they were our own. . . ."

"Egypt has sovereignty over Canaan, it should not be cause for suspicion."

"Egyptian sovereignty is collapsing here, it is well known that the Pharaoh's empire is disintegrating. No, we are strangers to them in all things: dress, weapons, habits, as well as speech. We cannot pose as Canaanites."

Joshua nodded, accepting the word of a man he knew to be wise. "And the walls?" he asked. "You and I once spied out this land for Moses. But that was forty years ago, when the earthquakes had only just begun. How are they now?"

"Still as we saw them then," Caleb said dryly, "built of cut and uncut stones all mingled in together, with no plaster to hold them except dried mud. They are very thick, yes, and once, no doubt, were strong. But they are very old, and falling apart."

The earth was shaking more violently than ever, and Caleb murmured, "The Egyptian seers tell me that these earthquakes will last for a hundred years and more, that they will culminate in one great shudder that will destroy the world, and us with it."

As if to punctuate his words, the constant tremors were suddenly augmented dreadfully, and Joshua was thrown from the rock he was seated on. To the north of them, a great column of dark blue smoke started rising from the ground, and there was a bright red fire in the sky that was livid even in the heat of the day. Even from so far off, as they stared at it in wonder, a sudden searing blast came at them, and they covered their faces against its heat.

Joshua picked himself up and said calmly, "The seers are Egyptians, who are heathen. Their knowledge is very deep, yes. But knowledge is of consequence only if it is correct, and theirs is not. They count the stars in the sky, and chart the movements of the sun and moon, and come to quite the wrong conclusions. These disturbances are sent by the one Lord God Yahweh to confound our enemies. They are not meant to confound *us*."

He sat down again as though nothing untoward had happened at all and said, "More of Jericho. Did you see soldiers there?"

"Without number," Igal said.

"And they have chariots too," Caleb added.

"Of course. I have always known this. The quivers they carry aboard . . . how many arrows?"

Igal said, blustering, "The quivers are well stocked, but how many—"

Caleb interrupted him smoothly, "I would say forty shafts to each. And they are made of the finest Egyptian reed, topped with re-curved heads of copper. There is a bar at the front of their chariots, which leads me to believe that the driver can tie his reins there and also serve as a bowman when needed. It would mean three bowmen, a hundred and twenty arrows, to each chariot."

"A single horse?"

"No, two. And very surefooted, working well in harness together."

"And the foot soldiers?"

"Armed with swords," Caleb said, "very much like those of the Egyptians, with daggers a span long, with bows made, I think, from yew. And each man has a circular shield perhaps two cubits across strapped to his left forearm."

"The length of their arrows?"

Igal said, bewildered, "Arrows! How long can an arrow be?"

But Caleb thought about it carefully and said at last, "Two cubits, I would say."

"A little more, or a little less?"

"A little more, I think. And yes, it presupposes a very strong bow."

Joshua nodded. "And therefore a very long range. And how many men would be required, in your estimation, to take Jericho?"

Caleb sighed. "We are not fighting men," he said, "and the enemy is very strong. I would say five thousand men at least."

Igal was silent, sulking; on this crucial point he was not being consulted. Joshua felt his anger, and said, "Igal?"

"More," Igal said roughly. "Five thousand will not be enough. Double that number. How can we fight on foot against heavily armed chariots?"

There was no immediate answer, and he was determined to be part of these decisions. Raising a finger and pontificating, he said, "Even if we could cross the river, we cannot hope to conquer them—"

"We *will* cross the river," Joshua said.

Igal went on, ignoring the interruption. "Even if we could, and we cannot . . ." He turned to Caleb, adding sarcastically, "There are a few among us who know how to swim. But it is a rare talent. The river is a barrier we cannot hope to overcome. If we must indulge this foolishness, we should move south again through Moab and into Edom."

"A journey of a month, at least," Joshua said.

Igal continued. "Yes, a month! We should cross the Valley of Araba to the south of the Dead Sea, at Oboth, perhaps—"

"In the dreaded Valley of Salt?"

"Yes! And then go north on the west bank of the Dead Sea."

"A journey of another month! No! We cross here, opposite Jericho, which is our first objective."

"Madness!" Igal said.

He saw the look in Joshua's eyes, looked to Caleb and saw the slow smile there, and he said hastily, "I exaggerate, of course, forgive me. What I mean to say is very simply that the Jordan cannot be crossed here by an army of fifty thousand men. It is not possible!"

Joshua's eyes were hard as granite pebbles. "You have four sons, I believe," he said.

Bewildered, Igal said: "Three. Three sons and five daughters. The sons are Elam, Barkos, and Dibri."

"Elam, I know—a young man of quality. I am giving him command of twenty men for our assault on Jericho."

Igal stared. "You are?"

"Meanwhile, to bring more honor to your family, Barkos and Dibri will watch the river for me."

"They will do . . . *what?*"

"Day and night, they will watch the river. A few days from now, a few weeks, a few months . . . It will cease its anger, and we will be able to cross over."

Caleb murmured, "The cliffs to the north of us?"

Joshua nodded. "Yes, the land is unstable. A few more tremors like the one we suffered but a short while ago, and those cliffs will collapse, they are made of sandstone. When they do—"

"*If* they do," Igal said sardonically.

Joshua scowled. "When they do," he went on, "all of the tribes will cross over into Canaan. Now leave me. I must think."

Dismissed, Igal and Caleb made their long way back up the hill to the encampment, and Joshua was left alone with his thoughts. He was thinking: *The conquest of Canaan will not be easy, we are not fighting men. And yet . . . we must learn how to fight. . . .*

He was right. The Israelites were poorly armed, undisciplined, a rabble of nomads, many of them not even wearing swords, armed only with clubs. And they were pitted against a community that had for generations maintained its strength and its own culture by the prowess of its arms. With sword and dagger, with bows and arrows, with javelins hurled from racing chariots skillfully driven, they had fought off attacks by hostile neighbors and had become strong, the strongest city in the whole of Canaan.

On the opposite bank of the Jordan River, Jericho was an emblem in the sky, perched high on its hilltop and surrounded by six-foot-thick walls that had served, already in this great panoply of time, for more than seven thousand years; this first walled city in the world had been built by unknown people five thousand years before the building of Egypt's pyramids, four thousand years before the first use of the wooden plough, the discovery of the sail, and the invention of the wheel. . . .

Joshua stared at the walls across the dense green shrubbery of the river's jungle, a distant challenge lit by the evening sun, and he brooded.

The sun went down at last, and he shivered in the cold night air. He remembered the time he had been sent, forty years previously, to spy out this fragrant land for his now-dead leader Moses, traveling from Kadesh-Barnea to the borders of Syria and back, a journey that had taken him, with Caleb and ten others, one man from each of the tribes, forty days and nights. He remembered the *Anakim* they had seen here, the formidable giants who were a tribe of Canaanites; and how could a simple bedouin fight against a man who was more than four cubits tall? Against a man whose strength matched his great size? Against a man who could wield a copper sword as though it were made of the lightest Egyptian reed?

And how many of the *Anakim* might there be in the Canaanite armies? (They were regarded with great contempt, he already knew, a contempt based on fear of their prowess; they were considered second-class citizens, but still . . . dangerous fighting men. How many were there of these fearsome adversaries?)

As he worried over these matters, the disturbance of the north seemed to him to be approaching, a live and very worrisome thing; there were red-hot stones falling down from the skies, and great clouds of pumice dust rising everywhere. And the earth was shaking more violently than ever before. But even though the calamity was moving south, Joshua was not yet ready to leave; he knew that it was directed against his enemies and not against *him,* and in a little while the great column of fire changed its course to the west, where Jercho lay, and he murmured aloud, "It is good. I thank thee, O Lord God . . ."

He fumbled at his waist-cloth and found a sticky mass of dates for a meal. The ants had found them, and he slid down the bank to the river's edge and let the swirling waters wash most of the tenacious creatures away. . . . He ate them, sucking the pits dry and carefully tucking them back into another corner of his waistband, to preserve them for planting one day, somewhere; nothing would be wasted that could eventually provide food for his people, a people who had been decimated by starvation for so many long years.

And when he had satisfied his hunger, he lay on his belly and cupped the furious water up into his dried-out mouth, remembering the years of the direst thirst when so many of his followers, the children particularly, had simply lain down on the hot sand to die because there was no moisture anywhere to strengthen their dehydrated limbs.

How many had died of thirst on those interminable wanderings? Or of hunger?

He could think only of swollen bellies that were filled with air, of huge black childish eyes staring at him in reproach at the moment of death.

He remembered a young woman who had buried her third son, the last of all three to die for want of food and water, remembered her words: *"A curse on you, Joshua, for leading us into this salt desert . . . !"* She too had died only a few weeks later, and for the life of him he could not remember her name; she was merely one of hundreds whose bleached bones still marked the route they had taken.

But the image of her accusing eyes would not leave him. Her fist had been clenched, and with her last breath she had whispered, holding it out to him: *"Manna,* give it to the baby of my sister Rizpah, he too is dying of hunger. . . ."

He had forced that dead hand open, and had found there twenty-seven coriander seeds that she had husbanded for this last emergency while dying of hunger herself, marching under a broiling sun as she clutched at twenty-seven seeds. "It will give him a few more days of life," she had whispered.

There had been one terrible moment when one Izaak of the tribe of Joseph had gone quite out of his mind with hunger and had thrown himself at Joshua, bearing him to the ground as he screamed, "Food! Food must be for those of us who can fight . . . !"

Lying under that wasted body, Joshua had drawn his dagger and had forced it up through the skin of Izaak's chest and into his heart. He had then fed the seeds, one by one, into the demanding mouth of Rizpah's child, who was named Benjamin. And four days later, Benjamin too had died, of starvation and thirst.

Manna was all they had to eat, and there was not enough of it. And how could a whole nation survive on the seeds of an herb that, itself, struggled in the killing sand against all the elements of nature?

Joshua sighed; and he knew that their destiny was in the hands of their one God, Whose name was Yahweh.

He sat there all day and brooded, and at last two young boys came to him and squatted on their heels close by, saying nothing, but just staring down onto the river. Joshua said at last, angered by their silence: "Well?"

They had been recognized by the great man, and they rose to their feet in a kind of unconscious respect. One of them said a little sullenly, "I am Barkos ben Igal, and this is my brother Dibri. We have been sent to look at the river."

"Not to look at it," Joshua said coldly, "but to *watch* it."

"An occupation," Dibri said, "for imbeciles. It is a pity that neither of us is an imbecile."

Joshua rose to his feet and struck him across the face so hard that the boy stumbled back and fell to the ground. "Respect for your elders!" he shouted. "The respect you owe your betters! You will watch the river, and when it subsides, as it will, you will hurry to me and let me know!"

Dibri was staring at him in shock; but Joshua

turned on his heel and stalked off, trying to contain his anger and wondering what was happening to the younger generation of his people. They were fifteen and seventeen years old, respectively, and very resentful of the established order. When Joshua had gone a few paces, he turned back and leveled a finger at them, and said furiously, "When we attack Jericho, you will both be in the forefront of the assault! Bring me news when the river subsides!"

He continued on his way, and Dibri looked at his brother in astonishment and said, "What did I say. . . ? He had no right to strike me!"

"He has every right," Barkos said sourly. "He is our leader. Get up, you look like an idiot lying there."

Dibri rose slowly to his feet, nursing a savagely bruised cheekbone; and suddenly he was laughing out loud. He shouted, "Do you know, Barkos? In all of my fifteen years, our hallowed leader Joshua ben Nun has never even known of my existence! But now, he knows me! When he hears the name Dibri ben Igal ben Gahar of the tribe of Issachar, he will say to himself, 'Ah yes, that is the young man I knocked to the ground once. . . .'"

He could not stop laughing and he shouted, "And what would have happened, Barkos, had I struck him back? Which I very nearly did . . . I am stronger than he is, and faster. . . . What would have happened, Barkos?"

Barkos said gravely, "He would have drawn his dagger, brother Dibri, and driven it into your heart. He is not a man who can easily be crossed."

Dibri was suddenly very serious. "You are right, of course," he said. "And perhaps that is the definition of a good general: a man who can easily kill."

They found rocks to sit on, and quite solemnly they stared down on the tumbling River Jordan, watching it just as Joshua had commanded them.

Chapter Four

Igal lay on the mule skin that was their bed, a coarse and heavy hide stretched out on a dozen pegs to raise it a few inches above the ground, and impregnated his sad and worn-out wife Azuza.

And in the act of love, he said cheerfully, "Joshua . . . ! The man is a fanatic! He believes, very firmly, that the River Jordan—quite impassable, mark you—will just dry up and allow us to pass over into Canaan! Madness! It means that we will be obliged to stay here in the desert of Ammon until he comes to his senses. It might be weeks, months, years! Who knows? And he has set his heart on the conquest of Jericho, a feat which cannot possibly be accomplished."

"And if he *tries* to accomplish it?" Azuza asked, lying quite still as she suffered his fervent onslaught, wanting only to go to sleep now. "How many of our sons will die in the attempt?"

It was not a question Igal was prepared to answer; there were other things on his mind. He was struggling mightily, and when he was satisfied he rolled from her and said, "Truly, it matters very little to him. For myself, I would be content to stay here in Ammon. The desert here is not as severe as that of the Wilderness of Zin, we are within reach of food and water in the jungle of the Jordan, more water than we ever thought possible, a great luxury. And do you know?"—he lay on his back beside her—"if we were to cross into Canaan, we would become city-dwellers, we would leave our comfortable tents and live in mud or stone houses; it is not a prospect that pleases me greatly. And yet, this is Joshua's dream. How can a man of spirit live in an immovable *house?* It makes no sense at all!"

He was suddenly conscious that Azuza had drifted off into sleep, and he shook her angrily and said, "Wake up, woman! Your husband is talking to you!"

She awoke and said, "No, I was not asleep . . ."

He had quite forgotten what he was saying, and he searched desperately in his mind for something of importance to say. He murmured at last, "Elisheva. We must find a husband for her soon. I thought of Ethan of the tribe of Reuben . . . He owns four hundred goats, a very wealthy man."

Azuza felt she had to protest, though it was really not her business: "But . . . Ethan is a very ugly man, and he is known to be brutal—"

"Brutal, ugly! What has that to do with it? He's a rich man! And when he came to sup with us last month, I saw how he looked at her. He would be an ideal husband! If his flock could be combined with ours . . . Can you imagine, six hundred goats in a single herd? We would be the envy of all the neighbors!"

On her own skin in a corner of the tent, Elisheva, wide-awake and listening, wept silently; she knew Ethan to be the most unprepossessing man she had ever met, and a man of sour and unpredictable temper to boot, who would beat her very often, she was sure. She was a dutiful daughter, and knew that the choice of a husband for her was none of her business. And yet . . . Ethan was a man who had boils all over his neck, and never stopped talking about the excellence of his goats. Quietly, she cried herself to sleep.

Igal said mildly, "Of course, there is always young Ahab of our own tribe. His father is not really very rich, but he dotes on his son, and it may be that I could get a very good price for her. And yet . . . Shall I tell you of a thought I had?"

All Azuza wanted to do was *sleep!* But she murmured, "Tell me, husband, I am listening."

Igal held his silence for what he thought might be an impressive moment and said, "*Joshua!*"

She did not immediately understand, and she mumbled, "Joshua? What about Joshua?"

"A husband," Igal said, "for my Elisheva! Can you imagine the advantages that would accrue to me if Joshua himself were to take Elisheva to wife? I would be made a commander of the army at the very least!" He was suddenly very angry, and he said, "You are only a woman, and perhaps more stupid than most! But you must have seen how he has looked at her! 'Find her a husband,' he said, and do you really think, foolish as you are, that he had no ulterior motive? No! He was sounding me out, he's a very devious man! Of course, Joshua has no money, but there are other considerations that are not lightly to be dismissed," he said deprecatingly. "I would almost certainly be made his second-in-command, and this too is of considerable value."

He was aware that she had dozed off, and he shook her angrily and shouted, "And will you wake up? Not only am I talking to you on most important matters, but I will need you again very soon. And I don't wish to lie with a sleeping woman, it is undignified for a man of my stature."

Azuza awoke and said hastily, "Yes, yes, I hear you. I was not asleep, husband."

"Good," Igal said, mollified. "Then turn over."

In a little while, they both slept, and when the dawn came, a startled Dibri was there, shaking Igal's shoulder and saying urgently: "Father, wake up . . . !"

Igal awoke, and the first thing he was conscious of was the dreadful itching of the flea bites on his stomach. He scratched at them irritably and said, "Son, I was sleeping . . . What is it?"

In the half-light of the tent there was a strange look on Dibri's handsome, boyish face. Awed, he whispered, "You sent us to watch the river . . ."

"You wake me to tell you what I did? I know it, child! It was Joshua's order."

It seemed that Dibri was in shock. He said hoarsely, "It no longer runs. It has dried up, Father."

"What has dried up?" Igal asked irritably; but suddenly the import of what his son had said struck him almost physically. He caught his breath and whispered, "The river?"

"Yes, Father, the river."

"The *Jordan?* Are you telling me . . . ?"

"Where only a few hours ago there was a torrent, there is now nothing but mud."

"No! It cannot be true . . . !"

"I swear it." Dibri too was trembling, and he said, "I walked across it, into Canaan and back. I too could not believe it."

Igal's eyes dropped to his son's feet; the sandals were hidden in caked mud that went as high as his calves, and the boy said again, "Into Canaan itself! I *walked* into Canaan!"

Igal took hold on himself, not knowing quite what to make of this, nor what to do about it. Azuza awoke and said querulously, "What is it, husband? What is happening?"

"Go back to sleep, woman," he answered roughly. "This concerns only men."

"No," she said crossly, "the sun is rising, how can I go back to sleep? I have to carry water, to make fire, to bake bread . . ."

Igal turned back to Dibri and, master of the situation now, said, "Does Joshua know of this?"

"Not yet. Barkos told me to tell you first."

"Good, it was a wise decision. Momentous events are upon us, it is befitting that *I* should inform our commander. Stay with your mother until you are sent for."

He strode to the tent's flap and lifted it, then turned back, frowning. He said slowly, "You are sure of this, Dibri? It was not, perhaps, all a dream?"

Dibri held up one foot and said, "Is this a dream, Father?"

"Yes, the mud . . ." He went out and dropped the flap behind him.

He paused for a moment in the cool fresh air of the morning, looking at the red-gold of the sky and wondering what great excitements this new day would bring. He heard the distant bleating of goats, where the shepherds were leading their flocks out to pasture, and the barking of their guardian dogs; a solitary crow was croaking its raucous, obtrusive cry somewhere as he found his way to Joshua's tent. He hesitated for a little while, trying to find the words he would use, and called out at last the warning: *"Mutar . . . ?"*

Almost immediately, the reply came back to him: *"Mutar!"*

He went inside and saw that Joshua was not in his bed as might have been expected, but was pacing back and forth, fully dressed and even wearing his sword and dagger. Igal knew that this was not a time for the normal preliminaries of polite discourse, and he came to the point at once. "You sent my sons to the river, Joshua," he said clearly, "to watch for its drying up. I am pleased to tell you that it has now come upon us."

"Ah . . ." There was no surprise in those dark and thoughtful eyes at all. "And how deep is it now?"

"A man may walk across it, into Canaan, as my son Dibri has just done. Where one man may walk . . . so may thousands, even our women and children."

He hesitated, but he could not contain his puzzlement. He said curiously, "And if a simple man may know how it was that you foresaw this?"

For a long time, Joshua did not answer him; he was wrapped in deep thought, but he answered at last, a little absently. "There are sandstone cliffs only a few miles to the north of us, where we saw the fire and the clouds and the torrent of debris from the skies . . . The cliffs have collapsed into the river, effectively damming it."

"Ah yes . . . there is always a logical reason, is there not, for the most illogical of events?"

He felt the anger in those cold hard eyes as Joshua stared at him. "It is not illogical, Igal!"

"No. No, I am sure of it."

"It comes from a very simple reason. I prayed to the Lord God Yahweh. He answered my prayers be-

65

cause I lead His chosen people, and He listens to me, as I do to Him."

"Yes, of course . . ."

He looked around the tent and wondered about its absence of furnishings. There was not even an ox hide for a bed! Joshua, it was apparent, preferred to sleep wrapped up in his gown on the hard sand. There was no cupboard, no possessions-box, not even a fire. What, did this man never eat? And why was it that he had not even one wife to look after him? Why was it that *nothing* was known of his family, his parentage, save that he was reputedly an Ephraimite?

Igal found it all very disconcerting, but Joshua said, a fierce light of triumph on him, "Call the Elders of all the tribes together, Igal. I will speak with them now."

He went to a corner of the tent and leaned on his almond staff and stared at the ground as though all the secrets of the universe were written there.

Igal nodded. "At once, I will do so."

As he moved to obey the order, he turned back, and not quite sure that he would be permitted to raise such a delicate point now, he said slowly, "And will it be remembered that it was my sons who first brought this news?"

Joshua did not move. "It will be remembered."

"Dibri and Barkos," Igal said, his heart beating very fast, "both *ben Igal* of the tribe of Issachar."

Joshua turned and said gently, aware of Igal's pride, "I will order the scribe to write it, my friend. We will all be eternally grateful to your house. It will not be forgotten."

Bursting with pride, Igal went from tent to tent in the glorious light of the early morning, calling out for runners to take the word to the Elders. From tent to tent, the shouted word spread like wildfire among the tribes, from the tents of the men of Reuben to those of Simeon; on to the distant Levites and the tribe of Judah; to Zebulun camped on the slopes of the hill; to Issachar and Dan; along the valley to Gad, Asher, and Naphtali in the great grove of palm trees. And as far as the tents of Joseph and Benjamin the cry went ringing out: *"Joshua calls us . . . !"*

It was midday under a broiling sun before the Elders could all be brought together on a stony hilltop, where basil and wild lentils were growing, with great masses of coriander, which they now scorned, because their bellies were filled with good dates and almonds and honey and barley bread, and even with meat from the gazelle which they hunted inexpertly with their dreadfully inefficient bows and arrows, or spears that would simply not fly straight.

Joshua told them, very quietly, that the great moment which Moses had promised them was now at hand. "The Lord God Yahweh," he said "has dammed the river for us, that we may cross over into Canaan, which is to be our home for all eternity. Soon, the waters of Galilee's great sea will break through the dam and create once again the dreadful torrent of the river as we know it. It behooves us, therefore, to move very quickly, lest the great wave descend on us as once it came down behind our people when Moses led us across the Reed Sea, and drowned our Egyptian enemies by the thousands. We must move at once!"

There was a fervent excitement on them all; but the striking of some ten thousand tents, the loading of them onto the backs of recalcitrant mules and donkeys, the apportioning among the slaves of the loads to be carried, the waxing of the wine, oil, and honey jars, the smoking of the meat for the journey

. . . All these things took *time,* which was in very short supply now.

And it was not until thirty-six hours later that, by the light of a half-moon, the long, undisciplined column began to cross over the River Jordan and into Canaan.

Joshua was at their head, and once the opposite bank had been reached, he said to Igal, "We wait here now, friend, till the last straggling children are safely on the western bank."

His dark, fiery eyes were on fire with his emotion, and he said softly, "The Promised Land! It is a moment of great importance in your long history and mine! We have arrived there!"

All through the long night, the column struggled through the clinging knee-deep mud that sought to suck them down. The babies were crying, and men who had crossed over were coming back to midstream to pluck them from their mothers' arms and carry them to the fateful shore. Some of the very old men were stumbling in the mud, and there were younger men there at once to help them. There were cries: "Your arm over my shoulder, old man . . ." "Give me your child, woman, I will carry her . . ." "Hold on to my wrist, do not let your feet remain in one place for too long, the mud will suck you down to your waist . . ."

Tribal enmities were forgotten in the urgency of this momentous event, and a man of the Levites, a tribe known for its harshness and cruelty, was saying to a woman of Gad, renowned for its great ability to overcome all evils, "Let me help you now . . ." A young man of Simeon, also known for its anger and intolerance, was saying softly to a very old man of Issachar (the Issachars were supposed to be the strongest of all the twelve tribes), "Your hand on my belt, we will reach the land of Canaan together, you and I . . ."

Even the slaves were being helped across, while on the western bank Joshua stood with Igal and two of his sons. They were staring to the north, where lightning was stabbing at the trembling earth; those dreadful fiery cinders were raining down again, and a planet in the darkened sky, where not a single star was to be seen, was moving majestically across the horizon, a long tail of fire from it that seemed to brush the earth itself.

And there was a mounting sound shattering the silence of the night, a thunderous roar that seemed to mix itself with the terrible sounds that came from the heavens. But they were all across the river now and struggling to higher ground; all save one woman —and who was she? A woman of the tribe of Zebulun?

She was dragging two children with her as she struggled through the deep mud, a girl of six or seven years and a boy perhaps a year or two younger, and she had ceased her struggles, turning to stare at the approaching wall of water; she knew that death was coming now, and there was a dreadful horror in her huge black eyes.

Dibri shrieked, "No . . . !" and hurled himself toward them. He stumbled through the clinging mud and reached out for her, and he shouted urgently, "My arms, hold my arms . . ." She would not let go of her children, and he scooped the girl-child up . . . And then the great wave, more than twenty feet high and advancing on them with the fearful sound of thunder, picked them up, and smashed them down to the riverbed with all that weight of water above them, grinding them into the riverbed and picking them up once more to hurl them over and over in its fury like rag dolls, with the great contempt that Nature holds for mere mortals.

But they did not know of this ultimate assault; the first great pounding had broken their bones and pulverized their skulls; and as the water roared on, it carried the four dead bodies with it, down to the murky depths of the Dead Sea, some ten miles distant.

Igal sank his head into his hands and moaned, and Joshua laid a hand on his shoulder and whispered, "Take comfort, Igal, my friend. He died bravely, with yet more honor to the tribe of Issachar, who was Jacob's ninth son."

Igal's cheeks were streaked with his tears. He said, "And how will I tell my dear wife Azuza? He was always her favorite. . . ."

Joshua could not answer him; and Igal began scooping up sand and pouring it over his head as he swayed back and forth with his prayers. He fancied that he had seen his son's eyes staring at him in reproach for long-forgotten indignities as he was swept away to his death; and he could not drive away the terrible feeling of *guilt*.

He had always been a good father, he was quite sure; but was he correct in his certainty? He came to himself again when he felt Joshua's strong grip on his shoulder, heard the voice that had lost its customary harshness. "Weeping will not bring him back, Igal! I too feel your great sorrow. Life goes on for our people, for your tribe as for mine. And it is the living we must think of now. Come with me. We go to Gilgal."

It was the best possible palliative for Igal's anguish, and he knew it, but he could not properly collect his thoughts, and he did not cease his moaning. Joshua watched him for a while, and he grunted at last, wondering why it was that the death of one young man, after so many deaths, should be of such great importance. He was not a family man, and a father's pain was sometimes strange to him.

He sent for Caleb, a man with whom he had much more in common, and said to him, "Let the people set up their tents, it may be that we will be here for a long time."

Caleb nodded. "Many of the tribes will want to camp by the river, where the jungle will hide them. But there are others who will want the security that higher ground offers them."

"The jungle will *not* hide them," Joshua said. "We are only a few miles from Jericho, and what? Can we hide so many thousands? No. Let them camp where they choose. But from this time forth, all of our men will carry their arms, will sleep with their swords close at hand, a few children from each compound to stay awake at night and give warning of any attack. We are very vulnerable now, and I did not bring my people over Jordan to see them slain for want of reasonable precautions. Have some of the dogs tethered at a distance, their enemies now are not wolves or bears, not even lions; their enemies are *men*."

"Of course. I understand."

"And men, remember, who are skilled in battle. In every one of our families, a child or a woman to sleep outside the tent to listen for the dogs' barking, to awaken the head of the household at even the slightest suspicion of intrusion."

"It shall be done."

"The younger sons of every family to prowl the outskirts of every compound, also to give warning of any unwarranted approach. We are in the land of the Canaanites now, a land which will shortly be *our* land. We must assume that they know this, and fear it. It means that we must expect attack, in great force. And with chariots, remember."

Caleb said dryly, "They cannot use their chariots in the Jordan's jungle, nor can they on the slopes of the hills."

"It is true. Let the people avoid the flatland as they would avoid the plague."

"I will see to it. And you yourself?"

"I go to Gilgal to wait for the dawn, that I may spy out Jericho on its distant hilltop and discover how it may be reduced. Summon me twenty men of the tribe of Issachar as a bodyguard."

Caleb said slowly, "Our own Ephraimites would be better."

Joshua flared at once, "No! The men of Issachar are stronger, and are destined to serve others!"

"So be it then. . . ."

"Let them serve me as a bodyguard! If the men about me are to be slaughtered—as well they might be—I do not want them to be Ephraimites!"

"Very well. Within the hour . . ."

But it was to be three hours later when Joshua and Igal, accompanied by seventeen heavily armed warriors from the tribe of Issachar, began the ascent of the hill in the darkness. And when dawn broke, they were in the deserted village of Gilgal.

Joshua said, "A man named Guni, you told me . . ."

Igal led him to the corner where the old man was propped up against a fragment of mud wall; his clawlike hands were clutched tightly around the haft of the spear that was embedded in his stomach. His eyes were still open and staring blindly, but there was a twisted kind of smile on his lips, and Igal whispered, "His last thoughts were for a woman named Tamar."

Joshua growled, "He could have helped us. But

now, he cannot." He stared out at the city on the other side of the valley, its walls beautifully gilded now with the rising sun, and murmured, "Jericho . . . a prize beyond compare, and our true entry into Canaan."

Within days, the Israelites were tilling the ground to the west of the Jordan, digging into the soil and planting millet, barley, leeks, and garlic. This new territory was to be their home; and a new home could not exist without husbandry. Almost overnight, they changed from simple bedouin into agriculturalists, no longer harvesting wild-growing crops which they stumbled on, but crops which they themselves grew and nurtured.

It was the beginning of an entirely new culture, embodied in their love of the land, that was to last for thousands of years.

Chapter Five

Three miles distant on the hilltop, a captain of archers was closeted with Jericho's senior commander, whose name was Belesh. He slapped his bare shoulder in a salute and said, "Whoever they may be, Commander, the strangers in our midst . . . they have crossed over the River Jordan and entered Canaan. They are spread out now from Gilgal all the way down to the river, in uncounted thousands."

The commander said sourly, "I want those thousands *counted*, Captain."

"Of course. It is being done now." There was a thin smile on the captain's aristocratic face. "There is a man named Anak," he said, "who has sent one of his herdsmen into their camp to discover just who they are."

Belesh said angrily, "Anak? It means that he is one of the giants?"

"Yes."

"And therefore . . . a civilian?"

"Yes."

The commander leaned forward and said with heavy sarcasm, "And will you tell me, Captain, why it should be that vital military information of this nature should be left to civilians?"

Not caring to mask his satisfaction, the captain said, "The herdsman, whose name is Jabez, is one of my spies. Anak does not know that he reports first . . . to me."

"Ah . . . And what has this Jabez told you? What are their armaments?"

"It seems that they carry only swords and daggers, a few spears . . . Hardly any of them wear the shield."

"Bows?"

"A handful, only, with quivers of perhaps three or four arrows of indifferent merit. Hunters, rather than soldiers."

"Chariots?"

"None at all. And no cavalry either. They have no horses, only mules and donkeys."

"Slingsmen?"

The captain stared. "With respect, Commander," he said, "the sling is a weapon the bedouin use against wolves and bears, it has no military significance at all."

The commander was a weary man, older than his years and very sick, and he was tired of the constant battles against Jericho's neighbors. "The Hittites to the north of us," he said caustically, "have incorporated slings into their weaponry, and it is said that they use them to fearful advantage, a long-range weapon that can kill a good swordsman at more than a hundred paces. And will you tell me, Captain, how good a sword is, even in the hands of an expert, at one hundred paces?"

"I will find out," the Captain said uncertainly. "I will send the man Jabez to them."

Belesh took a handful of raisins from the tray a slave girl offered him and chewed on them. "And will you tell me," he said, "how it came about that they crossed over the Jordan, which for generations now has been our eastern barrier against attack?"

"Some miles to the north," the captain said, "the river was blocked. It dried up for the space of two days. They took advantage of it."

For a long time, Commander Belesh pondered. At last he said, "And the city gates?"

"Closed, save those on the east. It is the time of the farmers, they must have ingress and egress, or we will starve."

"There is grain enough in the stores. Close the eastern gates too. All the troops to man the walls, the archers in the forefront. These people, whoever they may be, have not come here merely to pay us their respects."

"No, sir. Yes, sir."

He left the commander's hallowed presence, and within the hour, Jericho was a tightly sealed city, its heavy wooden gates closed, its archers manning the walls, its infantry and its chariots standing to arms and ready for a sortie if the time should come.

The people of Canaan were waiting. . . .

One of those people was the giant Anak.

He was a very lonely man, one of the *Anakim* who were both despised and feared by the main body of the Canaanites, and moreover, an orphan whose parents had been brutally killed in one of the interminable battles between the varied Canaanite city-states, a trauma that had left him with a certain distaste for war. And he lay now with a woman on the Street of the Brothels and opened his heart to her. Musing, he said, "How very easy it is to talk with you, Rahab!"

She was an attractive woman, and she murmured, smiling, "It is part of my trade, Anak. Perhaps the most important part. The body means little, but if I have the ability to open a man's mind, then I am pleased."

They were lying together on the skin bed in her tiny room, and on the table beside them there were the mugs of wine they had been drinking. Their clothes had been dropped carelessly on the ground by the bed, and a young goat had chosen them for a sleeping place.

"Body and mind," Anak said, "you have them both . . . And do you know of the dangers threatening Jericho now?"

"The hordes out there? The soldiers say they cannot harm us, they are not well armed."

He sighed. "Let us hope that they are right. I have fought in so many battles, and I am not even a soldier! I am tired of the constant killing. It means nothing to me anymore, and—can you believe it?—it is this aspect of our life that distresses me most of all, that a man can become *inured* to the killing."

The single tallow in the room was spluttering, and she whispered, "Forgive me, my love, that I must leave you for a very brief moment . . ." She found more oil, poured it into the little clay pot, and waited for the flame to find itself again. She said, "Almond oil, it smells so good. But oil of almond is so very expensive now."

He watched her as she moved like an animal in the half-light, finding great pleasure in the easy articulation of her limbs as she moved back to the skin and lay beside him.

"Yes, I know it," he said. "Everything is expensive these days. I had lunch today in the market, two very small loaves of bread, a little honey that was really not as sweet as it should have been . . . and a pitcher of beer. Eighteen shekels! This is mon-

79

strous! *Eighteen shekels!* I remember the good old days when such a meal would have cost perhaps four, five at the very most."

He was fondling her breasts, and he said, "And now . . . it may well be that we will shortly suffer the attack of that vast army out there. I dread it."

Lying on her back and finding great satisfaction in his caresses, Rahab shrugged. "We are strong here. We have fought off attacks before, without number."

"Yes. But this time . . ."

He took a deep breath. "They are Hebrews, from Egypt. I sent a herdsman to them, on the other side of the Jordan, which they have now crossed."

"Hebrews?" Rahab frowned. "I have very little knowledge of history, or, for that matter, of anything else except my trade. But did not the Hebrews leave Canaan many generations ago?"

Anak nodded. "Yes, they did, though some few of them remained here. Most of them went to Egypt— you know where Egypt is?"

Rahab said uncertainly, "To the north of us, is it not? The land of the Hittites?"

"Ah . . . no. The Hittites are indeed to our north, but the Egyptians, my love, are to the south. Beyond Gaza and the Wilderness of Shur. It is there that the Hebrews went in the years of the great famine. And it seems they they have now returned, in very great numbers."

"How good it is," Rahab murmured, "to have a man of learning to teach me these things! I have always believed that . . . well, knowledge is really very useful, is it not?"

"Indeed. It is often of great consequence."

"And do you also know why it is that these Hebrews came here?"

"Yes, I do," Anak said, worriedly. "Jabez tells me

that they have set their hearts and their minds on the conquest of Canaan. To achieve this, they must first take Jericho."

"No . . . !" Her eyes were wider than ever with her fear, and Anak said glumly, "They must, or we'll be a thorn in their sides, a great danger to them once they begin to drive to the west."

She could hardly find her voice. "To attack us here? And . . . are they good fighting men? Better than our own soldiers?"

Anak shook his head. "No, I think not. From what I could gather, they are an undisciplined rabble, badly armed and quite untrained in the arts of war. And yet . . ."

He was puzzled, and he said, thinking aloud, "My herdsman, Jabez, is a man of very devious quality who knows what question to ask, knows how to listen well. It seems that almost a generation ago, these people fought with the Amalekites in the Wilderness of Paran, and defeated them soundly, with very great slaughter, sparing none of them. Now, I know the Amalekites to be fierce and competent desert warriors, so how could this be? Yet Jabez tells me the Hebrews cut these famous fighting men to pieces, under a man named Joshua, who leads them still."

Rahab said slowly, "And if they should attack us here? Surely, our walls are strong?"

"Once, they were," Anak said. "No longer. You must have seen how they have collapsed, in so many places! Now they will scarcely keep our goats in, much less the Hebrews out! Our first line of defense from the east was always the river, quite impassable. But they have crossed over now; it gives me cause for deep thought."

Anak ceased his physical attentions to her and rolled over onto his back, staring up at the dancing

81

tallow shadows that lined the edge of the loft; a rat was there, staring down at them, its nose quivering. "Shall I tell you a story?" he said absently.

Rahab smiled. "I am listening."

He propped himself up on an elbow and looked down into her large, dark-as-night eyes that were filled with understanding. He said slowly, "Four hundred years ago, there was a man called Isaac, a Jew. He had a wife named Rebekah, who gave birth to twins, Esau and Jacob. Esau grew up to be a great hunter, and he took three wives from among the Hittites, whose names were Adah, Oholibamah, and Basemath; Adah was the daughter of Elom, and her firstborn son, by Esau, married the daughter of a man whose name, like mine, was Anak. He was Anak the Long-Necked, and the founder of our race, the *Anakim*. And I myself am one of the offspring of this . . . this twisted genealogy. All of the *Anakim* went their way, but one small branch of them, my own, followed a different bloodline and produced me—Anak, your devoted friend."

"Ah . . . a pretty story," Rahab said, wondering what he was trying to tell her. She added politely, "And I am sure it is of the greatest importance."

"Yes, to me it is important," Anak said. "From that time on, the *Anak* men married only with the Canaanite women, save among my own forebears. One of Adah's grandchildren married a Jew, as did one of *his* grandchildren. That grandchild was named Heber, and he was my great-great-grandfather. He died at the age of one hundred and forty, shortly before I was born." His eyes were very grave. "It means, my sweet Rahab," he said, "that I am at least in part . . . a Jew."

The moment of her alarm flittered away, and she said scornfully, "How can you be a Jew? You are

Anak, one of the giants, it is very apparent! And the kindest, most gentle man I have ever taken to my bed! And it is well known that the Jews are *not* kind and gentle! The Jews? I have heard of them! They *mutilate* themselves, did you know that?"

She gripped his genitals and said fiercely, "With flintstones, they cut off their foreskins, here. Can you believe what I am saying? Yet I know it to be true, I have been told so very many times!"

Anak nodded. "Yes, I believe it is so."

"Savagery!" Her voice was suddenly very soft. "And you are not a savage, Anak, but the most gentle man who ever entered my life. And yes, even changed it."

Anak sighed. "And the hordes who are camped by the river," he said, "are ready, my herdsman tells me, to wipe Jericho off the face of the earth, to reduce it to rubble, to put every one of us to the sword . . . These people, now Jericho's enemies . . . they are *my* people. It is very hard for a man of my conscience to know where his loyalties lie. There is always that strain of . . . very persuasive blood."

Rahab was quite frightened. But she clutched at him and muttered, "Forget your persuasive blood, Anak, and love me again."

"Ah yes . . . !"

He held her tightly in his arms, seeking the kind of skilled, professional comfort that only she could provide him with.

In a little while, he gave her some money and thanked her with a very old-fashioned kind of courtesy, and left her. And when he had gone, Rahab climbed the rickety ladder that led to the sleeping loft, and up the second ladder onto the roof to sit for a while in the cool night air. She stared out to the east and watched the thousands of pinpoints there of

83

flickering flame that were camp fires. She worried about her three children, to whom she was deeply devoted, and as she thought about Anak's casual words—*to put every one of us to the sword*—she wept for them.

Chapter Six

The multitude settled themselves on the rolling hills that rose from the Jordan's valley, marveling at the wealth of vegetation they found here. By the tens of thousands, their goats descended on the undergrowth, beginning their own kind of devastation.

The threatened attack that Joshua had feared did not develop, and he wondered why it was that the Canaanites would permit so large a horde of potential enemies at their doorstep without making at least an attempt of some sort to drive them away. He was a man of no military training at all and knew only what he had learned by himself in the field; but his instincts were sound, and this lack of activity puzzled him. Could it mean Jericho was so strong that its people felt a threat did not even exist? If so, was this contempt founded on solid reason—or was it merely Canaanite arrogance?

Day after day he sat on the roof of an abandoned mud house on the edge of Gilgal and stared at the distant outline of the city, brooding, planning, and praying for guidance. He saw, as he watched, that one of the gates had now been opened, that small groups of farmers and traders were coming and going, their numbers increasing as each new day broke. It did not mean that the defenders were relaxing their vigilance, he was sure.

He sent for Caleb, a man in whom he had great confidence, and said to him, "Come, sit with me here, let us learn what we can of Jericho by watching for a while."

The sun was high in the brilliant blue sky, and heat waves were rising up from the gray rocks. Joshua said, thinking aloud, "A single gate open, but it means little. It would take half a day for an army to climb that steep hill, and the gate could be closed in moments. There are still archers on the walls, though not as many as there were yesterday, less still than the day before. And yet, they make no move against us! I must know why, Caleb."

The old man shrugged. "I have visited the city before, I can do so again. There is always gossip in the marketplace."

"But the last time you were there, you met with a certain suspicion, I believe. Perhaps I should send someone else."

"Any of our people," Caleb said firmly, "will be suspect. Whomsoever you send there, Joshua . . . it will be known at once that he is one of the multitude which has crossed the river; we have no reason to believe that the Canaanites are fools."

"And therefore . . . ?"

"Therefore, *I* should go. It is work for a *thinking* man, a man with the ability to turn aside unwanted questions, a man who knows how to survive when survival may indeed be a difficult matter. It means that you should send *me*." He chuckled. "It is even work that demands a certain deviousness, a deviousness I was born with, a generation before you were dragged, screaming out your anger, from your mother's womb." He shrugged. "And it will not be too dangerous. After all, Jericho's market is filled with merchants from Bashan, Gilead, Ammon, Moab, and Edom; there are even a few Midianites there. And if we must, perhaps we can pass as Edomites."

"We?"

"I assume," Caleb said slyly, "that you will also send Igal with me once again, to contain my youthful impetuosity."

Joshua grunted. "You know as well as I do, friend," he said, "that Igal is in many ways a fool. But I suspect that he is also a natural-born leader of men. For some years now I have been watching him, waiting for that foolishness to drop from his shoulders like a cloak discarded in the maturing of the day, waiting for signs of that magical moment when a simple and likable man takes on his full potential." He dropped a hand on Caleb's shoulder and said gently, "Forgive me, Caleb, that I use you as a test of Igal's capabilities. I only do so because I am convinced that you can, and will, guide him."

"I know it. Then we should leave soon, I think."

"Perhaps at dawn tomorrow, when they open the gate and the traders enter."

"No. Shortly before they close them tonight." Caleb's leathery old face was wrinkled up, and his eyes were shining brightly. "We will be suspect again, without a doubt. And if we have to hide from our enemies, I will be happier knowing that darkness will soon be upon us. The darkness has always been my friend."

"So be it, then. Send Igal to me, and I will inform him of his duties."

When Igal heard the news, there was great elation in his tent, tempered with a certain awareness of the danger. He said to Azuza, "And I will be in command again! It is apparent that Joshua has great faith in my abilities."

"They will discover you and kill you," Azuza said heavily, but his enthusiasm would not be dimmed.

"No," he said, "they will not! I know exactly what has to be done, and I will do it. Successfully. You will see."

Elisheva's large, dark eyes were on him, and she whispered, "You will be very careful, Father?"

He felt a sudden sharp twinge of pain; her unspoken thoughts were not only for him, he knew, but for her dead brother Dibri too, the happy, cheerful brother to whom she was so attached; he felt her anguish and said softly, "Of course, my sweet! A family man's prime concern when he goes on such a mission, always, is to return safely to the family he loves."

He turned to Elam, standing there a little apart, his arms akimbo, his eyes very solemn, and said, "You are the man of the house, Elam. Take good care of your mother in my absence, remember that she is very old and therefore deserving of your respect at all times."

Azuza grunted and turned away to scrub the eating platters with sand from the floor of the tent. There was an almost inaudible murmur: "I am not so old, merely worn-out . . ."

But Igal ignored her completely. He went on. "The other children too, they are in your care, especially Elisheva."

"Elisheva," Azuza said, "always Elisheva . . ."

It was enough, and more than enough. Igal turned on her angrily and shouted, "Yes! Always Elisheva! And I have affection for her! What, you think it should be otherwise?"

And when he was climbing the hill toward Jericho

a little later in the evening sunlight, he turned to Caleb. "My wife is jealous of my daughter," he said, still smoldering. "How can this be?"

"Have you noticed," Caleb asked, musing, "that wives invariably grow old faster than their husbands? I wonder why? Perhaps it is the constant childbearing, every year a pregnancy."

"Oh, nonsense!" Igal said crossly. "Childbearing is a woman's duty, as much so as . . . carrying water or cutting wood for the fire. A duty! She accepts it! It should not make her grow prematurely old." But it was too splendid an evening for anger to last, with that glorious golden light on the hillside and the city walls. Igal said happily, "But there is a scent on the air! What is it?"

"Wild basil," Caleb said. "We are walking through a field of it."

"Ah yes, basil . . . How good it is to have settled in a place where food grows wild for the picking! You remember the Valley of Salt?"

"Yes, very well. My waterskin was almost dry before we even began the crossing. Just one day later, it was empty, and a day after that, it became brittle. There is nothing in the whole world I fear so much as a brittle goatskin."

"Yes, I know. The air itself in the Salt Valley can kill a strong man; it is well named."

"I remember," Caleb said, "that when at last we moved out of it, there were salt crystals on my beard, creeping all the way up to my eyes. I had the dreadful feeling that sooner or later they would blind me—Am I walking too fast for you?"

Igal could never be quite sure when Caleb was mocking him, and he merely grunted. Caleb placed a hand on his shoulder as they climbed together and said quietly, "And I have not told you, dear friend, how distressed I am at your son's death. Dibri was a good boy, a great future ahead of him. I saw what happened, I was no more than fifty paces away. And shall I—shall I tell you what I thought?"

There was an image in Igal's mind of the great wall of water, picking up the bodies and smashing them down again in unbelievable fury, and he said, "Yes, tell me. I am sure it will be a comfort."

"I thought," Caleb said gravely, "of a youth in the prime of his life—what, sixteen years old?"

"Fifteen."

"Fifteen then. Giving his young life so bravely for a woman and her children, even though they were not of his own tribe. He must have known that he could not hope to save them. And yet . . . he made the attempt. In that moment, I was proud to consider myself a friend of the house of Igal."

Igal tried to ignore the tears on his cheeks. He said roughly, "We are late, I think. We must hurry now, before they close the gates in our faces."

"Yes, you are right," Caleb said. Like a mountain goat, he scampered up the mountainside, and Igal found it hard to keep up with him.

They arrived at the gate at last just as it was being closed, and squeezed themselves through. Scowling, a guard challenged them: "Who are you?"

"Merchants from Moab, Excellency, with trade to Jericho's great benefit," Caleb answered.

"Pass then," the guard said, and with three other men closed the heavy-timbered gate behind them.

They were within the city, and there were pitch-flares being lit everywhere. But this was not a city that went to sleep with the setting of the sun. The drinking places were all full, and wandering troubadours were strumming their harps, thumping their drums, blowing their flutelike *zamouras* to entertain

91

the drinkers. The young women among them were dancing, holding out their arms as they swung their hips, clothed from neck to ankle in the all-concealing *abba*, and wearing necklaces of gold chain to proclaim their worth.

They found an open-air tavern, and Caleb said, "Here. This is where we will sit and listen to what the people are saying."

Igal whispered, "It will cost money. You still have money? I have none at all."

"Two and a half *minas* still," Caleb said. "Come, let us enjoy ourselves, the work of a spy should not be entirely without its compensations. And tonight, we will have wine."

Igal goggled. *"Wine?* Beer is so much cheaper . . . !"

"But there is a mood on me," Caleb said, "and only wine will satisfy it." He thumped on the table, and when the landlord came, he said, "We will have half a flagon of your best honey wine. Filtered and smooth to the taste."

"My wine," the landlord said, "is filtered four times through bags of charcoal made from the roots of almond trees. It is the best wine in all of Canaan."

"A whole flagon, then . . ."

"Your servant, good sir. And food?"

"No food," Caleb said.

"We have cheeses without number, pastry cakes by the score: filled with raisins or walnuts, some with a paste of almonds crushed with dates, others dripping with honey . . ."

"No food," Caleb repeated sternly, thinking of his meager funds. "We will have only wine. A whole flagon."

They drank together for an hour or so, acknowledging the friendly greetings of the passers-by:

"A pleasant evening to you, good sirs . . ."

"Your health, gentlemen . . ."

"Traders, I am told, from Moab . . . ?"

"And what think you, friends, of our fine city . . . ?"

This last was the sort of question Caleb had been waiting for, and it came from a man whom he sized up at once as *exactly* the kind of man he wanted to talk with. He was small and wiry, and very nervous, with darting black eyes and compulsive gestures with hands that fluttered like the wings of a Sinai butterfly.

He accepted Caleb's invitation to join them in a drink, and he said, "My name, gentlemen, is Helez, and as you see me, I am a Hittite."

"Caleb and Igal," Caleb said. "From Moab."

"Moab?" the Hittite asked. "I would have said, by your speech, from Edom."

"From the border of those two lands," Igal said wisely, and Caleb nodded. "Yes, from the border. Specifically, an oasis called Punon."

"Ah, from Punon! I have heard tell of it! It means then, as I see by your dress, that you are bedouin?"

"Yes indeed," Caleb said, smiling. "Nomads and tent-dwellers." Now that the story was accepted, he felt that a certain embellishment would be not only safe, but appropriate. He said amiably, "And in Punon we grow the best dates the world has ever seen. They are large and juicy, the color of the best bronze, and when a man eats them, the simplest pressure of his fingers is enough to slip off their skins. Truly, they are splendid dates!"

Helez raised the cup that Caleb had ordered for him, and said gravely, "I drink . . . I drink to the success of your importation into Jericho . . . of Punon's *bronzi* dates."

93

He had already been imbibing quite heavily, but he drained his cup and said thickly, "From Punon, you must have moved through a great horde of savages that has settled on the shores of the Jordan. I learn that they are called 'Hebrews.' "

Igal said politely, " 'Hebrews'? I do not know them."

"Tribes," Helez said, "who left Canaan several generations ago. But many of their people stayed behind and are still here." He glowered at his drinking cup and said, "Our enemies . . . I do not like the Jews."

Caleb found it necessary to throw a warning glance at a very agitated Igal, and he said quickly, holding Igal's angry look, "I have heard of them. They have nothing at all to commend them." Caleb put on an expression of deep concern and said, "But why is it that here in Jericho we have done nothing to prepare ourselves against them? Our enemies, as you say. And yet . . . we just sit here and do nothing!"

Helez leaned toward them, his eyes shifting slyly, conspiratorially, and he whispered, "Our king has sent for help against the invader. He will not move against them till he can be assured of help."

"Ah . . . A very wise decision."

Helez looked back over his shoulder, and when he turned to them his voice was hushed. "The king of Jericho," he whispered, "has appealed to the kings of Gezer and Lachish for help. He will not move against these savages until he is sure that once he drives them from Jericho's hilltop . . . it will be into the arms of Lachish and Gezer behind them."

Igal began to splutter, but Caleb threw him a look again and, tempering his voice to a deceptive mildness, said quickly, "One sees that the king is a thinking man, and let us all be grateful for it. And will you have more wine, my good friend?"

Helez looked up at the waning moon and sighed. "No," he said, "I may not. My family awaits me, I told them I would be home before dusk. And it is already night. But will you be here for a while . . . ? A pleasant place to spend an evening, I think, and perhaps, once I have assured myself that my women are safely in their quarters, I can return so that I may be permitted to repay your gracious hospitality? What do you say? New friends should not so quickly be parted."

"An excellent idea," Caleb said. "Yes, we will be here for a while, anxiously awaiting your return."

"So be it, then. And by your leave . . . ?"

As soon as he had gone, Caleb said calmly, "A spy for the Canaanites, beyond the shadow of a doubt."

Igal stared back at him. "No!" he said, exploding. "How can that be? He told us of the king's intentions, which is what we came here to find out!"

"A sop to hold our interest, as he wishes to hold us here! I suspect strongly that when next we meet—if we were to be so foolish—the questions would be his, not ours."

"You cannot be sure of that."

"No, I cannot. But the life of a spy, good Igal, depends not on certainties, but on suspicions."

"Ah . . . very well said."

Caleb was staring into the distance, and he said quickly, "Yes, as I suspected . . ." There was a look of amusement in his dark, shrewd eyes. "And it behooves us to leave this place at once."

"Very well, then. I have always known you to be a man of great competence in these matters." He called out, very grandly, "Landlord! The bill for the wine . . . !"

But Caleb grabbed him by the throat of his *abba* and pulled him to his feet, and hissed at him: "You never want to understand, do you? Come, *now!*"

Startled out of his complacence, Igal followed his partner's look and saw, no more than a hundred paces away, a small phalanx of soldiers trotting into the marketplace, a dozen of them in military order. Their swords were drawn, and they carried their shields on the left forearm; two of them, those in front, carried flares.

Igal stuttered, "But not—not for *us,* surely?"

"Yes, it might well be for us!" Caleb answered him.

With this he gathered up his gown and ran, and Igal followed him, shouting, "Wait . . . ! Wait for me!"

Together they raced through the dark alleys of the township, and Igal found it very hard to keep up with his octogenarian partner. He collapsed at last, gasping, "Here, we can hide here, it is dark . . ."

But Caleb dragged him to his feet again and whispered: "No, not here . . ."

A shout came to them from the distance—"That way, to your right . . . !"—and then there was the beat of the pounding feet again, drawing closer now.

They took to their heels once more, and found a broken piece of wall, an abandoned pen, perhaps, for sheep or goats. They climbed over it quickly and lay down on the stinking earth there, holding their breath as the sound of the running feet drew closer. It was a rhythmic, impersonal sort of sound, as though to the pursuers the quarry had no importance at all, as though completing the act of catching them was all that mattered.

As the two of them lay in the dark and the silence and the slime of long-gone animals, the ominous sound padded on, passing them and finally going beyond their hearing.

Crouching under his cloak, Igal whispered, "If we stay here . . . ?"

Caleb shook his head. "No. They will be back."

In the light of the rising moon, his face was limned with a strange blue aura that ran down his high forehead, his hooked nose, the firm set of his chin; and Igal thought, incongruously, what a sharp and alert old man he was. Caleb whispered, "Do my old eyes deceive me? Or is that door unbarred?"

It was the door to a house close by, the house, perhaps, to which the pen belonged. There were no animals here now, and three well-fertilized fig trees were growing close by. Igal squinted at the door, which seemed to be very slightly ajar. But he whispered, "After dark? No, it must be barred."

"It is not. Come, let us see what is behind it."

They moved across the compound and cautiously felt the timbers of the door, finding that it was indeed open. Caleb pushed at it gently, and the noise of the bronze hinges was loud in the silence. Moving like thieves in the night they crept inside and found themselves in a small dark corridor, at the end of which a faint yellow light was casting its glow over the stonework of the wall, an ancient archway there leading . . . to what?

Slowly, carefully, they eased their way toward it, and at a sound behind them, Igal gasped out his alarm and spun round; it was the unmistakable sound of wood on wood, the door's heavy bar being dropped into place. His eyes were still not accustomed to the darkness, and all he could make out

97

was the bent frame of an old woman standing there, almost doubled up on her staff.

They heard her voice, the whining, fragile voice of an old crone: "Straight on, to your left, where the light is."

Caleb said calmly, "I thank you, old woman. And if we may know the name of this house?"

"Its name?" She was cackling suddenly, the sound of a hen that has just laid an egg. "Its name?" she echoed. "Why, this is the house of Rahab, of course! You have chosen wisely."

Igal stammered, "Rahab . . . ?" It was a name he had heard before, though he could not quite remember where or when.

He could see more clearly now, and she was nodding at him.

"Rahab," she said again, "the harlot Rahab, the best in Jericho, perhaps in the whole of Canaan."

These were words she had been taught to repeat, and she went on mechanically. "The most skilled of all the prostitutes, with comfort in her hands, her thighs, her lips—even her words are honey to the wearied traveler. She is the most expensive of them all, and the best. To your left, gentlemen both . . ."

The darkness swallowed her up.

Worried, Igal whispered, "A prostitute? What, have we stumbled on a brothel?"

"The house of Rahab," Caleb murmured. "There was a guard who told us of her, you remember?"

"A harlot!" Igal said. He saw the humor in Caleb's eyes, heard his quiet laugh, and said, blustering, "A harlot, very well, I accept! But what, the most *expensive?* Caleb! How much money do we have?"

Chapter Seven

She was a woman of statuesque beauty, in her thirties, full-bodied under her long embroidered gown, with very large and fiery eyes and a smooth complexion with only a few pockmarks remaining on her face from the usual childhood sicknesses.

She was clambering down the ladder from the loft where the grain and oil were stored, the loft that was also her own private sleeping place, with an ox skin thrown loosely over a span's depth of good clean straw that would be changed every month or two for fresh buoyancy and resilience.

Her voice was very melodious, the voice, moreover, of a woman who was perfectly at ease with strangers; it was a very *exciting* voice. "I am Rahab," she said.

Here below, the bed was more conventional, a hide stretched tightly over twenty or thirty pegs driven into the sand to raise it a few inches off the ground. There were four chairs here made from olive wood and strips of leather, a cupboard of sorts in which were stored the platters and mugs her customers might require, and a low wooden table on which there were three tallows—fashioned from lengths of braided goat's-hair—in small clay bowls of oil; only one of them was alight now, and Rahab took a taper and lit the others.

In the augmented light, she looked at the two of them and said, smiling, "Are you nervous? You seem to be nervous; it is not necessary. May I ask who sent you to me?"

Caleb said, "A guard at the gate." He searched the recesses of his memory. "I think his name was Adriel?"

There was a veil over her lustrous eyes. "Adriel? He is a viper. None the less, you are welcome. And will you have wine first?"

In acute desperation, Igal stared at Caleb, and the sound that came from his throat was almost a moan. But Caleb said quietly, "A mug of wine, truly, would be very acceptable."

"Good." She clapped her hands, and the old crone came hobbling in, waiting for orders. Rahab said, "Wine for my clients, at once."

They sat modestly on three of the leather chairs and stared at each other. And Rahab said at last, "And which of you will be first?"

Flustered, Igal began to speak: "But we have not come here—"

"*I* will be first," Caleb interrupted him, "as befits my great age." His eyes were very hard. "But you spoke of the guard Adriel as a *viper*. Do you have reference to Adriel the soldier—or Adriel the man?"

For a long time she was silent. She said at last, very quietly, "You wish to make an issue of this?"

"I wish to make an issue of it, for reasons of my own."

"Very well, then. I speak of Adriel as a symbol of a hateful government. There! Does that satisfy you?"

"It satisfies me. But will you tell me why you call your government 'hateful'?"

"Another issue?"

"Yes, perhaps so . . ."

"The taxes," Rahab said flatly. "The soldiers come to collect the taxes, to take from me the money I earn by my labors. And when I have no money to give them—they take me instead, as though it were their right. But by your dress you are bedouin, I think, no? And therefore will know nothing of taxes."

"Once we suffered them," Caleb said, "a generation ago. But no longer. Now, we are free men, and yes . . . bedouin."

The old woman came in with a pitcher of wine and set it on the table, and took three pottery mugs from the cupboard and set them down too, then hobbled out again in silence. Rahab filled the mugs and said slowly, "I was on the rooftop when you took refuge in my compound, I saw you hiding. I saw the soldiers running past as they searched for you. Will you tell me why? Am I harboring criminals? Did you kill someone? It is only fair that I should be told."

"No," Caleb said calmly. "We have harmed no one, nor will we."

"The reason, then?"

"We are suspect, no more than that."

"Suspect . . . of what?"

For a long time, Caleb did not answer. Igal began to fidget, sure that this conversation could lead only to trouble for them both. He cleared his throat and said loudly, "If you will permit me to say so, Rahab, your wine is the best we have tasted for a very long time indeed. . . ."

But Rahab's eyes had not left Caleb, and she said very quietly, "Can it be that you come from the horde of strangers who have so recently and inexplicably crossed over the River Jordan? Can it be that you are . . . Hebrews from Egypt?"

Igal wailed, "No, we are merchants from the south—"

But Caleb shook his head. "Igal," he murmured, "our Rahab is a woman of understanding! Even if we wished, we would not be able to deceive her! And for my part—I do not believe it is necessary to try."

Suddenly, there was a thunderous hammering on the door to the house, and a muted voice shouted, "Open! Open to the soldiers of the king!"

Igal felt the blood draining from his face. He whispered hoarsely, "We are dead men, both of us. . . ."

But Caleb's old eyes were filled with a kind of good humor, and he said, "No, I think not. I think that we have found a friend." He turned to Rahab and said shrewdly, "I am sure that in your house there must be a place to hide, is it not so?"

The assault on the heavy door continued, and the old woman hobbled in to them and said, not worrying too much about it, "Soldiers. Shall I unbar the door? Or not?"

"One small moment," Rahab said swiftly, "and then, yes, open it."

She gestured at the unstable ladder and said, "The sleeping loft. Under the sleeping skin there is straw, and under the straw there are the rafters, a good hiding place between them. Go there, quickly. . . ."

Caleb was already clambering up the ladder, and Igal followed him, stumbling over his long gown, and as they wormed their way under the skin and into the straw, he was in great distress, and he wailed, "How can we trust her? A prostitute . . . !"

103

"Ssshhh . . ."

Igal fell silent, out of nothing more than fear. There were only bamboo canes tied below the rafters for a ceiling, and Caleb whispered, "Not a movement of any sort now."

They heard the sound as the old woman removed the timber bar across the door, and then there was a more fearsome sound, the clanging of metal against hide as two soldiers came down the corridor, striking their copper swords against their hard leather shields to announce their presence; it was a sound greatly dreaded throughout all of Canaan. And then, as they entered the room, the sound ceased and the voices began:

A man's voice first: "Your name, woman?"

Then Rahab's voice, mocking: "Ask your companion, soldier! His name is Amal, he has shared my bed a hundred times. And never a shekel paid for his pleasure."

The voice was harsher now: "I know *his* name. I demand *yours*."

"It is Rahab."

It was an incomplete identification, and the question came at once: "Rahab the daughter of . . . ?"

"The daughter of no man. Just . . . Rahab."

"A prostitute, then?"

"I live on the Street of Brothels," Rahab said scornfully. "Then what should I be? A seamstress? A leather worker? Yes, I am a prostitute."

"Two men, nomads from the desert beyond the river . . . Have you seen them?"

Frozen into immobility between the rafters, Igal was trembling as he thought of the three cups and the pitcher of wine down there; would she have found the time to dispose of them?

But the voices were wafting up to them, very clearly:

"They were here," Rahab said. "They were Hebrews from Egypt. But they had no money, nor had they come here for my services, but merely to hide. At night, my door cannot be barred to harbor criminals, it must be left open for those who search me out for the pleasure of my company."

The man again, harder still now: "But your door *was* barred. . . ."

"Against their possible return after I sent them on their way."

"You sent them away?"

"Yes."

"And you know where they went?"

"No."

"They did not stay to love you?"

"No."

"And why not?"

"They had no money."

"And I have no money either."

There was the tiniest of silences. And then, Rahab's voice, very soft and persuasive: "But you, Sergeant, are not a Hebrew, but an honest and hardworking Canaanite, as I am."

There was that little silence again, and then the sergeant's voice once more, filled with authority: "Search the loft, Amal."

A mumble, then, from the other man: "If you say so, Sergeant."

"And have you really slept with her so often?"

"There have been occasions, yes."

"And is she good?"

"She can take a man to the borders of ecstasy and far beyond them."

"Search the loft, then. And after that, the roof.
And then . . . you will return here only when I call
you, is that understood?"

"It is understood."

"Go now."

Lying motionless in their hiding place, Igal and
Caleb heard the creaking of the bound cross-pieces of
the ladder as Amal climbed up for the search. They
saw his feet within inches of their faces as they lay
there, holding their breath; they saw him climbing up
to the roof; and then the sounds were coming up to
them from the room below there.

First, the sergeant: "We are alone now. Take off
your gown, I wish to see your body."

Rahab's calm voice then: "Of course. As you
say."

In a moment, the sergeant's voice again: "Ah
. . . in a lifetime devoted to the pursuit of beautiful
women, I never before saw such breasts, nor such
thighs. . . ."

"If they give you pleasure, Sergeant."

"They will give me the greatest pleasure."

"Then take advantage of them."

"I will, I will. . . !"

Igal was stuffing the hem of his gown into his
mouth to stifle his moans as he listened to the sounds
of animal love below him, to the heavy grunting, and
the groaning, and—before long—the gasping of the
final release. There was a long, loud sigh, and then
all was official business again: "Amal! Come on
down, we go now!"

From the roof, there was the answering cry—"I
am here, Sergeant!"—and the heavy footsteps were
hurrying down the ladders once more.

Igal and Caleb knew that the danger had almost
gone, and then the voice of the sergeant came to

them from the room below, a harsh, officious voice: "If they should return, Rahab . . ."

She said swiftly, "They will not. I will bar my door again."

"So be it. But if they should, send your servant to the street; a single shout will suffice. There are soldiers on every corner now, searching for them."

"I will do so."

"Good night, then."

"Good night."

The sergeant and the soldier marched out, and in a little while there was the creaking of the ladder's rungs once more to announce Rahab's presence. They heard her quiet voice in the darkness: "My friends? And I do not even know your names . . ."

They came out from under the straw bedding, and Caleb whispered, "My name, Rahab, is Caleb, and my friend here is called Igal. And there are no words with which I can tell you how grateful we are."

"Come, we must talk now. We will drink more wine together."

She led them to the downstairs room and refilled their mugs, and Igal could not contain himself. He muttered, "I was sure that you would betray us, and you did not. My guilt is very heavy on me."

"And I was equally sure," Caleb said, "that you were our friend." His old eyes were very shrewd, and he was smiling. "There are certain classes, are there not—and please believe me when I say that I mean no disrespect—"

"I believe you," Rahab said, and Caleb went on. "Certain elements of any city's population are inherently opposed to those in authority over them. My young friend Igal does not understand this, because he has never lived in a city. He was born in a desert oasis called Kadesh-Barnea, and has been a tent-

107

ridden nomad all his life, one of the bedouin. I myself was born in Egypt, and I spent my youth——"

He laughed suddenly, a bright and very cheerful laugh that endeared him to Rahab, and he said, correcting himself, "Perhaps I should say that I *misspent* my youth in a great and glorious city named Rameses, after our Pharaoh, a city, I would have you know, that I helped to build.

"I was a slave then," he said with great dignity. And there were times when our slavemasters would not give us straw to bind together the bricks that we made, and yet . . . If, with his mallet, he could break one of them, we were flogged." He sighed. "I too was a rebel against the government. And I will say that many of the women I loved were harlots. I learned very quickly to understand the harrassment they suffer from a faceless entity known as . . . *authority*. It was very rife in Egypt, though I never understood why. But I am sure that it is rife in Jericho too, and will be so in every major city all over the world, for all of eternity."

Rahab said curiously, "And among the nomads, there are no harlots?"

"None," Igal said emphatically. But she paid him no attention at all.

Caleb nodded. "Yes, there are many of them." He looked to Igal and said, laughing, "Shall I mention the name Hannah of the tribe of Asher? Or the young woman Jalah of Gad? Or most of all——"

"Hannah seduced me when I was tired and not myself," Igal said hotly, interrupting him. "And Jalah . . ." he said, sulking, "I will not discuss Jalah."

"Then keep quiet, Igal! I have found here a woman of my own persuasion. . . . She is a woman of great quality, and I adore her."

Rahab was filling his mug again from the pitcher,

and Caleb was slowly and happily getting drunk. But he said, "We should not be discussing the women in our lives! Instead, we should be worrying about a very vexing problem. We heard that demanding sergeant say there is a soldier on every street corner now, searching for us. When we leave at the gate-opening in the morning, it might not be easy to elude them."

"Not in the morning," Rahab said. "But during the night, when the moon goes down."

Igal said, stammering, "But, but, but—the gates are closed at night! No one can leave the city. . . ."

"There is a way," Rahab siad. She poured still more wine, and said slowly, "My house, as you may have observed, is built into the city wall. There is a way from it to the outside."

"And you will show it to us in exchange for . . . for *what?*" Caleb asked. "We have very little money, Rahab."

"Not money," Rahab said. "For my life."

"Your *life?*"

Even Caleb was startled, and Rahab said, "I have a friend, a very dear friend, one of the *Anakim,* the giants. He tells me that your people will soon attack Jericho, he tells me that our defenses are weak, he tells me that our seven-thousand-year-old walls are crumbling. . . . In short, he tells me that soon the great city of Jericho will be no more. I have children, I do not wish to see them put to the sword. My own life matters nothing, but theirs . . . I do not want them to be part of the slaughter. And if it is so certain that our destruction is imminent, as my friend suggests, then the time to save my life and the lives of my children is *now.*"

It was to Caleb that she was talking, and she ignored Igal completely. She said very softly, "If I help you to escape from the city, will it become known among our assailants that there is one Canaanite woman in Jericho who is your friend? A woman who saved you from the soldiers? For if they had caught you, be assured that they would have cut off your heads!"

"Yes," Caleb said at once. "I will see that it is known."

"And will it mean that your people will spare me, and my family too?"

"Yes, I can arrange it. I have the confidence of our leader, whose name is Joshua."

"But in the heat of battle . . ."

"Ah yes," Caleb sighed. "It is true. The heat of battle is indeed a fearsome thing, a man easily loses control of his senses."

"And they will not stop every woman on the street and ask, before they slay her, 'Is your name Rahab?' Even if we hide ourselves in the house . . ."

"A sign then," Igal said urgently. "A sign, Caleb, by which the house may be known, as once blood from slaughtered lambs was plastered on the lintels of our people's houses in Egypt."

Caleb nodded. He thought about it for a while and said at last, "When the battle begins, tie a scarlet cloth to your windows, as a sign for our people. I will ensure that Joshua knows its meaning, that our whole army knows its meaning. They will say when they see it: 'This is the house of Rahab, who is to be spared.' "

Rahab's sigh of relief was very audible. "So be it, then," she said. "The moon will soon be down, and if you are to escape unseen, we should wait for absolute darkness. There are patrols outside the walls every night."

110

She called for her ancient servant and said, "There is a rope in the stables. Bring it."

She hobbled out, and when she came back with the heavy coil in her arms, Rahab laid it on the table and murmured, "A good rope, it is very strong. It belonged to my family for four generations."

There was a long, oppressive silence as they sat like three strangers, and at last Rahab said politely, "If you wish more wine . . . ?"

Caleb shook his head. "No, though I thank you. If there are patrols beyond the walls, we will need all our wits and our vigilance to elude them."

The silence again, and Rahab said quietly, her eyes cast down, "If you wish to lie with me before you leave . . . ?"

Blustering to hide his embarrassment, Igal said, "No, no, I think not." But she was watching Caleb and saw his eyes go to the bed on which the sergeant had so recently taken her, saw that he was smiling gently. She said quickly, "Not here, but in my own quarters on the upper floor. I find that I cannot regard you as . . . merely customers."

For a moment, Caleb did not answer her. He picked up the coil of goat's-hair rope, tested its strength, and murmured, "Yes, it is well made. And the window you spoke of that looks out beyond the wall? Is it the one in the upper chamber?"

"Yes."

"Then perhaps, while there is still a moon, you should point out for me the best way to go, so that the patrols will not see us."

Rahab nodded. "Then come."

She went to the ladder and climbed it, and as Caleb followed her he looked back and saw that Igal, uncertain, had risen to his feet, not quite sure what to do now. He was almost laughing, and he said, "Wait below, Igal, till I call you. Drink a mug of wine, it will not be long."

"Yes, yes, of course . . ." Igal said awkwardly. He turned away and reached for the pitcher, his heart beating very fast. He waited till they had disappeared and looked up at the darkness of the loft; he heard their muted voices there, guessing from their whispered words that they were at the window.

Rahab's voice came to him first: "Gilgal . . . it looks so beautiful in the moonlight."

Then Caleb: "An empty shell now. But our people are slowly beginning to occupy the houses there, many of them leaving the tents they were born to and sampling the pleasures of mud walls and roofs of thatch."

"And so many fires. They look like red stars there, and just as impossible to count."

"For each fire, a tent, for each tent, perhaps as many as a dozen people. Truly, there are very many of us. And down to the ground from here? Eight or nine cubits?"

"No more than that. A man can drop to it safely, but for your old bones, a rope is better."

"My bones are indeed old. But I am still strong."

"Indeed?"

"Yes, indeed."

Her arm was around him affectionately. "And you are . . . what? Ninety years old?"

"No, not yet. I was born eighty-one years ago, on the morning of the day on which the Pharaoh, in Egypt, took his young sister to wife." He laughed softly. "And still . . . I am very strong."

"And your friend downstairs?"

"A man," Caleb said, "of many great and admirable qualities. Unhappily . . ." He chuckled. "Unhappily, they are so deeply hidden that very few men even suspect that they might be there."

"But you do."

"Yes. My great age has brought me, as it should, a certain understanding. But . . . in the company of a beautiful woman, I do not choose to dicuss another man, who might well be a rival for my affections."

They were flirting together, like young children, and she whispered, "Then come to bed. Show me how strong you are."

He turned her round to face him, and embraced her, saying quietly, "But I should tell you . . . I have very little money, Rahab."

She sighed and said dryly, "It seems that our Canaanite gods have determined to deny me payment for my services tonight. Well . . . Come to bed. We will make love and rest awhile, as we wait for the darkness."

Listening and trembling, Igal could no longer hear their murmurs. He drank and tried to contain his anger, not even knowing what it was that he was angry about. He leaned back in his chair and closed his eyes, and without really wanting to, he fell asleep.

He could not tell how much time had gone by when he awoke with a start; had someone called his name? And where in Heaven's name was he? Then the voice came to him from above, quite sharply now: "Igal! What, are you forever sleeping? Come! It is time for us to leave now!"

The memories came flooding back, and he gathered up his gown and clambered up the ladder again, stumbling. In the light of the single tallow there, he saw Rahab and Caleb standing by the square of black night-sky that was the window, and there was

113

a gentle and quite strange look in the woman's dark eyes, a look of sadness and great pleasure both combined in enigma.

Caleb fumbled in his waist-cloth and found a coin. He pressed it into her hand and said quietly, "It is for the wine we drank, nothing more."

She looked at it and whispered, "You are very generous, but no. I will not take it."

"Take it," he urged her, but she was adamant.

"No. I do not take money from friends. Neither for wine, nor for anything else." She tucked it back into his belt and said, "Go now. Remember, as soon as you reach the ground, run quickly down the slope till you reach the bushes. And then . . . move east before you descend into the valley. Once you pass the stream, you will be safe, but not before."

The old man embraced her warmly. "We leave you in peace, Rahab."

"And go in peace. Whatever gods your people have be with you."

Caleb smiled, a kindly, gentle smile. "Only one God. And we will meet again."

He turned to Igal and said, "Go first, I will follow you. Remember . . . silence."

Igal looked at Rahab and said politely, "And our thanks for what you have done."

He eased himself through the window, seized hold of the rope, and slid down it to the ground; and in a moment Caleb was there beside him, staring up at the window as the rope was hauled up again. His old face was tired and drawn, but his eyes were very bright. He called out quietly, "Peace, always peace . . ."

Igal hissed, "Ssshhh . . . We are once again among our enemies."

As though to answer him, a distant shout came to

them: "Hey! You there! Two men . . . !" And then, the same voice, raised in a command and much louder: "After them, first squad . . . !"

Caleb was already half a hundred feet down the hillside before Igal recovered his wits and raced after him, falling over his gown again in his haste, picking himself up and staggering on, his heart pounding. He came to the cover of the shrubbery, and Caleb reached out and grabbed his arm, saying quickly, "This way now, to the east . . ." He was even laughing silently.

For a while, they heard the sound of pursuit behind them, and then there was only the silence of the night. They found the stream at the bottom of the little *wadi*, and lay on their bellies to slake their thirst, then rested awhile to catch their breath.

They climbed slowly up the hill in silence, and as they came to the ridge that gave onto the village, Igal felt Caleb's strong hand on his arm, and he saw that his companion was staring ahead into the darkness. Caleb could see like an owl at night. He dragged Igal down to the grass with him, and whispered so quietly that his words were almost inaudible: "Wait for me here. . . ."

He slithered off, silent as a fox, and when he returned a few moments later, Igal saw, to his astonishment, that he was carrying an extra sword. But Caleb only gestured for silence, and when they reached the village itself at last, he said gravely, "You did not see him?"

Igal shook his head, irritated as always when he was puzzled. "See whom? No, I saw no one."

Caleb held up the sword and said, "One of our sentries, fast asleep. The boy Joram from the tribe of Naphtali. If Joshua learns of this, he will have him killed at once. Take the sword to the Naphtali tents,

115

find Joram's father, and give it to him. Tell him the circumstances, a sentry sleeping on duty, let him settle the matter in his own way."

All the excitements of the night were crowding into Igal's mind now that they were safe again, and he said testily, "Caleb! How often must I remind you who is in command of this patrol? I will not have you give me orders!"

"Not an order," Caleb said soothingly, "merely a suggestion."

"Which I do not accept! Go yourself to the Naphtali tents and find the boy's father! Mark you, the suggestion is a good one."

Caleb sighed. "Unhappily, I cannot. Joshua will be waiting for me, to learn from me not only all that we have found out about Jericho, but also what I may have to say about your own potential as a leader. He's very anxious to know about that."

Igal stared. "He is?"

"Yes. Well, never mind! We will give the sentry's sword to Joshua and leave it all to him."

He turned away, but Igal stopped him. "Give me the weapon," he said gruffly. "How can I handle this affair if I do not have the sword as proof of this young man's negligence?"

Caleb nodded and handed it over, saying, "The tents of the Naphtalis are in the hollow that lies to the west of us above the banks of the river—"

"I *know* where they are!" Igal interrupted him angrily. "I *know* where the Reubens and the Simeons are, the tents of Dan, Gad, and Asher! Of Judah, Levi, Benjamin, and Issachar! I know where they all are! What, you take me for a fool?"

"I take you," Caleb said quietly, "for a man who will one day lead his people, in battle, to great victories. I take you for a man who will one day bring great honor, with his valor, to all the tribes."

Igal's voice was hushed. "You do?"

"Yes."

"In truth?"

"I swear it."

There was a short silence. And then, Igal whispered, "You are a good friend, Caleb."

"A good friend," Caleb said, "only to good men. And on this mission of ours, you have done only one foolish thing."

Igal stammered, "Only—only one? And that was . . . ? Tell me, Caleb!"

Caleb said, chuckling, "It was very foolish of you to have refused the woman Rahab. You would greatly have enjoyed her. Go now."

Igal mumbled, "Yes. Yes, of course." He stared at the sword and said, "Joram of Naphtali?"

"Yes."

"And the Naphtalis are . . . where? I seem to have forgotten."

"In the hollow that lies to the west of us," Caleb said.

Igal nodded vigorously. "I know, I *know*! Above the bank of the river! There is a stand of olive trees there that marks the entrance to their camp—"

"No," Caleb said. "The olive trees you speak of mark the camp of the Zebulun."

"Good night," Igal said with great dignity. "We will meet again, no doubt, in the morning."

When the night had swallowed him up, Caleb went off to find his impatient leader Joshua.

There was a great deal he had to tell him.

117

Chapter Eight

Joshua had been meditating again, worrying about the difficulties of overcoming Jericho and yet knowing that the city's destruction was mandatory if he was to penetrate any further into Canaan.

He sat with Caleb at his favorite viewpoint on the edge of Gilgal's bluff, where the sandstone dropped precipitously away into the green valley, spotted here and there with yellow climbing shrubs and little scarlet flowers, and the scent of wild thyme was strong on the evening air, cool, balmy, and satisfying.

The sun was turning to red-gold as it sank over the distant mountain, and Joshua said heavily, "We could take Bethel or Ai more easily, and either of these cities would give us a firm foothold from which to proceed south, to Jerusalem perhaps, certainly to Hebron and Lachish, and perhaps even as far as Gaza, which would be a prize indeed. But Jericho would always be behind us, a great danger to our lines of communication which we *must* maintain, all the way back to the River Jordan. It means that Jericho must be taken."

He turned his hard, fanatic stare on Caleb and said, "Jericho is strong. Their walls, broken as they are, are an insuperable barrier, since we have no catapults or battering-rams, nor do we know how to use them, even if we could make them, which we cannot. They have archers without number, using very long range bows, against which the puny bows our hunters carry will be of no service at all. They have chariots and cavalry, while we, who have become bedouin in our desert wanderings, do not even merit the honorable title Foot Soldiers."

There was a dangerous mood on him, and Caleb said carefully, "But . . . this does not mean that you have given up all hope of conquering Jericho?"

"No, it does not. What it means is we need a miracle, which only our God can provide."

"And our God is for us," Caleb said piously, not quite sure where this discussion was leading.

He was surprised at the reaction. "No!" Joshua shouted furiously. "He is not for us now, he is against us!"

"Oh? And why should that be?" Caleb was thinking: *He's been conferring with Yahweh again, Heaven save us. . . .*

For a long time, Joshua did not answer him, but just sat there scowling. He said at last, sullenly, "Cast your mind back, Caleb, into our people's history."

"I find it very easy to do," Caleb murmured.

Joshua went on. "When Moses heard the word of the Lord from the burning bush, and traveled in search of his brother Aaron to be his interpreter, he fell ill and was close to death."

"It is well known . . ." Caleb said politely.

"But his wife Zipporah," Joshua said, his voice rising, "knew the true reason for his sickness! It was because their newly-born son Eliezer had not been circumcised! And so, she took a sharp flint and per-

121

formed the rite, and Moses' life was spared by a wise and benevolent God."

Now Caleb knew exactly what was on Joshua's mind. He said slowly, "For forty years of wandering, our people have been dispirited, cast-down, and exhausted. And because of this, the rite of circumcision has been neglected. Our men all have foreskins, like the heathens."

"It is an affront to Yahweh," Joshua said. "And we need his help now."

There was quiet for a very long time, and then Caleb said, "It is not intended as criticism, but are you asking that all of our men circumcise themselves?"

"No," Joshua said. "I am not asking it, I am *demanding* it! You and I were circumcised at birth, as were all men of your generation and mine. But those of our people who were born in Kadesh-Barnea were not." He raised his strident voice and said, "I will not lead uncircumcised heathens into battle against Jericho!"

"It is a heavy task you put on them," Caleb murmured.

"Heavy or not, let them see to it!" Joshua shouted.

Caleb rose to his feet. "Very well. It shall be as you say."

"Within ten days! Not one man to be left uncircumcised!"

"I will so order it. By morning, the runners will go to the tents of all the tribes."

And for the next ten days, the holy rite went on. There was no metal in all of Canaan sharp enough for surgery, and now good flintstones were in great demand, passed from family to family, split with mallets time and time again to provide satisfactory

122

cutting edges. Fathers circumcised their sons, and then themselves, binding the wounds with rags over pastes of wood ash and water to inhibit infection. And in time, word came back to Joshua: *"All the sons of Zebulun are circumcised . . ." "The people of Benjamin, purified . . ." "The men of Issachar . . ."*

And when news of all the tribes had come to him, Joshua called a meeting of the Elders.

Raising his arms to the heavens, he shouted, "I have this night met with an angel of the Lord! And he raised up his sword and said to me, *'I am Captain of the Host of the Lord! And I will give you Jericho, and its King, and all of its mighty men of valor!' We are all circumcised now, and our Lord God Yahweh is for us and not for our adversaries!"*

He lowered his voice, no longer the fanatic, but a rational man—for the moment. "I want one thousand men from each of the twelve tribes, your finest warriors. And before the new moon, Jericho will be . . . *ours!"*

As he spoke, the earth resumed its fearful trembling.

Igal's sweet young daughter Elisheva had broken all the household rules; in defiance of her father's authority, she had left her pegged-out skin bed in the family tent, listening first to his heavy breathing to make sure that he was truly asleep. He had drunk a great deal of wine this night, and she had heard her mother Azuza say to him in that weary, disapproving voice she so often used: "Sleep, husband, you are tired. It has been a heavy day. One of the goats died this evening, stung by scorpions."

Igal sighed. "Then at least there will be meat to eat, instead of your damned bread."

"My bread is good, the envy of all the neighbors."

"And from its skin . . . I need a new pair of sandals."

"Your sandals need only new soles. I will stitch them."

"Do that. Elisheva?"

"Elisheva is sleeping, as she should at this hour." A touch of temper came over her, and she said, "Ask me instead about your son Elam."

"Very well. What about Elam?"

"He is out in the desert, hunting lion with a spear, in the darkness. If he finds one, he will be killed."

"Elam is a grown man, he does not need the fluttering of a woman's anxiety to inhibit his actions."

"Go to sleep, husband. If you need me, I am beside you."

"Why should I need you?" Igal said scornfully. "You are old, woman." He laughed shortly. "Ha! In Jericho there was a prostitute named Rahab, and she wanted me—you understand what I am saying? She *wanted* me, offered herself to me! But I refused her! It was a mistake. Even Caleb told me it was a mistake."

"Caleb!" Azuza said scornfully. "That man is an evil influence on you!"

"Her name was Rahab," Igal said dreamily, "a woman of startling good looks. Caleb lay with her. But I did not. And now . . . it's too late."

"Then go back to Jericho if you wish, why should I care?"

He said angrily, "Be quiet now. I want to sleep."

He slept deeply, thinking of the smooth-skinned Rahab, and in a little while Azuza shook him by the shoulder and said quietly, "Elisheva . . . she left her bed a while ago and has not returned."

He was only half-awake, and very angry at having

124

his pleasant dream shattered. He said sharply, "She went outside to urinate, no doubt. What, should she do that in the tent?"

"It was a long time ago, husband."

"She will be back, she's a good girl. Now go to sleep and let me sleep too. I'm tired."

Azuza sighed and closed her eyes, and listened to the animal sound of Igal's snoring.

But Elisheva did not soon return.

She was walking quickly through the cool night, climbing up the steep slope that led to Gilgal itself, a tall and slender beauty with all the charm of her tender years; she moved with a desert lion's natural grace, and her dark eyes were large and startling against a smooth complexion that was almost the color of almonds. Her hair was black and very long, dropping below her waist on those rare occasions when she let it hang free; most of the time it was fastened on top of her head with bone pins in glorious disarray. There was a quality about her that made all the young men stop their work when she passed them by, stopping to stare at her and wonder how it might be to lie with her; but she scorned almost all of them, jealously guarding her chastity and never letting any of them even touch her.

There was, however, one young man she knew, whose name was Tubal, of the people of Dan, and he was on sentry duty this night, standing in the shelter of an olive tree on the very edge of the bluff that faced Jericho. He was eighteen years old and quite unaccustomed, like most of the Israelites, to soldierly duty, preferring the easygoing life of the fields among the flocks, following the tinkling sound of the goat bells with no problems to worry him, and no responsibilities save the care of his herd.

He was slender and well formed, though a little

delicate, and very handsome indeed, his face only lightly bearded, his eyes thoughtful and introspective; and Elisheva looked at him with feelings much the same as those of the men who looked at her. . . .

When she came to him in the darkness, he laid his sword on the ground and embraced her. He whispered, "Elisheva . . . my love! I was not sure that you would come."

"I said I would come," Elisheva murmured, "and I came."

His arms were tight about her. "My love, my love, my love for all time . . ."

She laughed, a pleasant and friendly sound, and she mocked him: "What, '*my* love'? I am not yet yours."

"No. But soon you will be."

"Do not be too sure of it."

There was a sudden alarm on him. "But . . . you promised . . ."

"I did not promise. I said *perhaps*."

"But I love you, as you love me! The outcome is inevitable!"

"No, it is not! I am a virgin still, and I do not want to lose that happy condition to a man who may or may not marry me one day."

"Marry you? But I told you! If that is what you truly want, I will speak to my father—"

"And have you done so?"

He still held her tightly, but he could not meet her eyes. He said at last, "Well, no, not yet. I am a very dutiful son, I cannot just say, '*Father, I wish to marry Elisheva. . . .*'"

"Why not?"

"Why not? Well . . . He has a girl from the tribe of Asher in mind for me, and I must wait for the right moment to tell him that—that—that my heart is with Elisheva of Issachar, the daughter of Igal."

"Your heart!" she said scornfully. "What will your father care about your heart?"

He said hotly, "He might! We are on the very best of terms!"

"Yes, I know. All our people know it, you are a spoiled brat."

He laughed suddenly. "A brat, perhaps! But not spoiled until you love me! And then, yes! Spoiled beyond all imaginings!"

His hand was reaching for her breast, and she brushed it away, "No, Tubal! That is not allowed."

"But I love you, Elisheva," he said hoarsely. "And, honestly, I must have you! I *must!*"

"No, that is not allowed either."

He held her so tightly that he could feel the beating of her heart. He took her hands in his and whispered, "Then sit here under the tree, and let me lie beside you with my head in your lap."

"Well . . ."

"Please?" He said, urging her, "I will give no offense, I promise you."

"Well . . ."

She sighed. "All right, then. You are really very persuasive, Tubal."

She sat down cross-legged on the sand, and he stretched out happily beside her with his head resting on her thigh, and he murmured, "In all the world, Elisheva, there is no one else . . ."

She wrapped his tousled hair around her fingers and teased it. "Not even that awful girl your father has in mind for you? What's her name? Abigail?"

"Yes, Abigail. Honestly, I can't stand the sight of her."

"I should hope not! She has a wart on her nose."

127

"Yes, I know, it's quite dreadful. But I really don't want to talk about her, Elisheva. Let's talk about you."

"All right, then. What do you want to know about me?"

"I want to know if you love me, just a little bit."

"No. Not even a little bit."

"But . . ." He was desperate. "But could you *learn* to love me one day, do you suppose?"

"Oh, I suppose so," she said airily. "Everything is *possible*, isn't it?"

He took her other hand, kissed it, and held it to his cheek. She was transported and still determined not to let it show. He whispered, "Tell me what you truly think of me, I want to know . . ."

"W-el-l . . ." Her fingers were still entangled in his hair. "I think you're very handsome . . ."

"You do?"

"Oh yes! Very handsome indeed. But it doesn't mean very much, does it?"

"Of course not, I know that! But what *is* important? I mean, in your estimation?"

"Oh, I don't know. *Fortitude*, I suppose. Bravery . . . But you are nice, I really like you very much."

She was leaning down over him, and she could not understand why it was that his mouth had suddenly dropped open, nor what might be the reason for that dreadful terror that had come into his startled eyes. She twisted her head round to follow his look, and stared up in a darkness that was almost absolute to see the face of a Canaanite soldier.

She saw his spear raised high, saw it streak down and embed itself in Tubal's chest, saw the barbed head withdrawn, bringing flesh and blood with it, saw it driven home again and yet again.

All of time seemed to stand still as her would-be

lover screamed and clutched helplessly for the haft of the spear that had already killed him. His life was quite gone, but he was still thrashing as the nameless soldier withdrew the blade for the last time. The Canaanite reached out and seized her hair and twisted it into a knot, and pulled her face close to his own. He was grinning wildly, and he hissed at her, "I could as easily kill you too, child, but I have my orders and I obey them. They are . . . to let it be known among your people that the Canaanites are not sleeping. So *tell them!*"

As silently and as swiftly as he had come, he was gone.

Elisheva screamed and went on screaming, and men came running. One of them tried to pull her away, but in her hysteria she was clutching Tubal's head and twisting it this way and that, as though seeking to shake it back to life. . . .

Igal came at last, and stared down at her in shock, understanding nothing, and then, among the others, Caleb was thrusting his way to her. He bent down and took hold of her shoulders and said, with no gentleness in his voice at all: "Stop your screaming, girl! Stop it! It will serve no purpose now! Stop it, I say!"

But she could not; and suddenly, he slapped her face hard.

Now she was silent, and then she let a moan escape from her throat, allowed him to pull her to her feet, and collapsed into him, sinking her head onto his chest as she wept.

He said gruffly, "And do not turn to me for comfort, child! Your father is here. And he loves you even more than I do."

Igal came out of his bewilderment and took her in his arms, but all he could find to say was, "But why

. . . why did you leave the tent? You are not allowed to leave the tent at night. . . ."

He stared helplessly at Caleb, and Caleb said gently, "It is not a time for recrimination, Igal, good friend. Take her home, be gentle with her . . . She has been sorely hurt."

"Yes. Yes, of course . . ."

He began to move away with her, and his heart was breaking with her sobbing. But then, a powerful voice came out of the darkness, and it was the authoritative voice of Joshua himself: "Wait! I will talk with her!"

In the moonlit darkness, Joshua was striding toward them and shouldering his way through the little crowd that had gathered. He stared down at Tubal's body, and turned his hard eyes on Elisheva. He said coldly, "If you can contain your womanish tears, child, you will tell me now how this young man met his death."

Igal's arms were still around her. He drew himself up to his full height and said with dreadful dignity, "She comes with me, Joshua. *Home.* In the morning, if you wish it, she will talk with you. Not now."

"Now!" Joshua roared. "I will talk with her *now!*"

As if to match his fury, a clap of thunder came, and bolts of white lightning struck at the earth. Out of a dark sky that only moments ago had been cloudless, a heavy rain of hailstones beat down on them, striking painfully on unprotected heads. Over the sound of the storm Igal shouted, "No! Not now, for reasons which should be apparent to you. . . !" Even so, he could not forget the courtesies, and he muttered, "My tent is your tent, and you are always a welcome guest."

Joshua did not hear him, and Igal moved back a

130

few steps to confront him at very close quarters, saying, more calmly now, "Your anger, Joshua, does not frighten me."

Why was it that their leader seemed, for the first time ever, to be such a small and slight figure? The hailstones were pounding down, and the constant lightning lit up their rain-streaked faces as the thunder burst over them again. Igal shouted, "My daughter Elisheva, whom I love dearly, will come home with me now. She has been sorely hurt. You may talk with her in the morning. Good night, Joshua."

He turned away and moved off, and Joshua screamed after him, "Seven of our sentries have been killed this night! I must know who the raiders are. . . !"

Igal turned back. "Who they are?" he asked scornfully. "They will be Canaanites from Jericho, who else? They know that we are set on their destruction. What, you think they will sit there and wait for us to attack them? Sitting idly by and doing *nothing*? Good night, Joshua."

Joshua screamed, "Seven of our sentries killed! I must know!"

But Igal was gone, and Caleb said gently, "You have asked me so many times, Joshua, is Igal a man, or a fool? Is he of the stuff from which leaders are made? And I think you have your answer now."

Joshua glowered at him, and Caleb went on. "We have seen what it is that—that *touches* Igal, brings out the good in him. It is danger to those he loves. Tonight, a young boy named Tubal, who might or might not have been Elisheva's lover, was killed by a prowling Canaanite scout. She saw him die, and she wept, as she should weep. But for Igal . . . he knows that the same spear could well have killed her too, and that it is only by the grace of God that it did not. A raider, slipping quickly in for the kill, and as quickly slipping away again. And Igal wonders why he killed only Tubal. He wonders, in terror, why he did not kill Elisheva too." He smiled. "You and I both know the answer to that perplexing riddle, do we not? And by morning . . . Igal will know it too. He is a little slow of understanding."

"A witness left," Joshua said darkly, "to testify to their invincibility."

"More than that. A dead body is witness enough. But the terror of a young girl . . . it is contagious. The killer knows that it will spread among our people like the plague."

"Come with me," Joshua said.

He led Caleb to the edge of the cliff, and they stared across the intervening valley to Jericho, tightly locked up for the night now, its walls intermittently illuminated by sheets of lightning. He sat on his haunches and stared at them; and after an interminable silence he said, "I want one thousand men from each of the twelve tribes, just as we fought the Amalekites in the desert. They will be led by the priests with their ram's-horns, and we will march on Jericho."

"Very well," Caleb nodded. "There will be many breaches in their vaunted walls, I have seen them where they are crumbling."

"They will be flattened to the ground."

"Perhaps it is possible." He chuckled. "The earth tremor we suffered yesterday . . . One or two more like that and Jericho will have no walls left at all. And so . . . we march on the city?"

"We march *around* it. And then retreat."

Caleb frowned. "We show ourselves, and then retire without joining battle? It seems to make little sense, Joshua."

"Twelve thousand men," Joshua said, "climbing the hills to Jericho, in battle formation. Their first sight of us will bring the defenders crowding the city walls, their bows and arrows, their javelins, their catapults ready. But we will stay out of their range, and we will circle the city, once. And then, we will go back to our camp at Gilgal and the slopes below it."

"Yes, of course. I understand." Caleb thought for a while and said at last, "No, I do *not* understand! What good will this do us?"

"On the second day," Joshua said, "we will once more climb the hill as though we were about to attack. Again, we will circle the city once, and retire."

"Ah . . ." Caleb's eyes were gleaming in the darkness. "We circle it as though we were taking up positions for an assault?"

"Yes."

"And then . . . we retreat?"

"Yes."

"And how long do we play this game with them?"

Joshua rose to his feet and pointed with his almond staff. "A great prize awaiting us," he said. The thunderstorm, as quickly as it had come, had gone, and the clouds, scudding across the moon, were alternately casting it into shadow and lighting it with an eerie blue.

His staff was a projection of his thoughts as he pointed it down into the valley and said, "On the first day, the moment they see twelve thousand men climbing the slope, the alarm will sound, and every armed man among them will take to the walls. And then we retire; they will wait till they are sure we have gone and are not returning before they stand down. On the second day, it will be the same. Perhaps even on the third. But by the fourth, they will begin muttering to each other, 'What are those mad

133

Israelites up to? Here they come again, and they will go again, some strange rite to satisfy their gods; they will not dare to attack us. . . .' By the fifth day, they will be tired of the game, and the numbers ready and waiting for us will be diminished. You must remember—it takes a great deal of time and effort for an army of defenders to move into a state of readiness. The saddling of horses, the preparation of the chariots, even the stringing of their powerful bows and the selection of arrows that have not become hopelessly warped in the heat. . . . It can become very wearisome indeed."

"And we attack them . . . ?"

"On the seventh day," Joshua said, "we will not retreat. We will pour through the walls to find them unprepared."

Caleb nodded. "It is a good plan. I counted a dozen places where the walls have already crumbled and have been very carelessly repaired. Slaves have been filling the breaches with their bare hands, and with our hands . . . we can open those breaches again."

Joshua fell silent and Caleb waited. The leader's heavy brows were furrowed, and he said at last, slowly, "Our bare hands tearing down stonework will leave our bodies exposed to their swords. No, we will bring down the walls first, in twenty, forty, a hundred places."

Caleb grunted. "If we had siege catapults, it would be easy, but we have none."

Joshua moved away to the very edge of the cliff and stared up at the heavens in silence. Caleb was waiting, thinking: *A maniac! Communing with his God again!* But he said quietly, "Better that we try to fashion catapults, Joshua. One or two will suffice."

There was that long, oppressive silence again, and Joshua turned back at last and said, musing, "You remember when we were sent to Canaan by Moses, you and I? To spy out the land?"

"Of course."

"There was a traveler from the snow-covered mountains of Lebanon, an Aramean, I think. He spoke to me of mountain passes blocked with great walls of ice. He told me . . . a shout, sometimes, would bring them crumbling down, an avalanche of the most terrible proportions."

"I have heard of this," Caleb said. "But we are dealing with walls of stone, not of ice. With walls that have stood for seven thousand years or more . . ."

"And are therefore no longer strong . . ."

"But of *stone*, Joshua . . ."

"Stones that have been shaken by constant, continuing earthquakes for—how long is it? More than a generation! Fifty years!"

He threw out his arms and held them high, and his voice was a fervent shout as he stood outlined against the dark sky: "The sound of twelve thousand voices raised as one! The sound of all our ram's-horns blown as a single note! The walls will crumble, Caleb! I have spoken with the Lord . . . and He has told me . . . they will crumble if we do His bidding!"

He sat down suddenly, cross-legged, laid his staff across his thighs, and folded his arms. There was a sullen, angry look in his eyes as he stared out across the valley. He mumbled, scowling, "It will be as I say, because this is what the Lord God has told me. We will bring down the walls of Jericho with the sound of our ram's-horns, and our voices."

There was a mood on him, and Caleb knew that

135

he could not argue. He said quietly, "I am an old man, Joshua. I need my sleep. Good night."

When he reached the line where the trees began, he looked back and saw the silhouette of that distant, sad and lonely figure, motionless in the silence.

He sighed and went to his tent.

Chapter Nine

Elisheva slept very late in the morning; and it was not customary for her.

She awoke with a start to find that the tent was light, its flaps all open and the morning breeze drifting through to take away the night's accumulation of smoke from the tiny charcoal fire.

Her eyes were wide with the sudden fear that she had neglected her morning duties, but Igal was by her side. How long had he been squatting there? He held her hand and said gently, "Everything is well. You slept, and I am glad of it."

She was trying to struggle to a sitting position, though his hands were firm on her. "But . . . I have to bring water. . . ."

"Your mother is bringing the water."

"There is wood to find for the fire . . ."

"Azuza will do that too. She knows what you have suffered; she is a good woman. I said to her, 'Elisheva must rest today. You will perform all of her allotted tasks,' and she agreed at once. She has gone to the river now to fetch water, and later, she will bring wood for the fire. . . . You must rest now, and empty your mind of all thoughts of Tubal."

"Tubal . . ." There were tears invading her eyes.

"Was he your lover?"

It was as though she wished he had been. She shook her head. "No, Father." It was not easy to talk with him about these things. "He wanted to become my lover, but I would not allow it. I am still a virgin."

"And I am glad of it. For a young girl of such great beauty, the temptations are always very strong. He was a good boy, Tubal, always polite to his elders . . . Were you fond of him?"

"Yes, very fond."

She was weeping suddenly, and she clutched at him and sobbed, "I saw the spear come out of his chest, dragging flesh and blood with it, and yet . . . there was still life in his eyes. . . ."

"Ssshhh . . . You must forget you ever saw it, consign it to the limbo of unwanted memories."

"Yes, I know it. It is not easy. I did not truly love him. But perhaps . . . I *could* have been the mother of his firstborn. And now, he will have *no* firstborn."

She looked up at her father, for whom she had the greatest love, and she whispered, "Was I so wrong? If I had not refused him, there would have been a son of Tubal. But no, he died without issue."

"You were not wrong," Igal said. He stroked her hair. "Your chastity is very important to me. And one day soon we will find you a husband." He said fiercely, "A husband who will treat you with the respect you deserve."

Joshua came to see them, in his usual furious temper, and he said abruptly to Igal, "Leave us. I will speak with your daughter alone."

Igal remembered that last night he had defied Joshua, and yet the Lord God Yahweh had not struck him dead. He said calmly, "No. There is com-

139

fort for her in the knowledge that I am by her side. Speak to her, ask her whatever you wish, but I will stay with her."

"Very well, then."

Joshua turned his terribly contemptuous eyes on Elisheva. "A child of no consequence," he said sourly. "But you will tell me what I wish to know. The Canaanite who killed your Tubal. What arms was he bearing?"

"He was not *my* Tubal. He was a friend, no more than that," Elisheva said clearly, perhaps echoing her father's newfound assurance.

Joshua said harshly, "His armament?"

"A spear, the spear that tore into his poor body ..."

"A sword too?"

"Yes, in his belt."

"A dagger? A bow across his shoulder? A second spear? Javelins too, perhaps?"

His presence was awesome, and Elisheva was greatly confused. She whispered, "I saw only the spear, I saw only how it dragged out great tortured masses of his flesh as it was withdrawn. . . ."

"Ha! Then their spears are recurved? Barbed? A simple spearhead will not drag out flesh when it is withdrawn."

"Then I think they must have been barbed."

"A shield?"

"No, he carried no shield."

"You are sure, child?"

"I have memories only of the spear. But there was no shield, I am sure of it."

"Armbands on his wrists to counter sword-blows?"

"I saw no armbands. I saw only blood."

"And there was warning of his coming?"

"None."

"Had you not been fornicating, would you have heard him?"

Elisheva said hotly, "We were not fornicating! If you wish it, my mother will examine me, and she will tell you that I am still a virgin!"

"I want to know," Joshua said resignedly, "how well he moved in the darkness. A breath of his coming, only an instant before he was there?"

"Not a sound of any sort."

"A highly skilled night-marauder, then?"

"Yes, I think so."

Joshua turned to Igal. He said softly, "In a moment of anger last night, I told you, I think, that seven of our sentries had been killed."

Igal nodded. "Yes, I remember."

"The final count was made later, at dawn. I placed forty-two sentries on the hillsides between Gilgal here, and Jericho. Last night, twenty-three of them were killed! Without a single outcry from any of them! And from now on . . ."

He raised his voice again to its normal high ferocity and shouted, "Igal! You will assume my authority here! Summon forty-eight men, four from each of the tribes. They will be *commanders of sentries*! Every night, they will go from post to post to make sure that the sentries are wide-awake and alert! And any man found sleeping on duty . . ."

He glared at Igal and said darkly, "I have heard of a sentry found sleeping, whose sword was taken from him and given to his father, so that he might be chastised." His eyes were very hard. "Joram of the tribe of Naphtali," he said, "and whipping is not enough."

There was a little pause, and then he went on. "I have had Joram slain, as a lesson to others who might neglect their duty."

He turned back to Igal. "Your first position in authority," he said, "is to command the commanders of sentries. From Gilgal itself down to the banks of the River Jordan, they will patrol constantly to ensure that our guards are watching over us as we sleep. If *they* sleep . . ."

He broke off and in a moment went on harshly, "I will tell you the pattern. The commanders of sentries will approach, unseen and unheard, the guards who have been placed for our protection. And they will seek to kill them! Let every commander have only this in mind, the death of the sentry he is stalking! And any sentry who is not alert enough to defend himself, and therefore to defend *us* . . . let him then die!"

"You are setting Israelite against Israelite," Igal said.

Flaring, Joshua answered, "I am setting Israelite men of valor against Israelite laggards! There is no room now in our society for laggards! Laggards like those who allowed themselves to be killed so easily by our enemies the Canaanites!"

Elisheva heard him and wept for Tubal.

Joshua said quietly, "We are strong in numbers. We are very weak in military experience." He raised his voice and thrust out his arms, shouting now. "But we can learn! And by the one God Yahweh, I will make an *army* out of this rabble! Even if it should take me a lifetime! For soon . . . we will mount our assault on Jericho!"

He was the fanatic again, and Igal, the perfect host, said politely, "My tent is your tent. Will you take bread with us? My wife Azuza bakes the best bread in all of Kadesh-Barnea, flavored with honey and spotted with good raisins."

"We are no longer in Kadesh-Barnea," Joshua

said sourly, "though sometimes I wish that we were . . ."

"A slip of the tongue," Igal said.

Joshua went on, scowling. "In the oasis, our people were tempered by adversity. Today, the good life, with food enough, water enough, leisure enough . . . it has spoiled them! It has made them dependent upon creature comforts, comforts that will one day destroy us all." He grunted. "And you are beginning to talk like Caleb. I tell you of the most momentuous event in our long history, and all you can say is 'My tent is yours!' It is the way Caleb talks, exactly!"

He could smell the roasting bread, and fancied he could even smell the honey in it; and when Azuza brought a platter of the thin round loves, he said grudgingly, "I will break bread with you, a sign of our great friendship."

He tore a piece of the bread and wolfed it down, then said, "Indeed, I find that I am hungry. It often happens that I allow the mealtime to pass without eating. And the bread is very good."

"There is cheese too," Igal said smugly, "Azuza's cheese is the best you have ever tasted."

"Ah . . . I am very fond of cheese."

"It is well known. Azuza!"

"Patience, husband," Azuza said. "I bring it, can't you see that I bring it?"

She was at the goatskin that hung in a corner of the tent, digging in her hand and bringing out dollops of the rich curd. She slopped them onto a clay platter and brought it to Joshua, and Joshua wrapped the bread around it and feasted on it happily, saying, "Oh yes, it is indeed excellent."

He ate in near-silence for a while, belching once or twice to show his approbation, and his temper was greatly improved. He said, "Your son Elam, I am giving him twenty men to command in the assault."

Igal nodded. "Yes, he has told me. It is a great honor for one so young."

"He is worthy of it. And, really, the cheese is very, very good."

Azuza saw that his platter was already empty of it; and she scooped out a great deal more from the skin, filling her cupped hand three times, and hurried to bring more of the warm bread. "Ah, what a generous host you are, Igal!" Joshua said.

"You are an honored guest," Igal murmured courteously. "You bring great honor to my humble tent."

"A good tent," Joshua said, "a tent in which the old traditions flourish. And you yourself . . . I am giving you command of two thousand men."

"*What?*" Igal's mouth had dropped open, and he stammered, "Two—two—*two thousand* men?"

"The east wall," Joshua said. "The east wall will be yours. It is the most dangerous, because even though we will circle the city seven times, the east is the direction we come from, and it is there that they will be expecting the attack if we have not completely deluded them with our previous, feinted, assaults."

He looked back at Elisheva, sleeping again on her hide bed in fine defiance of Joshua's presence; she knew that for once in her hard, harsh life, there was reason to just . . . *sleep*. Sleep was a rare and precious commodity.

He said, "A husband for your daughter soon, she is of age now, and very nubile."

Igal nodded. "Yes, I know it."

"Her breasts are budding. It means that she is ready to conceive. And Israel *needs* children."

"Very soon now. I will choose among her many

144

suitors." He hesitated, not quite sure how he should broach this delicate matter. At last, frowning deeply to show how important it was to him, he said, "I am anxious that her husband should be a very *worthy* man, a man, moreover, who is not so old that he can no longer impregnate her on occasion, not yet so young that all his youthful foolishness is still on him." He said dreamily, "I see her future husband as a leader of men, respected by all the tribes and their Elders, a man whom everyone instinctively follows. After all, she is a prize beyond all reckoning, a child-woman not only of great beauty, but of both intelligence and understanding too."

He laughed deprecatingly. "And to such a man, the price would really not be too high. A few bales of cloth, a few goats, perhaps some jars of good olive oil, only the very purest, mind you . . . No, if her future husband were to be a man I personally respect, the price would not be high at all."

Elisheva was awake again; and for how long had she been listening? Joshua saw the solemn look on her wide-eyed face, and in his own dark eyes there was a strange look, a look that someone who did not know him better might almost have interpreted as a look . . . of *humor;* for Joshua, it was a very rare emotion indeed. He said, "Yes, she is a worthy prize. And I would marry her myself, save that all of my energies are needed for more important matters. And I have neither bales of cloth nor goats, nor olive oil."

"A token payment," Igal said wistfully, "providing the amount never became known to neighbors. . . ."

"No," Joshua said. "It cannot be. I will be celibate now, and pure in the sight of the Lord. Is there more cheese?"

He stayed with them, eating for a long time, and

he told Igal of his plan to bring Jericho to heel. Igal listened in silence, worrying about it as Joshua rambled on, sometimes quite incoherently, and he said at last, a little diffidently, "And if the walls do *not* collapse?"

"They will," Joshua said sharply. "The Lord Himself has told me so! And let it be known through all the tents . . . I want every man, woman, and child in Jericho put to the sword! I want the city burned to the ground! I want Jericho to become nothing more than a memory in the minds of the Canaanites, a city that no longer exists, a city of which there is not one house left, not one inhabitant still breathing, not one stone piled on top of another!"

His voice rose to a scream. "I want the next generation to ask themselves: *Was there indeed such a city once, for we see no sign of it anymore . . . ?*"

He rose to his feet and began striding around, gesticulating furiously, and he shouted: "Ai and Bethel, Lachish, Hebron and Eglon, Shechem, even Jerusalem itself! I want all of these cities to stand in awe of our fury, to know that they cannot hold out against us! I want their peoples to tremble when they learn of our approach. . . !"

At the sound of his angry voice, the men from neighboring tents were beginning to gather outside, wondering in alarm what it could be that so aroused their leader's wrath. Joshua saw them, and strode outside, addressing them all as he waved his staff at them. There was a deep, consuming virulence on his face as he shouted, "Yes! You have become soft, all of you! Living in a land of plenty that is not yet ours! You are irresponsible and undisciplined! And the men among you are women! But by the living God, the only God, I will make soldiers of you yet! In three days, we attack Jericho! In ten days . . .

it will no longer exist! It is what I promise you, it is what I have promised the Lord!"

They made way for him, muttering among themselves, as he stalked off and climbed the hill to where his favorite tree spread its olive branches over the sand, to sit there, and brood on the heavy burden the Lord he loved so dearly had seen fit to place on his shoulders.

One of the men there, Dathan of the tribe of Joseph, was mumbling, "He is a madman! I do not want to be a soldier, I am a herdsman, and very happy in that capacity." Another voice in the crowd answered him: "The land of milk and honey that Moses promised us. It will not be ours without a fight . . ."

Dathan answered him hotly, "A fight! I do not want to fight! Don't you understand what I am saying? I am happy as a herdsman. . . !"

Igal was very angry. He said, petulantly, "*Shoo! Shoo!* Back to your tents, all of you! I have had conversations with our leader, and they are very private! Save that . . . you must know that he is giving me two thousand men to command, it means that I am a captain now! And as a captain, I *order* you! Back to your homes! At once! *Shoo!*"

They were indeed undisciplined, as Joshua had said. But they broke away and went back to their duties, knowing that with the crossing of the Jordan, the harsh life of the desert where death from thirst or hunger was always a fearsome specter of the morrow, was gone forever; and that the new plenty of food and water would have to be fought for, if it was to last.

They knew too that all of Canaan was girding its loins against them.

* * *

Within the enclosed walls of the city, Anak was with Commander Belesh.

He had been sent for, and when he had said, "No, I am busy now, I will see your commander in the evening," the soldiers had beaten him severely, three of them holding him down while a fourth had struck him repeatedly across the chest with the flat of his sword, breaking three ribs and raising great bloodied welts on his flesh. They had then dragged him off and had unceremoniously thrown him to the ground in front of the commander.

Belesh sat in his sybaritic quarters, surrounded by young slave boys, not one of whom was less than beautiful, and he stared coldly at the giant who was struggling to his feet; and he said, "Anak of the *Anakim*. Let it be known at once that I hate and despise your people. They are thieves and murderers, all of them."

Anak was standing now, trying hard not to sway, and mopping at the blood on his face with the hem of his robe, he said with great dignity, "My people do not approve of thievery, nor of murder. We are good Canaanites. And as such, deserving of your respect, Belesh."

"*Commander* Belesh," Belesh said, and Anak remained silent.

"Word has been brought to me of the peoples camped on our doorstep, the Hebrews. I have been told that they sent two spies into our fair city, and that you knew this."

"Knew it?" Anak frowned. "No. I overheard them asking questions of a merchant, and it seemed to me that they were seeking military information. As a good Canaanite, I told the landlord of the tavern where they were drinking to send for the guards, which he did."

"The *Anakim* are *not* good Canaanites. If you were so sure of their evil intent, you could have killed them yourself. That you chose not to do so . . . is very suspect."

"Kill them? I cannot kill a man on so slight a suspicion."

"Exactly. A good Canaanite, as you claim to be, would have done just that. Do you know what a Hebrew is?" He reached out for the mug of wine one of the boys was holding out to him, drank, and waited. And he said at last, "Well? The Hebrews. Who are they, in your estimation?"

"They are men," Anak said, "like us."

"No!" The commander flared. "No, they are trash! Hebrews! And they dare to threaten us!" He gulped his wine and handed back the mug for a refill, and he rose to his feet and shouted, " '*Men like us'?* I could have you killed for that comment! They are swine, pigs, thieves, murderers. They hope—they hope—they hope . . ."

He was clutching at his chest, and two of the guards were there at once, holding him up, and he muttered: "My heart, my poor heart, the seers tell me . . . the doctors say . . ."

He could not continue, and he was draped between the guards' strong arms as he tried to find his speech and could not. His face was ashen, his breath coming in short gasps, and Anak said urgently, "A bed . . . Lay him on his back, a rag soaked in cold water at his forehead till he recovers . . ."

Belesh was beside himself. He screamed, "What, you are a doctor too? No! A traitor!"

He was shaking furiously, and the sergeant of the guard came running, saying in alarm, "We are here, Commander. . . . Tell us what must be done now."

Belesh raised an arm and tried to keep it there as

he pointed a finger at Anak. He said thickly, "This man . . . a traitor to the Canaanite cause . . . Take him, take him, take him . . ."

He gasped for breath and could not find it, and said at last: "Take him . . . to the deepest dungeon you can find. In the morning—the morning . . . when the crowds are at their thickest . . . hang him from the gibbet by the gates."

He fell into the arms of the soldiers and hung there, gasping out his anguish.

There were three more of them approaching Anak, three solid, disciplined Canaanites, their thin lips set in stern, disapproving lines; their quarry was one of the giants, a man not easily to be taken, and they were masking their fear with a show of great determination.

One of them, less fearful than the others, reached out with a short rope to tie those strong wrists together, and Anak picked him up without effort and broke his back, and hurled him into the other two.

He turned and ran, and in the corridor he found an embrasure that led out onto the marketplace, and he leaped through it easily. And in a very few minutes, he was lost in Jericho's milling crowds.

Chapter Ten

The assault on Jericho began three days later; and from a slow beginning it grew, over the space of one week, into a cruel and monstrous battle.

The Canaanite sentries gave the alarm in the very early hours of the morning, just as the sun was coming up; a large force of Israelites was slowly emerging from the shadows at the bottom of the valley and climbing the hill on which the city lay. Within an hour of the first sounding of the guards' horns, twenty thousand armed men were on the walls, filling the breaches, or gathered in reserve in the great marketplace. Captains were cantering their horses along the defenses, checking out the places where falling stones had left great gaps in the walls, calling out, "Fifty more men here . . . A score of archers there . . ."

The chariots were lined up in the square, the horses chafing at their bits, with the cavalry prancing into position for a sortie when the time came. There was a great deal of orderly confusion as the orders were shouted:

"Second Cavalry, all units to the east gate . . . !"

"Archers, ready for massed flights on command . . . !"

"Ready to repel scaling-ladders . . . !"

On the wall, one of the men mumbled to his neighbor, "What scaling-ladders?" He was staring down on the slowly advancing horde, and he said sourly, "Do you see scaling-ladders? I don't."

The neighbor was a rough, impatient man in his twenties, always spoiling for a fight, and he grunted. "No ladders," he said. "I see swords, daggers, clubs, and a few bows. And their quivers are not even properly filled."

He turned to look down into the market, where eight hundred horses or more were waiting. "Belesh should order a sortie now," he said. "Cut them to pieces before they reach the walls."

"Yes, he should, but he won't! You know Belesh, he likes to keep his cavalry in reserve. And it's not for the likes of you and me to question his tactics, foolish though they are."

His companion laughed shortly. *"Massed flights,"* he said, "I hate massed flights, it's a waste of good shafts. Three hours of every day at target practice, till I can put an arrow through a man's throat at eighty paces, every time. And for what? To put five shafts into the air before the first strikes home? Yes, it's foolish indeed! It's precision that makes a good archer, not massed flights." He stared out at the long column. "And they're turning, what are they up to?"

"More foolishness." The disgruntled archer snorted. "The sun's right behind them now, *this* is where they should try to break in."

But the column was indeed turning, wheeling to the north some two hundred paces from the great eastern gate. And for the next half hour they marched silently, slowly, solemnly around the city, always just out of bow-range. And when the circle was completed, they turned east and plodded just as

153

silently back down the valley they had come from.

On the wall above the gate, Belesh, recovering from his heart attack but still a sick man, said heavily to his aide, "They found us too strong to attack, good. It means that they will move on, and vent their rage on Bethel, or Ai. They will trouble us no more. I go to my quarters now. Wait till the last of them have reached Gilgal, then have the trumpeter sound the stand-down."

"Yes, sir."

Belesh retired, a weary man, and he was awoken the next morning in the first light of the dawn by the horns again, the call to arms. The aide came running and said, "They approach us again, commander," and Belesh swore. He strapped on his shield and the heavy leather belt for his sword and dagger, and mounted the wall once again. Below him, his men were arming themselves, the horses being harnessed to the chariots' shafts, the archers stringing their bows and running to their positions.

Once again, he watched as the Israelites circled the walls and quietly withdrew; and on the third day the picture was the same. By the fourth day, and the fifth, there were one or two units who simply disobeyed the call to arms; and by the sixth, a great number of them stayed in their barracks, sure that this strange event presaged no attack at all. . . .

Captain Nabab of the Eighth Horse said scornfully, "Did you see the old men who were leading them? Priests, I'll be bound."

His lieutenant nodded. "Or perhaps tribal elders . . ."

"No, priests! I've heard about these Hebrews, they're obsessed with the one God they hold in awe." A few of his sergeants were gathering around him, waiting for orders, and he said, mocking, "They are waiting for their God to strike us all dead, to win a battle for them that they themselves dare not even join." He paused for just a moment, and added, "The arrows of their one lonely God, it is told, are longer even than our own. . . ."

There was a great deal of raucous laughter, which seemed to set the limits of their expectations, and at dawn on the seventh day the alarm was a token sounding of a single horn and nothing more. Even Belesh himself merely sat on the edge of his cot, grumbling to himself as he waited for the report to be brought to him of the habitual retreat.

But when his aide arrived, it was with news of a different kind. He said urgently, "A different pattern, Commander. They have not retreated. Instead, they are marching around the city time and time again. What it means, I do not know."

Belesh swore and said wrathfully, "It's what I half expected! You know what it means, don't you?"

"No, sir . . ."

"It means," Belesh said, strapping on his buckler, "that they are trying to lure us out from behind our walls, tempting us to chase them down into the valley where they might well have several more thousand men waiting. Well, that's something we'll avoid like the plague." He could hear the horns calling the men to full readiness, and he nodded his approval. "Come," he said. "Let's see what they do when they realize we have no intention whatsoever of fighting them out on the hillside."

He strode off to his command post on the wall over the eastern gate.

The continuing earthquake had assumed terrifying proportions, a series of shocks each stronger than the last. They followed on each other at very irregular intervals, sometimes only a few minutes apart, sometimes as much as half an hour.

As the Israelites marched slowly around the city, Elam was close behind his father, and he said morosely, "I have twenty men to command, twenty frightened men. Frightened, you understand, not of the enemy, but of our own Lord God Yahweh who sends us these trials."

"If they are sent by Yahweh," Igal said sharply, "they are sent to try our adversaries, not us! The seers tell us that it was an earthquake that dried up the Reed Sea and permitted our people to cross, just as Moses had prophesied. You yourself saw the same thing happen with the River Jordan, just as Joshua prophesies. And now he prophesies—"

He broke off, and lowered his voice; his neighbor on the march was a man of Levi, and the Levites were never to be trusted. He said, whispering, "Now, Joshua has prophesied once again, to the effect that if we all raise our voices and . . . and *shout,* the walls will collapse even more, open up more breaches for us, enough to charge through. It really doesn't seem to make sense, does it? And frankly, I find it very hard to believe." He scratched at his beard. "But then, who would have believed the drying-up of the River Jordan, which you and I both witnessed? Or of the Reed Sea for Moses and your grandparents?" He said irritably, "I hate *prophesies,* especially when, against all common sense, they turn out to be true."

Another strong tremor shook the ground, and Elam, struggling to keep his balance, said, "At the last tremor like that, one of my men was thrown so violently that his leg was broken. Another put his foot in a fissure that then closed on it like the bite of a desert lion, and I had to send yet a third to drag them both back to Gilgal. So now, I have only seventeen men left, and though the battle has not yet begun, they fear the wrath of the Lord."

"Let them fear nothing," Igal said fiercely. "The Lord is with us, not against us."

They turned a corner of the broken wall, and a stone of monstrous size rolled down from its top and thundered past them on its way into the valley. Igal said, "In our assault on the east wall, I have a special task for you and your men. Find the house of Rahab, and stand guard on it against all disaster. Disaster, that is to say, from our own people, who may be carried away with the bloodletting. Rahab is our friend, and you will know her house by a scarlet cloth hanging from its window. Together with her family, she is not to be harmed."

Elam laughed, struck with sudden amusement. "Rahab the prostitute," he said. "My mother told me about her, the woman you slept with on your visit to Jericho."

"I did not sleep with her!" Igal said furiously. "Caleb did, but I did not! Though I could have done so had I wished! She wanted me, she invited me! She wanted to be loved by a man of consequence as I am, but I refused her! I am a good husband and father, and I do not sleep with strange women if I can avoid it, which I did! There, now! Let us have no more talk of sleeping with prostitutes!" He muttered, "And is this the fifth or the sixth time we have encircled this damned city?"

"Our seventh tour now," Elam said, and the column, untidily, was halting. There was a long moment of silence, broken only by the soft sibilance of twelve thousand swords being drawn from their scabbards, and then seven ram's-horns from each of the twelve tribes were blown, an ear-piercing note from eighty-four horns in perfect unison. And in the distance, Joshua screamed, *"Now . . . !"*

Well-drilled for this astonishing moment (which almost none of them believed in) twelve thousand voices were raised in a tremendous shout, and men were falling everywhere as the earth itself seemed to answer them with its shaking. They picked themselves up, suddenly convinced that it was the roar of their voices that had intensified the earthquake, sure that Joshua, after all, had indeed been talking with their God. For, as they stared, great sections of the wall that stood between them and their enemy were crumbling; breaches that were already open but no more than a few feet wide were suddenly gaping holes as rubble fell in clouds of dust, wide enough for twenty men abreast to race through; one entire corner was completely demolished, opening a gap more than forty cubits across, and fine particles of sand hung over it so thickly that it was shrouded in a kind of mist through which a man could only barely make out the forms of the soldiers on the other side.

The earth's shaking would not stop, and all around the perimeter the tired stones of a wall that was already seven thousand years old were falling still, shaken from their fragile mud mortar, just as the Lord had told Joshua they would. And there was that hysterical voice again, raised in a maniacal fury as Joshua raced like a madman along the scattered column: *"Now, men of Israel, now . . . !* Into the fray! Strike them with the edge of the sword! In the name of the One God Yahweh . . . Kill!"*

There were breaches in the vaunted walls now by the score, and through them the Hebrews were pouring with the swords and daggers drawn. And within minutes, there was chaos and mayhem in the great marketplace and on the streets; among the defenders

158

there was consternation and dismay as hundreds of the troops on the walls fell to their deaths in a crush of rubble and stone, and there was a frenzied scream from one of the senior captains: *"Archers . . . ! Shoot at will . . . !"* He died from an Israelite sword-thrust before he could complete the order with that all-important phrase: *"Targets of opportunity . . ."*

It would have meant *aimed* arrows, but the order was never given. And so, the archers responded blindly to the orders they had earlier received: *"Archers, ready for massed flights on command . . ."*

And they sent flight after flight in rapid, unaimed succession, down into the screaming mob; many of the Israelites died, but many of the Canaanites were killed by their own bowmen too. And they emptied their quivers too quickly and were left defenseless when the invaders fought their way up to the top of those sections of wall that were still standing. The air was heavy with the sound of screaming as, by the hundred, soldiers and civilians alike, men, women, and children too, fell under the crush of weapons.

The Israelites were not good soldiers; but they were imbued with a strange kind of zeal that would remain with them for two thousand years and more, and they had been told by the fanatic who led them: *"Kill, kill, and kill again . . ."*

Their blunt and heavy swords of copper or bronze smashed like cudgels into unprotected heads, and the streets were running with blood. The Canaanites fought back furiously as they began to recover from their shock, and men died in huge numbers. They drove their horses into the tight-packed mob, thrusting with their lances and finding men they thought of as unskilled bedouin slipping under the bellies of their mounts and driving up with their swords, a tactic they had learned in battle with the Amalekites of the dessert. The chariots fared worst of all; in this kind of close-combat fighting the enemy was not a separate entity at all, but locked hand in hand with their own people, and the chariots, drawn up in their charge formation, had nothing to charge at. Fight-crazed Israelites were dragging the drivers down from their platforms and opening up their skulls, stomping on their throats, or driving crudely pointed blades through their hearts.

Igal and Caleb were fighting back to back, swinging their weapons inexpertly like flails, and Caleb shouted, with a vigor that belied his own words: "I am old, Igal! My arms are tired, I can hold out no longer . . ."

"Then follow me!" Igal shouted. "We go to Rahab's house, my son Elam is there, it will be a strong-point where we can rest! And will the day be won, do you think?"

"It is already won, I am sure of it! Come then, close by the wall . . . !"

Caleb expertly turned aside a Canaanite spear that was being thrust at his groin, and Igal swung his sword with both hands and smashed the skull of the soldier who had aimed it. They saw a Canaanite woman crouched screaming over the dead body of her child, saw one of their own people—was it Eli of Judah?—with his weapon raised high to kill her; there was a look of hysteria in his crazed eyes as he struck her down, and they heard him scream: "Death to a Canaanite mother . . . !"

They ran, heading for the Street of Brothels, forcing their way through swordsmen tightly packed and hacking at each other. As far as they could see and hear there was the clash of swords and daggers and shields, and men were dying everywhere. They stumbled over dead bodies, slipping in blood. Igal fell, and when he picked himself up, there was a moment of panic when he saw that Caleb had disappeared. But then that welcome voice came to him, urging, "Over here, Igal! The compound!"

He ran and leaped over the wall of the little enclosure where the three fig trees were. Together, they hurried into the house and slammed the heavy door shut behind them, standing there for a moment and listening to the muted sounds of the fighting outside, the clash of weapons, the screams of the wounded, the savage shouts of anger.

They went down the corridor to Rahab's room and pulled up short in sudden alarm. . . .

Rahab was crouched in a corner, with three small children, her face pale and drawn as she held them to her, their eyes wide with fear. And beside her, Anak the giant stood with his naked sword in his hand, ready to do battle, but seemingly hesitant. He was very wary, watching them suspiciously, and when he looked back at the woman, she said hoarsely, "No, they are my friends. They are the men I told you of."

Anak turned his hard eyes back on them. "Is it true? You have come to save her? If not . . ." He waved the sword threateningly.

Scorning the danger, Caleb said, "We have come to save her, yes. But you . . . ?"

"Also my friend," Rahab said quickly, and Igal scowled. "He is a Canaanite."

"As I am . . ."

"And one of the *Anakim* . . ."

"And still a friend!" Rahab said desperately. "For three days, he has been hiding here."

"Hiding? From what?"

161

"From the soldiers," Rahab said, "from soldiers who have been told to hang him. And as I saved your lives before, I ask you to spare his now."

"And if we choose not to?" Igal asked, and Anak laughed shortly.

"What, choose not to?" he said scornfully. "You think that you can harm me, worm? I can wring your necks, both of them, with my bare hands if I have to. But *I* choose not to fight. And I ask, instead, as one man of honor to another, that when you take Rahab and her children from this place, I myself be allowed to accompany her." With great dignity, he said, "It is not an idle request, nor the vain hope of a man who is afraid to die, as I am not. I have good reason to ask for sanctuary."

Caleb was watching him narrowly. "And that reason is . . . ?"

"The blood of Isaac runs in my veins."

"What?" Igal stared. "You are a Jew?" He looked at Caleb in consternation. "How can a man named Anak be a Jew?"

Anak shook his head. He said gently, "No, not a Jew, but a Canaanite. And as you see, one of the giants. None the less, many generations ago, one of my forebears was Adah the daughter of Elom, a Hittite, one of the women Esau took to wife. So, one small part of me, yes, is Hebrew. It means that I will not fight you. It means . . . I sheathe my sword."

He thrust his sword into its red leather scabbard and waited.

But before Caleb could answer, there was a commotion outside, the door burst open, and their weapons were all ready again. But it was Elam, with five of his men, and his face was pale and drawn. There was a dagger-cut across his chest, bleeding copiously, and he pulled up short as he saw his father, stammering, "It was not—not easy to find the house, we had to . . . had to fight our way here. . . ."

Igal wailed, "Your wound . . ."

But Elam was staring at Anak, wondering who he might be, what he was doing here, knowing only that this was one of the dreaded *Anakim*.

Caleb said quickly, "A friend, Elam! And you have come in good time. The battle outside?"

"It goes on," Elam said. "The marketplace is carpeted with dead bodies. Some of them are ours, most of them are Canaanites. The city is ours, without a doubt."

"There are fires, I think? I smell burning timbers."

"Fires without number. On Joshua's orders, every house is to be burned to the ground, every man, woman, and child of Jericho to be slain."

"Then it behooves us to leave this place at once," Anak said.

Igal was still moaning. He looked at Rahab in desperation and said, "My son Elam, a rag to bind him with before the loss of too much blood kills him . . ."

"Of course."

Swiftly, she tore a length of cloth from her gown, and Elam allowed her to fasten it around his chest. Grinning broadly, he said to his father, "And this is the famous Rahab my mother told me of? She is very beautiful. I understand now why it was that you could not resist her."

"Elam!" Igal screamed.

Caleb laughed and said, "The rest of your men?"

"Eight of the seventeen have been killed in the fighting," Elam said, "three more badly wounded. I have six men left. The five here, and one at the doorway."

"It will be enough," Caleb said. "We leave now.

Your father and I, Rahab and her three children, and . . . Anak."

He said dryly, "The Jewish giant, Anak . . . I will go first, Igal will bring up the rear, Anak will carry the three children who otherwise might slow us down, with Rahab in the center. You and your men will be on our flanks with your swords ready. If we are attacked by Canaanites . . ."

"We will not be," Elam said. "There is great confusion in their ranks, and thousands have already been slain."

"But if we should be," Caleb said, insisting, "then you know what to do. If our own people should try to reach Rahab or Anak, then I will shout to them in no uncertain terms that by Joshua's order their lives are to be spared. If, in the heat of battle, they persist . . . then use your weapons, should it become necessary, even against them. Come, we go now."

"Yes," Igal said. "We will go now. Through the marketplace to the east gate—"

He broke off, biting his lip, and Elam said, grinning, "The east gate is shut and bolted, Father. But close beside it there is a breach in the wall fifty paces wide, where a man may drive a herd of goats through without even clambering over fallen stones."

"And that," Igal said, asserting his authority, "will be our way out."

He suddenly remembered, and said to Rahab, "But there was an old woman here before, your servant? She too must come with us."

Rahab shook her head. "Dead," she answered. "Oh, not at the hands of your people! She went to buy meat in the market, and a runaway chariot . . . She was more than ninety years old, she could not avoid it."

"Well," Caleb said, "shall we be on our way?"

They made their way out of the house, surrounded by their protective phalanx, and crossed the market square, where it became apparent that the city had indeed fallen. The Canaanite bodies could be numbered in their thousands, and the Israelites were going from one to another, making sure that they were dead, finding with their swords the hearts of those who were still showing signs of life. The surviving women were strangled with cords, and infants were merely picked up by the ankles, and their heads dashed to the hard ground.

Clutching three small children in his strong arms, Anak strode on, blinding himself to the killing that went on all around him, with Rahab by his side hurrying to keep up with him, and Elam's six men on their flanks. And on their way out of the city there was only a single alarming incident:

A man named Lotan of the tribe of Joseph saw the little convoy and stared at it in bewilderment for a moment. He was a fearsome fighting man, especially skilled with his dagger, tall and powerfully built, and quite fearless. Anak's great size was a challenge to him, and he screamed, "A giant! I will kill him!" He rushed forward, his sword ready as Anak, the children in his arms, stood his ground.

Caleb seized him by the upper arm and said, "No! No, Lotan! He is our prisoner, and will be taken to Joshua . . ."

"The whore, then!" Lotan shouted. "A Canaanite whore! Stand aside! Let me smash her skull for you!"

"No! I will not allow it!"

But Lothan shook himself free, and he stood in front of Rahab and raised his cumbersome weapon in both hands. Rahab sank to her knees in terror, and

165

Elam was staring, first at Lotan and then at his father, unsure of what he should do now.

"*Use your weapon if it should become necessary,*" Caleb had said.

But who was in command here? Caleb? No! It was Igal. And Igal was just standing there with his mouth open. . . . And this was not an enemy, it was Lotan, a neighbor, whose daughter Iscah, a pretty young child of twelve, Elam had twice tried, unsuccessfully, to seduce.

But Caleb said mildly, "Forgive me, friend," and swung his sword in a wide arc, striking Lotan across the face with it and breaking both nose and his jaw, and dropping him unconscious to the ground. He grunted and said to Igal, "Poor Lotan . . . not a bad sort of fellow, really. But he never was able to control his emotions. He will recover. Come. We move on now."

They went on their way, and behind them there was only bloodletting; Joshua had ordered it: "*Not one man, woman or child to be left alive,*" he had said. . . . And so, in blind obedience, they killed.

For their fanatical leader, it was an obsession, a compulsion that no man should ever remember the name Jericho, nor know that it was once a great city. He had even ordered that no individual spoils were to be taken, no weapons, no garments, no cloth, no ornaments or jewelry—only the gold and silver and metal vessels for the treasury of the Lord; even the stores of food were to be destroyed.

After this dreadful day, *nothing* of Jericho was to be part of current history.

The old men of the Canaanites stared up at swords descending on their heads, the women screamed as the strangling-cords were tightened about their throats. . . . Sometimes, the soldiers tried to fight back, but the Israelites, though out-numbered, were filled with the zeal of their God and imbued with all of Joshua's vicarious hatreds. Commander Belesh was discovered hiding in a cellar and was dragged out and hanged, and even the horses were killed; *nothing* was to remain.

And at last, the only scent on the air was the scent of blood.

Chapter Eleven

In all of man's violent history, there had never been anything in the world quite like the carnage at Jericho; for days after the battle the surrounding countryside reeked with the smell of blood.

It was a faint, elusive kind of smell, but very distinctive indeed, and in such great quantity it was ubiquitous. On the changing breezes, it was carried to all the surrounding hills; and in their hidden daytime lairs, the animals were wide-awake and sniffing the air excitedly, knowing from the very strength of it, that out there somewhere a great deal of warm flesh was ready for the taking.

There were jackals and hyenas by the hundreds, rats by the thousands, and a few desert lions too, all agitated now and ready to brave the dangers of daylight because they were hungry.

Down in the valley, only a little way above the stream, there was a small cave in the rock, its entrance hidden by overhanging sandstone from which a dark green creeper trailed, and it was shelter now to two lions, a male and his solitary female. It was a long time since they had eaten meat; the Israelites in their invasion of the valley had slaughtered gazelles without number, and there were very few of them left for the lions to feed on. The male, crouched below the overhang, smelled the air and licked his chops. His ears were pricked up, and he was watching every shadow; it was not yet hunting-time, though the sun was dropping to the horizon, and he did not like the sound of the distant screams that were still coming from the hilltop as the last of the enemy were put to the sword or strangled.

But that enticing smell was too strong a temptation. He moved aside from the entrance and looked back over his powerful shoulder; it was a signal to the female to move out . . . and hunt.

Jericho and its dreadful mayhem were far behind the little column as they halted at the stream and lay on their bellies to quench their thirst.

As they rested, Caleb said, "I'm glad we're on our way home, I really don't like to see so much killing, even though I personally killed five Canaanite soldiers and one woman."

He fell into a dark and worried mood and said heavily, "Will it seem strange to you if I admit that I do not like killing women? There can be no logical basis for this . . . this *distaste*. After all, a Canaanite mother breeds Canaanite children, half of whom grow up to be Canaanite soldiers, and it is therefore necessary! But still . . . However, I did not use the strangling-cord, it is too slow and painful a death, I simply broke her skull open with my sword, a very quick and merciful death, and I find that this speaks well for my sensitivity."

Igal said moodily, "And we have been forbidden to take the spoils of war! 'No looting,' Joshua says. It's unheard-of!"

Caleb nodded. "Yes, I agree. We could have derived so much benefit from this battle! Did you see their bows? Every one a work of art! And their arrows! I saw how straight they were flying, really, expertly made! We could have armed every fighting Israelite with a good bow, with twenty or thirty excellent shafts, with a lance, a better sword than those we carry . . . And daggers without number! And their sandals! Did you see the soldiers' sandals, Igal?"

"Of course I saw them," Igal said angrily. "What, am I blind?"

He was upset because he did not understand *why* there was to be no looting, and yet he was loathe to criticize Joshua's decisions.

"There was one soldier I killed," Caleb went on, "the soles of his sandals were made from at least *six* thicknesses of skin! I never saw anything like it, they would have lasted me for the rest of my days!"

He sighed. "I was tempted, sorely tempted, to take them and say nothing about it to anyone. But no . . . It's probably not much to my credit, but I find myself obeying Joshua's orders just as if I had no mind of my own at all."

Anak had set the children down, and Rahab was sitting on the grass and breast-feeding the youngest, a girl of two years or so who was standing at her mother's side on sturdy, wide-spaced feet, her pudgy little hands on her hips, as she suckled ferociously. He stared back at the once-great city they had left, the flames there rising high now. Miraculously, now that the Lord's work had been accomplished, the earth tremors had ceased completely, and there was a strange stillness in the evening air; there was still that frightening red light in the sky to the north of them, and below it the scrub was on fire; but it was comfortably far away.

Anak said, brooding, "Your leader Joshua, will you tell me about him?"

"A madman," Caleb said at once.

"No! No, no, no . . . ! A *visionary!*" Igal wailed.

"Sometimes," Caleb said happily, "the one is the same as the other, as it is in Joshua's case. He is a visionary, yes. And a madman too! He sits under a tree and communes with the Lord. And he prophesies . . . The matter, for example, of Jericho's vaunted walls, and their collapse when we blew our damned ram's-horns and raised our voices in a communal shout . . . He *foresaw* it!"

"Damned ram's-horns, you say? The horns of our priests?" Igal was shocked. "Caleb! One day the Lord will strike you dead for your lack of respect!"

"No, I think not." The old man chuckled. "Had that been his intention he would have done it a long time ago."

"I don't imagine," Anak said mildly, "that the noise you made, fearsome though it was, had very much to do with it."

"It was the will of our God," Igal said, and he was very angry, "which was disclosed to Joshua for our benefit. It's all very simple."

Caleb turned back to Anak. "You wish to know who our leader is," he said, "and I will tell you." He looked up at the mountain on which the ruined buildings of Gilgal stood, and said, "Joshua the son of Nun, an Ephraimite as I am, and a madman as I am *not!* We have the same forebears, and so we have a great deal in common. We are descendants of the same ancestors, we have the same faith in the one God. . . ."

He chuckled and said wryly, "Though perhaps I am not quite the fanatic that he is. And we are both survivors of the great Exodus from Egypt. He and I were sent by Moses to spy out this land of Canaan

173

and to report to him whether or not it could be taken. Joshua and I both said *yes*. The others, ten of them, said *no*. And for this show of abject fear, our Lord God condemned us to forty years of wandering around the oasis of damned Kadesh-Barnea in the desert. To wipe you out, you understand, a whole generation of those who did not trust Him, and await a new breed who might be more receptive to His teachings."

He could not stop laughing. "But the new generation is led by Joshua, who is a survivor, as I am, of that earlier generation which so displeased the Lord Yahweh! It leads me to suppose that the Lord does not always know what He's doing. . . ."

"Blasphemy again!" Igal screamed.

"Yes indeed!" Caleb said. "And let us go now to Gilgal and tell all the women, and the old men and the children, that Jericho is no more."

As they moved off, he spoke to Anak, a newfound friend, very confidentially. "The Lord God has really treated me very well, it's quite unfair of me to revile Him so. Perhaps it's because He doesn't fully understand that I don't really believe in Him as strongly as I'm supposed to. Joshua believes that we should all have *faith*, and his faith surpasses not only all understanding, but all reason too. My own stops somewhere on that indefinable borderline that separates faith from absolute idiocy."

He put a hand on Anak's shoulder. "I just don't *know* anymore, my friend! The older I get, the less clear these things become. At the age of eighty-five, I have learned that I have no *knowledge*, only *beliefs,* which are not quite the same thing! And is this the circumference of our lives? I believe that perhaps it is."

They were climbing the hill toward Gilgal, and

Anak had taken two of the children in his arms, with Rahab now carrying the youngest. They plodded on heavily, turning to look back at the burning city once in a while when the evening breeze carried those dreadful screams to them. Igal murmured, trying hard to hide his dismay, "How long, in God's name, does it take a city to die?"

"Not only to die," Caleb said, "but to disappear in its entirety from the face of the earth. As Joshua has said, in generations as yet unborn, the name *Jericho* will not even be a memory."

But Anak had stopped, and he was peering up at the high sandstone above them. "A woman there!" he said. "A woman, climbing down the hillside from Gilgal . . ."

Caleb stared. He laughed suddenly and said to Igal, "Your daughter Elisheva! She comes to meet us, and I am glad! She is a gazelle, a creature of great beauty, intelligence, and understanding."

Igal beamed. "Yes," he said, "the light of my life." He cupped his hands to his mouth and raised his voice. "Ho there! Elisheva . . . !"

At this great distance she could not hear him, and she was dropping down the mountainside, from one outcrop to another.

"Anak!" Rahab said suddenly, an edge of urgency to her voice. "To the right there! Where the bushes are! A lion!"

Anak looked and saw nothing. "I see the bushes. I see no lion. . . ."

"It is there! Crouching under the shrubbery!"

She held her hand out at arm's-length, the fingers spread wide. "Three fingers to the right of where you see the girl Elisheva, under the largest of the bushes, he's watching her." Her voice was raised in anguish. "There! Moving now . . . !"

175

Anak had set down the two children, and he copied her gesture, shouting, "Yes, I see her, a lioness, and she's stalking . . . !"

With no further word he began racing up the hill, clambering like a mountain goat over the rocks. Caleb followed, and Igal stumbled over his gown as he ran, but neither of them could keep up with his giant strides.

He was shouting at the top of his voice, "Elisheva! Go back! Go back to the village! Run for your life. . . !"

But with the vagaries of the wind she did not at first hear him; and when she did at last, she stopped in confusion, wondering what the fuss was about.

He shouted, "Elisheva! A lion! To your left, go back. . . !" When she turned and saw it, she stood frozen in terror; it was less than fifty paces away and padding silently towards her.

A lion could sometimes—though very rarely—be scared off, and Anak raised his arms high in the air to establish his dominance and yelled, "Raah! Raah! *Raaaah . . . !*"

The lioness turned to face this new threat, and she would perhaps have moved away from the enemy descending on her; but she was desperately hungry, and in all of the animal kingdom there was no creature more stubborn, nor more dangerous, than a hungry lion. She looked back at the young girl and licked her lips, looked back to where her male was, watching her, and turned her yellow eyes on Elisheva again. Her muscles were rippling in the evening sunlight as she speeded up her approach, and Elisheva's terrified scream only excited her more; there were only twenty paces to go, and her mind was filled with only one thought: *Food*.

As she sprang, Anak was on her.

His sword was raised high in both hands, and he brought it down in a furious blow, cleaving her skull in two; but before he could regain his balance, he heard the savage roar behind him. . . . Falling to the ground, he half turned and saw the wide-open jaws of the snarling male, felt the sweep of the sharp claws rending his chest, smelled the stench of its breath.

He had dropped the sword, a useless weapon at such close quarters, and he drew back his fist and drove it like a bolt of lightning onto that sensitive black snout, then threw his arms around the tawny, muscular body, straddled the lion's back, and hurled it to the ground. He slipped his hands quickly down under the forelegs and brought them up again, to clasp each other tightly at the back of the mane. . . . He held on firmly as he struggled to his feet, dragging the great beast, all four hundred pounds of it, with him.

Caleb was running to him, gasping and out of breath, and more than a hundred paces away. Igal had fallen even further back, and was trying to gather himself up again.

The muscles of Anak's arms were bulging, the veins standing out like whipcord, and there was sweat running down his face. Caleb was approaching, his sword raised, and Anak gasped, "No! Not your sword, you'll kill us both! Your knife, into its heart. . . !"

Caleb was dodging madly, trying to avoid those flailing paws, armed, he knew, with claws that could tear a man's stomach open in seconds. He thrust out with his dagger, but the hide was too tough to penetrate with such a blunt point, and he tried to find the throat where the skin was softer.

And then, he heard the sound he had been listening for: the sharp, incisive crack as the lion's tortured neck snapped under Anak's relentless pressure. Man and beast fell to the ground together, and as Anak disengaged himself he gasped, "Dead, I think . . ."

Igal's arms were around Elisheva, protecting her now that the danger was over, and she stared in horror at the blood pumping from Anak's fearful wound. She broke away and ran to him, and dropped to her knees beside his dazed body. She lifted the hem of her gown and tore a length from it, and began to bind it around his chest. Caleb crouched beside them too and said wistfully, "I was not much use, I'm afraid. But you're a strong man, Anak, even for a giant."

He watched Elisheva at work for a moment and turned to look at the two dead lions. He sighed and said, "They will never believe it in the tents when I tell them! But you have two good hides as proof of your prowess, well-earned trophies! Will you permit me to skin them for you?"

"You are very kind," Anak murmured; but he had eyes only for Elisheva. "Elisheva," he whispered. "I believe that is your name? I am Anak of the *Anakim*, a Canaanite, as you see, but the blood of your own people runs in my veins."

It startled her. "A giant? And yet you are a Jew?"

"No," Caleb said. He had taken his flint from the waist-cloth of his gown and was testing its edge with his thumb. He laughed. "A mere drop of Jewish blood, but that is far better than none at all, is it not?"

Her dark eyes were wide as she digested this astonishing information, and she turned back to Anak and wondered about the sheer size of him, admiring the muscles on his powerful arms and legs, thinking to herself: *And what a handsome man he is too. . . .* There were strange looks passing between the two of them, as though each of them understood that light in the other's eyes.

Caleb said amiably, "Esau the shaggy hunter, Esau the son of Issac and Rebekah who was born covered with red hair like an ape, Esau the firstborn of twins who surrendered his birthright to his devious brother Jacob in exchange for a bowl of lentil soup and some bread . . . That same Esau was one of Anak's forebears. And, therefore, he is one of *us.*"

With his flintstone, he was slitting open the lioness's belly, forcing his hand under the skin to bring it away from the flesh.

Elisheva could not take her eyes from Anak. Canaanite or not, she thought he was the most beautiful man she had ever seen. And with such great fortitude too! Bleeding half to death, he was still smiling up at her with a gleam in his eyes that made her heart miss a beat.

She whispered, "You saved my life, and how can I find the words to express my gratitude?"

Anak was not an overly modest man, and he murmured, "Yes, I suppose that is true. But I discovered long ago that there are too few lovely women on this fractious earth. . . . They should not be fed to lions."

"Ah . . . Turn over a little; the bandage must be tighter, or the wound will never heal. You have lost a great deal of blood, do you feel weak?"

"I feel strong." He whispered, "I will prove it to you if we can find a way to retire into the shrubbery."

She colored. "Ssshhh . . . Evil thoughts are not good for you now."

179

"My thoughts are not evil. They are good for both of us. And will you permit me to admire you, in silence? Even . . . even to touch you?"

He laid his fingers gently on her cheek, and he whispered, "The women of Jericho were always renowned for their great beauty. But I never saw skin so smooth and delicate, like the petals of a rose."

"Ssshhh . . . You must not say these things."

"And are you married? Or betrothed?"

"No. My father is looking for a husband for me."

"Still a virgin, then?"

"Yes, of course! Should I be otherwise?"

Igal was crouched on the sand with Caleb, helping him with the slow and laborious process of the skinning. He hissed, "They are *whispering* together! What are they whispering *about,* do you think?"

"Cast your mind back," Caleb said, "to the time when you were his age, and you met for the first time with a lovely young thirteen-year-old girl. . . . *That* is what they are whispering about . . . Your flint now on the inside of the foreleg. Yes, there. A cut all the way down to the paw. And tomorrow, we will ask your wife Azuza to peg these skins out for us, and scrape them of their fat, and then chew on them for a week or two until they are soft as silk."

"No!" Igal said irritably. "I will not *ask* her, I will *tell* her! What, you think I have no authority in my own tent?"

Anak said softly, "Your eyes are the eyes of a gazelle, just as large and lustrous. And the touch of your hands is enough to drive a sensitive man into delirium."

Her heart was pounding. "You must rest now for a while until your strength returns." There was a catch in her voice as she thought of that dreadful

180

moment of panic, and she whispered, "How can I ever thank you enough?"

Her voice was a zephyr, and he laughed softly. "I would answer that question, dear Elisheva, were your father not within earshot."

Elisheva looked back and saw Igal hauling on a lion's carcass as Caleb tugged away at the hide. Rahab had joined them with the children, and they watched the rest of the skinning, and then she sat and looked at Anak and Elisheva for a while, wondering in silence why it was that they seemed to be doting on each other. She stared at Elisheva and saw a very young girl of startling, youthful beauty; and she remembered, with sadness, her own lost childhood days. But she was not the kind of woman to brood too long over matters that could not be changed, and she tugged at the bandage around Anak's chest to make sure that it was tight enough for her own satisfaction.

"We still have a long way to go," she said. She looked at Caleb. "Perhaps we should send to the village for some young men to come and carry him?"

Before Caleb could answer, Anak said grimly, "I believe that all the young men from Gilgal are in Jericho, intent on other matters. But I can walk. I am strong."

"Good," Caleb said cheerfully. "I always admire a man who likes to stand on his own two feet. So, shall we proceed?"

Soon, the little column continued on its way up the grinding hill. The three men were in front, and the two women, with the children, walked a dozen paces or so behind them, as was fitting.

They pulled themselves slowly up with handholds of protruding roots where the going was difficult, and for part of the way they followed the goat-track that had been in use for thousands of years.

In a little while, Elisheva said, looking obliquely up at her companion, "You are Rahab?"

Rahab nodded. "Yes, I am. You know of me from your father?"

"From my mother, mostly. Igal spoke of you only very briefly."

"Oh?" She was smiling. "And what did he say about me?"

"He said—He said that on that second visit he made to Jericho, he was at your house, but he did not sleep with you, even though you invited him to do so. My mother says you are a prostitute. Is it true?"

"Yes."

"Truly?"

"Yes."

"Does it mean—does it mean you've slept with many men?"

"Oh yes, very many."

For a long time, Elisheva was silent as they struggled side by side up the escarpment. There were long, dark green thorn branches reaching out for them from the broken red sandstone, and tiny yellow flowers were sprouting everywhere. At last, Elisheva threw Rahab a sidelong glance and said slowly, hesitantly, "I've often wondered what it must be like. To lie with a man, I mean."

"When I was your age," Rahab said, smiling, "I also wondered about that. And I found out. As, in the course of time, you will too. You're a sweet and very lovely child, Elisheva, a girl to turn the mind and the heart of any man. So perhaps it will be quite soon now."

"My mother says it's very dull and uninteresting, but a duty for a married woman. Only . . . I sometimes wonder how that can be true, if so many young girls, who are not married, do it not as an obligation, but for pleasure. Some of them have told me that . . . well, it's anything *but* dull and uninteresting. I wish I knew whom to believe."

The shadows were lengthening as they reached the top of the bluff and clambered over it. A little crowd of women, old men, and children had gathered there; and at the sight of Anak they began to move hesitantly back, wondering who he could be and what he was doing here. A prisoner? No, he still wore his sword and dagger. They stared at the blood-soaked rag around his chest, and one of the old men called out, a touch of desperation on his voice: "One of the dread *Anakim* . . . ! Have you brought him here to hang him?"

Caleb said quietly, "He will neither be hanged, nor harmed. He is our friend."

"Take his sword from him, Caleb! Before his kills us all . . . !"

"No. He is our friend."

Another voice then, from one of the women: "And Jericho? How fares it in Jericho? The screaming reaches us even here. . . ."

"When the screaming dies away," Caleb said gravely, "then Jericho too will have died."

"A victory?"

"A victory, complete and final."

There was a roar of approbation from the crowd, and the women began clapping their hands rhythmically as the little convoy went on its way through Gilgal's narrow street and down the slope on the other side to the tents of the Ephraimites.

It had not been, for them, an easy day of waiting. Early in the morning, the men had left, led by their priests; and they had crowded onto the bluff to see

183

what they could of the battle there. They had heard the shout and the trumpets, had seen the collapse of so much of the walls, had heard the sounds of battle. . . . Some of them had even been able to make out the massed flights of arrows from the defenders, arcing up into the air and falling on friend and foe alike. Many of them, being women, had not been told what was expected to happen; and now they knew.

But they still hung back, containing their excitement. Anak's physical presence was a fearful threat to them. And when they had gone a little way, Igal found that he could contain himself no longer.

He turned and held up the lion skins and shouted, "Look! My friends and neighbors, look! Two lions killed by our friend the giant! One of them with his sword, but the other . . . with his *bare hands!* Two of them! We have two good hides now to make into sandals and belts and scabbards for our swords! They were out stalking, and Anak charged in among them, with no thought at all of the danger to his person. He was grievously hurt, and if my daughter Elisheva had not bandaged him at once with cloth from her gown—a good garment ruined irreparably—he would have died from the loss of blood, be assured of it! I weep when I think of her gown, the gown she put on at puberty which has to last her until she marries, with fully two spans ripped from its hem! Ruined! It means three months or more of hard work for her mother to fashion a new one, and the hair of our goats is very short this season, it will not be easy to weave. And my sons will have to make a new loom! And yet . . . I am not angry with her! Because it is certain that she saved his life! Elisheva my daughter! A true Issacharite of the house of Igal, even though she is only a woman, and a very young girl!"

He looked back over his shoulder and saw that the others had left him far behind on their way to the tents. He shouted, "Elisheva! Wait! Caleb, Anak, Rahab . . . Wait for me! Wait . . . !"

He began running after them, still shouting, "Wait! Wait for me . . . !"

Chapter Twelve

Anak had arrived, in dire distress, at the tents of the Issachar, which lay a little below the outskirts of Gilgal, on the eastern slope, sheltered and shaded by an acre of olive trees. But at the very last minute, he had collapsed completely, falling into a trembling coma; the loss of blood was heavier than they had thought, and a great deal more than even he could suffer.

He was stretched out now, quite naked, on the main skin-bed in Igal's tent; Azuza had insisted on removing his cotton skirt and even his sandals, saying, "Who knows where else he might have been mauled?"

She unwound the cloth from about his chest and said to Elisheva, grumbling, "Your own garment. Well, so be it . . . It is well you bound him so tightly. Had you not, he would have bled to death. And now, I need wood ash."

"Yes, Mother," Elisheva said. She found a clay platter, took it to the remnants of the fire in the corner, scooped ashes up onto it with a twig, and said, "They are still hot."

"Good, so much the better."

There were four great rents in Anak's torso,

stretching from his left breast down to his navel, the two center ones very deep indeed. She said to no one in particular, "He is lucky. Another span or two, and he would never have fathered another child."

A lion's claws were hollow and always filled with decayed meat which was highly poisonous; disinfection now was of the utmost importance. She spread the lips of the wounds as wide as she could, and rubbed the wood ash deeply into them as Elisheva watched and Igal poured beakers of the palm wine that Azuza had made, for himself and Caleb. He said, grimacing, "Grape wine is so much better, but we do not yet have it." He laughed suddenly. "We found a small grain pit in Gilgal that makes an almost perfect winepress."

Caleb nodded. "Yes, I know it. My own people found it too, but when they carried the grapes there . . . your damned Issachars already had it filled with the grapes they had gathered. Well, it matters little. We found another."

At this very moment, the empty grain pit in the village, cut aeons ago into soft limestone by who could know what people, was being put to its new use.

It was two paces across and more than three cubits deep, smoothly formed into a deep bowl. It was three-quarters filled with grapes now, and the Issachar children, boys and girls alike, were treading them, up to their bare thighs in the red juice as two other girl-children played music to help them, one with a harp and the other thumping a goatskin drum.

Caleb went on, musing, "And we are becoming civilized again, are we not? Many of our people are moving into the Gilgal houses now, with no respect at all for the division of the tribes. Reuben mixed in with Levi, Simeon with Dan and Gad, Naphtali with

189

the sons of Joseph or Zebulon . . . I wonder if this is desirable?"

He stared down at the unconscious Anak. "And now, we have welcomed a Canaanite among us. Not only a Canaanite, but one of the fearful *Anakim*."

"Because he is half-Jewish," Igal said firmly.

Caleb sighed. "*Half* Jewish? No, a hundredth part, perhaps." He brightened suddenly. "But it is enough, is it not? Though when he is fully recovered, he must be circumcised, so that he may truly become one of us. And shall I confess to you a considerable liking for this man? When he speaks with his elders, one senses a great deference, it's a rare quality in the young these days. Do you remember what he said when he asked if he might come with us from Jericho? 'As one man of honor to another . . .' he said. I like that. It suggests not only a certain correctitude, but also a liking for . . . what shall I call it? For the niceties of civilized behavior which, among our own people, are sadly lacking."

Igal said crossly, "Caleb, you talk too much, did you know that? Always *talking*! And half the time, it's nonsense!"

Caleb sighed. "Yes, you are right. It is a weakness that I like to think endears me to my friends."

"Although I will confess that I agree with you. Anak is indeed a good man, even though he's a Canaanite. It's that Jewish blood in him, of course."

Azuza had finished packing his wounds with ash, and was lighting the tent's three lamps with a taper from the fire as Elisheva squatted on the ground beside the bed and took Anak's hand in her own. He was very still and silent, and she whispered miserably, "Will he live, do you think?"

"He will live," Azuza said. "Let him rest now."

And then, very suddenly, and with no formal

190

warning, the flap of the tent was lifted, and Joshua himself was there; his naked copper sword was in his hand, and he was in a furious temper. He screamed, "The giant! They tell me you brought an *Anak* to your tent!"

They were all staring at him as he advanced on them, and he clamped both hands on the hilt and raised the weapon high above his head. His eyes were burning, and he shrieked, "I will kill him! Death to the Canaanite giant . . . !"

Elisheva screamed, "No!" and threw herself across the unconscious body as Igal reached up, grasped Joshua's wrists, and threw him to the ground.

The look of shock on Joshua's face was terrifying. He had dropped his sword in the brief struggle, and he drew his dagger and glared up at Igal and said venomously, "First—first, I will kill the giant. And then, I will drag you out and have you hanged, in front of all your tribe! The Issachars! I *hate* the Issachars! And they will watch you hang!"

As he climbed to his feet, Igal drew his own dagger and awaited the attack, terrified out of his wits. But the knife was weaving defensively, and Joshua, a small, wiry, and immensely muscular man, stood poised on the balls of his feet, his dagger held out in front of him. There was a dreadful scorn in his fiery eyes, and he screamed, "You dare to threaten me? *Me*? The best fighting man you ever met with? You know how many Canaanites I killed today? Seventeen! Eleven of them soldiers! And now I will add one more to the number, one of my own people, but an Issachar who dares to defy me! And then . . . perhaps your daughter too, who also defied my will!"

At the mention of Elisheva, Igal roared out his anger and thrust with his dagger at Joshua's stomach. The clumsy strike was easily deflected, not by Joshua himself but by Caleb. He interposed himself between them, the peacemaker, his back to his friend Igal, and he placed his hands on Joshua's shoulders and shouted, "No! Listen to me, Joshua! Jew must not be allowed to fight Jew, we have enemies enough among the Canaanites! From the pinnacle of my great age, a generation older than you, I say . . . listen to me!"

He was very conscious of the tension, and he went on, his voice low and persuasive now. "What? You will kill a guest in Igal's own tent? By all the unwritten laws of hospitality, this is not allowed! Take him out if you will, and hang him in a public place; it is permitted, but you cannot kill him here! And before you do that, I will tell you. . . . He is one of *us*."

Joshua stared. "*What?*"

"The blood of the hairy Esau runs in his veins, the son of Isaac and Rebekah. If you kill him, you kill part of our ancient heritage."

"What?" Joshua said again, "One of the giants? And he is a *Jew?*"

"In part, yes," Caleb said. He took his hands from Joshua's shoulders and turned away. "Now slay him," he said, "I will turn my back so that I may not witness this offense to Yahweh, who is your God and mine."

For a long time, Joshua held his silence. He turned his eyes on Igal at last, and seeking to assert his superiority just as Anak had done with the lioness (and with just as little success), he said, "Pick up my sword, Igal, and give it to me."

"No," Igal said coldly. "I will not."

As though his commander were no longer there, he went to the bed and squatted on his haunches beside it. He took Elisheva's hand in his own, and whispered, "Do not bleed for Anak, my sweet. He will soon recover. And I swear by the one God that no harm will come to him while he is our guest."

He looked back over his shoulder at Joshua and said in a very formal tone of voice, "My tent is your tent. Will you take bread with us? Azuza will bake it for you with honey and raisins, the fire is a good fire, and the platters are hot."

Joshua stooped (knowing that for Igal this would be a symbolic gesture, and hating it), and picked up his sword. Not even sheathing it, he strode out of the tent without another word.

Caleb breathed a deep sigh of relief. He said, "Well! That man really is a maniac! But you did well to stand up to him, my friend! I suspect that he might even respect you a little more because of it. And did I hear you speak of bread baked with honey? And raisins too? I find that I am suddenly very hungry. . . ."

He watched as Azuza kneaded the barley flour and water, stirred in the honey with practiced fingertips, and tossed the paste in the air to let it fall in perfect rounds onto the upturned clay platters and then carefully, one by one, spotted it with the raisins.

When it was ready, very slightly burned on the underside and crisp to his outworn yellow teeth, Caleb munched on it happily and said, "Truly, Igal, you are a very good host."

Azuza and Elisheva were crouched in a darkened corner of the tent, waiting for their turn to eat after the men had finished, and he turned to the old woman and said cheerfully, "Yes, Azuza, there is no one in the whole camp of the Israelites who bakes better bread."

Anak was stirring, and Elisheva hurried to him at once, holding his hand as she whispered, "Are you well again? Are you recovering?"

He was suddenly aware that he was naked, and he said in desperation: "My skirt . . . Where is my skirt?"

Elisheva retrieved it from the floor where Azuza had dropped it, draped it over his loins, and said quietly, "Are you hungry? If you are, I will feed you . . ."

He shook his head slowly. "No. I wish only to sleep, knowing that you are by my side."

"Then sleep. I am here."

She would not let go of his hand, and she touched it to her cheek as he drifted off once again.

Caleb said, in a very offhand manner, "The woman Rahab. What have you done with her?"

"In the second tent," Igal said, eating, "to sleep with the children. Why do you ask?"

"I just wondered. And may I have one more mug of your excellent palm wine before I go about my business? It really is very good indeed."

In a little while, he rose to leave them, though Igal urged, "Sleep here with us tonight, there is a good bed you can share with Elisheva, a very large skin, there is plenty of room for two . . ."

"No," Caleb said, "though I thank you. I need the solace that only the tents of my own tribe can provide."

"Sleep here," Igal said. "Your Ephraimites are a long, long way off in the darkness."

"The darkness is my friend, I enjoy the night. But . . . if I might take a round of bread to eat on the way?"

"Of course! Azuza!"

Azuza peeled two more rounds of bread off the platters, her fingers dancing because they were very hot, and she looked back over her shoulder at her husband, occupied now with Elisheva, and she whispered, "One for each of you . . ."

"Er . . . yes. I thank you." He raised his voice and said, "Good night, Igal, and I thank you for your hospitality. Elisheva . . ."

"Good night."

Caleb went out into the darkness and breathed in great gulps of the cold night air, refreshing after the smoky interior of the tent.

He found the secondary tent where the children slept, and crept skillfully among the sleeping bodies till he found Rahab, wrapped in her gown on the sand floor. He slid his ancient hand under her robe and held her breast, and he whispered, "We go to the bushes now, the night is warm, the air very pleasant."

She was not in the least surprised, and she nodded in the darkness. "Yes. Very well, old man."

As they left the tent together and smelled the pungent scent of the wild coriander that was everywhere around them, Caleb said softly, "And I have honey bread, the best bread you ever tasted in all of your young life. With raisins."

"Ah . . ."

The darkness swallowed them up.

Scowling and still smoldering under his defeat, Joshua said, "He would not even pick up my sword when I ordered him to! Your friend Igal threatened me, with his dagger! A threat against my life!"

His voice was rising as he convinced himself of this dreadful denial of his authority, and he said darkly, "I still think I should have him hanged, a lesson for those who might want to stand against me."

195

"No," Caleb said firmly. "Igal stood against you because you were in the wrong."

"What? You dare . . . ?"

"Yes, I dare."

Caleb's eyes were gleaming in the darkness as they sat together on the edge of the bluff. The moon was low, though still very bright; poised on the rim of the mountain; its shadows were sharp and incisive.

He said mildly, "When I think you are wrong, Joshua, I will tell you so. My great age gives me that prerogative. To have killed a guest in Igal's tent, whatever the cause . . . it would have been unforgivable, as you must know. Igal was only defending his honor. I will admit that he surprised me too. . . . But it is greatly to his credit that for the sake of that honor, he was prepared to defy even you."

"He threatened me with his dagger," Joshua said, brooding.

"It is evidence of a strength in him that has long remained hidden from most of us under the patina of his foolishness. You yourself were the first to recognize it."

"I should hang him . . ."

"No."

"And call out all of his damned tribe to watch him squirm as he slowly strangles at the end of a good rope. A damned Issachar! I have nothing but contempt for them! On his deathbed, Jacob blessed his ninth son Issachar and said he was a strong ass, crouching between the sheepfolds. . . . Well, I don't know. Asses, yes, but *strong*? I would rather call the Issachars stubborn mules. Hanging Igal would have a very salutory effect on them."

"No."

"And his daughter too. Did you see the way she interposed herself between my sword and the *Anak*? Defying me to kill him!"

"She is a woman of great quality."

"Not a woman, but a child."

"No, she is thirteen years old now, and ready for marriage."

"Ha!" That unexpected flash of humor was on Joshua again, and he said, "Poor Igal wants me to take her to wife."

"Oh?" Caleb raised his eyebrows. "Really? Well, why don't you do that? She's sweet and kind, and fairly obedient. . . . She sews marvelously well and has almost all of the other wifely virtues. She has a mind of her own, I think, which is not desirable in a woman, but to a man of your temper, this should not raise any insurmountable problems." He shrugged. "Just beat her more often."

Joshua grunted. "I have the Lord's work to do, and it requires my undivided attention. I will not take a wife now."

Caleb said slyly, "Not even one so young and lovely? To marry her would be to tell all the tribes that you really are the strong man you consider yourself. Their respect for you, considerable though it may be, would be increased a hundredfold."

Joshua's voice was frigid. "I sometimes wonder," he said, "why it is that I regard you as my friend."

But that moment of good temper would not so easily leave him, and he said, laughing softly, "Fortunately, I have no goods to offer Igal for the purchase of his daughter. As you use your great age as an excuse for your sometimes quite remarkable arguments, so . . . I use my poverty, in the same good cause."

The bright moon, in a dark and cloudless sky, was shining down on the hilltop where once the proud walls of Jericho stood; there were still fires burning there, and Joshua said, with great satisfaction, "By morning . . . there will be nothing left. Within a few days, the crows and the jackals, the hyenas and the lions will have devoured the dead bodies. . . . *Nothing* left."

Caleb sighed. "And no spoils remaining, either . . ."

"No!" Joshua was suddenly very angry. "I want *nothing* to remain of Jericho!"

"Their pottery is so much better than ours . . ."

"All smashed into shards!"

"Their cloth is so very well woven . . ."

"All burned!"

"Their arrows so straight and well-fashioned . . ."

"All broken!"

"Their gold earrings, the necklaces of their women . . ."

"All cast into the flames!"

"Their garments . . . Six months at the very least into the making of every one of them . . ."

"All destroyed! *Nothing* to remain! No vestige of Jericho that was!"

Joshua's wild eyes were turned Heavenward, and there were tears streaming down onto his beard; he was moaning as he whispered, "Dear God . . . I have done what you ordered me to do! Stay with me, dear God, I beg of You! Listen to my prayers . . ."

Caleb said softly, "I almost took a pair of good sandals that would have lasted me for the rest of my life. But I remembered your instructions, and I refrained."

Joshua did not even hear him; he was communing with Yahweh again, and for a little while Caleb sat with him in silence. Caleb rose to his feet at last, and his voice was a zephyr: "I leave you now, my friend. But before I go, will you listen to my advice?"

"No, I will not."

"Find yourself a woman," Caleb said, urging. "The physical love of a woman is a great cure for all vexations."

"I am not *vexed* . . ."

"But you are! It is the only word to describe your condition! *Vexed!*"

"It is not true . . ." Joshua was flaring.

"It is! And all of Israel knows it! A pernicious and very burdensome failing you have! So find a release for your emotions! Go to the tents of Asher and search out a woman named Hannah. Or to those of Gad, and find a young girl named Jalah. Or, if you will only fornicate outside of your race, take the woman Rahab, who sleeps in Igal's secondary tent."

He went on, his voice rising with unaccustomed acerbity. "In God's name, Joshua, lie with someone! Know only that there is not a woman, married or not, who will not happily take you to her bed! They all believe that the sun shines at your behest, that the darkness falls when you command it! In God's name, take *someone,* Joshua!"

Joshua echoed quietly, " *'In God's name?'* You blaspheme in my presence, Caleb."

"Yes," Caleb said. "And I will do so whenever the urge is on me. Good night, Joshua."

He left the august presence, and when he looked back, Joshua was still squatting there under his tree, his almond staff embedded in the sand beside him; and he was watching the dying flames on the opposite hilltop, all that was left of Jericho.

In a moment, he raised up his arms and shouted,

"Lord God Yahweh! Jericho . . . is dead! *Nothing* remains of it! In generations to come, as yet unborn, the name will have been erased from all of history. . . ! I have done Your bidding!"

Quietly, Caleb went on his way.

Chapter Thirteen

In spite of Azuza's wood ash, Anak's wounds festered terribly. Elisheva saw the spreading inflammation and wept over it. She said to her brother Barkos, "He's dying, I know it! Only two days ago, there were deep slashes across his chest, but now, his whole body is swollen, and I just don't know what to do! He's dying, I tell you, he's *dying!*"

Barkos was very sensible young man, and deeply devoted to his sister. Igal had sent them to pick wild figs together for the family table, and he was crouched in the branches of a sycamore tree to pluck the small, hard fruit, tossing them down to her as she filled the wicker basket she herself had woven. It was a splendid basket, woven from palm fronds split with her thumbnail, and fashioned so tightly that it would even hold water.

He dropped lightly to the ground and lay on his back beside her, chewing on one of the tough fruit; when it was thoroughly softened and beginning to give forth its juices, he took it from his mouth and handed it to her saying glumly, "I don't honestly know why we have to eat these damned things, they're really not very good, you know."

She took it from him, popped it into her mouth,

and she shook her head. "No, this is a very good one."

"And about your Anak . . . Do you remember that about four years ago, when almost half our tribe turned out to look for some lost goats? One of the men, I've forgotten who it was, fell down a steep slope and scraped half the skin off his body?"

"Yes . . . I think it was Simeon. . . ."

"A week later, his whole body was inflamed, a poison in the soil, and one of the seers made him sit in an evil-smelling pool of yellow water that was bubbling there, smelling to Heaven like rotten eggs. . . ."

"Yes, yes!" Elisheva said excitedly. "I remember! And in a space of a single day, he was cured! Magic water!"

"No." Barkos scowled. "It is not magic, there is always a logical explanation even for those things we do not fully understand, remember that."

"I will never forget it," Elisheva said meekly. "But tell me what that explanation is, if you will."

"The spring water there was ripe with brimstone."

"Brimstone?"

"A strange substance with an evil smell to it. But immersion in it cures the most terrible wounds."

"And so . . ."

Her face fell. "But that magical spring was in Kadesh-Barnea, in the Wilderness of Zin! A week's journey from here, two weeks' perhaps! Even if father would let me take Anak there, which he would not, he would die before we could reach it!"

"The water of the Dead Sea," Barkos said, "is thick with the same brimstone. And it lies only half a day's walk from here."

"It is?"

She could only stare, and Barkos nodded. "I have

spoken to the seers about this. And though they treat me with the greatest contempt as a man who knows nothing, they have at least told me of the healing properties that lie in the waters of the Dead Sea." He shrugged. "I cannot be sure, but perhaps it will help him. I suggest that you take your Anak there."

"*My* Anak? Her eyes were shining. "He is not *mine*. Not yet."

"Take him there. It will cure him."

"It will not be easy. Father will not allow it."

"I will persuade him."

"You will? Oh, Barkos, *please* . . . ?"

And at supper that night, as they squatted on the tent's sandy floor around the spread ox skin that was their table, Barkos said very gravely, "I am worried about our guest Anak, Father."

Igal nodded. "Yes. I fear he will not be with us for much longer."

He went into one of his little speeches, and said, "A lion's claws poison the blood, it is well known. And how can a man live when his blood is poisoned? Our blood is our lifestream, and if it goes bad, then we die. Everyone knows this."

He sighed. "And for my part, I will miss him. He really is a very nice young man. He told me yesterday that he was called into Jericho's army, but that he flatly refused to serve. How can a man do that? It indicates a certain strength of character, I think. Yes, we will all miss him sorely. In this very short period, I've honestly become very fond of him. What a pity."

A goat had died after eating a poisoned shrub, and Azuza had broiled it over the coals of the constant fire. Igal chewed happily on a leg and said, "He was one of my best goats, he really was. And true to his promise in life, he tastes delicious in death. Truly, I am a very happy man when there is meat."

"Father," Barkos said earnestly, "we have to think of Anak now!"

"Ah yes, Anak." Igal shrugged. "Well, he is as good as dead. We should decide now whether he is to be buried as a Canaanite, or as a Jew. It's a very vexing problem. I went to great trouble to work out the actual amount of Jewish blood in his veins. Esau was really a very long time ago, and it is quite remarkable what a knowledgeable man, as I am, can do with figures. If his solitary Jewish progenitor was Esau, who lived twelve generations ago, then . . . there is a little more than one four-thousandth part of Jewish blood in him. Somewhere along the line, he says, one of his male forebears took a Jewish wife too, so . . . Very well, let us call it a two-thousandth part, it's still very little."

"We should save his life if we can, Father," Barkos said. "Well, of course!" Igal answered, a little crossly. "But we cannot. So, we have to think about his funeral."

"No. We can take him, or send him, to the healing waters of the Dead Sea."

Igal blinked his eyes. "The Dead Sea?" He suddenly realized what his son was talking about, and he said, beaming, "Why, yes, of course, what an excellent idea! I have indeed heard of the Dead Sea from the seers, they tell me its waters have miraculous powers, truly miraculous. Perhaps they can save even Anak. If they do . . . it will reflect very well on the house of Igal that we sent him there."

A thought came to him, a little late, and he scowled. "But who among us can take him there? Half a day's march south, and another half day north on the journey home? A whole day? I cannot,

205

I have my duties to attend to. Elam is out all day and night hunting his damned lions, you must continue your supervision of the herdsmen, and Dibri . . ." It was a slip of the tongue, and he bit his lip, the tears welling into his eyes as he recalled Dibri's death in the waters of the Jordan. . . . And the tragic memory stayed with him.

"The last water we had to cross," he said, moaning, "and it was there that the Lord God Yahweh chose to take my son from me. It is very hard to bear. For all of us."

"Anak is too sick," Barkos said, "to go alone. But Elisheva can go with him."

Igal stared. "What? Elisheva? All the way to the Dead Sea? And unaccompanied save by a stranger?"

"He is not a stranger anymore, but one of us, almost part of the family."

"A Canaanite!"

"But a man of honor, as you yourself have said. He will not lay a hand on her."

"And if he should?" Igal was very worried.

"Then he will have to answer to me," Barkos said. "To Elam too, and even to you yourself. If they leave in the early morning, they will reach the Dead Sea well before noon. Three or four hours of immersion in the healing waters, and they will still be home before dark. And Azuza can very easily take on Elisheva's duties for a single day."

"Well . . ." He looked at Elisheva. Her eyes were cast down as she picked carefully at her meat with her fingers, very delicately slipping it into her mouth.

"And you, daughter?" he said, frowning. "What do you have to say about this?"

Elisheva said quietly, though her heart was beating very fast, "I have nothing to say, Father. What you tell me to do . . . I will do. I am a dutiful daughter, as you must know."

"Ah . . ."

He looked at his poor wife Azuza, piling up their platters with more meat now so that they could fill their bellies with more and still more of the unexpected bonus a dead goat offered. He said happily, "You see, woman? You see what a dutiful daughter you have? It is my training, not yours. She has learned to respect the values her father holds so dear."

"Canaanites in our tents," Azuza grumbled. "The family has not been the same since this man arrived."

"A guest," Igal said sternly. "And he will be treated with the respect he deserves."

He turned back to Elisheva. "Take a full skin of water with you, your mother will bake bread for your journey before you leave, four or five loaves should be sufficient. I am told that there are date palms without number on the shores of the sea, so there will be food there when you arrive; be sure to carry enough, when you leave, for the journey home. Be home before dark. Remember, as you have cause to, the predatory lions. There are also wolves, bears, and wild dogs, so be careful to return before the sun sets. There may even be robbers, you will be in the land of the Amorites, who are few, but very dangerous people. Remember that Anak, a sick man, will not be able to protect you. So . . . home before dark. Is it understood?"

She would not raise her eyes, even though she knew that Barkos was looking at her with that stupid grin on his face. She murmured, "Yes, Father, it is understood."

And in the very early morning, when the sun was

no more than a red-hot ball on the horizon over the mountains where the land of the Amorites met with that of their constantly warring neighbors the Moabites, Elisheva and Anak left for the Dead Sea.

Igal was still asleep and snoring in his bed, hung over from too much palm wine; but Elam was there, tall and straight and wide-awake after a night of hunting, and he showed them proudly the beautiful skin of a desert leopard he had killed with his lance. "I was not even stalking him," he said, "but stalking a gazelle the leopard was stalking too. . . . And to his sorrow, we came together."

He embraced his sister and held her tightly, and he whispered, "I have spoken to Barkos, he tells me where you are going. It is a wise decision."

He looked at Anak and saw the red and horribly swollen limbs. Anak was hobbling on a long staff of olive wood that Barkos had cut for him, and Elam said (though his voice was very gentle), "You must be aware that when you return, our mother will examine Elisheva?"

Anak nodded. "I know it. It is the custom."

"If she is not still intact, it will mean dire trouble for her, and for you too. I will have to kill you. Big as you are, I can do it, I am capable with both sword and dagger."

"It will not be necessary," Anak said. "What, she takes me to the sea to save my life, and I will abuse her? No! It cannot be!"

"There was a phrase," Elam said, "that my father told me you used in Jericho: 'As one man of honor to another,' he said."

Anak nodded. "I remember it well."

"I use it again."

"You have my word."

"And I accept it. Go then, in peace."

"In peace," Anak said. "And if I do not return, if I should die before those waters can embrace me . . . know that I am honored to have counted myself a dear and grateful friend of your family. Peace on you, and on all of your people. May the fighting soon cease."

"I doubt that the fighting will *ever* cease," Elam said dryly, "Our enemies are too numerous, with a kind of hatred for us that will *never* die. But go now. Keep the sun in the left corner of your eye, and watch it rise till it is directly ahead of you. By the time it is above your head . . . you will have arrived."

He sat on a boulder as he watched them move off together. He saw that Anak's legs were swollen to monstrous proportions, and had turned to a deep and frightening purple; his arms too were in like condition, and young as he was, he was walking like an old, old man.

He thought to himself: *By the grace of the good Lord, he will walk back well again. . . .*

He turned at a sound behind him, and saw Achan of the tribe of Judah approaching. He did not like Achan very much, but he said courteously, "A good morning to you, neighbor."

Achan nodded a response. He was a big man, nearly as tall as Anak, though much older, and as skilled a fighting man, almost, as Joshua himself. He tended to swagger, and he wore his long brown robe with part of it thrown over his head in a manner he thought of as fashionable. He was very wealthy, owning more than five hundred goats, a herd which, on the long journey from Kadesh-Barnea, had grown from a mere ninety by careful and selective breeding into one of the largest of them all.

He squatted on the ground beside Elam and said,

making conversation, "I was born in Rameses in Egypt, in a house with floors of the finest marble. And yet, I have spent most of my life in a tent, like a damned bedouin. But now . . . I have taken over one of the Gilgal houses, the grandest of them all. I can tell you, it's good to live between stone walls again."

Elam wondered where this talk was leading, and he said politely, "My own family still lives in its tents."

"Yes, I know . . ."

He looked at the diminishing figures of Elisheva and Anak, disappearing now into the distance, and he said slowly, "I have been told that they go to the Dead Sea together."

"Yes." Elam nodded. "It is possible that the waters there might cure his wounds. If they do not . . . he will die, his blood has turned to poison."

"And he goes there . . . with Elisheva? Could he not have made the journey alone?"

"No, I think not." Elam was a little uncomfortable at this questioning. He said, "Alone, he may well have died on the way there, but . . . Well, Elisheva has been taking care of him in our tents, and we thought . . . Yes, we decided she should go with him."

"And you should not take on this responsibility yourself? Nor Barkos? Nor Dibri?"

"Dibri is dead," Elam said angrily. "He died when we crossed over the River Jordan."

"Ah yes, of course! I heard of it, but I had forgotten. Forgive me."

He saw the anger in Elam's eyes and said, condescendingly, "It is not for idle curiosity that I ask."

He took a rag bundle from the cloth around his waist and unfolded it to display a sticky mass of dates, and he said, breaking them apart, "I find that I am always hungry at this hour of the morning. And will you join me?"

Elam shook his head. "No, though I thank you."

"A robust man, as I am, must constantly feed his appetites. In the wilderness, I suffered gravely, far more than most of our people, simply because I do not like to suffer deprivation any more than I would wish my wife to."

"Your wife?" Elam frowned. "I did not know that you had a wife, Achan."

"I do not, I find my pleasures where I may. But I am nearly fifty years of age now, and it has occurred to me that perhaps I should marry, find myself a wife to cook my food, weave my garments, make the fire, gather wood, carry water, do all the things that a dutiful wife must do. Frankly, I am tired of an ever-changing procession of young women to do these things for me. And I have decided, instead, to take a wife."

"And I am sure," Elam said, "that it is a very wise decision."

"Yes. I have decided on your sister Elisheva."

"Elisheva?" Elam was startled.

Achan nodded gravely. "For some time now, I have been observing her, and I am very pleased with what I see."

"And have you . . . have you approached Igal, my father?"

"Not yet."

Achan slid a date into his mouth and spat out the pit, and he said, "Really, the Jordan dates are so good! Far better than those I remember in the oases. Are you sure you will not share them with me?"

"No, I think not."

Elam was very upset at the thought of this arrogant man marrying his sister, and he said stiffly, "It seems to me, Achan, that both custom and good manners demand an approach to the father, first."

"Yes, of course, I know that." He waved a hand airily. "I happen to know, also, that Igal does not much care for the men of Judah. It may be that I will need help, if the price I have to offer for her is not to ruin me."

With no apparent change of tone, he said, "You know the big goat in my herd that I call Wolf? Brown and black with splotches of white on his chest?"

"Yes, I know him," Elam said, and he was happy now that he could get a blow in, "I have heard it said that Wolf was once the prize goat in a herd belonging to the Zebulon people."

"Once, but no more!" Achan said angrily. "He left the Zebulon herd and impregnated seven of my females, so I claim him as my own! Let Zebulon complain if it will, that goat is now mine! But . . . I am happy to offer him to you, a present, to show my respect and my goodwill."

"A present?"

"Put in a word for me with your father," Achan said, "and that splendid animal is yours."

Elam was a little unsure; Achan had the reputation of being a very wily man indeed. He said uncertainly, "Really, Achan, this is a matter for my father."

"Of course, of course!" Achan said. "All I need from you is a word in my favor. And let me set your mind at rest . . . I am prepared to offer a very generous price indeed for her. Fifty of my best goats, two bales of cloth which we brought all the way from Rameses, six jars of olive oil, the new oil we have

212

pressed since we came to the Jordan Valley. And most important of all . . ."

He lowered his voice, looking back over his shoulder as though someone with evil intent might be listening to his words. "Most valuable of all . . . a garment made of scarlet linen. Not of goat's-hair, but *linen*. It is embroidered with gold wire and embedded with tiny turquoise stones, truly a work of art and of incomparable value. And it will be added to my offer for your sister Elisheva. I do not believe that Igal can refuse me, but to make sure . . . a word from you in my favor, and you will be the owner of the best breed-goat in the whole of the Israelite flocks."

Elam could not easily gather his thoughts together. A garment of scarlet linen, decorated with gold wire and precious stones? He had heard of these gowns, used by the aristocracy of Egypt and of Assyria, but he had never actually seen one, and it was hard to conjure up the vision of so much wealth.

He said hesitantly, "I am sure it is a very good price for a bride."

Achan nodded. "A very generous price indeed," he said. "I am aware that your father does not really like me very much, I don't think he likes *any* of the men of Judah. But the gown alone, from Babylon, should surely demand his respect."

Elam frowned. "From Babylon?"

"No, from Egypt," Achan said. "Did I say Babylon? A slip of the tongue. No, it came from Rameses, where I was born. It is the garment my mother, and her mother before her, wore when they first reached puberty."

It was not very likely that a woman of the Israelites would wear such a gown; even though he had never been in Egypt, Elam knew that his people had lived for the most part under great hardship there, certainly not showing off so ostentatiously what little wealth they may have had.

Why, then, was Achan lying?

But Achan rose to his feet and said, "I leave you now, dear friend. Remember that my prize goat will be among your herd tomorrow morning. He is the most valuable goat you ever saw in your life, a formidable breeder. All of his kids . . . they are invariably large and strong, so use him as a stud, it will pay you well."

"Good day, Achan of Judah," Elam said.

"And good day to you too, Elam of Issachar. It is good that our tribes are so friendly."

Actually, the tribes of Issachar and Judah detested each other with an undying hatred; but for Achan, the time had come for a certain diplomacy; it was something he liked to think he was very good at.

Elisheva and her charge Anak had reached the Dead Sea.

With his swollen, painful, limbs, the journey had been purgatory for him. He stood now on the crest of the mountain and looked down on the dark, dark blue expanse of water. He leaned heavily on his staff, and he whispered, "Are my wounds perhaps too advanced to be cured, do you think?" He had seen cases before of men's blood turning to poison; it was a constant danger, and death often came very quickly.

"We must have faith," Elisheva said fiercely.

He sighed. "It is not a quality I have been blessed with," he said, "But now that I find I have so much to live for . . . Yes, I too will have faith to match your own."

214

Together, they clambered down the hillside and reached the point at which the River Jordan was pouring into the sea, and Anak was scarcely capable now of more movement.

"A few moments of rest, then," Elisheva said, "but no more." She touched his skin and felt the awful heat in it. The swelling had progressed immensely, and both the legs were swelling up now to monstrous proportions, the throbbing ankles nearly the same size as his thighs. He was very, very weak, and his voice was almost inaudible.

"I can move no more, Elisheva. . . ."

"You *must*! A few hundred paces to the water, and we have come so very far together!"

"Thus far, and no farther . . ."

"No! A few hundred paces only! Come, I will support you."

For a while, he staggered with her, his arm over her shoulder.

She was carrying the heavy goatskin bag with water now, and when they were fifty paces or so away, Anak lost consciousness completely and fell to the ground.

Elisheva gritted her teeth and dragged him by the ankles to the water's edge. She wondered for a moment if she should remove his skirt, but she decided against it. She took off his leather belt with its dagger and heavy sword, and rolled him over and over into the gently rippling shallows until, save for his head, he was almost totally immersed. She crouched on her heels beside him, up to her knees in strong-smelling water that left her hands sticky; she wondered why it seemed to burn her so. But it was cool and refreshing, and it made her feel drowsy. She held Anak's swollen hand and closed her eyes, trying not to fall into too desperate a sadness. In a little while, it was a

215

movement of the hand that awoke her from semi-sleep, and she saw that Anak's eyes were open now, and that he was watching her, a very grave expression on his face.

He smiled. "I fell, I remember. You brought me here?"

"Yes . . ."

"You are strong for so slight a woman."

"It was not far. How do you feel?"

"The water is comforting. It seems to take away the pain."

There was a strange stillness on the air, and she looked at the variegated green of the lush vegetation, at the white sand beach and the bright blue sky above them, dotted with puffs of cloud that looked like scatterings of kapok. She said quietly, "And it is so beautiful here. The shadows on the mountains . . . I never saw shadows so purple."

Anak used his arms to push himself farther out and floated there, and he said, "Come, join me. It's good . . ."

"But I cannot swim!"

He laughed. "It is not necessary. You cannot sink in this water. Come! Try it!"

Taking him at his word instinctively, Elisheva paddled herself out into deeper water. She felt the sand beneath her disappearing, but the brine cradled her so that she bobbed like a cork on its surface, and she said, astonished, "It's like sitting in a deep chair made of the softest fleeces. . . !"

"As it works its wonders on us!"

They held hands as they moved up and down on the gentle swell together; and they could not yet know it, but a hundred different minerals of which they did not even know the names were already at work on Anak's infections. Stinking though they were, they were substances of which the healing powers had been well recorded for generations, had been known even since the days when the first cavemen crept out of their lairs to bathe there the wounds thay had sustained in bloody fighting with wolves, lions, bears, and their neighbors.

Anak said quietly, "Your family has been so good to me—Igal, Elam, Barkos, Azuza—even the children, they have all treated me so well."

"It is because we are all very fond of you, Anak."

"A fondness that is well reciprocated. Rahab came to see me a few days ago, while you were out collecting figs, I believe. . . ."

"Yes, with my brother Barkos."

"She tells me that she too has been treated with great respect and affection since we came to the camp."

"Azuza told me Rahab had visited you." She hesitated. "My mother tells me you have lain with her many times. Is it true?"

"Oh yes. Very often. Rahab was the most famous of all the prostitutes in Jericho. Fortunately, I was a very wealthy man there."

"Oh, really?"

"Yes indeed. I had nearly eight hundred goats, thirty mules, fifty-two donkeys. A small vineyard, a large olive grove, and a very good stand of date palms. In my coffers, there were more than two hundred bars of silver and jewels for barter without number." He sighed. "All gone now."

"But . . . how can it be *gone*?" Elisheva asked. "The silver and jewels, yes. But the land? Land can't just . . . go away!"

"It was all down in the jungle of the Jordan River, and I believe that the tribe of Zebulon is camped in my olive grove, the people of Dan among my palms, and that the tribe of Asher is, at this moment, making wine from my grapes. But I cannot, under the circumstances, make any claim, and I will not."

She was silent for a little while. Then, very quietly, she asked, "And what will become of you now, Anak?"

"What will become of me now?" he echoed. "I have given the matter a great deal of thought while I lay sick in your tents. My earnest wish is to become truly one of your people. Caleb . . ."

He laughed suddenly. "Caleb, whom I greatly admire, told me that one single drop of Jewish blood is enough to make a man a Jew, and perhaps he is right, as he thinks he always is. It means that if I can find myself a wife from among your people, then the wheel will have turned full circle, it means that I will truly become one of the descendants of my forebear Esau the hunter. And yet . . ."

He still held her hand as they floated, half-sitting and half-lying on the heavily saline water, and he said, "And yet, there is a problem that seems to me, at this moment, to be quite insuperable."

Elisheva nodded. "Yes," she said. "The bridal price."

"Exactly. I have no property now. So how can I purchase myself a bride? I am reduced . . . almost to the stature of a slave, dependent upon others even for sustenance."

But suddenly he was in a very good humor. He tried to draw her to him, and found himself sitting in the water with only his head and the barest part of his shoulders above the surface; he clutched at her upper arms, and they swung together from side to side in a motion that he could only regard as quite ridiculous.

He shouted happily, "An insuperable problem?

Yes! But I will find a way to overcome it! I will take for myself the bride I want, a woman of incomparable value!"

Elisheva's voice was a whisper: "And have you chosen her already?"

"Yes. I have chosen her."

"And will you tell me her name?" She found she was trembling.

"No, I will not," Anak said happily. "Not until the proper time comes." He held up his arms, and he was laughing, a different man altogether in so very few hours. He shouted, "Look, do you see? Do you see how the swelling has gone down? In no time at all I'll be fit and strong again. . . ."

He struggled around and positioned himself so that he could hold both her hands, and he rocked her from side to side as she bounced around in the brine, and laughed as she tried to steady herself and could not. The water cradled them, like babies; and like very young children, they gloried in the endless game they were playing together.

Chapter Fourteen

It was that time of day when the brilliant copper of the afternoon's last minutes were being infused with the almost luminescent silver of a bright full moon; neither day nor night; a twilight that would last not long, but, while it lasted, would cast strange shadows and a flickering aura over the mountains.

And in that eerie light, Joshua sat under his favorite tree on the edge of the bluff and worried about his next move.

For the establishment of a Hebrew state in Cis-Jordan, as ordered by Moses, the occupation of the Central Massif seemed to him to be essential. Its mountains made a natural fortress from which the inexpert and poorly armed Israelites might hope to defend themselves against the massive counterattack of well-armed and competent Canaanites who—sooner or later, he was sure—would band together to drive the invaders out.

And so, he *brooded*.

He turned, his dark eyes boring into the darkness at the slight sound of a shuffle in the sand behind him; and Achan of Judah was there, creeping up on him almost silently, a man to whom stealth was second nature.

"Never approach me in the darkness so stealthily, Achan," Joshua said, contenting himself with a mild reproach. "It can mean your death: these are troubled times when every shadow might be an enemy."

"I come to you quietly," Achan said, "because I know how important your thoughts are, and I do not wish to interrupt them."

"As you do. What is it you have to say that cannot wait until morning?"

Achan squatted down on the sand, not in the least put out. He was a man of very strong character, and one of the best of the commanders. The cowl of his long brown cloak was tossed carelessly over his head, and his long olive-wood staff stuck up between his crooked knees. He said, "Our next objective. Have you decided on it? My people are still inflamed with Jericho's blood, they want more fighting. We should take Bethel now. Its garrison stands in our way."

"Not Bethel," Joshua said, "but its sister town Ai, which lies two thousand double-paces to the southeast of Bethel."

Achan grunted. "The walls of Ai are stronger than those of Bethel. We should take Bethel first."

"Do not try to teach me the arts of war," Joshua said angrily. "It is precisely because of Ai's strength that we strike there first! The men of Bethel will come to her aid, but by the time they have mustered their forces the town will be ours! And we will be in a strong defensive position. We smite Ai just as we smote Jericho."

"Success in one battle," Achan said dryly, "is always a commander's weakness in the next. He assumes that he will again be victorious, when it may not be so."

"We will succeed," Joshua said stubbornly.

He was waiting for Achan to leave him, but Achan did not move. Instead, he plucked at his beard and said mildly, "Ai or Bethel, whichever it might be . . . do we know the strength of their defenses?"

"We know that Ai is less strong than Jericho was."

"Do we know how many chariots they have?"

"We know that they cannot use them to advantage within the confines of the town, their streets are too narrow."

"Do we know the number of their archers?"

Joshua was becoming progressively more and more angry; he hated this trespass on his responsibilities. He said coldly, "We can never know these things unless I send spies in to them. And this, I cannot do. After Jericho, every town for a hundred miles around will be on the lookout for our spies. It would mean sending men to certain death."

Achan knew when to withdraw before attacking again. He sighed and murmured, "Yes, I suppose you are right. What a pity, a spy's report would be so useful now. Have you thought of possible interference by the Egyptians?"

"The Egyptians rule Canaan only with the greatest reluctance, and their nearest garrison is nearly three days' march from here. They left Jericho to its fate, and they will do the same with Ai."

Achan rose to his feet. "Yes," he said, "you are right, of course."

"As always."

"As always. I will leave you now. Good night." When he had gone a few steps he turned back and said, frowning, "A thought has just occurred to me. The question of sending a spy to search out Ai's defenses. And how right you are in choosing Ai over Bethel; truly, I would never have thought of this myself! But there is one man in the camp who would be accepted as a friend by the Canaanites, since he is a Canaanite himself. I speak, of course, of Anak. For reasons of his own, he has chosen to throw in his lot with us. But this cannot possibly be known to Ai's defenders, since there is not a living soul left in Jericho to tell them about it."

Joshua was silent for a while, and Achan pressed home his advantage. "Anak the giant, a survivor of the Jericho massacre, moving to Ai in search of a new life . . . He would be accepted immediately."

"He would still be suspect. Canaanite herdsmen will have reported the news that he is in our camp."

"I think not. Since he came to us, he has not left the tents of the Issachar. He was badly mauled by a lion, and has been very close to death."

"A sick man cannot be a spy, Achan."

"He has gone to the Dead Sea, where, as is known, the waters have miraculous healing powers." He tried to hide his anger but could not, and he said tightly, "He went there with Igal's daughter Elisheva . . ."

"I know her well. They went there together?"

"And by now, they should have returned. They have not."

"But they were accompanied, no doubt, by one of her brothers?"

Achan said icily, "No, they were not."

"Alone?"

"Alone."

Joshua thought about it for a moment. "I find it remarkable," he said at last, "that Igal would trust his daughter to a stranger."

"Not only a stranger, but a Canaanite! Not only a Canaanite but one of the *Anakim*! '*Return before dark*,' he told them. The sun has long gone down and they are not here. Who knows what they are doing together? A young girl, unmarried and at puberty, with a strong and virile young man . . ."

"Badly mauled by a lion, you said, and very close to death."

"We both know," Achan said harshly, "the healing powers of those waters."

"And what is it you are trying to tell me?"

"Nothing. I am merely speaking my thoughts aloud. Forget them. Good night, Joshua."

He moved off again, but Joshua stopped him. "Achan?"

Achan turned.

"News has been brought to me," Joshua said mildly, "that you seek Elisheva as a bride."

It was a surprise that Joshua knew, but Achan said steadily, "It is true. In the morning, I make my offer to her father. It is a very generous offer."

"I am sure of it." Was there a touch of sarcasm in Joshua's voice? "You are known, Achan, for your generosity. Leave me now."

"Of course."

"Wait for Anak's return. If he should come back to us a healthy man, which is possible, send him to me."

"I will do so. Good night again, Joshua."

"Ai, not Bethel."

"I know it."

Achan went on his way, and once more he was as stealthy as a fox, his sandaled feet falling soundlessly on the soft red earth.

Joshua fell into one of his moods again; he closed his eyes, and began communing with his God, seeking a very militant kind of inspiration.

* * *

226

There was a reason for the nonarrival of Elisheva and Anak.

For more than three hours he had soaked himself in the brine as she floated comfortably beside him, delighting in his presence and in the strange sensation of the buoyancy. And she could not believe the speed with which Anak's infection seemed to be leaving him. His limbs were reduced almost to their normal size, and that fiery redness had quite gone.

He looked up at the sun and murmured, "A walk along the sand to dry ourselves, and then . . . Then I fear, we should start walking back." He sighed. "Though I could stay with you here forever."

They walked hand in hand along the beach, under the tall palms that leaned over the water, in the silence of very close companionship. The residue on their bodies was drying to a yellow-gray dust, almost like a thick coating of wood ash, and when Elisheva began flicking it off her arms, he said, "No, this is the healing brimstone, leave it on as long as you can. Even where there are no wounds, it is very good, they tell me, for the skin."

"All right. But my gown . . ." It too was caking as it dried.

Anak laughed. "On the way home, we will bathe in the fresh waters of the Jordan."

"And are you strong enough now for the journey?"

"As strong as ever I was."

"A miracle."

"No, not really. The only miracle is that which brought us together."

He towered over her, his arm around her shoulder as they strolled along the hot sand together, and he saw that she was staring out into the distance, a touch of anxiety in her dark eyes. He followed her look and saw a black speck in the distance, moving very slowly across the field of their vision, a long way to the north of them against the mountain.

He said, frowning, "A man? Or an animal?"

She had been born in the desert, and her eyes were desert eyes, like those of a hawk. "A man," she said, "but he is crawling, and very slowly." A fold in the ground swallowed him up, and he was gone.

"An Amorite without a doubt," Anak said. "Better we leave him alone, they are very dangerous people."

"Yes, I think so. Shall we go now?"

They moved off in the same direction where the figure had been, and an hour later, as they crested the top of a small hill, they looked down to one side and saw the body there below them, only a few hundred paces from them. It was an old, old man, gnarled and skeletal, dressed in a tattered black robe with a broad leather waistband. His hair was gray and his long, flowing beard was white.

"I see no weapons," Anak said, and Elisheva shook her head. "No sword nor dagger, and no waterskin either."

"Then come," Anak said. "Amorite or no, we must help him."

They hurried down the slope together, and found that he was on the very edge of consciousness, a rasping sound to his breathing. His lips were swollen, and it was a sight that Elisheva had seen too often in her family's wanderings, the old and infirm lying down to die for want of water.

But there were also other very disturbing signs; one of his eyes was blackened and swollen, it seemed that his nose might have been broken, and there was dark caked blood at his chin.

Anak was already squatting on his heels beside him, taking the rag stopper from the bloated skin and trickling water into his mouth. He revived very quickly and reached for the skin in a kind of panic, gasping, and Anak said, "No . . . There is water enough, old man, but you must not take it too fast." He splashed the withered chest and wet the long hair, and the old man lay back on the sand and let them minister to him. They saw then that both his legs were broken at the shins, and Anak said gently, "Can you tell me what happened?"

The voice was slow and uncertain, the eyes clouded with pain. "First," he said, "I will thank you . . . My name is Merari, a Moabite, and the tents of my family lie beyond the ridge there. A small spring, twenty-four date palms, enough grass for a few goats to feed on . . ."

Haltingly he told them of his family, three wives, eighteen children, and a grandchild brood of which he had long lost count. Some days ago, he said, he had gone off to search for a goat which had wandered away, and down on the plain he had been attacked by a roving band of Amorites, four young bedouin who had beaten him severely, taken his sword, his dagger, his staff, and his waterskin, and left him to die in the desert.

"But I will not die," he said, his voice quavering, "until I reach the tents where my family awaits me anxiously, not knowing what has happened to me. There is great love for me in my family, from my grandchildren especially."

Anak was frowning. "And how far is it to your home?"

"For a strong man," Merari said, "as I was till recently, it is a matter of two hours by the sun. In my present state, it will take me one more day. So be

229

it. I have crawled, dying of thirst, for three nights and two days. Now, thanks to your generous help, my old belly is filled with water. And before I die . . . I will see the family I love once again."

He was spitting dark red blood as he spoke, and he touched his chest and whispered, "Not only my legs . . . They broke many of my ribs with their blows. *Amorites.*"

Anak rose to his feet and took Elisheva's hand. He said quietly, "I would rather face Igal's justified wrath than my own conscience if we were to leave him here. He has very little time left now, I am sure of it."

There were tears for him streaming down her face, even though she had seen a great deal of death in the long desert trek, the death of many people who were far closer to her than this sad old stranger.

She nodded. "Yes. I know what is on your mind. And you are right. I will tell you that there will be no wrath from Igal, nor from Barkos, not even from Elam, because, what we do now is *right.*"

Anak stooped down and picked up the fragile, wasted form, light as a bundle of dried sticks. He said softly, "Hold onto your life for a few more hours, old man. And I will carry you home to your family. Guide me while you rest in my arms."

Anak was not yet wholly cured.

The caked minerals were still a thick coating over his entire body, a disinfectant of tremendous potency. But even so . . .

There was a strength on him that was purely spiritual, an urgent need to do what he knew had to be done now; and there was a great stubbornness derived from the close presence of the child-woman he loved so dearly.

He said, gasping, "Stay close beside me, Elisheva. . . . I must not weaken now."

She whispered, "I am beside you. Forever, if you wish it . . ."

Slowly, they moved off in the direction of the ridge, a little to the west of their true course.

It seemed almost as if Merari had given up the ghost, but it was not so; he had merely resigned himself to a position in which, dying, his last hours would be in the hands of strangers who had already given him good evidence of their charity. He closed his eyes, but opened them again almost at once, and said, "Your names . . . If I may know your names?"

"I am Anak," Anak said, "and the woman is Elisheva. We are your friends."

There was still a spark left in those tired old eyes. "A young girl of great beauty," he said. "Your daughter?"

"No." As they moved off, he said, "Not my daughter. But the girl whom, one day, I will find a way to marry, even though I have lost all my property."

He looked at Elisheva and saw the sudden burst of light in her eyes, and she reached out and held onto his belt as they walked over the rocky, broken ground.

Merari murmured, "Ah . . . my blessings on you both," and fell into a deep, deep sleep.

Anak was strangely silent, and when the sun was low on the horizon they had reached another little peak and they looked down on a camp of seven small black tents in a tiny grove of date palms where a score of goats were wandering in the scrub, scrub that was sparsely watered by a gentle spring that rose out of the rocky soil and disappeared again almost immediately. There were children playing in the dirt, the youngest of them quite naked, and a few grown men, with very many women and young girls, and they were all staring, fearfully, it seemed, up at the rise on which Elisheva and Anak were standing, perhaps five hundred paces above them. They saw three of the young men buckle on their swords, an instinctive need for defense against intruders, as they began to climb the hill.

Elisheva whispered, "It is good that he lives to see his family before the end comes," and Anak shook his head.

"No," he said, an unaccustomed harshness in his voice. "Merari is not sleeping. He died in my arms an hour ago."

Elisheva caught her breath, and moaned as Anak laid the frail body down on the sand and stood up, tall and straight and almost as strong as he ever was. He took Elisheva's arm and turned her away from the sight of the old man, the purple blood caking at his lips from punctured lungs as he had gasped out his last few breaths. "His family is on its way here," he said. "His sons, or perhaps his grandsons. It will be best if we leave them alone in their sorrow."

"Yes, I am sure of it."

"Come then. The darkness will be on us soon; your hand on my arm at all times. Should we encounter wolves, or bears, or other predators, have no fear. I am strong again, and you'll be in no danger."

Strong, he was . . .

The yellow-gray brimstone still caked his body; and with every step he took, it worked its wonders on him, the best medicine known to the world of the Middle East. He looked back once and saw the three young men climbing still, and he said, "At least he will be buried among his own people. Not left to die in the desert . . ."

"Yes, I know. The jackals would have devoured him."

"Feasting on him even before he was dead."

But there was another thought on her mind. She said hesitantly, "You told Merari you would one day find a way to marry me. Was it the truth?"

"With your father's consent, it will become the truth."

She held him tightly, and he was very conscious of her trepidation. She whispered, "There is a great love for you in my heart . . ."

"And perhaps it will count for something with Igal. He dotes on you. But it will not be easy, Elisheva. Your Father is a *good* father, it will be hard for him to marry his favorite daughter off to a pauper. With every passing month there will be other suitors, I am sure, all of them far wealthier than I am. It saddens me."

"Both Elam and Barkos, my two brothers of age . . . they both admire you, Anak. And they will speak to Igal on your behalf."

"They . . . *admire* me?" Anak laughed. "I cannot think why they should."

"Then I will tell you. In the matter of your escape from Jericho, your care of Rahab's children impressed them enormously. Your fight with the lions that saved my life impressed them too. And since then . . . your gentle behavior in our tents has endeared you to them still more."

When they were only a mile or two from Gilgal, they bathed in the moonlight in the waters of the Jordan, washing away the salts that had accumulated on their bodies and their clothes. Deep in the water, Anak embraced her and whispered, "There is nothing in the world I desire now more than to lie with you." His hands were at her immature breasts, and he said, "But I may not, I must deny my almost insuperable urging."

"No!" Elisheva was feeling for him, a strange sensation for her, and her voice was very hoarse: "If you want me . . . take me now. I am a virgin, it means little to me."

"No, I may not. I gave my word to your brother."

She lay still under his caresses, quite ready to surrender herself to him, remembering Rahab's words: *"When the time comes . . ."* But he would not take her, and he said at last, very quietly: "I think we should go now, Elisheva. Already, your family will be worried about you."

"Very well . . ."

They went on their way, and within the hour they met with a rescue party which had come to find them. It consisted of Caleb, and Elam, and Barkos, and four young men of the Issachars, all armed and mounted on mules.

Caleb shouted happily, "We thought the Amorites had slaughtered you both!"

Elisheva told them about the ancient Moabite Merari. Caleb listened gravely, and when she had finished, he nodded his grizzled head and said, "Yes, you were right. The desert is the enemy of us all, he should not have been left to die there with only dry sand for company. But come now. We return to Gilgal, which is *ours*."

The little convoy turned north again, and shortly before sunup they found themselves in Gilgal again. They dropped down the slopes of the hill to the Issachar tents, and a dark figure was crouched under the olive trees there, rising like a ghoul out of the ground as they approached.

Achan said tightly, "Anak?"

Anak turned. "Yes?"

"Joshua is waiting for you on the bluff. Go to him now."

"At this hour?" Anak was surprised.

"Joshua himself, our leader. He demands your presence."

"Then I will go to him."

"Do so."

Achan waited till Anak was on his way; and then he disappeared into the darkness, creeping silently to his own tent, where a young girl from the tribe of Reuben was waiting for him.

Chapter Fifteen

The sun was coming up over the hills as Joshua said sourly, "Sit down, Anak. Sit down and listen to me."

He was in a foul mood. All night long he had been sitting there, dozing off only once or twice for a few moments of restless sleep, thinking about Jericho and its complete destruction. There were some in the Israelite camp who did not really believe that he was quite as strong a man as Moses had been; but now, he was sure, this decisive victory would earn for him a place in history that could not be denied.

And yet . . . In his communion this night with the Lord, he had sensed a deaf ear turned to his pleas for guidance, and it had disturbed him deeply; if God was not on his side, then how could he hope to succeed in this struggle?

And so, his dark brows were drawn together in a furious frown as he looked up at the giant and said, almost snarling, "Sit down, there are words we must have together."

In the short time he had been in the Israelite camp, Anak had heard a great deal about Joshua, and he fancied—not entirely correctly—that he knew all the strengths and weaknesses of this fiery man. He sat on the sand and said amiably, "First, let me express my gratitude for the hospitality that has been shown me by your people."

"Yes . . ." Joshua scowled. "A whim of Igal's. I myself wanted to kill you. I would have done so, had his daughter not interposed herself between my sword and your body."

"They told me of it," Anak said. "They considered it, and rightly I would say, a monstrous thing to do. Are you a monster, Joshua?"

Joshua exploded. He was not accustomed to disrespect, and he shouted: "No! And I can have you killed for a question like that! I am a man of God, never forget that!"

"I am not sure," Anak said politely, "what a man of God really is. Are we not all God's creatures? But I am sure you did not call me here to discuss so trivial a matter as your godliness. What is it you wish to tell me?"

The interview had not started well, and it was not easy for Joshua to compose himself. "I wish to know," he said angrily, "why it was that you decided to come over to us, why you chose not to fight for Jericho, but instead to seek shelter with Jericho's enemies?"

"I think you already know this," Anak said. "I am sure that Igal has told you."

"None the less, you will answer my question."

"I sought shelter among the Hebrews because I am part Hebrew myself."

"Ah yes. The blood of Jacob, who was a scoundrel."

"Not of Jacob, but of his brother Esau, who was a worthy man."

"And an infinitesimal part at that."

"Caleb likes to say that a single drop of Jewish blood is enough to make a man a Jew."

239

"If that be true," Joshua said sarcastically, "then we must avoid miscegenation like the plague, or it will mean the end of our race!"

"Perhaps. It might, of course, improve it, like the yeast that is added to the flour to improve the bread. . . ."

"We do not eat leavened bread!" Joshua shouted, but abruptly he calmed himself and said, more quietly, "But I did not bring you here to discuss these things either. I am told that you come now from the Dead Sea, where you went with Igal's daughter Elisheva."

Anak held out his arms for Joshua to see. "Yesterday," he said, "my arms and my legs were red and inflamed, swollen to more than twice their natural size, and I believed that I was dying. Today, I am almost cured."

"You were alone with her there. Does it mean a certain intimacy?"

"It does not. I gave my word to her brother Elam."

"And you kept it?"

"Of course."

"It is not for idle curiosity that I ask."

"I am sure of it. I am convinced that not for one moment ever in your life were you idly curious."

"That is true. If you have lain with Elisheva, I must know of it. *Now.*"

Anak said steadily, "I have not laid a hand on her."

"You swear it to me?"

"No. I merely tell you. I see no need for oaths, and if you choose not to believe me—it is a matter of complete indifference to me."

Joshua knew well when to control his anger, when to replace it with conciliation. He said, "It is important to me, Anak, for reasons that will soon be apparent to you. As a friend, as your commander, I ask you to swear to me that Elisheva is still a virgin."

"I cannot do that," Anak said. "For all I know, though I think it extremely unlikely, Elisheva might have slept with every lusty young man in the tents of Issachar. I repeat, I do not believe that her chastity has ever been impaired. And since it seems so important to you, yes, I will swear to you that I have not touched her."

"Good. Do you know a man named Achan of Judah?"

The sudden change in the questioning puzzled Anak, but he shrugged and said, "Achan? I spoke briefly with him once. It was he who sent me to you."

"Achan," Joshua said, "seeks Elisheva as a bride."

"Oh?" Anak shrugged. "Is that important?"

"If it were not, I would not have mentioned it."

"Of course. Well, I too hope to marry Elisheva one day."

Joshua grunted. "But you have no property. How then can you take a wife?"

"I pray for a miracle," Anak said dryly. "I am told that your religion is full of miracles."

Joshua's voice was heavy with sarcasm. "And your bride payment will be what? A hundred goats?"

"I no longer have my own herds."

"Then five bales of good cloth?"

"I own no cloth either."

"What then? Seven virgins to comfort her father?"

"I no longer have any slaves."

"And yet—you still wish to marry Elisheva."

"It is more than a wish. It is a determination."

"Even though it makes a rival of Achan? He is a

241

powerful man, Anak. A determined man, a cunning man . . . I myself would not like him as an enemy."

"To the devil with him," Anak said.

Joshua fell into one of his silent spells and thought deeply for a while, and when he continued, it seemed to Anak that he had left this matter altogether. He said, "Soon we will attack Ai, which lies some ten miles to the west of us here."

"Yes, I know the town well."

"Very little is known to us about the strength of their garrison. And knowledge of the enemy's strength has always been important to me."

Anak could not resist it. "And will not your God," he said, "the God you commune with so long and so earnestly . . . Will He not tell you these things?"

To his surprise, Joshua took no offense at him. He shook his shaggy head and said unhappily, "No. All night long, the Lord spoke not a single word to me. He is angry, and I do not know how I have offended Him. It is a very heavy burden to bear."

"Then perhaps I can help you," Anak said, conscious that Joshua was watching him closely. "At a guess, I would say that Ai is garrisoned by maybe four or five thousand men, or even less. Perhaps only two or three thousand."

"A guess is not enough. And I must know a great deal more than just the size of the army. And yet . . . I cannot send one of my own people there as a spy, he would immediately be suspect. They will have learned the lesson of Jericho, and I *must* know the extent of their preparedness. I *must* know the number of their chariots and horses, the strength of their armaments. And most of all—their *mood*. Are they waiting for us in terror? Or girding their loins in the sure knowledge that they can defeat us? These are the things I must know."

"Very well," Anak said, understanding at long last where all this was leading. "I myself will go there for you. I am obviously a Canaanite, there will be no difficulties."

"Your loyalty to Jericho?"

"It was never strong. In any case, both Ai and Bethel have broken their treaties with us. Neither of them, as you yourself saw, came to our help when you attacked us."

"But there was a treaty?"

"A treaty we made with scoundrels, and worthless."

"Do this for me," Joshua said, "and I will count you as a friend. More, I will make you one of my commanders."

Anak rose to his feet. "It would be best if I go there in two days' time," he said. "It is a feast day for Canaan, and the market there will be crowded, everyone will be drunk. . . . There is nothing like wine to loosen a man's tongue."

"Good. So be it then. You know the questions that must be answered?"

"I know them, and more. Good day, Joshua. God be with you."

"He always is." As Anak turned away, Joshua said quietly, "Perhaps there is one more thing I should tell you." Anak turned, and Joshua went on. "The suggestion that you might be the only man I can safely send into Ai—which I admit had not occurred to me—came from Achan of Judah, your rival for Elisheva's hand."

There was suddenly a thin smile on Anak's handsome face. "Really?" He laughed suddenly. "I don't consider that important."

"If they should discover the reason for your visit, it would mean a cruel death. A slow strangling, perhaps, or an even slower disemboweling."

"There is no danger. There are many of the *Anakim* in Ai, I will merely be one of them. None the less, I am glad you told me. It seems that Achan is a very devious man."

"He is a disgrace to his honorable tribe," Joshua said sharply. "But he is a good commander of troops, one of my best, and I need him. Be very wary of him. Go now. I must think."

"By your leave, then . . ."

When he had gone, Joshua stared at a slight motion in the broken rock at his feet. He saw a scorpion there, one of the dangerous ones, and he found a stone and ground it to a pulp.

The sun was once again low in the sky, sinking into a purple horizon, when a young goatherd from Ai was guiding his flock back to the safety of the pens for the night.

One of his charges had fallen into a crevice opened up by the continuing earthquakes, and he was using his shepherd's crook to reach for it. A shadow fell across him and he looked up in sudden alarm to find three men standing over him; they were strangers, and strangers in these troubled times were always enemies.

They were Achan's slaves, young, strong, and violent, and one of them took the boy's arms and twisted them up behind his back and marched him off, not saying a word, to where Achan was squatting on the ground under a tall bush. His captor threw him down, and then the three of them took up their positions around him, crouching on the sand and just staring at him.

"Your name, child?" Achan said.

He was frightened, but not entirely without courage. "I will tell you mine," he said, "If you will tell me yours."

One of the men reached out and struck him a furious blow across the face, and the boy said sullenly, "My name is Heth, the son of Meshach, a Hittite."

"And you come from Ai?"

"It is my home."

"Good . . ."

"And if it is your intention to kill me, I ask only that it be quick."

"I did not have you brought to me to be killed," Achan said. "But to do me a service."

"Which is?"

"You know of the *Anakim?*"

"The giants? Of course."

"In the next few days, one of them will come to you in Ai. He is a survivor of the slaughter in Jericho, perhaps the *only* survivor, whose life was spared so that he might be sent here as a spy."

"To spy on *us?* Does it mean that the hordes will attack us next?"

Achan forced a dry laugh; He had to be very circumspect now, since he was a Commander and would be heavily involved in the assault. "You are wise for your years, boy," he said. "How old are you?"

"Nine, I think."

"Well, set your childish fears at rest." He said carefully, "The hordes who destroyed Jericho have no intention whatsoever of attacking Ai, but only Bethel. However, they wish to know if Ai will go to Bethel's rescue. And this *Anak* is being sent there, a spy, to find this out. Do you understand me?"

The child said steadily, "I understand. But I do not know why you tell me this."

"You will tell your master, who will inform the garrison."

He stared. "And I am not to be killed?"

"No. Give the message to your master. He will reward you, I am sure. Now repeat to me what I have told you."

"A man named Anak," he answered, "one of the giants as his name indicates, is coming to Ai to find out if our people will go to the aid of Bethel when it is attacked."

"Good. Go now."

"First, I must rescue a goat which has fallen into a hole. *Then,* I will go."

"My men will help you."

He signaled to them, and one of them took the child's crook and dragged the goat out with it. Its leg had been broken in the fall, and the young boy tossed it across his shoulders and strode off, not looking back even though he half expected a lance to be thrown at him and embed itself between his shoulder blades.

When he reached Ai, he passed on the news to his master as he had been ordered, and was given a fine leather belt for his pains.

Chapter Sixteen

For Anak and Elisheva, the next two days were a delight.

His strength returning almost hourly, he helped her gather dried wood for the fire down in the Jordan Valley, piling it up into huge bundles which he let her carry up the hill on her head, since this was woman's work. He scooped up water from the river to fill the daily pottery jar, and helped her balance it on her hip for the long climb up to the camp.

They were young people in love, with heavy restrictions placed on that love by custom and Anak's rigid sense of his honor; there was an implied oath he had sworn, and a very strong awareness of his obligations to the family.

He walked with her once to the top of the mountain simply for the sheer pleasure of the startling view from the summit that was laid out below them all the way to the coast on the west, and to infinity in the scorching, limitless deserts of Moab to the east, over the ridged, striated red-gold sand that went on forever, and over which hung upturned oases shimmering in the heat, mirages of oases that were nonexistent . . .

Almost nothing lay to the east of the Jordan, for as

far as a man could imagine; and Elisheva, staring out at the emptiness, murmured, "For forty years my people wandered there, can you imagine it? I myself was born in one of the oases we found. Even when at last we left Kadesh-Barnea, we had to search constantly for food and water, which often just could not be found. For days on end, we had nothing to live on, and so many thousands died. My own brothers and sisters . . ."

She stopped, and looked down on the abundance of water below them, the Jordan raging between its lush green banks.

"There was one sister," she said, "a girl named Naomi, who was seven years old. She was always a weakling, and I remember that one terrifying day, when all our waterskins were dry, she was crying quietly to herself, her belly swollen from hunger, her lips cracked from thirst . . . And there was nothing we could give her. We had lived for two weeks on the sap of some trees that we found, and the seeds of a wild herb; but there were none of these left for Naomi, who was dying as other children had died. And I remember watching my father slice his arm open with his flint and give her the wound to suck on. In this fashion, feeding her daily with his blood, she was kept alive for nearly another week. And then . . . she was gone. I hate the desert! I will always hate it!"

"It is behind you now. You must forget it." He took her in his arms and embraced her, and he said quietly, "May I tell you, Elisheva, how much you mean to me? These last days have been the happiest in my whole life. Your beauty, your gentleness, the deep feeling you have for others . . . They've brought me a kind of contentment I've never known before."

She rested her head against him, and the harsh days of the wandering seemed to be nothing more than a nightmare that had passed and could indeed be forgotten. There was the comforting tinkling sound of goat bells floating up to them below, no two of them alike, each bell hammered out by the owner or his slaves, and each as distinctive as the herdsman's own voice.

"Barkos," she said. "Barkos is below us there with our herd."

In a little while, he released her, and he said, lifting her to her feet, "And we must return now. I promised Azuza that I would build an oven for her."

She was suddenly very happy again, and she laughed. "An oven? But why on earth should Azuza need an oven? We have a very good fireplace. . . ."

"No, you do not!" Anak said. "Any ordinary fireplace consumes far too much wood."

"But there is plenty of wood here now!"

"And how long does it take to gather it, to carry it home? All that you can find in one day is consumed that same day, and the next morning you must begin your search for kindling all over again, and this goes on day after day. With the kind of oven we used in Jericho, a few twigs will suffice for a whole day's cooking, the amount you can carry on your head will last for ten days at least."

"Oh, really?"

"Yes, even longer. You see the saving in time and trouble?"

He took her arm and helped her down the steep slope, red sandstone interspersed with gray granite, and red-purple rocks that had been twisted up out of the earth's fiery depths.

He said enthusiastically, "And it's so simple! We

need fifteen or twenty baskets of clay, which we'll carry up from the edge of the river; I know a place there where the clay is excellent. We build a little pottery cave, a cubit wide, a cubit high, and two cubits long. In the space of one day, it dries hard in the sun, and then, we cover it with sand, leaving an opening in the front. Careful now, there are thorns here."

"I see them. Go on."

"Into this clay box, we throw a few burning twigs, just a mere handful, and place there whatever has to be cooked—bread, meat, vegetables. We close the opening with a flat stone, throw on more sand to seal it completely, and then . . . Well, then we just forget about it for a few hours until it's time to eat. There's no constant turning of the meat, no ceaseless replenishing of the wood which has been so laboriously collected."

"But . . ." Elisheva frowned. "A handful of twigs? They will very quickly become ashes and grow cold."

"No. Inside the oven there is not enough air for them to burn properly, and so, they will just *smolder*. Believe me when I tell you that even a whole day later, the oven will still be hot. I built one of these for my own house in Jericho. There is no reason why I should not build one in a tent too."

He had clambered down to a lower level on the rockface, and he held up his arms to catch her as she jumped. When he set her down, she said, "Yes, your home in Jericho . . . Will you tell me about it?"

They moved on together, hand in hand. "Well," he said, "it was a handsome home, a large room for myself more than four paces across, furnished with a comfortable bed made of leather straps fastened to a wooden frame, quite unlike the beds you have in your tents. . . . There was a cupboard for my eating and cooking utensils, and a wooden table—"

"And who did your cooking? You had a wife?"

"No, no wife, I never before wanted to marry. But I had eight or nine slaves, three of them young girls, really quite attractive, who did most of the household work and comforted me in my bed when I needed them, with four young men who looked after the watchdogs and kept the house in good repair. It was a very old house, you understand, perhaps as much as a thousand years old, made of mud bricks. On one side there was a very large stable where the mules were kept and the slaves lived, and on the other side a granary where I kept the oil, wheat, barley, millet, the jars of wine and so forth . . . And on the roof there was a shaded place where I used to sit in the evenings and drink the wine one of the girls poured for me, it was truly a very pleasant spot indeed."

"Then you were a very rich man in Jericho."

He sighed. "Yes, I suppose I was considered so. I traded in skins, in wine and oil too, but mostly in hides. And my treasure chest . . ." He sighed. "In my treasure chest I had nearly three hundred shekels of silver, as well as two small bars of gold, and four beautiful Egyptian gowns I had bought from itinerant traders. Against the day, you understand, when I might want to marry."

He looked down at her feet, shod in crude sandals of mule leather, and said sadly, "And there was a pair of sandals from Assyria that would have delighted you. They were made, very skillfully, from camel skin, which outlasts even the hide of a goat, and decorated in gold wire and scarlet thread. And all I can think of at this moment is the light in your eyes had I been able to present them to you! Truly, you would have been so very pleased with them!"

They reached the bottom of the green valley, and climbed again to where the Issachar tents were, just below Gilgal.

And when they arrived, Achan was there, squatting in the shade of a tamarind tree as he carefully, assiduously, plucked the lice, one by one, from his robe and squashed them between the nails of his thumbs, passing the time as usefully as he might.

Anak said courteously, "A good day to you, neighbor," but Achan merely looked up at him and scowled.

A few hours later, Elisheva summoned Igal's three male slaves. Under Anak's supervision, they dug the clay at the river's edge with wooden shovels, and piled it into tightly woven wicker baskets.

Four times they filled them and climbed the steep hill, sweating in the cooling evening breezes, and dumped their loads close by Igal's tent; and while all this hard labor was undertaken, Igal walked with Achan among the lengthening shadows of the olive grove, talking on matters of the utmost importance. . . .

Achan said, growling, "Your daughter Elisheva is spending far too much time with the Canaanite giant. I do not approve."

"Whether you approve or not," Igal said tartly, "is a matter of complete indifference to me. Unless, of course, you can give me a good reason for your concern."

"My concern is prompted," Achan said, "by reasons which, I am sure, are already well known to you."

"I cannot *imagine* what they might be."

253

"I want her for my wife."

"Ah, that . . . ! Yes, I will confess that I had heard rumors. But I am not the kind of man to pay much attention to the camp's idle gossip."

"And your reaction?"

"My reaction is," Igal said, playing his first card, "that you are quite the wrong man for my most cherished daughter. She has many other suitors, some of them very wealthy. Why, Nekoda of Benjamin approached me only two days ago, offering me a price for her that I really found very hard to refuse."

"Nekoda!" Achan said scornfully. "I can buy Nekoda himself, and all his women, ten times over!"

"Perhaps. But it means that I am scorning the usual offers altogether. 'Forty goats,' someone said, and I am happy to report that I have even forgotten who that was."

"I do not offer forty, but fifty," Achan said. He had determined to restrain himself very severely in this bargaining, but as he thought of the lovely Elisheva, all restraint seemed to drain away. "Together with two bales of good cloth and six jars of the finest olive oil from the new pressing."

"Yes . . ." Igal tried hard not to show his excitement. "I am not a fool," he said, "and so I will not attempt to deny that this is a fair sort of price. . . ."

"Fair only!"

"Well, perhaps even generous. But I have always regarded Elisheva as really quite priceless. Her accomplishments are deserving of the highest respect."

He picked up the hem of his robe and showed Achan a piece of embroidery that Azuza had stitched in there for him and said: "Look! An example of her work with the loom! She also cooks very well, and the bread she bakes is second only to Azuza's."

He lowered his voice. "And I will tell you that Joshua himself approached me, and wanted her for his bride. But I refused. Joshua is a pauper, and I will not allow my daughter, the light of my life, to be wasted on a pauper, however powerful a man he is. No! I said to Joshua, "I will not allow it." And there are others too, far too numerous to count."

"Not only the goats," Achan said. "There is silver too."

"How much silver?"

Achan hesitated. He had three full bars of silver buried in the floor of his tent, and he said, "I have two bars. I will add them to the goats."

"Though silver is not as good as gold. I never owned any gold at all, ever in my life."

"I have no gold."

"What a shame. I am sure that were there a little gold in the offer, my resistance to it would be considerably weakened."

"Well . . . it may be that I have an undersized bar buried somewhere. Perhaps I could melt down a quarter of it."

"Half of it."

"Igal!" Achan was almost screaming. "It would make a poor man of me! You said yourself that you do not want your daughter to marry a poor man!"

"But a quarter seems so little! A denigration of her qualities, which are very considerable," he said earnestly. "It is not only a question of her cooking and sewing, nor of her strength when it comes to carrying wood or water. Indeed, I have female slaves who are almost as competent in this respect. But . . . it is a question also of her own personal beauty, which is very considerable. When your neighbors say, 'Achan has taken himself a thirteen-year-old bride,' they will say it with envy in their hearts, because her name is Elisheva of Issachar. It is a matter of some importance. You will have seen that her skin is almost without blemish. Her legs, I assure you, are very long and quite straight. Her breasts are immature, but well shaped, and her waist is very small indeed. Remember the envy of your neighbors, Achan."

"Then we are agreed? On all that I have offered you?"

"No, we are on the verge of agreement now, but not quite there."

"Very well."

Achan had been holding back his final strategem till the very last, and he said, lowering his voice, "There is one more item, more valuable even than all the others. It is a Babylonian robe, made of the finest linen . . ."

"*Linen . . . ?*"

"Yes, *linen*. And dyed to a glorious scarlet color. It is embroidered with gold wire . . ."

"*Gold wire . . . ?*"

"Yes, a masterpiece of the weaver's art. Moreover, it is thickly embedded with tiny turquoise stones, perhaps two or three hundred of them."

Achan was not a fool, he had brought his final argument with him, wrapped up in a piece of sackcloth. He unwrapped it carefully, and laid it out on the sand. The turquoise stones were glistening in the evening sun, and he whispered, "Can you believe the value of this robe? For you and me, a garment is the result of a month's work or more for one of our women. The sheep to be sheared, the wool to be woven, the cloth to be cut and stitched . . . But can you imagine the work that went into this? A family of ten people at least, working for no less than a year. And it comes all the way from Babylon."

"Babylon?"

"Did I say Babylon? I meant, of course, Egypt. All through the long wandering, we carried it with us, my family carried it."

"But . . . Elisheva could never wear such a gown! She would be stoned to death if she ever dared to appear in it!"

It was a last effort to raise the price, and Achan said, shrugging, "Why should she ever want to wear it? Why should she ever even know about it? It is not for her, it is for you! Just think how many goats you can buy with this garment! A hundred at the very least!"

Igal did not want to make up his mind too fast, nor, indeed, to give the impression that he had too readily accepted a purely business proposition. He said, "Well . . . if you will agree to half the bar of gold instead of a quarter, I will accept your offer for my daughter Elisheva."

Achan smiled thinly. "But there is one more matter, Igal."

"Oh? And what might that be?"

"The question of your daughter's chastity. She spent a night with the foreigner Anak at the Dead Sea. I understand he gave his word to Elam that he would not touch her. But he is Canaanite and therefore a scoundrel. If he did not keep his word . . ." Frowning, he said, "I will not take a woman to wife, Igal, who has already been opened."

"She is intact."

"Can you be sure?"

"On her return," Igal said, "I will confess that I had the same fears. On my instructions, Azuza examined her, and she assures me . . . Elisheva is still a virgin."

"Good. Then we are agreed?"

"Two full bars of silver, then," Igal said, "each to weigh not less than a talent. Agreed . . . ?"

"Agreed."

"Half a bar of gold, to weigh not less than a whole *mina*. Agreed?"

"Agreed."

"One hundred goats . . ."

"I said fifty."

"It is not enough. Think of your first night with her, in your bed."

"A hundred, then,"

"And the Babylonian garment."

"The *Egyptian* garment. Agreed."

"No donkeys? A few donkeys should be included in the purchase price, it is customary."

"No donkeys," Achan said firmly. "I have already paid too much for her."

"One mule, at least, that I may not be shamed in front of my neighbors."

"Very well, one mule, but no more," Achan said. He rose to his feet. "The marriage within the month?"

"The sooner the better," Igal said. "We have very serious problems with Anak of Canaan."

"Keep him away from her, she is my betrothed now. And we will have a wedding feast of not less than two weeks. I am a wealthy man, I must make an impression."

"We are in a state of war with Canaan," Igal said. "Perhaps the festivities, in deference to the difficult times we live in, should be cut down to . . . shall we say ten days?"

Achan shrugged. "Very well. But not less than a hundred guests to attend the ceremonies." There was a very hard look in his eyes. "And make sure that Anak is one of them."

"Anak?" Igal said apologetically. "Perhaps, under

the circumstances, it would be kinder to exclude him."

Achan said harshly, "Invite him. I want him to see me take Elisheva to the bridal chamber for the consummation."

There was a nagging discomfort at the back of Igal's mind, but he thought of the very handsome price that was to be paid for his daughter, and he nodded, albeit a little uncertainly. "As you say then, Anak shall be one of the guests."

"And when will you announce the betrothal?"

"Immediately," Igal said. "Runners will be sent out at once."

"Make sure the price I am paying for her is known."

"Of course, that is as it should be, and will be."

"One month from today, we will already have conquered Ai, and perhaps Bethel as well. As one of the commanders in that battle, I will be treated with a great deal of respect, and this can only reflect well on your own house. Truly, you are a very fortunate man that I have chosen your daughter."

"And she, of course, is fortunate too," Igal said.

"Yes. Make sure that she knows how lucky she is. And I leave you now. Rahab, the Canaanite prostitute, is waiting for me."

"Ah . . ."

Achan went on his way, and Igal returned to his own tent. He found Anak there, sweating over the heavy loads of clay he had carried up from the river's edge, patting it into place, forming a dome of adobe to be turned, by tomorrow's hot sun, into pottery. Elisheva and Azuza were helping him as he worked, and he said happily, "An oven of the kind we had in Jericho."

Igal looked at his daughter and saw the bright happiness in her eyes as she patted at the clay, following Anak's directions. He knew that what he had to tell her would not please her in the least, and for a moment he worried. But he thought of the price, of the goats and the cloth, of the oil and silver and gold that would make him a wealthy man. He thought most of all of that remarkable garment. . . .

A garment of any kind was of great value, the result of months of hard work by the women of the family; the shearing, the looming, the weaving, the stitching . . . But this one? Spotted with turquoise, threaded with gold wire as only the Babylonians knew how to make it, thoughts of the garment hardened his heart, and he said to Elisheva, quite brusquely and feigning a smile that did not come to him easily, "I have just spoken with Achan of Judah, who will shortly be your husband."

He saw the sudden shock on her face, and he raised a conciliatory hand and said, "He will be good to you! Though he is one of the men of Judah, he is a *good* man! A commander in Joshua's army—it is not a title to be treated with disrespect. He has slaves without number, so you will be well cared for, the wife of a very wealthy man and, therefore, the envy of all our neighbors!"

He was conscious that Anak was staring at him, and for no reason at all Igal dared not look him in the eye. It seemed that Elisheva had lost her voice completely; all that came from her throat was a moan as she sank to her knees and tried to control the sudden nausea. Anak, his lips set in a tight line, was trying to help her to her feet, and for a moment she clutched at him and sobbed. He too was on his knees, beside her, and he stared at Igal with a look in his eyes of surprise, consternation, and a deep, deep anger.

Elisheva would not stop moaning, and Igal said crossly, "Oh, don't make such a *fuss*! I have always known you as a dutiful daughter, and you have always known that I think of nothing but your welfare. . . ."

Before he could continue, Elisheva stumbled to her feet and pushed Anak away as though he were suddenly her enemy. She ran to the tent and threw herself down on the skin bed and wept; and in a little while, Azuza came to her.

Azuza was a sad old woman, much older than her years, and most of the sadness came from the tragedies that seemed to follow her family wherever it went. The death of Naomi and the others from thirst in the desert (but most of all Naomi, whom she adored), the drowning of Dibri who was her favorite son . . .

She whispered, clutching at Elisheva's hand, "There is nothing I can say, is there? And yet . . . you know how much I love you."

Elisheva turned over onto her back and wiped at her cheeks. She stared up at the top of the tent, where a lizard was hanging upside down on the fabric, its tongue snaking out like lightning to capture unwary insects. "Achan," she said. "A hateful man, you know how much I detest him."

"Yes, as I do too. But the decision is your father's, as it must be. And he has made it. Life was never easy for a young girl, nor indeed for any woman. But you must learn to accept it."

"I cannot . . ."

"You must! There is no alternative."

"I am in love with Anak, deeply in love with him."

"I was sure of it. I have seen the look that passes between you sometimes, and I know that he is in love with you too. But this . . . it means very little, a girl does not marry for love."

"Yes, you are right, of course."

"And Anak? What does he think of this?"

"I saw only a look of consternation on his face when Igal told us."

"He is such a good man," Azuza said. "But he has nothing now! No money, no property, not even a herd of goats! So how can he take a wife? No, the dice have been cast, and you must learn to accept the divination of their numbers, simply because nothing we can do can change them."

There was a voice outside, a strangely cold and angry voice: *"Mutar . . . ?"*

They were both properly covered, and Azuza called out, *"Mutar . . . !"*

It was Anak.

He raised the flap of the tent, entered, and looked at both the women, his eyes lingering on Elisheva. He turned to Azuza and said, in a very formal tone, "The oven is finished. Do not touch it till this time tomorrow, it must harden for one day of hot sun. There is a thin slab of rock ready to put in place for the door . . . I leave for Ai at dawn tomorrow, and when I return in the evening, I will show you how to use the oven. Good night now."

Elisheva looked at him and saw the hardness in his eyes, and she said, wailing, "Anak! The fault is not mine. . . !"

He could only stare down at the ground at his feet. He mumbled, "I know. It is not your fault." He took a long, deep breath. "But I love you so dearly, Elisheva. Good night."

He turned on his heel and was gone.

Azuza embraced her daughter, sensing her pain, and she said fiercely, "Resign yourself, child! There is nothing that can be done now! Nothing!"

Chapter Seventeen

As the tip of the sun came over the distant Mount Nebo, where Moses had died, nearly a thousand people were waiting at the gates of Ai, waiting for the guards to swing them open, waiting for the start of another day.

They came from Bethel, from Gibeon, from Hebron and Shechem, and from Jerusalem itself. They were traders, farmers, shepherds, merchants, dealers in wine, oil, flour, fruit and vegetables, goats, chickens, and mules; and they were squatting on the sand outside the gates with their wives, children, and animals. The famous feast day in Ai brought them from as far afield as Lachish, Gaza, and even Joppa. There were thirty or forty tribes represented here, each with it distinguishing dress, brown robes and gray, long and short, simple and more sophisticated, some with headdress and some without; it was a colorful, cosmopolitan crowd, all drawn together from all over Canaan for a market day and a chance to make a little money.

And, lost in the waiting crowd, Anak was one of them.

He had already walked around the town's perimeter three times as he waited, casually looking over the stone walls; they were not as ancient as those of Jericho, and had been kept in better repair, though there were still great cracks in them, plastered with mud, where the earthquakes had rocked their foundations.

And now, the people rose up out of the sand in their hundreds as the heavy gates creaked open, and they began to gather themselves together, searching out their wandering children, lifting up the heavier loads onto the heads of their women, slinging the squawking chickens—their yellow legs tied with raffia—over their shoulders in great feathery noisome bundles; they shouted out their grunts to the animals as they crowded, sweating, into the marketplace, belaboring the mules with pointed sticks as they searched out the best places to squat with their produce.

And Anak was standing head and shoulders over most of them, but unconcerned in his sure knowledge that there were forty or fifty of the *Anakim* living in Ai, and that three others (from Jerusalem, he guessed by their clothing) were among the waiting crowd.

He had thought long and deeply, as he waited, about that drop of Esau's blood in his veins that made him a Jew; but now he was suddenly faced with a strange circumstance that seemed to place him once more, and perhaps more firmly than ever, among the ranks of his own people. . . .

It seemed that *all* of Ai's *Anakim* were in the marketplace, a fact that in itself would not have been extraordinary, except that so many of them were there so early in the day. Anak was a shrewd and perceptive man, and it seemed to him that every single one of them had eyes only for him and for the other giants. It worried him momentarily, as something he did not fully understand and could not find a reason for. He saw one of the three from Jerusalem being quickly approached by another *Anak*, saw a whispered conversation and a look of surprise, a shake of the head. . . . And as he wondered what this could possibly be about, there was a hand on his arm, a giant's hand, hard as bronze, and a voice in his ear: "Your name, friend, quickly. I am Jezer of Ai, an *Anak* as you see me. . . ."

But before Anak could answer, two soldiers barred their way, and one of them said to him, very roughly, "In the name of the king, identify yourself."

Smiling, Jezer said quickly, "He is my cousin Arba, officer, from Gibeon. And as you know, I am Jezer of Ai."

The soldier growled. "What, he cannot answer for himself?" He thrust the hilt of his sword into Anak's stomach and said angrily, "Your name, fellow, when I ask for it!"

Holding back his anger and not quite sure what was happening now, Anak said, "I am Arba of Gibeon, sir, a merchant from that city, and I have come here to buy wine. It is said that the Ai presses have been very generous this year."

"Generous?" he grunted. "How would I know? I am a simple soldier, and paid a pittance any honest merchant, if there be such a creature as an honest merchant, would find barely enough to keep his favorite concubine's stomach filled. I know nothing of our harvest, I cannot afford to buy wine."

The throng was pressing around them, jostling, everyone minding his own business, and Jezer said, "The shame of it! The mighty warriors of Ai, who are famous throughout the length and breadth of Canaan, denied the pleasures that can be bought so easily with just a few more shekels!" He produced a narrow bar of silver, the size of a woman's little finger, and said, "I hope you will not take offense . . . but a valiant soldier of the king should drink to that king's health on a day like this."

The silver disappeared with miraculous speed, hidden away in the tight folds of the guard's waistcloth. "Then be on your way," he said, "and if you learn of a giant named Anak, after his people, report it at once to the first soldier you see; you will be rewarded handsomely. Anak . . . Anak of Jericho, sent here to spy on us."

When he had gone, Jezer said quietly, "You are truly Anak of Jericho, I believe?"

Anak nodded. "Yes. And how did you know me?"

"Your sandals. Such sandals are only made in Jericho."

"And how can it be that they know I am here?"

"For two days now, this has been the major gossip in the marketplace. An *Anak*, they said, spying for the Israelite hordes for reasons that are known only to him." His eyes were very hard. "We held a meeting, all of the most important *Anakim* in town, and we decided that, whatever the reason, we could not allow you to be taken. Upon capture, you were to be crucified, and disembowled. We could not permit it."

There was a question in his voice, and Anak said quietly, "I am part Jew, Jezer my friend, and one with the Hebrews who came from Egypt."

"Ah . . . We should have guessed. Will you tell me why it is that you came to spy on us?"

"To find out the strength of Ai's garrison. Ai is shortly to be attacked."

"Say no more. There are others who must hear this, others of our own people. They are waiting. Come with me, and stay close."

Jezer was tall and very thin, but powerfully built, with very tightly corded muscles on his bare chest and shoulders. He wore a very expensive looking skirt of wool, yellow and heavily embroidered with an Egyptian design in blue, green, and scarlet. His copper sword was in a scabbard of leather highly ornamented in the Egyptian pattern.

He took Anak to a potters' workshop and led him through the artisans at work there on the double wheels and the clay cones, some of them sitting at benches under the palm-frond shelters as they worked the lower stone wheels with their feet, others treading the deep red clay in pits; there were naked children there, turning the rods that spun the wheels, working from sunup to sundown, many of them only seven years old but already skilled at their allotted tasks.

Jezer said, "My brother Shema owns this potters' shed, a very good one, the most successful in the town. They come here all the way from Gaza to buy his products."

There was a small house at the back, a single room built from clay bricks, and three elderly men were already gathered at the table and waiting there, dignified and somber men with long gray beards.

Jezer introduced them: "Anak of Jericho whom we have been searching for. The Elders of Ai's *Anakim*, Zaham, Nebat, and Hakupha."

There was a certain hostility in their eyes as they nodded gravely at him; this was one of their own who had chosen to go over to an enemy sworn to destroy the Canaanite empire; and much as they hated their Canaanite rulers (even though they were also Canaanites themselves, though having no say in government), this bordered on treachery.

270

"I will speak for us," the old Zaham said. "Your name is Anak?"

"Yes, after the name of my people."

"And why is it you spy for the Hebrews?"

"I am part Hebrew myself."

There was a subdued murmur at this surprising information, a muttering that might perhaps have indicated a certain contempt, and Hakupha said, "And have you always known this?"

"Yes, I have."

"And you have now decided to join forces with the people who are set on our destruction?"

"With my own people, yes," Anak said stubbornly. "And as for the matter of Ai's danger now, you must know that there is little love between Jericho, my own city, and your town of Ai."

"But there are forty-seven *Anakim* living in Ai. Are they to be put to the sword too, as all the people of Jericho were? Save yourself?"

"No. Part of my purpose in coming here was to warn the *Anakim* to leave the town, for Bethel, perhaps, or Gibeon."

"And leave behind us all that we own here? To be destroyed at the whim of the fanatic who, we have learned, leads the Israelites?"

"As I lost everything," Anak said.

"Except your life."

"Except my life. Our Canaanite overlords have long kept the *Anakim* in a kind of slavery, allowing us no say at all in the matter of ruling a country which we, by our skills, have helped to make rich. We are despised, scorned, and hated. It is time to turn against them, all of us."

"You cannot decide for all of us."

"Your pardon," Anak said. "It is merely a suggestion."

"Very well. And what is it, precisely," Zaham asked, "that you came here to find out?"

"The strength of Ai's garrison."

Zaham fell silent, and thought about this for a long time. He looked at Nebat and Hakupha, and was quite sure that he could read their thoughts with great accuracy. He was a man of wealth and position here, with a great deal to lose, and his twin concerns were that Anak, one of his own people, should not be harmed; and that Ai, which was his home, should not fall to the invaders . . . Like all the *Anakim*, he was a man of high intelligence and intellectual skills.

He said quietly, "Ask me questions, Anak. And I will answer them as best I may."

"The number of your soldiers," Anak said promptly.

"Two thousand," Zaham replied. "Perhaps a trifle less."

"So few?"

"It may be only fifteen hundred. Recruiting recently has been very difficult."

It was a lie; there were nine thousand armed men in Ai.

"The number of your chariots?" Anak asked.

"One hundred and forty."

Another lie; there were four hundred and ten.

"How many shafts to each of your archers' quivers?"

"Thirty." It was the truth.

"And the number of your horses?"

Zaham pretended to think for a moment, and said at last, "I would say about two hundred." He turned to his companion on the right. "What do you think, Nebat?"

Nebat said, smiling, "I happen to know the exact number, since I supply their feed. Apart from the horses for the chariots, which number one hundred and forty as Zaham has said, there are two hundred and twenty-seven, numbering the calvary."

In truth, there were more than seven hundred of them, and the game of deceit went on. "And the state of the army?" Anak asked. "This is very important. Are they expecting an attack, or not? And if so, are they waiting in terror, or in the absolute knowledge that they are stronger than their enemies?"

Zaham turned to his companion on the left. "Perhaps you can best answer that question, Hakupha," he said.

Hakupha nodded. He plucked at his beard and frowned darkly, enjoying this charade and understanding perfectly the reason for it. "The army," he said, "will not fight. At the first sign of an attack, they will lay down their arms and surrender. They have learned the lesson of Jericho. And as we all know, they are arrant cowards."

"Well," Anak said dubiously, "perhaps not cowards. The men of Ai are known to be very courageous. . . ."

"Yes, it is true," Zaham said swiftly. "But the slaughter in Jericho has demoralized them completely. They know that if they should be attacked, surrender is the only sensible response."

A young girl entered unobtrusively and moved from one to the other of them, setting before them five of the beautiful ceramic pots for which, among other wares, Ai was famous. She filled them with wine from a pitcher, and just as quietly left them to their business. She returned a moment later with rounds of thin bread, stuffed with dates and honey.

For Anak, the bread was a great relief. He had sensed their antagonism at once, even though he knew that his own people would never betray him;

but the breaking of bread together was a sign not only of hospitality, but of trust . . . and therefore, for him personally, of safety.

And the questions went on . . .

"In battle," Anak asked, "do your infantry run with the cavalry, as the men of Jericho were wont to? I have heard it said that they do not."

"No," Zaham said, tipping back his head and clicking his tongue in the universal negative. "Only in Jericho and Gibeon. Our cavalry are not trained in the canter, they go at once from the walk to the gallop, an infantryman cannot keep up with them, even holding onto the saddle straps in the fashion of Jericho."

"Can the chariots be used within the walls of the town? Your streets are very narrow, it leads me to believe that they cannot."

"Only in the marketplace at the gates. As you say, the streets are too narrow elsewhere."

"And they carry, what? Two men? A driver and an archer?"

"Yes, two men each."

"Is the driver also a bowman?"

"No. He occupies himself only with the reins."

This too was a lie; on Ai's chariots, there was a frontal bar that permitted the reins to be tied, so that the driver could use a bow and thus double the war chariot's effectiveness.

In a little while, Anak said, "Perhaps I should leave you now. I have discovered what it is I wanted to know. Can I be assured that in the next few days all the *Anakim* here will leave for Bethel or Gibeon?"

"You may be so assured," Zaham said. "And will you stay and drink wine with us for a while? The wine is good, I think."

Anak shook his head. "No, though I thank you. Every moment I spend in Ai is a moment tempting Providence. I must return to my camp and report what I have learned."

"And Ai itself is to be attacked? We were told . . . Bethel."

"By whom?" Anak said swiftly.

"By one of your own Israelites. The shepherd he spoke to did not know his name. He wore a robe of linen, not of goat's-hair, with the cowl thrown over his head, and the belt was of leather embroidered with yellow thread."

"And this man told you of my coming here?"

"He told one of our shepherd boys."

"He was tall, as tall as an *Anak*?"

"Almost exactly the words the boy used to describe him."

"Did he say his name was Achan?"

"You do not listen to me. . . ."

"Your pardon . . ."

"The boy did not know his name."

"If he wore a gown of linen," Anak said, "with the cowl thrown over his head . . . A man as tall as an *Anak* can only be Achan the son of Carmi of Judah. He wishes to marry the woman I have determined will be my wife."

Zaham stared at him for a moment. "On so fragile a thing as jealousy," he asked, "rests the question of an *Anak*'s crucifixion?"

"Yes, it would seem so. And by your leave, I will return to my camp now, there is much that has to be done before nightfall."

"Then I will escort you," Jezer said. "So far, we have eluded the guards. My presence beside you, a Canaanite of known loyalty to the king that you and

I both despise, will assure a continuance of that happy state."

He escorted a troubled Anak to the gate, and when he returned to the room behind the potters' shed, he sat down and said heavily, "We have condemned him to death, I think."

Zaham nodded gravely. "Yes, it is true. But he will die in battle, as an *Anak* should, bravely, fighting against those he considers his enemies. It is better than capture as a spy, and the torture they would put him to."

"And should we take his advice and leave Ai now?" Hakupha asked.

Nebat grunted and said, "Are you mad? What, leave all that we have built here? Run like cowards when a few thousand savages, who have scarcely a score of good bows among them, choose to threaten us?"

"Those few thousand savages destroyed Jericho and ground it into the earth."

"They will not be so fortunate with Ai."

"And did we discover," Zaham asked, "when the attack will come?"

"No," Nebat said, crestfallen. "It is indeed a question we should have asked, but we did not. And shall we tell the king of the impending attack? Or not?"

Hakupha pondered the problem for a while, and he said at last, frowning, "Perhaps the king, whom we all cordially detest, should listen to his own spies. It means that perhaps we should say nothing, take no side at all in this coming battle." He raised a cautionary hand. "And yet . . . if our fair city were indeed to fall to the invaders, simply because the garrison was caught unawares, it could mean disaster for all of us. Let me give the matter more thought. We will meet again this time tomorrow."

*   *   *

The supper that night in Igal's tent was a veritable feast.

Igal was chewing on a fine leg of roast goat, and he held it up and waved it at Azuza and said happily, "I never tasted a better piece of meat in all my life! Is this Anak's new oven?"

Azuza was standing discreetly behind the men, waiting to serve them, with Elisheva squatting in a corner of the tent in case she should be needed too, rising once in a while to refill their beakers with palm wine. The old woman shook her gray head. "No, the new oven is finished, but Anak has not yet shown me how to use it. When he returns from Ai, if they have not killed him there."

It was a very oblique remark, but Igal chose not to let it ruin his good temper. "What then?" he asked. "Roasted on the coals?"

"Of course. The same way I've cooked your meat for more years than I care to count."

"It's so tasty. . . ! And so much of it! I never saw so much meat on a goat's thigh!"

A sudden thought occurred to him, and he said to Elam, "But . . . the size of him! You didn't kill off one of my breeders, I hope?"

"No, Father," Elam said calmly. "He was a present to us from one of the neighbors."

"Oh really? Well, how nice."

But why should any neighbor want to give them so fine an animal for supper? In exchange for *what*?

It made little sense, and for a while Igal worried about it. He said at last, frowning, "What neighbor, Elam? I must thank him, perhaps even send him a small jar of our new oil."

"Achan," Elam said happily. "Achan of Judah. We are eating his prize goat Wolf. And doesn't he make a splendid meal? And his skin! Within a week or two, we'll all have new sandals. . . ."

Barkos, always in league with his elder brother Elam, roared with laughter, slapping his thigh; and Igal could only blink his eyes, not knowing in the least what was going on between them.

Chapter Eighteen

When Anak returned to the Gilgal camp, he went at once to find Joshua, and he reported to him, in all innocence, the whole tissue of lies he had been fed in Ai. . . .

"Less than two thousand soldiers," he said. "One hundred and forty chariots. Two hundred and twenty-seven horses to form their cavalry. The chariots carry two men, but only òne of them is an archer, the other is occupied with the horses. . . ."

He told Joshua in great detail all that he had learned in Ai, and carefully omitted any mention of the danger he had been in there.

"And most important of all," he said, "they think in terms of surrender. After Jericho, they are completely demoralized."

"Surrender?"

Joshua thought about it for a while. "Yes," he said at last, "I will accept surrender. But let them first see the strength of our arms, let them know that we are capable of wiping them off the face of the earth, as we did with Jericho! A force of three thousand men, then, no more will be needed. We will make scaling-ladders for their walls, and with the help of the Lord God Yahweh, within half a day I will accept Ai's surrender. Their king and his captains to be killed, together with all the officers of his army. The women and children to be spared if they submit to us. For those who do not—the strangling-cords. By this means, Bethel, our next objective, will not dare stand against us. Go now. Go to the tents of Judah and send Achan to me. He is to be my supreme commander in the coming battle."

"It is to the tents of Judah that I go now," Anak said. "And, indeed, to seek out Achan. Whether or not I will send him to you . . . whether or not he will be capable of accepting your invitation when I have finished with him—that, I cannot promise. I think you may not see Achan today. Good day, Joshua."

He turned on his heel and moved off, but Joshua stopped him, screaming, "Wait! If there is bad blood between you and Achan, I must know of it!"

"No," Anak said. "It is between the two of us."

He strode off, conscious that Joshua was screaming after him, "One of my best commanders! I must know what you hold against him!"

He did not even turn back, but went on his way down to the tents of Judah, and found an old man there close by where he knew Achan's tent to be. He was in his nineties, perhaps, a kindly old man, sitting now in the sand and doing nothing, just staring out into empty space and plucking at his long gray beard with nervous fingers.

He stared at Anak as he approached, well aware, with the wisdom of his years, of the anger there, and he said, a little fearfully, "You have come to the tents of Judah, young man. I am Carmi, and how can I help you?"

"I look for Achan," Anak said.

Sighing, Carmi answered, "My son, the troublemaker." (In Hebrew, this was what the name meant, and it was a constant source of sorrow to Carmi that he had thus named his screaming, fighting son at birth.)

"If you will tell me where he is, old man?" Anak asked. But before he could answer, the flap of the black tent behind him was raised, and Achan was there, knowing that there was a fight on his hands now; and perfectly prepared to accept it.

He said to Anak, "Canaanite scum that you are, you came looking for me?"

The gratuitous insult simply made the confrontation easier for Anak, and controlling his anger, he said, "You betrayed me to the people of Ai, and they were waiting for me."

Achan said, mocking, "And still, they did not hang you? What a shame! Well, next time, perhaps."

Anak balled up his fist and swung it in a clumsy blow to the side of Achan's head; inexpert though it was, it knocked him to the ground, and Achan stared up in momentary shock. He clambered to his feet and said, a little unsteadily, "I cannot, and will not, fight you now, neither of us carries a sword. And strong though I am, I find it difficult to kill a man with my bare hands."

"I find it very easy," Anak said.

"Then kill me now if you will," Achan answered. "But if you are a man of courage, meet me at dawn tomorrow, with weapons, and we will fight."

"With weapons? Good! Sword and dagger?"

"No. With slings."

Anak stared. "With *slings?*"

"I am told that you were a shepherd once, as I was too. It means . . . you know the use of a sling."

"Yes, I do. Against wolves and bears and even lions. I have never used it against a man."

"It is your chance," Achan said, "to kill a man who detests you. If you are not a coward . . . we will fight with *slings*. Among my people, it's an ancient and honorable way to settle quarrels."

"Your people are now my people too," Anak said. "So be it then. At dawn?"

Achan nodded. "At dawn, by the banks of the Jordan so that the loser can be toppled into the river, to be carried on its torrent all the way to the Dead Sea, which you so recently left."

He laughed shortly. "But it is known, is it not, that we are truly not fighting because I tried, unsuccessfully, to have you killed in Ai? But because of the love of a woman?"

"For Elisheva," Anak said tightly. "The winner will take her."

"Good. It is all I ask."

Achan was a very wealthy man, the owner of the largest herd of goats among the Israelites. But he had come to his great wealth with difficulty, starting his life as a simple herder at the age of six. In a very few years, Carmi's herd, with Achan as the head herdsman, became a model for all of the Israelites, growing stronger month by month until he owned, at last, more than five hundred head.

And in his early days, one of Achan's foremost accomplishments was with the sling, a talent which no shepherd who hoped to protect his herd from marauding animals could be without. . . .

The sling was made up of a pouch at the end of two leather thongs about a yard long. A stone was centered in the pouch, the thongs were wound round the head with increasing velocity, until one of them was let go, with a sharp, incisive crack like the sound of exploding charcoal . . . whereupon the missile would fly to its target with astonishing speed, with force enough to smash open the skull of a desert lion, or break the neck of a gazelle.

It was a formidable weapon, and had recently been incorporated into the armaments of some of the Hittite forces.

Achan, with long years of poverty as a herdsman, was highly skilled in the use of the sling; Anak, an aristocrat who had always hired herdsmen to do his bidding, was not. But this was a challenge to his personal dignity, and he said, his face a mask to hide his emotions, "For Elisheva. We meet at dawn tomorrow by the bank of the river."

He turned on his heel and strode away, and in a little while he found Elam setting out from the Issachar tents for his nightly hunt. He put out a hand and stopped him, and said, amiably enough, "Elam, good friend . . . do you have a sling I could borrow? I had one once, a long time ago, but it was left behind in Jericho."

"Of course," Elam said, reaching into his waistcloth and bringing it out. "A good sling, the thongs are very supple, I oil them regularly. And what, you are hunting lion? I know where there is a small pride hiding in the long grass. . . ."

"No," Anak said. "I hunt a man, in the morning."

He told Elam of Achan's challenge, and saw his face paling as he spoke. . . .

His voice hushed, Elam said, "Before he became a wealthy man, Achan was known as the best herdsman among all the tribes. He earned this reputation by killing thirty or forty wolves, more than a dozen bears, and several lions, and all with his sling. . . . Anak, Achan is the best slingsman in the whole of the

Israelite horde! You cannot fight him with this weapon!"

"I must," Aanak said. "I have accepted."

"A sword, yes, I would agree," Elam said, wailing. "Or even daggers at close quarters . . . But the *sling?* In Heaven's name, no! There's not a better slingsman in the whole of the Israelite camp!"

"I accepted," Anak said stubbornly. "And if you have them, I will need good stones."

Elam threw up his arms, and knew that there was nothing he could do to dissuade his friend. He said, resigned, "I have twenty or thirty carefully selected river-stones. You will only need three or four, because if Achan does not kill you on the first strike, he surely will on the second or third. I will give you only my very best. . . ."

He squatted down on the sand and emptied his leather stone-bag and began picking up the round pebbles one by one and weighing them in his hand, fingering them, testing their roundness and their weight, matching them carefully; and he said at last, "There! Six identical stones of perfect weight and size. And you know how to kill a man with a sling?"

Anak shook his head. "No. A blow at the heart, I imagine."

"No! Aim for the forehead! Never for the heart! And if you should be a span or so too low you will hit the throat, also a killing blow. The chest is not important, always remember that, a strong man, well-muscled, can take a half-dozen stones in the chest with no great damage unless they are very formidably thrown. I saw a man killed once with a stone to the precise middle of the torso; but this was a very rare case, and the slingsman was the champion of all the Hittites. You yourself cannot expect this kind of success. So aim always for the forehead." He added politely, "Unless, of course, you are also expert. Are you, Anak?"

Anak shook his head. "No," he said, his voice dulled. "I was never an expert. I killed a wolf and a bear once, but that was many years ago."

"Then let me teach you," Elam said urgently. "Over the years now, in our long wanderings, we have become bedouin. And a bedouin herdsman very quickly learns how to use his sling, or his herds are soon wiped out."

And so, the lessons began. . . .

Elam showed him how to place the selected stone precisely into the center of the leather pouch, saying, "The tension on each of the two thongs must be exactly equal, or the stone will not fly straight. Now, show me how you wind it around your head. . . ."

Anak obediently swung the sling around and around, and Elam shouted, "No, no . . . ! Twice as fast, at the very least! Faster, faster . . ."

Anak wound it up faster still, till it was whistling around his head, and Elam said, "The tree there, any point on the trunk, hit the trunk for me!"

Anak let go, and the stone went flying at very high speed toward the target, and missed it by more than three cubits.

"Again," Elam said. "You must let go the thong the briefest moment before the pouch lines up with the target. Try it again."

At the thirtieth stone, Anak hit the tree, and Elam was diligently recovering his stones and replacing them in the leather pouch. At the fiftieth cast, Anak began hitting the trunk almost every time, and Elam took his bronze dagger and cut out a piece of bark to make a blaze.

After half an hour or more of practice, Anak hit

the blaze three times in a row; but Elam was still not satisfied. He shouted, "It was a strike, and you perhaps have given him a headache! Faster! The windup much faster! Here, let me show you. . . ."

He took the sling from Anak and wound it around his head so fast that the sound of it was an angry whistle. He let it fly, and the pebble hit dead center on the target so hard that it embedded itself deeply into the wood and had to be prized out with Elam's knife.

Handing back the sling, he said, "*That* is what you have to do. That patch of stripped bark . . . imagine it is Achan's forehead. Now, try again."

Hour after hour, under Elam's expert tutelage, Anak practiced; but the time to make an accomplished slingsman was measured not in hours, but in *years*.

"And for defense," Elam said, "do not wait for the sharp crack of the sling to tell you that the stone is on its way; by the time you hear it, and react, the stone will be already reaching you at tremendous speed. Instead, keep your eyes always on the first finger of his right hand. The moment you see it straighten . . . it means he is releasing the stone and letting fly. That is when you drop to the ground or sidestep. And you must vary your evasions. If you step always to the left . . . then he will know how to counter the move. Believe me, Achan is very expert. Now, try again. This time—far more speed to the swing around your head, the stone must kill, not merely hurt!"

By the time the fading light made it impossible for him to see what he was doing, he had reached a point at which he could hit the tree trunk perhaps once out of five strikes, and the target-blaze itself once out of twenty.

Elam wailed, "You die tomorrow, Anak! On the third or fourth strike, he cannot fail to kill you! You must give him two or three strikes, no more! And you are allowing him twenty."

Stubbornly, Anak began winding up the sling again. "It seems to be a question," he said calmly, "of releasing the thong at the precise moment . . ."

"Of course. That, and the speed of the wind-up."

The sound of it whistling through the air was formidable; and when Anak at last straightened his index finger and let go, the stone flew straight to its mark, and sank deeply into the trunk of the tree, exactly on the blaze, just as Elam's had done.

"Good," Elam said. "Now show me that you can do it again."

Once again Achan hurled his missile; and this time, it missed even the tree, by more than thirty degrees.

"A dead man," Elam moaned. "Dead in the first few strikes . . ." He sank to his haunches on the ground, and Anak set aside the sling and joined him.

"And will you tell me," Elam asked, "what it is you fight over?"

"Over your sister Elisheva," Anak said. There was no surprise at all on Elam's face, but Anak went on, "Oh, that is not the ostensible reason. Ostensibly, we are fighting over the fact that Achan tried to betray me to the people of Ai."

Elam stared. "What? A traitor among us?"

Anak shrugged. "But we both know that the fight is over Elisheva." He stared into Elam's eyes. "Under your rules of personal combat, will she be mine if I kill him?"

"*Rules?*" Elam echoed. "Rules of personal combat? I don't know what you mean by this."

"In Jericho, under like circumstances, all the property of the loser goes to the victor."

Bewildered, Elam shook his head. "First of all," he said, "Elisheva is not yet Achan's property, not until they are married. And secondly, I don't even know the rules, this is not a very common occurrence among us. But I fear . . ."

He was deeply troubled, and he said heavily, "I fear Achan will very quickly kill you, his reputation with the sling is quite formidable." He thought about it for a while, and he said at last, "Although . . . in the last few years, with the doubling, the tripling of his herd, he has become very rich, and now has slaves without number to work for him. Perhaps his arm has lost its cunning, who can tell?"

He grunted and said philosophically, "Perhaps it has. And in this possibility lies your only hope of survival. Because, if he is still as expert as once he was . . . then within the first few minutes, he will kill you."

"To the devil with him," Anak said angrily. "We fight for Elisheva. And if I cannot win her for myself . . . then my life means nothing to me."

Chapter Nineteen

Word of the coming fight had spread like wildfire through the tents of the Israelites; and by the time the sun had shown the first sliver of red over the top of the mountain, there were great numbers of them gathered by the bank of the River Jordan.

The women who came here every morning for water or firewood had elected to stay for a while; the herdsmen had left their flocks to their own devices and were waiting; those who were treading the grapes in Gilgal's grain pits had decided to let the juices rest . . . and the bank was crowded with them.

During the night, news of the duel had been brought to Caleb, and he had promptly elected himself as referee, startled though he was by this unexpected development. He wondered what Joshua would think of it; but Joshua was up on his bluff, communing with his God, and had absolutely forbidden *anyone*'s approach, an injunction most of his people were more than happy to obey; he was not an easy man to talk with.

The shortening shadows on the red-gold sand where the deep green trees were sparse enough to permit the sun's beams heralded the arrival of the contestants; Achan with his father Carmi, Anak with

Elam. Gathering around them were others closely connected to the combatants—Elisheva, Igal, Barkos, and Caleb's daughter Achsah on the one hand; and Achan's other family members on the other: his mother Timna, his two sisters Miriam and Helah, and his old uncle Massa, who was reputed to be one hundred and seventeen years old, so frail and decrepit that he had to be carried by two of his multitudinous grandsons to the site of the contest, there to be set down in a shallow hole scooped out in the sand to support his withered body.

He was cackling to himself, and it was a strange kind of laugh. He said, to anyone who would listen, "It is sixty years since I witnessed a combat with slings, sixty years! That was in Zoan in Egypt, when I was a young man." His voice was a croak, and he chomped with his empty gums on a piece of bread, spread with garlic, that he had brought with him. "No, eighty years ago, and it was not Zoan, but Sile."

Caleb raised his hands and called out, "Sons and daughters of Abraham! Israelites who are known as Hebrews! Listen to me!"

The murmuring crowd fell silent, their excitement rising, and Caleb went on. "Your attention, my friends! This is a fight to the death, over a matter of honor, between Achan of Judah, and Anak of the *Anakim* who is none the less an offspring of Esau ben Isaac, and therefore one of us. The matter in dispute is that Anak claims Achan betrayed him to the people of Ai."

There were very strict formalities to be attended to, and Caleb was one of the few people who, by virtue of his age, understood them. He called out, "Achan of Judah! Do you deny the charge?"

Achan said stolidly, "I do. It is a lie."

"Anak of the *Anakim*, do you withdraw your charge? If you do, the ordained punishment for a false charge of this nature is a flogging, not less than twenty strokes of the cane."

"I do not," Anak said. "On the contrary, I repeat it. Achan told the people of Ai that I had been sent to spy on them. And thus; betrayed not only me . . . but your leader Joshua as well."

There was a little surge of consternation in the crowd, and Caleb said, shocked at this flouting of good manners, "Enough, Anak! It is sufficient to state that you do not choose to withdraw the charge."

"I do not withdraw it."

"Very well, then."

He looked over their excited faces as they drew nearer to him, hanging onto his words, and he enjoyed their attention. "There has not been a case of personal combat among our people—and I say again, Anak is one of *us*—since Keros slew Peleth in the Wilderness of Shur, shortly after we left Egypt with Moses. A matter, I remember, of the seduction of Peleth's daughter Serah . . . But the rules remain the same. The distance will be thirty paces, each of the contestants to be allowed as many strikes as necessary, the combat to begin on a signal that I will give. When a man is hurt and falls, there is no restriction on his opponent, save that once the fallen man is declared to be dead, there will be no further desecration of the body. The contestants will now take up their positions."

Barkos had already paced out the distance, and with three of his friends had set out two lines of limestone chips. Anak and Achan went to them, and stood there with their slings held in the right hand, the longer thong wound three times around the thumb, the shorter wound once around the index finger and held in place with the tip of the thumb. In the left hand, they held four or five stones ready for instant loading, and in the open leather pouches that hung from their belts there were twenty or thirty more pebbles, all meticulously matched for size and roundness to ensure equal accuracy of flight.

Caleb said, "The signal will be a falling stone. As it strikes the ground, the contest will begin. Are you both ready?"

"Ready and waiting," Achan said.

"I am ready," said Anak.

Caleb took a stone and hurled it up into the air. . . .

Instinctively, Anak watched it, and when it fell to the ground he quickly placed a pebble in his sling's pouch and began to swing it around his head as Elam had taught him. But Achan's weapon was already whistling as he wound it up; Achan had kept his eyes on his opponent and was trusting to his ears to tell him when the signal came, while Anak, unskilled in these matters, was watching the falling stone.

Anak heard the deadly crack of the leather thong and threw himself to the side as the stone hurtled past him. His own strike went wild as he stumbled, and missed Achan by more than a quarter of a circle, and he saw that Achan was laughing. He heard the mocking voice: "Shall I come closer, fool, to make it easier for you?" and as he dropped quickly to his knees he heard the pebble whistling over his head. . . . He was on his feet again in the minutest fraction of time, and as he let fly he saw his stone strike home in Anak's groin; he had aimed for the head, but the bellow of rage that came from his adversary was reward enough.

He heard someone in the crowd shout, "A strike, a strike . . . !" Was it Caleb's daughter Achsah? No, it was his lovely Elisheva.

Two stones hurtled past him in rapid succession and a third struck him in the shoulder, momentarily paralyzing his arm, before his next was ready; and this too went wild, flying (though at great speed now) more than three paces to Achan's left.

He remembered Elam's injunction—"*Watch his first finger . . .*"—and he did so, learning that he could begin his evasive action even before the stone left the sling.

There was a dreadful tenseness on the watching crowd as the opponents flung their stones, the slings cracking viciously as they sidestepped or suddenly dropped to their knees. . . .

Anak was hit in the chest three times in a row, but he was well muscled there, and though there was great pain, there was no lessening of his capabilities. He was very fast on his feet, and giving all of his attention now—too much of it!—to the movement of that index finger that would signal the strike.

Achan had fired fourteen or fifteen stones (and Anak some seven or eight) when he made a decision that almost gave him the victory. *Why should I take any evasive action at all,* Achan asked himself, *when this foolish man has hit me only once in eight attempts?* And so, he stood his ground and concentrated only on his target. He would up his sling seven, eight, nine times, until he was quite sure that the velocity of his stone would quite inhibit any evasion. Two stones from Anak whistled past him, one half a cubit to his left, the other very close indeed on his right, but he did not take his eyes off Anak's forehead.

There was even time for him to reflect that the

stone in his pouch was the best of all his stones, a river-rounded pebble of perfect symmetry, rather heavier than most, a stone that had already killed, more than a year ago, a monstrous bear that on its hind legs was almost six cubits tall, a bear that had made the mistake of lowering its head at the whistling sound of the sling and thus had died for its curiosity.

The perfect stone left the sling with a *crack* that could be heard all the way up to the village of Gilgal. It was not only a perfect pebble, but a perfect shot too, minutely timed and meticulously executed, the secondary thong released at precisely the right moment. . . . It sped at tremendous speed to Anak's throat, and he saw it coming and swung his whole body around in sudden alarm, knowing that this . . . he could not avoid.

He was already throwing himself to one side, his own sling neglected, as he felt the glancing blow over his left ear.

Glancing, yes . . . But it was heavy enough to drive the consciousness from his mind, and he fell heavily to the ground, the stars exploding in his orbit of vision. He was barely conscious as he heard Achan's maniacal shriek: "And now, Canaanite scum, I kill you. . . !"

He heard the harsh sibilance of the whirling sling, saw through dulled eyes the winding-up, knew that the next strike would drive its pebble into his forehead. In perhaps half an hour of combat, he had hit Achan only twice, while he himself had been hit at the very least seven times, often quite severely. And now, he was lying on the sand on the borders of consciousness with his adversary poised and confident, swinging those deadly thongs around his head in ever more potent circles. . . .

He tried to struggle to his feet and could not; he even tried to move his head back and forth, but his muscles would not answer the commands of his brain; all he could hear was that dreadful sound of Achan's relentless leather thongs.

And then, suddenly, there was a bellow of rage coming to them, loud enough to worry Heaven itself, and Joshua was racing toward them down the hill, waving his almond staff, his wiry legs pumping. He screamed as he approached them, at the top of his voice: "Stop . . . ! Stop it, I tell you! Desist! How dare you? How *dare* you . . . ?"

He threw himself bodily at Achan and swung his staff with both hands, knocking him, startled, to the ground, and beat him again and again, shouting, "You dare? Jew fighting Jew in my camp when we are surrounded by so many enemies? Personal combat? I will not allow it!"

He dropped his staff and ran to Anak, only semiconscious as he lay there, and raised him up by a handful of hair. He slapped him repeatedly across the face and screamed, "And you! A guest in my camp! I could have you hanged for this. . . .!"

The fury fell from him like a worn-out cloak, and he folded his arms and stood there, glowering, staring at the crowd with a dreadful malevolence in his dark and angry eyes. He singled out Caleb and said, "And you, whom I always trusted! You lend your dignity to this boorishness?"

Caleb nodded. "I lend it my dignity," he said calmly, "because it is an affair of honor that may not otherwise be settled."

Many among the crowd, frightened by Joshua's anger, were already moving away, and Joshua found his stick and waved it at them, shouting, "Be gone with you! Back to your tents! What, have you no work to do? Be off with you. . . !"

Slowly, Anak was recovering his senses, and he was aware that Elisheva was on her knees beside him, binding a rag around his head, wiping away the blood from his chest. He saw Achan take her by the arm and pull her to her feet, saying roughly, "Enough! You are my betrothed! Leave him alone!"

She turned on him like a vixen and tried to slap him, but he caught her wrist easily and held it; and he was laughing at her now, a laugh that he did not feel, a laugh that was entirely devoid of any good humor. She spat at him and said furiously, "When I become your wife, Achan, not before . . ."

She pulled herself away and dropped down to her knees again to finish the bandaging.

Achan was about to strike her, but Igal's hand was on his arm; for a moment, he held Igal's quiet look, and then he turned away and strode off, muttering to himself.

Massa's grandsons were gathering the old man up and carting him away, Achan's father Carmi and his mother Timna were grumbling to each other because their son's victory had been snatched away from him; and in little groups the crowd was dispersing, knowing only that the contest, unresolved as it had been, was something they could all talk about for a long time to come.

And soon, all of them had gone, save Anak and Elisheva.

They sat together on the sand, commiserating silently with each other; there was not much that needed to be said now, but Anak murmured at last, "Perhaps it was a mistake that I came to the Israelite camp, what do you think?"

"No."

"Perhaps I should leave now and go to . . ." He sighed. "Well, Jerusalem, perhaps?"

Her voice was a whisper: "No, it would make me very miserable if you went away."

"I have been so happy here, and yet . . . to see you married to another man, a man we both detest, it's more than flesh and blood can stand."

"We have one more month. Perhaps, in that time, something will happen." She was trembling.

"Something? Such as?"

For a long time, she could not bring herself to answer, but she said at last, not meeting his eye, "If you were to love me, physically, I mean, and we let it be known . . . Achan would surely refuse me if he knew I were no longer a virgin."

Anak shook his head. "No," he said quietly, "it would be a betrayal of Igal, of Elam and Barkos, of your dear mother Azuza. I could not reward them for their generosity to me in this fashion."

"No, I suppose not . . ."

She was in tears suddenly, and he embraced her and held her close. She took his hand and put it to her cheek; and that heavy silence came over them both again. She lay down on her back and rested her head in his lap and closed her eyes, deriving what comfort she could from his presence and wondering what marriage would be like with that hateful man, wondering what, if anything, might be done to avoid it.

And *nothing* could be done.

Except . . . There was only one man who could help her, she thought, and that was Joshua himself. In his devious mind, perhaps he could find a way out of the dilemma. . . .

But the more she thought about it, the more

strongly she realized what his reaction would be should she approach him with the problem. He would hear her out, and then say, in that sour, sardonic voice of his, "Achan is one of my commanders; what he wants . . . is what *I* want." It would not only be demeaning, it would also be quite useless.

Suppose, then, she should run away with Anak? To Jerusalem, or one of the other fine cities of Canaan? To Gaza, perhaps, a city close by the sea of which she had heard tell a great deal . . . or to Joppa, or Acco, Tyre, or Sidon (and of these northern cities she had heard even more, legends of their ancient history, of the flowering of their varying cultures . . .).

But would Anak consent? No, this too would be a betrayal of the trust he had spoken of, without a doubt, and she murmured, lost in a flow of semiconscious thought, "If only you were not so honorable a man, Anak . . ."

It did not surprise him in the least. As if he were reading her thoughts, he said quietly, "Yes, if my sense of honor were less than it is, if I were a rogue as Achan is . . . yes, we could perhaps leave this camp and flee to the island of Tyre, where there are many of the *Anakim*, some of them members of my own family. We would be welcome there, I would once again be a rich and even a powerful man, and you yourself would be lost in a delirium of happiness. And yet . . . what would Igal think of this? I cannot play false with a man who had been so good to me."

"Elam, I am sure, would approve. And so would Barkos."

"The head of the family is Igal. He too is a man of honor. I cannot betray him."

"No. You are right, of course."

"Our happiness together," Anak said, "for all of our years, would be marred by the remembrance of my dishonor."

"Yes, I know it."

She fell silent again, and in a while he took her hands in his and said, forcing a smile, "But while we have time together, shall we stroll along the river-bank? I know where there is a nest of humming-birds. . . ."

Childlike, she was immediately excited, all her worries behind her for the moment, almost forgotten in the pleasure of a fleeting moment. *"Humming-birds?"*

He was delighted by the enjoyment so evident in her eyes, and he said, laughing, "There are three eggs there, the palest of blues and smaller than the nail on your little finger."

She could not wait, nor constrain her emotion. She leaped to her feet and took his hands, pulling him up, and said excitedly, "Show me, show me . . . !"

They ran to the edge of the water and walked slowly and quietly along its brink until they came to a tangle of creeping flowers that were clambering up into lower branches of a thorn tree. He whispered, "Softly now . . . You will see the male protecting the nest, hovering close by."

They crept on in silence, and Anak reached up and moved a thorn branch away very carefully, and there was the nest, tightly knit and very small indeed, no wider across than half the span of Elisheva's hand. He took her by the elbows and lifted her up, and he whispered, "You see the eggs? You see them?"

"Yes, I see them . . ." She could not contain her

excitement. "They are so small! May I touch them?"

"No! If you do . . ."

He broke off, "And there is the father . . ."

The smallest of all hummingbirds, no more than an inch long, was sweeping in on Elisheva's face, the green blaze at its throat shimmering, and Anak dropped her to the ground at once. He said, laughing, "He feels his family is being threatened."

But suddenly he was frowning, and he said, puzzled, "But he is not worried about *us*. There is something else."

The hummingbird was darting back and forth at furious speed, and Anak looked up to the sky and said, "A hawk . . ."

Elisheva followed his look, and saw it, a large and very beautiful bird with mottled brown feathers, circling easily and very low above the nest. It settled on a nearby branch, and the tiny hummingbird made two or three passes at it, flying within a few inches of that murderously curved beak until it, too, came to rest on a thorn branch closeby.

For a moment or two, it seemed to be concerned only with preening itself, raising a wing and scratching under it. The hawk was watching the nest, and the hummingbird was feigning complete indifference. . . .

Anak held Elisheva's hand tightly, and said sadly, "I fear that we are about to witness a small tragedy. . . ."

Almost as if in answer to his thought, the hummingbird suddenly flew, as straight and as fast as a slung pebble, toward the hawk and drove its sharply pointed, minuscule beak into that feathered head. For a brief moment, the hawk reeled back and almost lost its clawed footing; it was hurt but not killed, and the powerful beak opened once and closed once, and Elisheva screamed as she saw the dead hummingbird held there, still fluttering as the hawk devoured it.

She turned her face away, unable to watch, as the hawk hopped lazily to the nest and ate the eggs. Anak held her tightly, and he whispered, "Come. It is over. We must return to the tents now."

Slowly, they wound their way up the hill to the camp; and there was Joshua waiting for them. . . .

He scowled at Elisheva, and said to her, "Go child. Leave me alone with your lover, I must talk with him."

Elisheva met his angry look, and she said calmly, "He is not my lover. Though I will say that I wish he were."

Joshua struck her sharply across the face for her impertinence, and he screamed, "Go, woman! Leave us alone. . . !"

Daring even more of his anger, she embraced Anak briefly and whispered, "Every moment I am away from you . . . I dream of you."

"My love . . . We will find a way . . ."

"Enough!" Joshua shouted. "She is betrothed to Achan!"

"I know it," Anak said. "And if you wish to talk with me on other matters . . . I will listen."

"Come then," Joshua said.

He left Elisheva standing there and strode off, and in a moment Anak followed him further up the hill and onto the habitual bluff.

Joshua squatted on his heels at the edge and stared across the valley to the ruined walls of Jericho, as though deriving comfort from his victory there. There were huge scavenger crows circling,

304

black as death; and even though it was the middle of the day, the cries of jackals could be heard as they fought over meat that was quickly rotting in the heat of the sun. And when the wind changed once in a while, they could smell the decomposing corpses there.

Joshua plucked at his beard, searching out a louse there. His eyes were touched with madness as he turned to Anak and said, "You are a Canaanite of Jericho. Do you know how to construct a scaling-ladder?"

Anak nodded. "Yes, of course. They were always part of the army's equipment in Jericho. I myself was never a soldier there, but I sometimes supplied the slaves for the army's work. Yes, I know how to make them."

"Tell me how."

"We go down to the jungle of the Jordan," Anak said, "and with flint knives we carefully cut bamboo poles, twenty cubits or so in length, and fashion cross-pieces from other poles that must be an inch or more across in order to carry the weight of a man. We bind them to the uprights, half a cubit apart with cord made from plant fiber, a plant that grows well by the river."

"And how long to make a hundred of them?"

"A *hundred?*" Anak was startled. "With how many men and women?"

"As many as may be needed."

"Well . . . the cutting of the wood takes a very long time. The work can be hastened if the cross-pieces are burned into sections with fire, rather than cut with knives—"

"I am not interested in *how* it is done," Joshua said. "I asked how long it would take."

"I will remind you," Anak said, "that your exact

words were 'Tell me how.' That is what I have done. As for how long . . . five or six men or women, working from sunup to sundown, can make three such ladders. With ten times the number of workers, perhaps thirty or forty can be constructed in a single day. For a hundred . . . four days, I would say."

"Not ten times the number of workers," Joshua said, "but a hundred times, if necessary. Go to the men of Zebulun, of Naphtali, of Dan, and Asher. Tell them my orders. Show them how to make these ladders."

He was almost snarling now. "And by this hour tomorrow, I want to see my hundred scaling-ladders ready. Then, one more day, because . . ."

He rose to his feet, and his voice softened. He went on, sighing. "One more day, Anak, to accustom my people to them, under your instruction. We are bedouin, there are very few among us who have ever stepped off the hot sand of the desert floor. To climb a high ladder . . . it may be difficult for them. They must learn how to carry their arms as they climb."

Anak nodded. "Yes, you are right."

"I always am."

"Perhaps. In Jericho, the swordsmen drew their swords as they approached the top of the enemy wall, and therefore used only one hand for climbing. When they reached the walk at the top of the wall itself—that is when they drew their daggers. It is indeed the crucial time, the moment of stepping from bamboo rungs onto stone blocks in the face of opposition that can be very heavy."

"You will tell them these things," Joshua said. "Tell them also that you speak in my name, so that you will be obeyed at all times."

"You do me great honor, and I am grateful."

"Your Canaanite knowledge can be useful to me now."

"I am sure of it."

"We Israelites are unskilled in the arts of war, and very simple people."

"And I am sure of that too," Anak said.

Joshua raised his voice, and he was angry as always when he felt that not enough *respect* was forthcoming.

"My plan for the second assault on Ai," he said, "is as yet unpolished. I need a night or two more of thought; it is a very complicated strategy. But we will attack in three days' time. You will command the one hundred laddermen, showing them where to place their ladders to best advantage. Your immediate superior will be the commander who leads the assault on the walls."

There was scarcely any pause at all, then Joshua said, "He is Achan. Achan of Judah. Go now. I wish to be left alone."

"Until we meet again," Anak said sourly, "peace be on you."

But Joshua did not deign to answer him.

Chapter Twenty

The assault on Ai was a disaster.

All through those long nights, Joshua had sat alone on his bluff, sad and alone, worrying about his assumption of Moses' God-given mantle and asking himself why it could be that the Lord no longer wanted to commune with him.

And the only comfort he could find lay in the falsity that Ai, as best he knew, was prepared to surrender to him.

There would be—and he gloated over the thought—the laying down of the enemy's arms, the ritual hanging of their king and his officers, followed by a token slaughter of perhaps a quarter of the city's population . . . and the way into Canaan's four-thousand-foot mountains would be open.

But not only had he been grossly misled; it was far, far worse than he could possibly have imagined. Under the senior Elder of the *Anakim*, the decision had been made that they would not flee (they had far too much to lose in Ai) and would, instead, warn their king of the impending attack.

And so, when Joshua was ready, the garrison of Ai was standing to its arms and eagerly awaiting the onslaught.

Joshua was not to be allowed a battle within the confines of the city's narrow streets, but would be attacked on the ground outside the walls, where the chariots and the cavalry of the defenders could be used with great advantage.

Thus it was that as soon as the Israelites reached the beginnings of the plateau on which the city was built (with not a movement to be seen on the walls, just as if the place were empty and undefended) the heavy wooden gates were swung open. . . .

First, some three or four hundred horsemen cantered out, splitting up at once into two columns to ride to positions on either side of the attackers, where they halted and sat their mounts in expectation of their orders. Next, forty or fifty chariots were driven out, to take up a wheel-to-wheel line in front of the walls.

And then, four thousand men or more poured out through the gates in battle order, their swords drawn, their shields buckled on. Behind them, a small—but still formidable—force of mounted archers and lancers followed, all of them trotting to the north and wheeling round towards a position behind the Israelites.

Joshua was in shock.

He stared for a moment at the advancing infantry, and even though his military knowledge was limited, he saw at once that in a very few minutes his inferior numbers with their inferior weapons would be cut off, forced to fight not only against vastly greater numbers of infantry but against cavalry and the dreaded chariots as well.

Joshua was not a fool. Some of the assault force had already turned to run, in a desperate effort to get through the encirclement before the ring could close, and he raised his staff and his voice and bellowed, "Retreat! Children of Israel, hear me! Retreat!"

The order was taken up by the commanders (some of whom were in the forefront of those already fleeing), and the word echoed back from the walls of the valley: *"Retreat . . . Retreat . . . Retreat!"*

Surprisingly, in the escape, only thirty-six of the Israelites were killed, though one hundred and eighty were wounded, some of them quite severely. And as they climbed slowly back toward Gilgal, Joshua turned to look across the valley at the distant enemy he had been so sure of conquering; they were still there, though reforming their ranks now and beginning to move back into the town. He squatted down and stared at them as his people, sullen and angry, stumbled past him.

Within the hour, all the hapless forces had reached the fragile security of Gilgal's ruined walls, and the gates of Ai were being closed again.

Joshua looked up to see Caleb standing beside him, and Caleb said softly, "The danger now is that they will attack us here. Better we warn the commanders."

Joshua did not answer, and Caleb went on, "Our walls are not strong, but they cannot use their horses here."

"Go away," Joshua said roughly. "Why do you pester me when I must think now? Leave me!"

"Very well."

Caleb moved away, and Joshua screamed after him, his fanatic's voice vibrant with his fury, "Only the Lord God can help us now! And He is not with us! I will find out why! I will find out!"

He leaped to his feet and strode off after Caleb, shouting like a madman, "Once I know what it is

312

that we have done to offend Him . . . I will rectify the mistakes we have made! And He will no longer be our adversary . . . ! Not *against* us, but *for* us, as He was at Jericho. . . !"

His rage was awesome, and he waved his staff at Caleb's back and screamed, "A defeat! And news of it will spread like wildfire through the cities of Canaan! We will be discredited as a fighting force in the eyes of our enemies; they will laugh at us, mock us, scorn us! When they should cower in fright at our approach! And, listen to me, Caleb, when I talk to you! A plague on you for your silence. . . !"

Caleb turned back. He said quietly, "I am listening to your ravings." He could not hide the distaste in his voice. "If, as you say, the Lord God is displeased with us, then talk to *Him*, and find out why."

He went on his way and left Joshua there, shaking in fury.

Ai was a disaster; but it was to have a strange effect on the lives of Anak and Elisheva.

A clear and cloudless sky that night was suddenly overcast with dark clouds that seemed to brush the tops of the mountains, and where the moon had been bright, the land was now black as the pitch that bubbled around the shores of the Dead Sea.

The thunder came, great rolling blasts of thunder that shook the earth itself, and then hailstones the size of walnuts, pounding down onto the earth; and the sky was rent with sheets of white lightning that lit up the land and seemed to split the hills themselves.

Under the deadly deluge, Joshua crouched on his knees, his back bent, his arms over his head for protection as the hailstones beat down on him. His gown

313

was soaked, and the earth under his knees and his feet was wet and viscous mud.

For more than an hour the hailstones pounded down on him, and still Joshua would not seek cover; he remained crouched in the same position, almost as though he regarded this beating as a flagellation at the hands of his Lord God. And when at last they stopped, he rose to his feet in the heavy rain, and raised his arms to the Heavens, and he shrieked, "Speak to me, O Lord God! I am your servant! Speak to me! Speak to me. . . !"

And he was sure that he heard the voice answering him.

By dawn, the skies had cleared again, and Joshua was calm and even amiable, all his problems solved now. He said to Caleb, "I spoke harshly with you yesterday, will you forgive me?"

It was an unusual gesture, and Caleb was surprised. Smiling, he said, "Of course. And in all the years we've known each other, it's the first time I've heard you seek my forgiveness. Or anyone else's, for that matter." He shrugged. "You've been harsher with me in the past, it's never really offended me."

"I was angry with you, with my commanders, and most of all with myself. But that's all past now."

They were strolling together among the olive groves by the tents of the people of Judah, and they saw Achsah, Caleb's daughter, struggling up the hillside with a heavy jar of water on her hip. Joshua paused to watch her for a while, a graceful and attractive woman, still young, though fast approaching her thirties. She wore a long and modest gown of light brown wool, decorated with hems of red cloth and bound at the waist with a red waist-cloth. So heavily laden, she could not turn her head, but her dark eyes, very large and slightly slanted, moved to the side to smile at them as she went toward the tents, and Joshua said, "A daughter to be proud of, my good friend."

"Yes, I am indeed proud of her." He looked at Joshua and said, faintly mocking, "And will you tell me the reason for your unusual good humor?"

Joshua would not immediately answer him. Instead, he looked down on the millet field there below them and murmured, "It is strange, the young grain is still standing. After last night's storm, I would have imagined it flattened to the ground. It means that the Lord is ready to be with us again, once I have done His bidding."

Caleb frowned. "Last night's storm? What storm? There was no storm last night."

Joshua bit at his lip and stared at the ground. He said at last, "Your own tent is nearby, I believe?"

"Yes, it is."

"And would you have bread? I have not eaten for two days."

"Of course. Achsah made bread before she went to fetch water. Come."

They went to Caleb's tent together, and sat outside it on the sand in the welcome shade of the flap, and ate together as Caleb waited for whatever it was Joshua wanted to talk to him about; he knew that Joshua expected to be prompted, and so he held his peace.

Joshua wolfed down three flat loaves of bread and went to the water·jar and drank deeply from the wooden ladle there (a very nicely made ladle of olive wood that Caleb himself had carved more than seventy years ago, in Egypt), and at last he made up his mind to say what had to be said; and he was very serious now.

He sat down again, gathered his robe about him, grasped the staff between his crossed knees with both hands, and began. "I talked with the Lord last night, during the storm."

He waited for another denial of the storm from Caleb, but none was forthcoming, so he went on. "I learned the reason for His displeasure. No, for His *anger,* He was very angry indeed, He smote me with hailstones till I could bear it no longer."

"And now, He is for us again?"

"Not yet. He will be when I have done His bidding. Do you recall that when we destroyed Jericho, I gave orders that no spoils were to be taken save the symbolic metal vessels?"

"Of course. Many among us were very angry. Looting is part of a fighting man's privilege."

"Not in this case. I wished, as the Lord God wishes, that *nothing* should remain of Jericho to remind future generations that it had ever existed. Indeed, this is why it seemed necessary to me to slay Anak, even though, as you so rightly protested, he was a guest in our camp. But when I learned of Esau's blood in his veins, I realized that he could not truly be called a man of Jericho, but a Jew and one of us. One might almost say a captive, rescued."

Caleb nodded. "Yes, I will agree."

"But . . ." Joshua scowled. "There is one man among us who disobeyed my orders and the Lord's, and took spoils of great value from Jericho. And so . . . Jericho's name lives on."

"Oh? And who was that?"

Joshua shook his head. "I do not know. But I will find out. This is the Lord's bidding that I must obey if we are to succeed in our next attack on Ai."

Caleb sighed heavily. "Yes," he said, "I was sure

you'd want to try again. And our second attempt might be just as calamitous as our first."

"No," Joshua said quietly. "You will see. Call together the Elders of all the tribes, one man from each of the twelve, I will talk with them. Bring them to me at the bluff as soon as the sun goes down. Bring also twelve good straws."

Caleb stared at him. "Straws? But for what purpose?"

"Eleven of them to be of equal length," Joshua said calmly, "the twelfth . . . shorter than the others by half a span."

Caleb could not believe his ears. He said, almost exploding, "So serious a matter, and you expect to decide it by *chance?*"

"Not by chance," Joshua said. "By lottery."

"And what is lottery if not chance?"

"The hand of the Lord God Himself will place the shortened straw in the hands of *one* Elder, from *one* tribe. That tribe will be the one sheltering the man we are searching for, the man who lost us the battle of Ai, the man to whom, directly, the deaths of thirty-six of our best warriors can be attributed." His voice was rising, and he shouted, "I will find him, Caleb! And not by chance! But with the guidance of the Lord God! Go now!"

"What, *go?*" Caleb said angrily. "This is *my* tent, and you are my guest, not I yours!"

Joshua leaped to his feet with the agility of a young man half his age. He said tightly, "For the second time, I apologize! I am indeed your guest, and I thank you for your hospitality, the bread was very good." (In truth, it was very gritty, and quite awful. Achsah had dropped the dough accidentally onto the sand, and had not cleaned it sufficiently before going on with the kneading.)

317

"At sundown," Joshua said coldly, "bring the Elders to me. I will be waiting for them." He strode off in great dignity.

And as the sun, still red-hot, was touching the tips of the mountains where Jerusalem lay, that well-fortified Jebusite city, Caleb led the little procession of eleven other old men to where Joshua was waiting.

He said, not at all pleased with this charade, "I represent my own people of Judah."

Joshua nodded. "Good. I would have expected no one else. And the straws?"

"I have them."

"Give them to me."

"I do so under protest."

He handed them over, and Joshua checked them carefully, making sure that they were all of equal length save one, which was two inches shorter than the others. "And who will hold them?" he asked. "I will not let it be said that by a trick I influenced the outcome."

"Igal will hold them," Caleb said. "Igal of Issachar, representing that tribe."

"So be it, then."

He gave the straws to Igal, who was also very unhappy about this, and Igal held them out and let one Elder after another take a straw from his clenched fist. And when the plucking was finished, they all held them out for Joshua to see. There was a sharp clap of thunder from a distant sky, and the ground shook as Joshua took the short straw from Caleb's hand.

As he stared at it, Caleb said furiously, "What? What idiocy is this? Does it mean that *I* am the man who took spoils from Jericho? If so—"

"No," Joshua said, interrupting him coldly. "Can

318

you not understand, blasphemer that you are, even the word of the Lord God? It means . . . a man of your tribe, and the Lord God has spoken against Judah. Come, we go now to their tents."

"What, to the tents of Judah?" Caleb had quite lost his habitual calm. "For what purpose?"

"The Lord has shown us the way," Joshua said.

"What, with *straws?*" Caleb shouted.

"He has put us on the right path," Joshua said, insisting. "He has shown us the way. The man we seek is sheltering in the tents of Judah, and we will find him now."

"Madness!"

Joshua's fury arose, and he struck Caleb across the face and knocked him to the ground. Caleb clambered slowly to his old feet and said again, more quietly now, "Madness. But if you wish . . . I will follow you, as I have always followed you. Though sometimes wondering why, at my age, I should be so foolish."

And now began a search of the most extraordinary aspect. . . .

There were more than eight hundred tents of the people of Judah, spread out over a wide area that began with the shelter of olive trees and went on down almost to the banks of the River Jordan itself, where the trees were date palms.

Joshua said to Caleb, "It is your tribe; you alone will enter the tents with me."

"Very well, if your heart is set on it."

"Not only my heart, but my mind too. The Lord God is with us."

"I hope so."

"He is, I assure you. And He will guide us."

The first of the tents they came to was that of a man named Asa, and scorning the correct use of the request *"Mutar?"*, Joshua raised the flap and stepped inside, with Caleb close behind him. Asa was there with four of his sons, playing a game of dice in the light of half a dozen tallows, and he looked up in alarm at this unexpected intrusion.

Joshua said harshly, "The matter of the spoils you took from Jericho . . ."

Asa, a hard-headed and very angry young man, answered, "What spoils? Your orders were to take none, and I obeyed. Are you mad?"

Joshua stared at him for a moment, searching into his eyes for the truth, and then stalked out with a deeply embarrassed Caleb hard on his heels. The others of the Elders were there, waiting, looking at Joshua for some sign; but he gave none and went to the tent of Jeriel, one of the wealthier men of Judah.

Again, there was the same accusation: "The matter of the spoils you took from Jericho . . ."

And when Jeriel recovered from his surprise, he laughed and said, mocking, "Spoils? I took no spoils! I am a wealthy man, you see me here with two wives and four concubines; what, I need the stuff of Jericho to buy my pleasures?"

Hemdan next, who fell into a raging temper at the unwarranted intrusion and took his sword from its hanging place on the tent pole to drive them out. And then Cheran, and Lud, and Nepheg, and Hagri, Darkon and Oreb . . . and very many others.

There was always the same phrase: "The matter of the spoils you took from Jericho . . ." But the answers were varied, sometimes angry, sometimes jocular, sometimes whining. They woke up those who were sleeping, with no apology at all, even when they were in the arms of their wives or concubines; and by sunup, they had visited more than a hundred and forty of the tents; and Joshua, it seemed, was content with all of their answers.

A man named Othni, then, who shared his sleeping quarters with two young boys; and Jetheth, Hakkoz, Omar, and Heled; and still the search went on. Until . . .

Only a few moments after the sun had risen, Achan was leaving to go about his day's business; and as he opened up the flap he was astonished to see the weary tribal Elders gathered at the entrance to his tent. Joshua, untiring, made his habitual accusation: "The matter of the spoils you took from Jericho . . ."

For a moment Achan stared at him in alarm. But then he recovered his arrogance and said brusquely, "The spoils I took are *mine!* It is a soldier's prerogative to take booty in time of war!"

"My orders were that there would be no looting," Joshua said mildly.

"A fig for your orders!"

"They were also the orders of the Lord God Yahweh."

"And how can a soldier live without the spoils of war?" Achan said hotly. "I am one of your commanders, your best commander! You cannot deny me my rights in battle!"

Joshua was still very quiet. "And will you tell me," he asked, "what it was you took from Jericho?"

"A gown," Achan said angrily, "a Babylonian gown that is now my property!"

"And what else?"

"A little gold and silver . . . And why do you ask?"

"Where are they now?"

"Where you will never find them! The devil take

you, Joshua! They are *my* spoils, *my* rightful property, won in honorable combat!"

"And you will not tell me where you have hidden them?"

"No! I will not! Never in a thousand years!"

Joshua turned on his heel and stalked out, and Caleb spread his arms wide and said to Achan, "A man of my own tribe! Shame on you, Achan!"

Achan only stared as Caleb followed Joshua out into the harsh morning sunlight, and he heard Joshua say to the assembled Elders, "Our search is over. Go to your tents, comfort your wives, your concubines, or your slaves. What happens now . . . is in *my* hands."

Less than an hour later, eleven burly young men, one from each of the tribes, save Judah, appeared in Achan's compound. They were led by a man whose name was Helez, which meant "strong" in Hebrew, and they carried with them short lengths of rope made from goat's-hair.

Helez, a hairy and powerful young man with bulging biceps and a temper as well developed as his muscles, said stolidly, as though reciting phrases he had learned by rote, "Achan of Judah. By order of our leader Joshua, for crimes committed against your own people which have resulted in the death of thirty-six of our finest warriors and the wounding of one hundred and eighty others, to whit, the looting of valuables from the destroyed City of Jericho: a mantle from Shinar in Babylon, two hundred shekels of silver and fifty of gold. And the word of the Lord is that you, and all you have, be burned with fire, because you have done a shameful thing and transgressed the covenant of the Lord."

Achan paled and felt the blood leaving his face. He whispered, "You are mad. . . !"

Helez ignored him and went on. "The Lord Himself has told Joshua: *'Whoever rebels against your commandment and disobeys your words, whatever you command him, shall be put to death.'* Therefore, you are condemned to be stoned to death, together with all members of your immediate family, and with token numbers of your animals. The stoning will take place tomorrow at dawn, after which your bodies will be burned with fire, as the Lord God has commanded."

Achan, in a paroxysm of rage, threw himself at Helez and seized him by the throat. At once, there were a dozen other hands on him, tearing him away and binding him tightly with cords. And then, the young men went through all of Achan's tents and found his relatives. They were all bound and dragged down to spend the night at the stoning ground, there to await the spectacle in the morning.

Tied as they were, three of the young men were detailed to guard them all night long as they lay there helpless in the long grass.

Toward dawn, the ancient Massa moaned, "Water? A little water for my parched mouth, in the name of the one God Yahweh?"

One of the young men moved over and kicked him in the face. He said roughly, "Be quiet, old man! In a few hours you will not need water, nor anything else except a pile of sand over your dead body. . . ."

Until the sun came up, they lay there on the hard earth, trussed like chickens for the market, and awaiting Joshua's pleasure: Achan, his father Carmi, his mother Timna, his sisters Helah and Miriam, and the old cripple Massa, six of them all told. Close by, the token animals had also been tied up—two

323

mules, a single cow, and four goats, all destined for the stoning.

Helez inspected the bindings and found them to be good. He squatted on the sand and waited for the sun to rise over the hills.

Once it was fully cleared from the silhouette of the mountain ridges, the ritual of the stoning would begin. Helez was a very young man, only sixteen years old, and he had never seen this before; he could hardly wait to find out what it was all about.

Inexorably, the time crept on.

Chapter Twenty-one

When the sun rose, there was a strange tint of purple in the broad streaks of copper that limned the horizon. According to the seers, its cause was a volcanic disturbance very, very far away. "Beyond the two rivers," they said wisely, "the earth is belching out its fire, and great clouds of dust are rising to the skies. . . ."

Perhaps they were right. But one of the effects, here in the Jordan Valley, was that the normal early-morning gilding of the greenery had taken on a quite different tint; the green and the purple had combined to form a strange and deathly pall that seemed to embrace the whole of the riverbank.

The young men digging the holes looked up at the sky and muttered each other, "The Lord God Yahweh is either angered with us for what we do now . . . or perhaps showing us His pleasure."

There were thirty of them working with their shovels, all from the men of Asher, whose destiny was to become tillers of the soil, as their ancestor Jacob had said on his deathbed. The holes they dug in the hard red sandstone were two cubits deep, deep enough to bury a man up to his waist.

Their wrists bound to their thighs with cords, the

victims were placed in the holes and the sand was shoveled back in to contain them there, the upper portions of their bodies exposed for the stoning.

There was Achan himself, together with Carmi his father; there was Timna, his mother, who suffered from a painful affliction of her bones; there were his two sisters Helah and Miriam, and his two sons and three daughters; and there was his decrepit old uncle Massa who was lowered, bound, into his grave by two of his grandsons, themselves greatly relieved that a benevolent Joshua had consented to spare their own young lives.

As the sand was spaded back in to confine him, Achan looked up and saw Anak standing there, a very somber look in his troubled eyes. At the point of death, he had not lost control of his emotions, and he said, mocking, "Anak! My natural enemy! Will the first stone thrown at me be yours?"

Anak shook his head. "No," he said quietly. "I will not join in the stoning; I do not approve of this slaughter. But I am helpless, I can do nothing to save you now. Joshua has spoken, and when Joshua speaks . . . his people listen, and agree. Go with your God, Achan of Judah."

"May I ask a favor of you?"

The sand was up to his waist now, confining him firmly.

Anak nodded. "Yes, of course."

"I have seen stonings in my time," Achan said, "and though I have always considered myself a man of courage, I will confess to a certain fear of dying this way. Slow strangulation would be easier."

He laughed shortly, a brave man on the point of death. "And do you hold it against me that I fear pain? I am a commander in Joshua's army, and yet . . . Am I a coward at heart?"

One of the men piling up the sand said roughly to Anak, "Stand aside, friend. We are finished now."

Buried up to his waist, Achan said urgently, "They are almost ready to begin. Joshua, without a doubt, will throw the first stone, but will you throw the second? A small stone to my temple, I beg of you, hurled with enough force to kill me instantly. A quick death instead of a lingering one . . ."

"I cannot," Anak said tightly. "I will not be one of those who kill you."

"And Carmi my father. Dispatch him quickly too."

But Anak, deeply distressed, moved away; and it was indeed Joshua who threw the first symbolic stone. It was a piece of granite the size of a lemon; well aimed, it smashed into Achan's face, breaking his nose and his cheekbone.

More stones followed immediately from the crowd, a torrent of them. And one of them, hurled by a man of Benjamin who wanted to prove to his friends what a strong man he was, was a huge river pebble twice the size of a man's clenched fist; it flew straight to Achan's chest and shattered several ribs, so that he began coughing up blood from punctured lungs.

By the twentieth strike, Achan was blinded completely by stones that had smashed his forehead and pulverized the bridge of his nose again, and yet he was still alive. Another flew straight to his throat and destroyed his vocal cords completely so that the tone of the screaming was altered to a rasping, whining sound. And he was still *living* . . .

Anak, watching, picked up a small round stone and hurled it with great force and unfailing accuracy at Achan's temple; it smashed through the skull and buried itself in the brain, and put him out of his misery at last.

But the spectacle was not yet over; there were others to be killed. As Carmi's old bones began to break, his jaw pulverized and his yellowed teeth dropping to the sand around him, Anak dispatched him quickly too; and all the while, the ancient Massa was shouting imprecations: "A plague on you, Joshua the son of Nun! May the one God send leprosy down on you! May your genitals fall off with the sickness! May your only offspring be the despised daughters of whores and mules!"

Joshua screamed, "What? You dare to curse me, Massa of Judah? A pox on all your people!" He picked up a boulder so heavy that he staggered under its weight, and smashed it down on Massa's head.

The stones were falling around and on Timna now, and she died very quickly when a stone hurled by one of the men of Benjamin broke open her forehead.

Miriam lasted longer, and Helah longer still. Miriam died when a piece of limestone the size of a pomegranate, thrown from behind her, found the back of her neck and broke it, and someone shouted jubilantly (was it Helek of Naphtali?), "Did you see that? Only my seventh throw, and I found her spine . . . !"

Helah was still not dead, and she was screaming in pain and terror. Anak, sick at heart, hurled a small stone to her temple and killed her.

Now there were the sons and daughters, though two of them had already been mortally wounded and the other three did not last for very long. And then, the animals . . .

They were not buried, but merely trussed up and

laid out on the hard earth, the cow, two mules, and four goats, bound and laid out for the slaughter. Within an hour, their skulls were shattered. And then, the righteous men of Israel, their duty done, went from one to another of their victims and poured pitch over their bodies, setting them alight to erase, forever, the name of Achan of Judah.

Over the charred and still smoldering remains of Achan, they raised a cairn of stones to mark the spot for all of history, and as the pyres were burning fiercely, Joshua went to his tree on top of the bluff, and knelt down, and raised his almond staff up to the skies, and he screamed at the top of his voice, "The crime, Lord God, has been expiated! I have done Your bidding! I have followed Your orders. . . !"

He fell into a frenzy and lay on his stomach on the hard ground, hammering at the earth with his fists and shrieking, "I have done Your bidding, Lord! How else can I serve you?"

He was moaning, thrashing in his delirium; and an hour later, Caleb found him there, quite unconscious. He laid him carefully out on his back, and swabbed the tormented forehead with a wet cloth. And in a little while Joshua recovered, and he whispered almost inaudibly, "In three days . . . Caleb . . . my friend . . . we mount a second attack on Ai. And this time . . . we will conquer, the Lord God has promised me . . . We will conquer."

Caleb, an old man but a good friend, picked him up in his arms like a baby, wondering how fragile a weight such a strong man could be. Joshua's tent was a long, long way off, and Caleb chose to stop, instead, at Igal's secondary tent, where his guest was Rahab, the Canaanite prostitute.

He laid Joshua, only barely conscious, down on her skin bed, and said to her softly, "Our leader. I believe that he is not a man for women, though I may be wrong. I know him to be a man sorely in need of comfort. It may be that you are the only woman in the whole Israelite camp who can comfort him now. Will you do me a personal favor, and care for him?"

He thought that he had never before seen such glorious eyes as she stared at him. She whispered, "I will care for him. All I have ever heard about him . . . is admirable. Yes, I will care for him."

"Good night, Rahab."

"Good night, dear Caleb."

He was gone.

Her children, half-awake, were stirring, and she whispered fiercely to them, "Sleep! Go to sleep, all of you! You are in the sacred presence of a very holy man."

It was still early evening, and Anak lay with Elisheva in the long grasses below Igal's tents. She was sick at heart, and he was trying to comfort her. He said somberly, "I never liked Achan, much less admired him . . . But, up till the last moment of his death, his courage was very apparent. Do you know that it was I who flung the last stone that killed him?"

She was in tears. "Yes, they told me. They told me that he was in such agony . . ."

"He asked me to throw the first stone, with the same intent, to kill him quickly. But I could not bring myself to be his executioner, not till I saw the torment he was in." He said tightly, "Your Joshua is a very unforgiving man, perhaps even an evil man."

331

"But a great leader . . ."

"And do you know what he has done with the loot that Achan took?"

Elisheva shook her head. "No. I heard only that some of the young men were digging up the floor of his tent, searching for it."

"They found a Babylonian robe of great beauty in a sack under his bed, buried in the sand there, and two bars of silver weighing a hundred shekels each, and a bar of solid gold weighing fifty shekels . . . Joshua had the gown burned, the turquoise stones it was decorated with scattered in the river. As for the gold and silver bars—they were hurled from the top of the cliff out into the valley, which he has named Achor, to be lost forever. It is madness!"

Elisheva shrugged. "It matters little. What can we do with gold and silver?"

They fell silent for a while, and Anak said at last, musing, "And did you know that he wants to attack Ai once more?"

"Yes, my brother Elam told me."

"I fear it may well mean the end of us all."

"This time," Elisheva said, "the Lord is with us, not against us."

Anak said dryly, "Because of the massacre of Achan's family?"

Elisheva was a little confused, and she said defensively, "Because . . . Well, horrible though his punishment was, his crime has now been expiated."

"According to Joshua."

"Yes. According to Joshua."

There was a longer silence now, and he felt her distress; she was too young to reconcile the fact of Achan's death with its apparent result, the bringing, once more, of the Lord God onto their side. *Even if it is true,* she said to herself and wondered if she were blaspheming.

Aloud she said desperately, "And with Achan gone, there is only one thing that stands between us now."

"Yes, I know it. The matter of the bridal price."

"But your family . . . Surely they will help you?"

"I am an orphan," he said. "My parents were killed in an earthquake many years ago, when I was a child. True, there is an uncle in Shechem, a very wealthy man indeed. But if I were to ask him for goods, then I would have to explain what I need them for, and once he learned that I want to marry outside of my tribe, he would refuse. He's very rigid in these matters. My grandfather too, who lives in Joppa and trades there . . ." He said glumly, "Even more strict, a veritable bigot."

"It means, does it not, that we have no hope at all of marrying? Ever?"

"I think not." Her eyes were wide on his, and he said slowly, "I've thought a great deal about this, and it may be that there is one solution. A drastic one, perhaps, but I myself find very little against it, in view of the great reward."

"And that is?"

"It occurred to me that if I were to indenture myself to Igal for say, seven years . . ."

He heard her gasp, and he took her hand and said gently, "If I were to offer this as the purchase price."

"*Indenture?* But this would make you a slave! And for seven years . . . ?"

"A small price to pay," Anak said, "I am prepared to pay it. And I don't think Igal can possibly refuse. He knows that I was once a wealthy and successful man, he would not merely put me to herding

333

goats! No, I would *manage* his herds for him, and his other business matters as well. Igal is shrewd enough to realize that a man does not acquire a fortune such as I once had without considerable talents. Those talents would be put to work for *him*."

Elisheva was wailing. "But why cannot you put them to work for yourself, and become rich again. . . ?"

"Oh, I could," he said swiftly, "if I had only a few score goats to begin with, but I have not. And in any case, think of the time it would take! Igal will not wait indefinitely before marrying you off. . . "

"But a slave . . . !"

There were tears flooding into her eyes, and she brushed them away angrily. "No," she said, "I will not permit it! Our slaves are from the—the common herd, men and women of very low esteem, hardly better than animals!"

"Well then," Anak said cheerfully, "your father will have an articulate animal to command them."

"No! You cannot become one of them. . . !"

"I will become a slave," Anak said carefully, "but *not* of low esteem. And my mind is made up."

She was crying as she embraced him. "There must be a better way. . . ."

"If there is," he murmured, "I have not been able to find it."

"The skins," she said suddenly, and he frowned. "The skins?"

"The two lions you killed after Jericho."

Anak laughed. "Yes, mine by right, but Igal has long since regarded them as his own and put them to good use."

"I know, but . . . a few more skins, if you were to join Elam in his nightly hunting . . ."

"A few more? A fair price for even the lowliest

wife would be a score of good lion skins at least, and it would still be very little. And how long would it take me to find and kill a score of lions? As many weeks, perhaps as many months. For years now, he tells me, Elam has been a hunter. And in all that time, he has killed, I think, four lions."

She was searching the deepest recesses of her mind for solutions, and she said suddenly, "I have it!"

"Tell me, then . . ."

"Under our laws,' Elisheva said carefully, "if I, as a free woman, marry a slave, I can instantly give him his freedom. There!"

She saw the look on Anak's face, and she sighed. "Yes," she murmured, "that too would be a betrayal, wouldn't it?"

He nodded. "It would indeed."

"Then, will you promise me something?"

"Of course."

"Will you give this matter more thought? Much more thought?"

"Very well. For a few days . . ."

"It's all I ask."

The lengthening shadows were turning the land to darkness, and they kissed and said good-bye.

As Anak went to the small tent that had now been allocated to him, Elisheva found Barkos skinning an iguana he had caught and told him what had happened between the two of them. . . . Barkos told Elam, and Elam told Igal, and Igal told Azuza, saying in astonishment, "Seven years of indenture! Can you understand what this means? It means I will have a man of enormous talent working for me for seven years! And in that time and far less, do you realize how very much our fortune can be increased? The Canaanites are the world's best herdsmen, their knowledge of selective breeding is unsurpassed; it means that in no time at all I will own not a mere four hundred goats, but perhaps as many as a thousand! Can you imagine how jealous our neighbors will be?"

"My daughter," Azuza grumbled, "married to a slave. What will the neighbors think about *that?*"

"They will understand," Igal said calmly, "that I have made a very shrewd bargain. I can't wait for him to approach me! But meanwhile, woman, say nothing. I don't want you gossiping about this."

"Of course. I'll say nothing about it, if only because it's a disgrace to all of us."

Igal slapped her face and shouted angrily, "It is *not* a disgrace, woman! It can bring us wealth beyond your stupid imaginings! Bake bread now, I'm hungry."

"Very well. We have an iguana Barkos caught . . ."

"Ah, splendid! What a good son Barkos is, I'm really very proud of him! Cook it in Anak's new oven. And remember, you will say nothing about my upcoming negotiations with Anak."

"I told you already, husband."

But in the morning, when she was fetching water from the river, the gossip time for all the women, she complained to her friend Maacah of Benjamin. Maacah told her husband Pildash, Pildash told his friend Elika, and Elika told Shobal . . .

And in the course of time, Joshua sent for Anak, and sat with him on the bluff, and took a very long time coming to the point that was the true reason for the meeting.

He said somberly, "Our defeat at Ai, Anak . . . Not only will the whole of Canaan soon know of it and mock us, but—far worse—our people have lost faith in our prowess. I cannot allow this. We must attack

336

them again, and very soon, and this time—we must win."

His dark eyes were glazed over, searching out the distant mountains to the west as though trying to convince himself that soon they would all be his.

"Now," he said, "a mile to the northeast of Ai lies the town of Bethel, and I have learned that the next time Ai is attacked, Bethel will come to its rescue. Therefore, we will defeat both these twin cities in a single campaign, and so reestablish our military superiority."

Anak listened and said nothing, and Joshua went on. "Bethel, my spies tell me, is very strongly defended, and we cannot hope to take their walls and slaughter them within the town itself. But . . . there is no need for us to attempt this, since the troops of Bethel will pour out of their gates the moment they see that Ai is under attack again. The garrison at Ai too will no doubt repeat its last maneuver if we repeat ours. In other words, the moment our attack begins, they will pour out of their gates to repulse us. Good. This is what I want."

Anak still said nothing, and Joshua began tracing lines in the sand with his staff, drawing up a battle plan. He said: "Here, our own camp. Here, Ai. Here, Bethel. Now, to the southwest of Ai, I want a body of picked troops to hide, under cover of night, beyond the brow of the hill. I want a second force to the north between Ai and Bethel, also hidden. Our main force, which I myself will command, will attack Ai just as we did before; and when, just as *they* did before, they open their gates and drive down on us, we will turn and flee again, only this time . . . less precipitously, turning to fight once in a while, quite halfheartedly, you understand, so that they will be encouraged to pursue us, down to the valley where we can more easily fight, because their chariots will be of little use on the broken land there."

His eloquent hands were gesticulating, and suddenly, like a flash of lightning, he drew his sword from its scabbard and held it up high in the air to illustrate his point, saying, "And when the right moment comes, I will be on a small hillock where all my people can see me, and I will flash my sword in the sunlight, like so. . . . It will be a signal, whereupon two things will happen. One, our main force will turn and fight. Two, your force will enter the now defenseless town of Ai and burn it."

Startled, Anak echoed, "*My* force?"

Joshua peered at him and said mildly, "Did I forget to tell you? Your pardon, then! Yes, you will be in command of the picked troops who will take Ai and burn it to the ground as soon as the defenders have left it to pursue our main body. Once this task is finished, you will lead your men to strike the enemy in the rear. At which point, the third force will descend on the men of Bethel as they pour down the mountainside to the rescue of their beleaguered comrades. Is that all clear?"

"It is clear," Anak said, "and I thank you for the honor you do me. The command is greatly appreciated."

He rose to leave, and Joshua said politely, "And it is deserved. I know the fighting abilities of the *Anakim*, I understand their worth. A captain no longer, but a commander."

With no change of voice he said, smiling shrewdly, "And as for my army commanders . . . I will never permit one of them to become a slave."

Anak turned back and stared at him, and Joshua went on. "Word has been brought to me. There will be no indenture, not for seven years, not for one. I

338

will not have it said among our enemies that my troops are led by slaves. Leave me now."

It was the habitual dismissal, and Anak went disconsolately back to the Issachar tents to search out Elisheva.

Chapter Twenty-two

The night was dark and thunderous, and the earth had renewed its violent shaking.

Here and there, flames were flickering out of fissures in the ground, sometimes leaping up suddenly to heights of a dozen feet or more before extinguishing themselves in puffs of smoke. Lightning opened up the sky, setting the trees in stark and momentary silhouette, lining the faces of the people gathered there, many of them frightened, even though, over the years, they had become accustomed to these recurring phenomena.

There were forty or fifty of them squatting there under the pouring rain as Joshua strode among them, shouting to make himself heard over the storm, waving his staff for emphasis, his arms thrown out and his eyes on fire.

He laid out for them, in the most minute detail, his new plan for the reduction of Ai; he appointed his leaders, captains and commanders, and gave them the most careful instructions. . . . And as he spoke, the fires died down, the thunder ceased, and the ground they were on was still again. There was a strange and somehow comforting silence around them, and the people's spirits were raised again.

Joshua said, more quietly now, "I myself will lead

the main force of four thousand men. Anak the giant will lead the picked troops who are to lie in wait beyond the crest of the hill that lies to the south of the town, while Igal of Issachar will lead the third force, which will lie, also in ambush, above the route the men of Bethel must take if they come to Ai's rescue, as they surely will. These two forces will number . . . three thousand to Anak, and four thousand to Igal. Caleb, a man whose advice I respect, will stay by my side at all times."

Elzaphan the Levite called out, "And the matter of spoils of war? Is there once again a prohibition against taking them? My people were deeply offended the last time; it is a soldier's right to take booty. . . !"

"There will be no prohibition," Joshua said. "Spoils will be taken. For the rank and file . . . simple garments, including sandals and belts, vessels of pottery but not bronze, bales of cloth, weapons, artifacts of decorative value such as tiles and the like. For the officers, any gold or silver that may be found there, together with garments decorated with these metals or with precious stones, swords and daggers with their hilts so decorated, shields of bronze or leather, recurved bows and all arrows made from Egyptian reed. These things only to the officers, with slaves too if they desire them, all slaves not so taken to be strangled. The officers may reward their troops, if they so wish, with captured female slaves, but only for conspicuous valor in battle. This is the word of the Lord God, and my order."

"And the route," Igal asked, "to the place of ambush?"

"Along the gorge of the Wadi Muheisin, in stealth and silence."

"And the main force begins its attack . . . when?"

"At dawn. Once we have engaged the enemy, we will turn and retreat a distance of not less than three miles, and not more than five."

He scowled, knowing that the precise moment to turn on the pursuing enemy would be vital, and he said, "When the time comes to wheel about and attack, then I will climb up on an eminence and flash my sword in the sun, a signal for all to see. It will also be the signal for those lying in wait to the south."

"And the signal," Igal asked, "for the third force, which is mine, to move in on the Bethelites?"

"You attack," Joshua said patiently, convinced that this was already clearly to be understood, "as soon as you see their rescue column has completely entered the gorge, thus cutting off any hope they may have for a successful retreat. The tail of the column itself," he said, insisting, "must be in the gorge, so that all your troops are above them, and none of theirs above you."

"I understand, I understand," Igal said peevishly. "We will charge *down* on them. And cut them to pieces! Have no fears that any of the relief force will reach you! With you in front of them, and my men behind them . . . they will be caught in a trap. One sees that there can be no escape for them!"

Joshua sighed, and answered all the questions they asked him as they argued among themselves for more than an hour, debating the wisdom of this and that, the folly of the other. And Joshua said at last, raising his voice to silence their chatter, making his carefully prepared little speech to exhort them to their highest endeavors:

"There is one more matter of importance! On the field of battle itself, it is my order that not a single soul escape with his life! Go now to your troops, as I will go to mine, to hearten them and raise their spirits. And when the time comes, lead them to glorious victory in the most decisive battle our people have ever been forced to fight! With the fall of Ai, the way into the heart of Canaan's highlands will be open to us! And when the news of our victory is spread over the land, as it will be, then not Makkedah nor Libnah, Lachish nor Gezer, Eglon nor Hebron will dare stand against us! These are the cities we take next! Go now! And the Lord be on you all. . . !"

He strode off in the darkness, to be with his warriors for the final hours before the battle.

The second assault on Ai, by all military standards, quickly degenerated into a slaughter. Joshua, sure that the Lord God was with him now, was confident of success. His troops were equally sure that the fulfillment of all Israel's cherished ambitions for a Promised Land was now to be negated, entirely, by far superior forces they simply could not hope to overcome.

They were convinced that their attack meant nothing less than national suicide; and yet . . . they were prepared to follow their charismatic leader to the death.

It was part of their national character; even though they were not yet a nation. . . .

The sun was scarcely over the ridge of the mountains when the main force took up its position on a ridge facing Ai across the gorge; they stood there, waiting in battle order, and it was less than an hour before the gates of the city swung open and the chariots, first, came riding out. They too took up battle positions, and the cavalry came next, with two of the infantrymen running with each horse and holding on to the saddle straps in the fashion of Jericho. They waited, lined up and ready, and then the bulk of the infantry trotted out and formed itself into three columns, and they too waited for their orders.

The king, mounted on a splendidly caparisoned mare, said to his commander-in-chief, "What, three thousand men, Emis? What do you say?"

Emis was a short, squat, and very powerful man who took his name from his own tribe, the *Emim*, who came from beyond the Jordan. He grunted and said, "A few more, perhaps. We outnumber them. And this time . . . we should teach them a lesson."

"Then move to the attack," the king said, "at your leisure."

Emis spurred his horse and rode up and down the ranks of the infantry, exhorting them with both malice and humor; he was a very good commander. He shouted, "Soldiers of Ai, our beloved city! We are threatened, as we were once before, by a horde of savages who eat their own children!"

There was a burst of laughter from the troops at this opening sally; the men adored him.

And he went on, shouting, "They are simple bedouin, thrown out of Egypt, most of them born in the desert and knowing nothing of the cultivated life which we, the people of Canaan, have enjoyed for generations! They carry very few bows, and their arrows are made by cobblers and swineherds!"

There was more laughter as he continued. "As for their swords . . . Well, some of their swords and daggers came with them from Egypt, but for the most part . . ."

He paused for just the right length of time and raised his voice. "I have it on the highest authority that, for the most part, their swords and daggers are whittled out of olive branches by their harlots!"

It seemed the laughter would never stop; and a voice came from the assembled troops: "Long live . . . our great commander Emis. . . !"

The cry was taken up by four thousand voices, till the valley was ringing with the sound: "*Long live . . . our commander Emis . . . Long live . . . ! Long live . . . !*"

Emis raised his javelin and shouted, "Infantry in column of fives to the center! Cavalry in two echelons to the flanks! Chariots to the rear in reserve! All the mighty men of Ai . . . *Forward!* Slay them! Smite them with the edge of the sword and with arrows! Grind them into the earth! Let not one single man among them escape with his life! *For . . . ward!*"

Joshua watched the army moving down the steep slope of the hill, and he turned to Caleb beside him and said, "A few minutes before we advance, I think. No?"

Caleb shook his gray head: "No, we must reach the bottom of the valley before they do. If they are to pursue us, they must be in the advantageous position. That is to say . . . above us."

Joshua raised his sword high to the heavens, and screamed, "Children of Israel! Into battle against the hated enemy! *Forward!*"

They began clambering down into the deep gorge, jumping from rock to rock, four thousand of them in their heavy brown robes covering the mountainside like ants. At the bottom, they faced the Canaanites and fought for a few brief moments before, true to their instructions, they turned and ran. . . .

But they ran down the deep gorge, and the men of Ai followed them, and Joshua was racing furiously ahead of those who were fleeing the savage onslaught. He found an eminence and climbed up on it, and drew his copper sword, freshly polished for this endeavor. . . .

He waited, watching the men fighting below him, his people turning once in a while to engage the enemy very briefly and then fleeing once more. He saw the cavalry enter the gorge, and he waited for the chariots. . . . And when they too had galloped into the chasm, he stared over to the west where Bethel lay, five miles distant from his point of vantage. There was a moment of deep worry when he could not see whether or not the town's gates had been opened; but in a moment he saw Igal's troops, two miles closer to him, beginning their move over the ridge; and he knew that the Bethelites too were entering the trap.

He was very sure of himself now, and absolutely certain of final victory. He shouted, "Now, Children of Israel! *Now . . . !*

He lifed up his sword and flashed it this way and that; and on the signal, the fleeing army made a 180-degree turn and fought back.

The infantry of Ai was stopped in its tracks, and both the cavalry and the chariots overran them, creating chaos as they fought together. And on the distant ridge, watching, Anak saw the reflected sunlight on the sword too and rose up from the ground where he had been lying. He said to his five captains, "You have your orders. Ai will be burned to the ground now. And I have other orders of my own: Those who challenge us will be put to the sword. Those who, instead, attempt to flee, will be allowed to do so."

One of the captains protested, a man named Jeriel of Issachar, and he said angrily, "But Joshua's orders were . . . every man, woman, and child to be killed!"

"There will be no wanton slaughter," Anak said calmly. "Those who flee or submit to us will be spared."

"Madness! And who are you to deny Joshua's orders . . . ?"

Anak drew his dagger, and drove its heavy bronze hilt into Jeriel's stomach, doubling him up in pain.

"I am your commander," he said, "a rank given me by Joshua. You will obey my orders. Only those opposed to us will be killed."

He laughed shortly. "It may be that where force will not win this land for us, a certain restraint will. Lead your men now. The slaves are ready with their pitch?"

"They are ready," Jeriel said sullenly. "Two hundred slaves with wicker baskets ready for the firing."

"Good. We go now to set Ai on fire. And when that has been done, we do not strangle their women and children, but instead, we march on to join Joshua in the valley, where our enemies are . . . soldiers."

Three thousand men moved on at the trot to the city of Ai, its gates open now, its walls undefended, and not a single soldier left there.

Within the hour, it was burning furiously, as the slaves ran from building to building firing their woven baskets of pitch. This duty done, they began herding out the cattle, the mules, and the goats. And, in spite of Anak's instructions, many of the remaining inhabitants were killed, and the sour stench of death was very heavy on the air. *"All to be put to the sword,"* Joshua had said; and who was this upstart to countermand their leader's instructions?

And so, the killing went on, of the old men, the women, the children; the men of military age were

349

engaged elsewhere in a struggle for life or death, which they were slowly, inexorably, losing. In the space of a few hours, there was hardly a living soul in Ai.

The flames were crackling around Anak as he moved through the town, his sergeant, Ofazi, by his side. Timbers crashed, half-burned, to the ground, and the air was rent with the screams of those who had been trapped in burning houses and could not escape. He found himself in a great room of some quality, nearly twenty cubits long and half as wide, with a vaulted ceiling decorated with ceramic tiles, and he knew that it was part of the king's own quarters; the flames were licking up the carved timber supports of the roof.

And there were three young people there, two youths and a girl, terrified out of their wits. The girl was perhaps fifteen years old, the boys a little younger. They were all brown-skinned and good-looking, dressed in the simple loincloths that proclaimed them to be slaves. They had been carrying a heavy box of cedarwood, it seemed, which they had now set down on the tiled floor because . . .

Because Nezziah the Gadite, drunk with the wine he had found, had lined them up in front of him on their knees, and he was weaving his sword back and forth over their heads as they cringed before him. The intensity of the burning building's heat was monstrous, but he paid it no attention at all.

He looked up at Anak and grinned stupidly, and he shouted, his voice slurred, "Three slaves of the king himself! Watch me now as I dispatch them with three quick blows of my sword! Not even the edge, but the flat of it to smash their skulls! Watch me . . . !"

As he raised the sword high above his head, Anak struck him a fearsome blow to the side of his head

350

and knocked him, unconscious, to the ground. He crouched down beside the girl and said quietly, "Your name, child?"

She was whimpering, sure that her young life had come to its end, and yet aware that this strange *Anak* seemed to have a certain sympathy for her.

"My name?" she whispered. "It is Mahala, sir, a Hittite and slave to the King."

She was very sweet and childlike, with large and slanted eyes of a strange honey color, filled now with fear.

"And your King?" Anak asked. "Where is he now?"

"In the valley below us, I think, sir." She blinked those lustrous eyes at him, and he found her quite charming. "Fighting against your people," she said.

The tears were streaming down her cheeks. "And will you kill us now?"

"No!" Anak said harshly. "I will not!"

Nezziah of Gad was recovering, and he snarled, "But I will!" He reached for his fallen sword, and Anak kicked him very hard in the side of his head and silenced him once more, sending him back into the realm of his dreams.

Anak looked at the wooden box, and saw that it was decorated with beaten copper in very intricate designs, with the King's crest on it, and he said: "The chest . . . what does it contain?"

The child Mahala was quite sure now that her life was to be spared, and she was taking on once again the coquetry of her calling. She fluttered her eyes at Anak, and said, "Garments, Excellency, the robes in which it pleases the King to dress His favorite women from time to time. I wore one of them myself, once. . . ."

"And you hope to steal them, is that it?"

She was horrified. "No, sir, no! We were taking them to a place of safety, they're very, very valuable."

Anak said wryly, "In Ai, today, there is no such thing as a place of safety. Soon, there won't be a house left standing."

One of the boys plucked up his courage, sensing that there was a man of goodwill here, and he said quickly, "It's what I told her, sir, but she wouldn't listen to me. She wanted to take the box to the granary and hide it there."

Wondering if he had spoken out of turn or had said too much, he bit his lip, and Anak said, "Your name, boy?"

"Zattu, sir," He indicated his companion. "And this is Ira."

"And where is the granary?" Anak asked.

But before the boy could answer, Sergeant Ofazi said stolidly, "It's on the other side of the town. But it's a heap of burning timbers now, all that good grain gone to waste."

Anak nodded and gestured at the box. "Break it open," he said.

Ofazi drew his sword and smashed it down onto the chest's lock, three times in all before its mounting shattered. Using the blade as a lever, he pried the top back on its bronze hinges, and Anak looked briefly at a shimmering mass of linen and silk, with pinpoints of lapis lazuli and turquoise, with silver and gold thread shining brightly in the reflected heat of the flames.

The fires were burning fiercely now, and roof timbers were crashing to the ground. Anak closed the lid and said to Ofazi, "Find rope and bind it. I claim the chest and its contents, and the three young slaves, as spoils of war. Take them outside the walls of the city and place a guard on them in my name.

Then, when the fighting is done, take them to Gilgal to await my pleasure."

"Your servant, sir . . ."

"Our work here is finished, I think. I go to take my troops to Joshua's assistance. It may well be that he does not need it."

And his assumption was correct . . .

Three thousand men under Anak the Canaanite, jubilant with their first easy victory, charged down into the valley and discovered that it had become a killing ground. A small force had indeed come out from Bethel to go to Ai's assistance, but when they saw the burning city, they realized that they had been tricked, and they turned back, only to meet head-on with Igal's four thousand men racing downhill to attack them.

Very soon, the warriors of Bethel and Ai, mightily confused, were mixed together in the gorge, with furious Israelites assailing them both from the front and from the rear. And in five hours, the battle was over. The scavenger crows were circling, the jackals and desert lions gathering in their hollows and waiting patiently as Joshua's men, carrying out his injunction that not one enemy soldier was to escape with his life, went relentlessly from one body to another, cleaving heads open with their swords and smashing wounded backs with heavy stones or with their clubs.

The King was captured, and taken to the top of a small hill, and hanged on the ancient oak tree which was there. His body was left hanging till sundown when it was removed to the remains of the town, where a great cairn was built over it at the ruined gates; and the battle for Ai, in which twelve thousand of its inhabitants had been killed, was over.

The army reentered the still-smoldering city to

complete its sacking and to carry away the spoils of war; and when night came, the victors clambered down into the gorge and wearily, by their thousands, climbed up the steep cliffs to their camp at Gilgal.

They were loaded down with pots, vessels, bolts of cloth, garments, weapons, sacks of grain, jars of oil, furniture, ceramic tiles, and other booty. Some of them were drunk with the wines they had found in the vanquished city; many more were drunk with the realization of complete victory.

And all of them knew that now, as Joshua had said, nothing could stand for very long in the way of the Israelite advance.

Anak went straight to Igal's tent.

Igal, he knew, was still out there in the darkness somewhere, mustering his troops and trying to get a casualty count.

"Mutar?" he said urgently, and in a moment Azuza came out from the tent. She was secretly very fond of Anak, and she whispered, "But you came to see my daughter, I think?"

Anak nodded. "Yes, if I may be permitted . . ."

"You are permitted." She looked back into the tent and whispered, "Elisheva? Anak is here."

Elisheva was there at once, and Anak embraced her as Azuza moved quietly back inside. Unexpectedly, his voice was broken, and he whispered, "Elisheva my love . . . I am sick, sick, sick at heart. There was so much killing in the battle, and not all of it was necessary. I saw children, only a few months old, swung by their ankles into stone walls so that their heads would be smashed. I saw old women strangled with the cords, soldiers who had lain down their arms and submitted to us, wantonly killed. I am sick, and only you can comfort me now. Will you walk with me for a while?"

"Yes, of course . . ." she whispered. "But surely, it was a great victory?"

"If victory is measured in carnage, yes. Come, we will talk of other things."

Arm in arm, they strolled among the olive trees in the moonlight, all the way down to the bank of the great river itself. Nighttime Nature was making itself known, and there was the repeated cry of an owl *hoot-hooting* at them. There was the distant sound of a lion's roar, and Anak said, sensing Elisheva's sudden alarm, "No, it is a very long way away. . . ."

The night was cool and very pleasant, and as they walked together, Anak told her of the distant cities he had visited, once traveling in search of trade as far afield as Tyre and Sidon on the coast of the Great Sea. "Tyre," he said, dreaming, "is perhaps the most beautiful city in the world, an offshore island that was once called Usu, only a hundred or two years old and yet fast becoming the most important center for all our region's commerce. . . . They build great ships there, the like of which you can surely never have seen."

"The *like* of them?" Elisheva said, laughing. "Anak! I never saw a ship of *any* sort, in all my born days!"

"Ah yes, of course. You were born and bred in the desert, a true bedouin. . . . But I swear to you solemnly that one day, somehow, I will show you parts of our world that you cannot even imagine now."

He held her tightly and whispered, "The time is very close now, Elisheva."

When she prompted him, he would say no more.

And when the moon went down and the absolute darkness came, he took her back to Igal's tent, whispered with her for a while outside it, and then left her.

He found that he was intolerably aroused by his gentle wandering with Elisheva, and he went to Rahab's tent and confided in her, saying, "She excites me beyond endurance, Rahab! And yet, I may not touch her till we marry, she's a virgin and an honest woman."

"Lie down beside me," Rahab said. "We both know, you and I, the cure for all these ills."

When he left her at last, there was only one thought coursing through his mind: *The time for marriage now is drawing very close. . . .*

He went to his own tent, and found his new slave girl Mahala waiting for him expectantly; but all he wanted now was sleep.

Chapter Twenty-three

"Will you come with me, Caleb, my friend?" Anak asked. "The most important moment in my life is approaching. And shall I tell you, frankly and without shame, that in trepidation I need the support that only you can provide me with?"

They were sitting together under the raised flap of Anak's black tent, sharing a pitcher of wine as the new slave girl Mahala filled their cups, and Caleb chuckled. "So," he said happily, "the day is upon us! And no sooner than I expected, indeed, I have been waiting for it! Yes, of course I will come with you, to speak in your behalf, as is customary."

Old as he was, Caleb had been fighting at Joshua's side, with the main force, acquitting himself very well indeed, and he had been quite badly wounded; a Canaanite javelin had pierced his thigh, and though the wound had been disinfected with copious applications of wood ash, he was still hobbling on his staff.

"And is it the fashion among your people, as it is among mine," Anak asked, "for a good friend to speak in support of a prospective bridegroom?"

"It is," Caleb said gravely. "And whatever eloquence I may be blessed with . . . will be at your disposal."

"Good. It is all I ask. If you can find good things to say of me, I will be grateful."

He turned to Mahala. "Ira and Zattu," he said, "send them to me."

She rose silently to her feet and went out, and Caleb's eyes followed her. "She's very sweet," he said softly, and Anak nodded.

"She's a Hittite, their women are really quite beautiful. She was born, she tells me, in Carchemish on the Euphrates River. Her father was a soldier." He shrugged. "He needed money, and so he sold her into slavery when she was a child."

When she returned with the two young men, Anak indicated the rope-bound cedar chest that carried the mark of Ai's late king, and said, "Come with me. Bring the box."

He turned back to Caleb, smiling. "Is there, shall we say, an air of confidence about me?"

Caleb nodded. "Yes, I would say so."

"And do I present an imposing appearance?"

He was dressed in his short Canaanite skirt of brown wool hemmed in a deep scarlet, with a broad belt decorated with copper rivets and sandals in the same heavy leather, cut from the hide of Canaan's famous cattle. The hilt of his copper sword and dagger were both of bronze, deeply incised, a few turquoise stones embedded in each of them. A broad leather band with gold wire running through it was around his forehead, confining his dark, shoulder-length hair. Tall and straight and muscular, he was indeed a very imposing figure, and Caleb said, his old eyes shining brightly, "Enough to turn the heart and mind of any impressionable young girl . . ."

"It is not Elisheva we have to impress," Anak said seriously. "It is *Igal*."

"The cedar chest," Caleb said, highly amused, "is what will impress Igal! And, of course, my own honeyed words."

"Yes."

Anak took a long, deep breath. "It is only a few paces to Igal's tent," he said. "And yet, for me, they are steps into an eternity of the most sublime happiness."

There were very few secrets kept for long among the tents, and Igal had been waiting impatiently for this moment ever since, shortly after dawn, his son Barkos had said to him, grinning stupidly, "It may be, Father, that a certain giant of Canaan, whom we all know and admire, will be visiting you this evening on a matter of the greatest importance both to him . . . and to you."

Now Igal, Elam, and Barkos were seated around the hide stretched out on the sand floor of the tent that served as a table, while Azuza hovered in the background ready to bring them more food when they might demand it.

Igal glared at his fractious son. "Who? Anak? And a matter of *what*?"

"He is not as impoverished today," Elam said, "as he was before the battle of Ai."

He wrapped his bread around a mess of heavy pottage made from leeks, lentils, and garlic, and chewed on it. "He has set his heart on marrying Elisheva."

"As I know," Igal said irritably. "As a matter of fact, I have gone so far as to make certain discreet enquiries myself. I understand that with the division

360

of the animals taken as spoils, Anak has been given four cows and a bull, two mules, and thirty-two goats taken from the Canaanites."

He passed the platter to Azuza and said crossly, "More of the pottage, woman. Your men are hungry, and you just sit there, daydreaming! More garlic this time . . . You *never* put enough garlic in my food!"

"I am sorry," Azuza said humbly. "I'll see to it."

She went to the fire and scooped up more of the slush with the wooden paddle, and found garlic to chop up with her flint blade and dropped it into it, and brought it to them.

"Better," Igal said benevolently, "far better. Never skimp on the garlic, woman."

He turned back to his sons and grumbled, "Anak got far more than his fair share, if you ask me. I led the force against the Bethelites, and honestly, Joshua did not treat me well at all. I was given two cows and forty goats, not a good breeder among them! Indeed, half of them seem to be suffering from the mange, and will have to be killed."

"Then they'll keep us in food," Elam said, "for a very long time to come. And I've seen them. There are seven or eight very good females among them; we were not treated too badly."

"And two cows!" Igal said miserably. "What will I do with cows? I know *nothing* about cattle! I don't even like them! From what I've seen of them since we came here . . . No, I *hate* cows."

"Their milk is very good," Elam said equably. "And one good cow gives as much as a dozen goats. I'll find a bull among our neighbors and breed them. . . . And in the course of time, we'll have so much milk to make into cheese and sell . . ." He laughed shortly. "Moses told our people," he said, "of a land flowing with milk and honey. He *knew* about the Canaanite cattle."

"Well," Igal said, "be that as it may. But if Anak hopes to purchase Elisheva with thirty-two goats and four more damned cows, then I have every intention of sending him away with a flea in his ear. Much as I like Anak, my first duty is to my daughter. And I will not sell her to a pauper."

"Your concern, Father," Barkos said, "does you justice. But I learned that Anak has other spoils. From Ai."

"Oh?" Igal was suddenly very excited. "What, he found silver? Even gold, perhaps?"

"No, I think not," Elam said. "By all reports, there was precious little silver to be found in Ai, and no gold at all. It may be that whatever bars they had were stored in a building that burned down on top of them, lost forever."

"Oh."

"None the less," Barkos said, "it seems that Anak now considers himself a very rich man. And this evening . . . he will visit you, with marriage on his mind."

Igal was very suspicious. "And how could you know this?" he shouted crossly, "when I myself have heard nothing of it?"

Barkos grinned. "I spent part of this last night with Rahab," he said calmly, "and there is no one in the whole of our camp who knows our gossip better than she does."

Igal could only stare, wide-eyed. "What?" he screamed. "At your age, you spend your nights with prostitutes?"

Very sure of himself, Barkos answered, "We have a harlot sleeping in our tents. It would be most discourteous of us to deny her the only life she knows. . ."

"Discourteous . . . !"

"In fact," Barkos said, catching his brother Elam's amused look and taking comfort from it. "In fact, I am wondering if I should make an honest woman of her."

"An *honest woman*. . . ?"

"That is to say . . . I might take her to wife."

"No. . . !" Igal was wailing. "A concubine, if you insist . . ."

"No, with the honorable title of wife." Barkos said earnestly, "She's a woman of great quality, Father, truly she is."

Igal's hands were at his cheeks, and he was weaving his head back and forth and moaning. "My son," he whispered, "marrying a harlot . . . ! The shame that will come on our family!"

"There will be no shame," Elam said steadily. "When you and Caleb first went to Jericho, it was Rahab who saved both your lives. And, therefore, I echo the sentiment that Barkos has expressed; she is indeed a woman of quality."

"And in bed," Barkos said, "she is irrepressible. . . ."

It seemed that Igal was about to faint. But now. . .

At the entrance to the tent, Elisheva was quietly listening to their conversation. She was crouched over the pegged-out skin of Achan's prize goat, using her father's best flint to scrape away the fat the day's sun had brought out.

She said quietly, "He comes now."

Anak and Caleb were approaching the tent, and behind them, the two young male slaves were carry-

363

ing the heavy cedar box, followed by the girl Mahala.

Caleb called out the obligatory "*Mutar . . .* ?"

"*Mutar*," Igal said quickly recovering from his shock, and they entered, all of them. The two young men dropped the chest to the floor, and with Mahala, they squatted on their haunches, awaiting their further orders.

And then, the courtesies began. . . .

"Peace on you," Caleb said. "And your house is well?"

"My house is well if yours is," Igal said impatiently.

"And the world treats you well?" Caleb answered.

"For the moment, at least, it treats me well. And to what do we owe the honor of this visit?"

"We come," Caleb said (a little put-out because the obligatory courtesies had been so short), "to make an offer for your daughter Elisheva, for her hand in honorable marriage. And as a friend of the prospective groom, I will speak now in his behalf and enumerate for you his sterling qualities, if you will be gracious enough to hear them."

"I will hear them," Igal said. "And will you take bread with us?"

"We will be pleased to take bread, and we thank you."

It was all very formal indeed.

Igal looked up and saw Elisheva standing there, and he said crossly, "What, you are listening to us? This is no matter to concern you, child, but for men only. Find your mother Azuza, tell her to bake bread at once, the best, with oil and honey, and raisins in it. When it is ready, bring it to us. Go now."

"Yes, Father. . ."

Elisheva moved away, and Igal said, "The young

364

people today, they have no understanding at all of what is correct."

He said hastily: "Though she is, of course, very obedient when she is told how to behave. You saw how promptly she obeyed me. And you were saying. . . ?"

Caleb cleared his throat. "Anak of Canaan," he said, "one of the *Anakim*, as can plainly be seen, but a Jew none the less. Now, Anak is the offspring of Esau the hairy, the son of Rebekah and Isaac, who was a skilled hunter and a man of noble character who took for his pleasure three wives from among the Hittites, who were women of the Canaanites. Of course, as is known, he also took to wife a Jewish woman named Mahalath, the daughter of Ishmael, who was half-brother to Isaac himself, who was also called Basemath, as was one of his Hittite wives—"

"Yes, yes, yes," Igal said. "You talk too much, Caleb, as always! His *present* qualities, move on to his *present* qualities!"

"Very well," Caleb said. "Anak, as we know him today, is a young and virile man, very strong and courageous. In the first instance, he slew two fully grown lions with his bare hands in order to save Elisheva's life; his bravery cannot be doubted. In the second, he walked, almost unaided, all the way to the Dead Sea to cure the wounds he suffered in that encounter, on which long journey, he kept his promise to lay no evil hand on Elisheva, a fact that attests to his sense of honor—"

"His wealth," Igal said peevishly, "come to his wealth!"

"His wealth? Well, as part of his booty from the battle of Ai, in which he played so successful a part, Joshua has awarded him with a number of cattle and goats. . . ."

His eyes on the chest, Igal said, "I will not sell my daughter for thirty-two goats." He added hastily, "Much as I respect him, and cherish him as my own son."

Anak was silent, listening to all this, and Caleb went on. "He offers no goats at all, nor any other animals. Indeed, if he is to become the wealthy man we all want to see as Elisheva's husband, he needs all of his animals to start his own herds, which, in the course of a few years, might well become the finest in all of Israel, since his experience in this field is not to be denied."

"His offer, then?" Igal asked.

He saw Elisheva standing at the tent's entrance again, and he said furiously, "What, are you still here? I told you! This is none of your concern!"

"The bread," she said, "Azuza is baking it now. But there are no raisins, we finished them at supper last night."

"Is your mother an idiot, then? Tell her to use sesame seed or coriander! And really, I cannot concern myself with these trivial household matters!"

"She mixed the dough with honey. She says sesame seed will not go well with it. . . ."

In a fury, he picked up the ladle from the water jar and hurled it at her, screaming, "It is your concern and your mother's! Not mine! All I demand is that the bread be good!"

The ladle had caught her in the stomach, and he was ashamed. He said gruffly, "And bring us wine and beakers. You may pour it for us yourself."

Elisheva picked up the ladle and placed it carefully back where it belonged; she caught Anak's eyes and exchanged a look with him, and neither of them said a word.

When she had left, Igal turned back to Caleb and

said deprecatingly, "Children! A great joy to a father, and yet . . . a pain too. And you were speaking of Anak's wealth."

Now Caleb's eyes were alight with pleasure as he said, somewhat slyly, "In the case of the late Achan of Judah, whom none of us mourn, there was an offer that included a little silver and gold, but most of all centered around a Babylonian gown."

"Ah . . . I remember it well," Igal said, still eyeing the chest.

"And Anak has brought you . . . garments of the same kind, made in Babylonia's famous center called Shinar, which lies between the Two Rivers."

He turned to the slave boy Zattu and said, "The chest . . ."

Slowly, with infinite patience, Zattu unwound the ropes and opened up the box. Igal gasped when he saw the bright, gold-and-silver-threaded silks and linens there. . . . And, one by one, very meticulously, Zattu laid them out with loving care on the sand floor of the tent.

The first was made of scarlet linen, with gold wire running richly through it from neck to hem, and tiny slivers of lapis lazuli worked into it very skillfully. The second was of blue silk, a dark blue color that Igal had never seen before, with horizontal bands of silver wire tied here and there in little 8-shaped knots of the most exquisite artistry.

And Zattu, it seemed, was very knowledgeable about these garments . . .

"This one," he said, "was a favorite with the king for a concubine named Ebla, whose hair was very long and the color of dried straw. The blue is a dye that only the dyers of Shinar have, unknown to anyone else. . . ."

The next was also made of silk, but not dyed; its

367

natural off-white color was decorated with minuscule patterns in red, green, yellow, and violet thread, and Zattu said, "Again, we do not know what dyes they could have used. Only in Shinar of Babylon . . ."

He laid out the next robe, of very heavy linen dyed to a brilliant yellow, with a strange nap to it that felt like velvet, and changed its texture when it was brushed this way or that. Along its hems, at the skirt, the neck, and the sleeves, there were tiny acorns fashioned in pure gold, each one a masterpiece of the goldsmith's art, and Zattu said, "In all, four hundred and thirty-two of the acorns, each one priceless. This, the king liked to have his concubine Mibzar wear when he loved her, which was very often, almost every night."

A dark green robe then; and green, in cloth, was not a color known to the Israelites. It too was heavily bound in gold thread, with tiny oak leaves of gold and silver wire, expertly interwoven.

And then . . . a multicolored robe of red, blue, yellow, and violet silk at which Igal could only stare in amazement. Zattu lifted up the hem and said, "To make it drape correctly on the body of your beloved, Excellency . . . Eighty-five nuggets of gold stitched into the skirt, all identical in size and weight. This gown was one of his favorites, worn often by Ebla, Moren, and Shebna, three of his very favorite concubines. Sometimes, he would even give it to his wife to wear, the Lady Toah."

One after the other, the garments were laid out on the floor of the tent, eleven of them all told, each beautiful beyond words, each exquisite beyond price.

Pacing up and down among them as they lay there, Igal stared at them and tried, with great difficulty, to compose his thoughts; he had never before in all his life, seen such beauty and wealth displayed in garments. But he gathered his senses together, knowing that this was a time for bargaining, for showing how clever he was at haggling, and he said, with great dignity: "I take it that I may have my choice of these garments? There is one there that particularly appeals to me, the yellow silk with those strange stones woven into its decoration. . . ."

He could not know the definitions of the stones, but they were garnets, shining like rubies, green tourmaline with striata of red running through them, amber-colored topaz, and shimmering, luminescent opal; for the most part, they were gems that only the distant Babylonians knew of and used for trading on their long caravan routes. And they were cunningly stitched into the robe to give it value . . .

He saw no objection in Anak's face, and went on, pursuing the bargain, hopefully. "And perhaps the multicolored robe as well; what do you say? Those little lumps of gold could easily be removed, and buried in a safe place. . . . I do not wish to appear greedy; truly, greed is not part of my character. But my lovely Elisheva is a prize without comparison, I really should not part with her in exchange for one garment alone, however valuable. What would the neighbors think? They would say to me, 'What, you traded your daughter for a single garment?' And I would be obliged to explain to them, one by one, what an exceptional garment this is, even *show* it to them to explain why I received so very little for a daughter who is acknowledged to be, through all of our tents, the most desirable of all our daughters."

He held Anak's look and said, "Two of the garments, then. The yellow silk with the stones, and the multicolored robe, which is really very pleasing to look at."

He lifted it up and felt the great weight of the gold

369

nuggets at its hem, and dropped it to the sand again in the vain hope that its enormous value might not become too apparent.

"Two of the garments, then," Igal said. "At my own choice, this one or that, regardless of their value."

Anak said calmly, "My offer is not one, nor two garments, Igal, however valuable they may be. My offer is all of them. *All* of them."

Igal's mouth dropped open, and his senses seemed to have left him completely. He stammered, "All— *all* of them? All. . . *ten* of them?"

"Eleven, actually," Anak said. "And I offer you all of them in exchange for the hand of your daughter Elisheva."

Igal was unable to contain his excitement. He stared at his friend Caleb and said, beside himself, "Did you—did you hear that, Caleb? *All* of them! Eleven garments of incomparable worth! And all of them mine! All of them! Ah . . . !"

Caleb was a little disgusted; he felt, moreover, that his eulogy had been unnecessarily interrupted; and so, he took up the speech again. "Anak the giant, a man who has proved himself in battle, a man who has shown us all that he is fearless, a man we all know to be beyond reproach, seeking the hand now of Elisheva *bat* Igal of the tribe of Issachar, sponsored by me, Caleb of Judah, a friend of Igal's family for more than thirty years, recommending in all sincerity that Igal, whom I love and admire, a commander in Joshua's army and therefore a man of consequence, as Anak himself is with similar title, accept this generous offer for her hand, to whit . . . eleven garments from Shinar in Babylon, until lately the property of the king of Ai and taken as legitimate spoils of war—"

Igal said crossly, "Oh, shut up, Caleb! How often must I tell you that you talk too much?"

Smiling quietly, Caleb fell silent, and Igal said, assuring himself, "It is understood, then? And in front of Caleb as witness! That the purchase price for the bride has been agreed upon? *Eleven* Babylonian garments?"

"It is agreed," Caleb said, and Anak echoed him, "Agreed."

Igal could hardly hold himself in check, and he fingered the robes one after the other, whispering, "Beautiful . . . and really quite priceless . . . One better than the other . . ."

Elisheva was entering the tent again, with a platter of bread which she set down on the skin table before them. She went out and reappeared with a pitcher of wine and beakers, and very delicately set the mugs down on the floor beside them. She poured in silence, and caught Anak's eye again, their looks hanging on, one to the other; and in absolute defiance of all good manners, scorning protocol completely, Anak reached out and took hold of her fragile wrist.

"Sooner than you think," he said, "you will be mine."

Igal said loudly, "Ah . . . yes, the question of the marriage. What do you say, Caleb? One month from today?"

Caleb's eyes were on Elisheva, and he said, understanding, "One *week* from today. There are political agitations of great moment going on now, and when they are over . . . it will be a good time for a marriage."

Igal frowned. "Political agitations? I honestly don't know what that means! Nor do I understand how it should affect this marriage!"

371

"It affects this marriage," Caleb said, "because we need Joshua's blessing on it. And at the moment . . . he is concerned only with the devious Gibeonites."

Gibeon was a town some twenty miles to the west of Gilgal; and it was the wealthiest city in all of Canaan.

But the city Elders had received word of the fall of Ai, and they met together in silent terror; and one of them whispered, "We must persuade him that Gibeon is a small and impoverished town. It can be done very simply."

One of the others answered him, "Then tell us how? Anything, *anything*, to stop this maniac Joshua from throwing his savage forces against us."

"We send a deputation to him," the Elder answered. "Dressed in rags, carrying patched water-skins which we will make, wearing worn-out sandals and torn robes . . . And we will tell him how poor and empty a town Gibeon is, with nothing here to make for spoils of war. It will deter him. . . ."

And so, fifteen of them found the thinnest, most ill-nourished donkeys they could gather together, and they rode to Gilgal and made an alliance with Joshua, which, hearing of their poverty, he swore to.

It was three days before he discovered the truth; but the oath he had sworn with them was binding, and he could not deny it. In his righteous fury, he condemned them, instead, to be "hewers of wood and drawers of water" for the Israelites; and this was to be their fate for all eternity.

Anak said, "I will not wait a month, nor yet a week, to enjoy the pleasure of my bride-to-be. The marriage will take place tonight."

372

There was a startled silence; it was quite an indecent proposal.

"Tonight," Anak said firmly. "Igal has accepted the bridal price, and Elisheva is now mine. It is my wish to consummate our marriage at once. *Tonight.*"

Caleb said gently, "It is against all of our customs, Anak."

"But against none of ours," Anak answered. "The purchase price has been decided; there is no more argument! She is mine now, and I wish to enjoy her tonight. It's all really very simple."

Elisheva's hand sneaked out and took his, and she whispered, loking at her father, "If he so wishes . . ."

"No!" Igal said furiously. "In all of our history, such a travesty has never happened before! A month at least . . . ! Or two weeks, if you insist!"

"Very well, then," Anak said. "Since you are adamant . . . But then, only four of the garments for a marriage in two weeks' time."

"No . . . !" Igal was wailing again. "All of them, as you have promised!"

"Eleven garments," Anak said steadily, "with all of their gold and silver decorations and their gold and precious stones. But the consummation will take place . . . *tonight.*"

Igal plucked at his lip and looked at Caleb for help. "What do you say?" he asked. "Is there justifiable precedent?"

Caleb nodded. "Asran of Zebulon," he said, "married Hisha of Dan at such short notice, though she was heavy with his child. And in Kadesh-Barnea, Piran of Benjamin married Prutah of his own tribe, without such urgency. Yes, there is precedent."

And so, it all became permissible. . . .

The marriage ceremony was not religious, but

purely secular, and very simple and straightforward. The father of the bride—in this case Igal—said in front of witnesses, "Do you take my daughter to wife?"

Anak, standing firm and straight, and trying, in the name of common decency, to hide his eagerness, answered clearly, "I so take her, to live with me and obey me in all things, to do my bidding at all times."

He could not take his eyes from his bride. . . .

Asserting her rights as a woman for the first time in her young life, she had chosen her wedding gown herself from among the garments (albeit with the help of her mother, both of them trembling with excitement).

And they had decided at last on the off-white silk with its tiny patterns here and there in brilliantly dyed threads, in colors she never dreamed could possibly exist. "It's so beautiful," she whispered.

It was not an easy decision.

"The yellow with the gold acorns," Azuza said, urging her; but Elisheva shook her head, and said, smiling gently, "Father has set his heart, I am sure, on those tiny gold carvings . . . more than four hundred of them! And if I marry in that dress, then my daughter must wear it to her wedding, my daughter's daughter too . . . And what will poor Father do without his gold acorns? No, I will take the white. It's the most beautiful garment I could ever imagine. . . ."

Now she stood a little apart from the others, close by the yellow flames of the tent's tallow flare that seemed to dance over her features, illuminating the lovely olive sheen of her skin; her dark, almond-shaped eyes picked up the light of the flames, and there was a quality about her that was both ethereal and earthy at the same time.

374

The white robe, made in Babylon for a king's concubine, clung to her young and nubile body almost like a second skin; and Anak was sure he had never in all his life seen so lovely a vision. She seemed somehow to have lost her childish insouciance, and there was more of the *woman* about her.

Had the gown done this to her? A concubine's dress on a virgin body?

Or was it the excitation of the moment, a subconscious awareness of the transition she was about to make from child to *wife?* Her eyes were moist now, and shining brightly, lustrous and beautiful.

The formalities were quickly over. . . .

Anak picked up a trembling Elisheva in his arms and strode off with her in the darkness to his tent, there to impregnate her with his strong seed in a long moment of furious passion, repeated time and time again; their love together was very strong.

In the weeks and months that followed, Joshua's conquest of Canaan went on apace, with one notable victory followed by another.

The scribes, wise men all of them, were to write for posterity:

So, Joshua defeated the whole land, the hill country and the Negev and the lowland and the slopes, and all their Kings, he left none remaining, but utterly destroyed all that breathed. . . .

Joshua and his army of Israelites, determined to find a new home for their people after so many long years of bondage and the most appalling suffering in Egypt, with every man their enemy, could not be stopped now. They had shaken off the shackles of

375

slavery, and were in search of personal dignity; that search was not to be denied, cost what it might.

The Canaanites were fine husbanders, and the Israelites learned from them, and improved on what they learned, building water-channels, terracing the ground where it was not hospitable, growing their crops now where nothing but scrub had grown before.

As they defeated one enemy after another, driving out the Canaanites, the Hittites, the Hivites, the Perrizites, the Girgashites, the Amorites, the Jebusites and all the other tribes, Canaan became, inexorably, the land of Israel.

And the children of Israel began, very slowly and painfully, to change from nomadic bedouin into agriculturalists and urbanites, giving up their goat's-hair tents for the houses they found in the cities they conquered. They became accustomed to roofs over their heads, and learned the value of defensive stone walls around them.

They were using the higher-quality weapons of their vanquished foes now, and learning how to make their own; they were adding more cattle to their herds of goats, and learning how to manage them; they were using vessels of bronze as well as of clay, and learning how to cast them.

And during this time, the Israelites—Anak among them—became rich with the legitimate spoils of war. The days of desert wanderings, forty years of them in acute tribulation, were behind them now, but would always be remembered; how could it be otherwise?

In this time, too, Elisheva conceived. Nine months after her marriage, she gave birth to a loudly screaming and very angry baby girl.

At the time of her labor, honey bees from the

hives that Anak had set up in the garden of their house invaded the bedroom itself; and so, they called the girl-child *Deborah*, meaning "bee."

It was a name that, in all of Israel's tormented history, would never, ever, be forgotten.